MY FINE FELLOW

Also by Jennieke Cohen

Dangerous Alliance

MY FINE FELLOW

JENNIEKE COHEN

HARPER TEEN
An Imprint of HarperCollins Publishers

HarperTeen is an imprint of HarperCollins Publishers.

My Fine Fellow

Library of Congress Control Number: 2021946939
ISBN 978-0-06-304753-2

Typography by Jessie Gang
21 22 23 24 25 PC/LSCH 10 9 8 7 6 5 4 3 2 1

First Edition

For the immigrants, children of immigrants, and anyone who's ever attempted to make a better life for themself in the face of formidable odds. May your journey and success go hand in hand.

MY FINE FELLOW

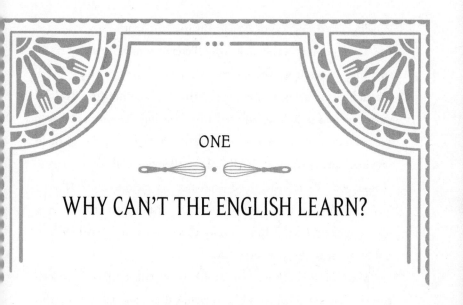

ONE

WHY CAN'T THE ENGLISH LEARN?

In the year 1833 of the Common Era, a fair ten years since King George IV died and his much beloved daughter, Princess Charlotte, succeeded him as Queen Charlotte of England, Ireland, Hanover, and so on and so forth, one Miss Penelope Pickering stood in the shadowed portico of St. Paul's London, wondering how much longer she'd have to wait for her dear friend Helena Higgins.

Of course, as even Penelope would admit if pressed, Helena had never been what one might call the epitome of charm. Nor would one characterize her as a lady of grace, for her sharp tongue offended nearly everyone she met. She was, however, well on her way to becoming the foremost authority of their generation on the culinary arts in Britain, and therefore considered herself entitled to tell people when they harbored incorrect assumptions about Culinaria, or indeed the world. And, to be quite honest, Helena was very often right. Most of Helena's schoolmates found this trait downright irritating, but

Penelope Pickering was of a decidedly tolerant bent.

This perhaps explained why Penelope now found herself standing across from the Covent Garden Market, wishing she'd remembered to bring an umbrella on this chilly evening in early January. She had only just returned from touring the Americas with her parents, and after not seeing Helena since the final day of their previous spring term at the Royal Academy of Culinaria Artisticus—a good six months since—most of her memories of Helena's less-than-ladylike manners had softened. Distance and time have a way of making friends forget each other's faults, and Penelope was not immune to this phenomenon.

She looked about her once more, then pulled a piece of paper from the pocket of her navy blue traveling dress. She held it up to the flickering gas lamp to her left with one gloved hand as she did her best to shield it from the rain with her other.

Number 9, Cavendish Square   *January 5, 1833*
Marylebone, London

My Dear Penelope,
What a pleasure it is to welcome you to Cavendish Square!
It seems an age since we first concocted this scheme to spend
our final term at the Royal Academy living away from
those dreary girls at school, and the day has <u>finally</u> come. I
am pleased your parents relented at last! My own parents
and brother continue their sojourn on the Continent, and
therefore I must apologize for not being able to greet you
myself, but I trust the staff has welcomed you with great

*ceremony and that you are now settling into the violet
room with your every comfort well attended. I daresay
your journey was decidedly unpleasant, but I hope you will
be sufficiently recovered from your travels to join me this
evening in some research. I shall await you at eight of the
clock at St. Paul's Church, and we shall sample London's
most authentic taste of the Americas. Bring your appetite
and coin purse as the night market has markedly improved
in your absence.*

    Yours as ever,
    Helena Higgins

Penelope glanced across the street at the vendors hawking their
wares and food by the light of the gas lamps. The usual assortment
of unaccompanied young men and ladies her own age milled around
the purveyors who had set up on the street—those who couldn't
afford stalls inside the columns of the market building. Hats,
umbrellas, or hooded capes shielded most of the patrons from the
worst of the rain as they bought goods and food from the roaming
hawkers. Unlike Penelope, *they* had come prepared for the weather.
None of them looked particularly like Helena, however. Penelope
stuffed the letter back into her pocket and her hands back into her
fur-lined muff. With the rain, many of the vendors now had a cap-
tive audience as ladies and gentlemen emerged from the theaters
only to huddle under whichever awnings and porticos they could.

A party of three stopped next to Penelope and blinked at the
rain. The girl, who looked to be a year or two younger than Penelope's ten and seven, huffed. "Oh, it's too, too tiresome. Can't you

get us a cab, Frederick?" She turned to the young man next to her. Judging by their similar looks, Penelope guessed him to be the girl's brother.

"I'll get deuced wet out there!" he exclaimed in a way young men reserve for sisters who irritate them. Then he seemed to remember a stranger stood nearby, for he inclined his head to Penelope. "I beg your pardon, miss."

"I must apologize for my son," said the third of the party, a middle-aged woman with a tall feather protruding from her coiffure. "He is a heathen, I'm afraid."

Penelope nodded at the lady. "Quite all right." She'd hardly call the young man a heathen for using the word "deuced" in her presence, but the woman couldn't know that Penelope had heard far worse language in her travels. "The weather shows no sign of abating, I fear."

"Freddie, get this lady a hackney as well."

Penelope shook her head. "I thank you, but I'm meeting someone."

The older woman frowned. "Here? At this time of night?"

Penelope gestured at the carts in the street and at the sheltered stalls beyond, inside the market building. Steam from the food the vendors were cooking dissipated into the dank evening air as a multiplicity of scents wafted toward Penelope. "A school friend invited me to join her here at the stalls for some culinary research. It seems this is one of the few places in London where one can find an authentic taste of the Americas." Though Penelope rather thought she'd be the judge of that.

"The Americas?" the woman repeated as though the thought of

anyone seeking out food from the continents across the ocean had never occurred to anybody in the whole history of human relations.

"Are you a Culinarian, then?" the young man asked Penelope as he swiped a piece of damp hair away from his dark blue eyes.

She nodded. "I soon will be. I'm in my final term at the Royal Academy."

"My sister dabbled a bit but decided to go to the Royal Conservatory of Commoditas and Design in the end," he said with a gesture at the young woman.

"I never dabbled, Freddie. My design improvements to Lady Hammersley's chaise and four had her bragging to her neighbors for weeks. If anything, *you're* the dabbler." Freddie's sister wrinkled her nose.

"Well," said he with a rueful smile, "perhaps I am, but I make a dashed fine pheasant pie." He tipped his tall hat to Penelope, murmured something to his mother about going to look for a cab, and bounded off into the rain. As he stepped off the curb, he collided with a bedraggled young man in a shapeless brown coat carrying a wooden tray covered in cloth.

Penelope winced as two half-moon-shaped pies fell from the tray and plopped onto the dirty, wet cobbles.

"Watch yourself, why don't ya?" the young man said, throwing a glare at Freddie.

"I beg your pardon," Freddie said. He touched his hat and hurried down the street.

"Two pasties trod in the mud," the boy yelled at Freddie's back. He made a great show of covering the remaining pies with their protective cloth. "Some gentleman, jostling poor cooks and knocking their livelihoods onto the street," he said loud enough for anyone nearby to hear.

"Here, boy," Freddie's mother called. "I'll pay for what my son cost you." She turned to her daughter. "Clara, give the young man a shilling."

"Oh, he's your son, is he?" the boy said, approaching. Penelope figured he must be about her age, yet it was difficult to say, considering the quality of the gaslight flickering to the left of them. "Might have raised him better than to pay for his mistakes yourself. Fella might as well pay for his own mistakes, my ma always said."

"Do you care for the shilling or not, boy?" Clara asked, holding out the coin between gloved fingers.

"I'll take it, miss, and thank ye for it." The boy winked at her then, and Penelope looked away from the exchange, realizing that the young man might have been attractive if he washed the dirt from his face and had the waves of his brown hair cut into a semblance of a shape.

"Well, I never," Clara said, and pulled her mother's arm so they stood farther away from the boy.

He smirked. His gaze then landed on Penelope, now standing alone under the portico. She scanned the stalls for Helena again, but saw no one resembling her.

"Buy a Faraway Pasty, miss?" the boy asked. He lifted the cloth off his tray, and the smell of fried dough, beef, and oregano wafted toward her.

Penelope blinked. "Empanadas?"

His light brown eyes, framed by thick lashes wet from the rain, widened. "What a clever one you are! Not one person in twenty knows 'em by their right name. Just fer that, I'll give you two fer the price of one."

Penelope raised a brow. She doubted she was getting much of a discount, but she *had* come to eat, after all. "How much?"

"Just tuppence, miss. Not a penny more."

Penelope riffled through her pocket and handed him two copper pennies. He held out the tray for her to choose from. She pulled out her handkerchief and used it to take two plump, medium orange ones with a few browned spots from the center of the tray. Despite the cold evening, they still held some warmth. He covered them again and raised an eyebrow as though waiting for her to taste. Penelope took a bite from the flat end of one of the pouches so she could perceive the filling's flavor. The perfectly fried corn-based dough and well-spiced minced beef, diced potato, and onion mixture yielded under her teeth. Surprised, she glanced at him. He grinned back with a slightly crooked smile.

The spices sang to Penelope of heat and love and generations of hardship. "Salvadoran?"

"Not I, but"—he tilted his head as if to tell her a secret—"I learned it from a Salvadoran."

Penelope raised her brows. She hadn't even known there *were* any Salvadorans in London. She took another bite. "Paprika in the masa instead of achiote?"

His eyes lit up. "Best I could do."

Penelope nodded and wrapped the rest in her handkerchief. She wouldn't think many London purveyors would carry achiote, anyway—let alone sell it cheaply. "Your Salvadoran friend taught you well."

"These aren't even my specialty. You should try my squash-blossom corn pasties. Best in London when they're in season."

Penelope raised an eyebrow. It sounded like something she'd had with her parents during their time in Mexico. The ones she'd eaten had been uncomplicated, but clean, straightforward food at its most delicious. "And where did you learn those?"

He shrugged with one shoulder. "Now, now, a fella can't reveal all his secrets, can he?"

Penelope raised a brow. Cooks, chefs, and Culinarians alike often kept their special recipes to themselves, but so few people in Britain had any but the smallest knowledge of the cuisines of the Americas that she found herself wondering why he didn't care to reveal his source. "I suppose not."

"Course, for a lady so pretty as yourself, I might be persuaded . . . if you saw fit to buy another." He lifted the tray nearer Penelope's face as the corner of his lips kicked up at one side—the kind of smile she imagined rakish gentlemen used to attract naive girls who had greater dowries than judgment. On him, though, she didn't know if it was anything more than a way of enticing her to buy more empanadas.

She had to hand it to him; the young man was a good salesman. "I'm afraid I've hit my limit for Salvadoran empanadas this evening." After all, she had a night of tasting in front of her, and a lady had to preserve her figure somehow. Her trip across the Americas had already added more curve to her shape than she'd departed England with.

"Balderdash! Utter balderdash!" a voice boomed from behind a column.

The young man and Penelope swiveled back to look at the speaker.

"Here, what's this?" the boy said.

A slight figure under a hooded cape emerged from the shadows. "Learned it from a Salvadoran, my foot. Why, anyone who tasted them could tell that those empanadas are Peruvian. No doubt this boy stumbled upon the combination on his own, and he's taking advantage of your knowledge, Pen." The lady pushed back her hood, revealing black ringlets minimally frizzed from the rain, and green eyes that tipped up slightly at the edges like those of a cat. "I am disappointed to see you making such a trivial mistake," she stated.

Penelope smiled despite herself. "Have you been hiding behind that column this entire time? I've been waiting an age, Helena."

"Seven minutes, to be precise. I had some notes to jot down on this fellow's Peruvian pasties." She waved a palm-sized notebook in the air. "Flavor good, but sloppy execution."

"Who are you?" the young man asked with a frown. "And what right do you have to take notes on me?"

"As to your first query, I am Lady Helena Higgins, top of my class at the Royal Academy of Culinaria Artisticus, and soon to be the most sought-after Culinarian in Britain. Most recently, I have acted as a culinary consultant by royal appointment to Queen Charlotte *and* the Royal Navy. As to your second question, the same right as any creature alive, I'm sure." Helena reached under her cloak, revealing the reticule hanging from a cord over her shoulder. She dropped her notebook and pencil inside and closed it.

The boy sniffed. "Culinary consultant, eh? Well, I don't take kindly to people trying to steal me recipes—especially puffed-up

Culinarians who haven't even *graduated*. Fella's gotta make a living somehow, and next thing I know, you'll be cooking me empanadas for the queen and not paying me nary a ha'penny for it! Meanwhile, I have to hear you tellin' me I don't know me own business."

Helena's green eyes widened. "How dare you insinuate that *I* would steal your accidental recipe for a *Peruvian* empanada. Why, the very idea—"

"I must say I agree with him, Helena," Penelope cut in. "Those empanadas taste far more like those I ate in Central America or Colombia. My parents and I spent weeks in each region. We didn't make it so far as Peru, but according to my research, most Peruvian empanadas are made with a wheat-based dough."

Helena turned to Penelope, all her outrage melting like candy floss in water. "Did you really go all the way to Colombia? I wonder if I should have taken you up on your offer to accompany you to the Americas, primitive as they are. But then I would not have been able to consult for the queen, and I daresay that will prove far better for my future culinary career."

Penelope tried not to roll her eyes. "The Americas are not primitive, Helena. I might, perhaps, characterize some places as a bit rural, but not primitive."

Helena waved her hand in the air. "I meant no offense, I assure you. Only how can you possibly think this street rat knows his Salvadoran anything from his Peruvian?"

The young man had had enough. "Here, how do you know what *I* know? You some kind of busybody? What sort of lady comes 'round Covent Garden looking to deprive a poor young cook of his livelihood by telling his customers he don't know where his own food comes from?"

Helena stretched to her full height, which was admittedly not much, but she wore it well. "Young man, *I* am a Culinarian. I have no intention of stealing your so-called recipes or telling your customers anything at all. This lady, however, is my friend and a fellow Culinarian, and as second in our class at the Royal Academy, she should know better."

Penelope let out an amused breath. Helena never took too long to bring up the fact that Penelope held a constant second place in their class to Helena's first. "I really think you ought to take another bite of this empanada, Helena."

"Oh, very well." She held out her hand for the unbitten pasty, and Penelope obliged. Helena chomped into it with little delicacy, chewed a few times, and tilted her head to the side. "Ah, this one's different from the one I ate earlier." She nodded at Penelope and then at the boy. "You see, lad, she *does* know better."

The young man frowned. "So you agree it's Salvadoran now?"

Helena nodded and swallowed another bite. "Undoubtedly." She weaved her arm through Penelope's. "My friend, you know, is working toward becoming an expert on the cuisine of the Americas. Come, Penelope! The rain has practically stopped and there's a delightful little Hungarian stand across the way that I've been longing for you to try." She pulled Penelope off the curb and into the street.

The boy followed. "Hey! Just because you're *almost* a Culinarian, that don't make you the Queen of Sheba. You may have a right to take down notes on me food, but you got no right to insult me. People coming from all around tell me my pasties are the best in

London. Faraway Pasties, they call 'em."

"That may be," Helena said, pulling Penelope to the left to skirt a pile of muddy refuse, "but you sell them for two pence apiece."

"So what if I do? It's an honest living."

Helena spoke over her shoulder. "Honest it may be, but not very profitable." They ducked between two columns and into the shelter of the market building.

"I can't sell them for no more—I'll get priced out."

"Helena, do leave the lad alone," Penelope interjected, starting to feel uncomfortable about how the young man had interpreted the conversation.

"Penelope, I have no intention of doing anything else," Helena said with big, innocent eyes. "I only mean that if he had the training, he could easily open his own shop, be *the* Faraway Pasty Man, if he so desired, and end up pulling in hundreds of pounds a year."

"Here, what's that ya say?" the young man asked.

"But instead he's forced to walk the streets with his wares, making barely enough to live on. If we could but educate these poor souls to a higher degree, just think how society would flourish."

Penelope brushed droplets of rain from her shoulders. "But surely not everyone could make a success even if they had the education."

"No, but they'd have a better chance." Helena walked farther into the market. "Just take this bedraggled young man, Pen." She cast a glance over her shoulder. "If I had a mind to, in six months I could turn him or anyone else into a first-rate gentleman culinary artist. One even our classmates would find impressive."

"Hey! You saying I isn't impressive?"

Both girls stopped and looked at him then. His eyebrows knit together as he glared back.

"Your flavors are excellent," Penelope said.

"But nothing out of the common way," Helena qualified. "At any rate, they're not impressive enough for you to own your own shop or even a stall of your own—of course, you are still quite young, I suppose." She eyed him up and down. "How old *are* you?"

He frowned. "Why would I tell you that?"

Helena cocked her head to the side. "Ten and seven?"

"Thereabouts," he grumbled.

She turned to Penelope. "There, you see, he is your age, Pen, and just look at the unfortunate fellow."

"He's your age, too, Helena," Penelope stated, tilting her chin down.

"Have you forgotten that I shall be eighteen in nary a month? Dear me, what a little education might do for this creature. I've a good mind to write a book on the subject. One day. I mean, if you think about it, had King George not given his assent to Lady Bramley's Freedom of Female Education Bill, we might not be able to become the preeminent Culinarians we are destined to be. Truly it boggles the mind, Penelope."

King George IV, though universally disliked by his subjects, did manage to do one good thing of note before his death, which was to grant royal assent—in person, no less—to the aforementioned bill when Parliament passed it in 1820. The fact that he only did so at the urging of his daughter, Princess Charlotte, surprised nobody.

Penelope opened her mouth to reply, but the boy spoke first.

"Just cuz you're educated, that don't give you the right to be insulting."

Helena stared at him. "Was I insulting?"

Penelope cleared her throat. "He's quite right, Helena. You were."

Helena gasped. "I had no notion I was *insulting* the poor fellow." Her cat eyes stretched into guileless green orbs. She reached under her cloak and sifted through her reticule. "As a show of good faith, young man, please accept this donation to the betterment of your culinary education." She dropped three half crowns onto his tray, and he ogled them. "Now, good evening to you." Helena threaded her arm through Penelope's again. "Was everything quite satisfactory when you arrived?"

Penelope threw a glance at the money and then at the boy's face. Judging by his wide eyes and slack jaw, she doubted he'd ever had so much value in his possession at one time. "Er . . . yes, the room is lovely." She looked at the coins again and wondered what he would do with it all.

"I knew the violet room was for you! I can hardly believe we *truly* get to stay at Cavendish Square together this term instead of squeezing into that ridiculous dormitory at school with the likes of Mabel Pilkington. I fancy I've grown used to the privileges of being a fourth-year far too easily. Now, come along. There is so much to taste," Helena said, dragging Penelope into the market and leaving the young man staring after their wake.

TWO

A ROOM SOMEWHERE

Late that evening, after all the stalls at Covent Garden had shuttered for the night and the theater patrons had disappeared into their homes and even the pickpockets had gone on their merry ways with springs in their steps from the accrual of more coin than they deserved, Elijah Little trudged down the stairs to the door of his uncle's basement-floor room in Old Fish Street. The creaking on the second-to-last step always made Elijah wonder if it would give out, but again, tonight, it held his weight. He pulled out his key and opened the door to the small room.

The short wooden bed that was barely long enough to support his heels sat against the wall under the tiny window that looked out onto the street level. He'd scrunched the pallet he slept on when his uncle wasn't at sea into the corner to make the room seem bigger, but the effect was marginal. Elijah set his empty tray down on the rickety wooden table, opened his tin tinderbox, and set about striking the cold flint and steel together until enough sparks lit the tinder. He let a brimstone match flare to life and used it to light a tallow candle before tamping down the tinder. Then he lit a few small branches in the grate with the candle and moved to the washbasin, where he set about scrubbing the food particles and other residue of the street from his hands. Since he had no looking glass, he swiped his wet hands over his face a few times, then dried everything with a piece of cloth. It was a tedious process for so late at night, but one he was well used to.

He sat at the table, pulled every coin from his pockets, and emptied it all on the table's surface. The copper and silver he'd earned stared back at him. He took a deep breath. All told, it was more than he'd ever made in a single night, even if two-thirds of it was basically charity.

Elijah scratched his earlobe as he considered the coins. Part of him wondered if he should feel ashamed at taking so much money from a rich girl who'd belittled him multiple times in one evening. On the other hand, how many principles could a fellow have when he was as poor as he? With this money, he could buy twice or even three times as many ingredients as he was usually able. If he kept up his hours working with his neighbor Charlie in exchange for the use of his kitchen, and with this fortunate influx of funds, Elijah could do some right good business. Maybe he'd even make as much as his uncle did as an able seaman.

Elijah shrugged off his coat and waistcoat and hung them over the chair. He untied his neckcloth and placed it on top of his outer garments. Lowering himself onto the bed, he ignored the lumps and yanked off his boots. Then he lay back, cradling his head in his hands. He frowned as the face of the lady who'd given him the money appeared in his mind. One trouble Elijah had never had was trouble with the ladies, but that Helena Higgins, as she called herself, had been one of the rudest, most insulting young females he'd ever met.

Her pretty friend with the brown eyes (and superior taste in empanadas) had been kind to make her apologize, but the fact that Helena Higgins hadn't seemed to realize how offending she'd been galled him even more. Yet what had actually kept running through his brain all night was her comment about what she could change him into if she tried. Being London's "Faraway Pasty Man" sounded like a bloody tempting prospect when you were always counting your ha'pennies.

Elijah peered into the water stains above him. Though brown, mottled, and ever present, they were nothing compared to the black mold spread across the window casing and the moth-eaten, threadbare carpet covering the slats of the floor. The four walls barely kept the cold night air at bay. What had he here to stay for? His uncle was at sea and would likely be gone for another six months yet. He'd been kind enough to take Elijah in, and he'd given Elijah enough coin to keep the roof over his head until his uncle's voyage to the West Indies returned, but a lad still had to eat. Besides, naval voyages had a way of extending longer than anyone expected, and Elijah couldn't be living under his uncle's charity forever—it just didn't sit well.

And that girl had said she could turn him into a first-rate culinary artist. For a moment Elijah dismissed the thought as madness. What kind of fellow took up a lady on a proposition like that? Possibly the kind of fellow Elijah never wanted to become. He didn't really think she'd meant it as a sincere offer anyway. But he'd already raised himself much higher than society thought a boy like him should climb.

She herself had said that with a little education he might go far, and who was to say that Miss High-and-Mighty Culinarian wasn't correct? Certainly not he, an ignorant cook.

A knock sounded through the door. His landlady's voice followed. "You awake, luv?"

Elijah closed his eyes. It had to be past one, and he had to wake with the dawn to help Charlie with his baking. Though, maybe now with this abundance of coin, he could *pay* Charlie for some time in the kitchen instead of working for the privilege of using it.

"Coming, Mrs. Willet," Elijah said, swinging his legs out of bed. He pulled the door open, though not all the way so she didn't take it as an invitation to enter, and tried to smile.

Mrs. Willet's chins jiggled as her gaze dropped to his chest, which was half-exposed without his neckcloth.

He suppressed a grimace. "Rent's not due fer another two weeks, Mrs. Willet."

The old lady sniffed, then batted her eyes. "Ah, you and your uncle is always good for the rent, young 'Lijah, I know that. No, I wanted to see that you're well. We haven't seen you for a week or more, and Lucy's been askin' fer ya."

Lucy Willet had been after him for months—ever since he'd come across her at the local market one day and walked her home. But since they lived in the same building, he hadn't thought she'd take it as him paying her special attention. "Just been busy, Mrs. Willet. A fellow's gotta make plans for the future."

"Of course, of course. Nothing better a young man like you should be doing than thinking of the *future*. I know my Lucy would agree. Just remember you're always welcome fer tea." She winked.

He swallowed. He certainly hadn't meant to imply he was thinking of marriage or Lucy in *any* future of his. There was nothing really wrong with her, but if there was one thing he disliked more than her mother's ogling, it was the taste of her mother's cheap Indian tea. He'd rather drink no tea at all than that bilge water. "You're real kind, Mrs. Willet. Now, if you'll 'cuse me, I gotta get some sleep."

She grinned at him wide enough that he could see the space where her missing molar used to be. "Always thinkin' of work, you enterprising young fellow. By all means, rest. But don't be a stranger upstairs, mind."

"Course not, Mrs. Willet."

She turned from the door. "I'll tell Lucy you said 'ello," she called over her shoulder.

"G'night, Mrs. Willet," Elijah said, closing the door. He swallowed once, looked about the room, and sighed. Then he yanked his satchel out from under the bed and started throwing his belongings inside.

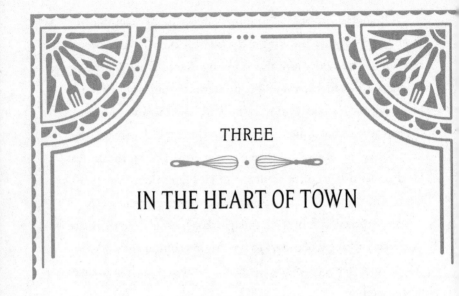

THREE

IN THE HEART OF TOWN

The following day, in the dining room of Number 9, Cavendish Square, Helena gestured with both hands at the table. Only three plates of food and two place settings sat upon it, but Helena enjoyed acting as though things were lavish even if they were not—it gave her a sense of joy in the everyday course of events, especially since, in her mind, so many things in life were utterly mundane. Though she knew her future as a Culinarian of the highest echelon would be anything but routine, the fact that she still had a final term left to finish before her fascinating new life began irked her whenever she bothered to dwell on it.

"There, you see, Penelope, are three different versions of Jägerschnitzel. As you may or may not be aware, much debate exists throughout the German states as to the correct way to make this dish."

Penelope raised a delicate eyebrow. "Though I don't pretend to be an authority on Continental cuisine, I was aware of this particular debate. You wrote about it in one of your letters."

Helena didn't remember ever having mentioned it, but she'd written Pen quite a few letters in the months her friend had been abroad, so it was certainly possible. "So I did."

"I take it this has some bearing on your final project?" Penelope asked.

Each student at the Royal Academy needed to create an original research project during their fourth year in order to be certified as an expert in Culinaria. Fourth-years usually spent their autumn term consulting under a Culinarian's supervision, or in Penelope's case, gathering information and experience abroad. In spring, the girls would compile and complete the project to be presented to their headmistress at the end of term. The ladies with the most imaginative projects went on to become the most sought-after Culinarians after commencement, and Helena had every intention of devising the most innovative project the Royal Academy had yet seen.

"I am still weighing the possibilities. This may become the first part of it. Well, I hope your knowledge of the issue doesn't skew the experiment, but since we are here anyway, do see what you can identify."

Penelope nodded and the medium brown curls framing her face bobbed. "So I am to taste the differences."

"Of course, but beyond that, you must determine which version is the most authentic." Helena's eyes widened with excitement.

Penelope sat at the table and picked up the silver fork and knife lying next to the first dish. "Surely any version that comes from somewhere in the German states would be authentic."

Helena moved around the table to sit across from her. "Not at all, I assure you. In any case, *I* have prepared these myself."

Penelope tilted her head. "Then they are all *your* interpretation of Jägerschnitzel?"

"*At least* one is my interpretation, and at least one is as authentic as I could make it, given the ingredients I could find in London. You must determine which is which," Helena pronounced, unable to suppress a smile.

"Very well." Penelope cut into the first plate, a version made with venison pounded until it was thin, lightly dusted in flour, and pan-fried in butter.

Helena had decided to keep the chanterelle and chestnut mushrooms in the sauce consistent in all three dishes as they would be the easiest for Penelope to identify, but each sauce had subtle differences.

Penelope chewed the venison, then used her knife to scoop some mushrooms and sauce onto her fork. "The venison pairs quite well with the chanterelles, but I count no less than twelve variations that you've made to the dish. The lemon thyme and the"—she licked her lips—"saffron is particularly obvious."

Helena nodded, though she'd thought the lemon thyme a rather clever addition considering it was much less robust than English thyme and often easily overpowered by other strong flavors. Still, a part of her would have been disappointed had Penelope missed it.

Penelope moved on to the next dish. "Wild boar fried in what I presume is its own lard. Unadulterated by flour this time. Same mushrooms, but the sauce contains cured pork belly, which complements the mushrooms and the boar. I believe I detect a fruity wine that could be from the Rhineland, but it could be French as well."

Helena smiled but gave nothing away.

Penelope cut into the third plate. "Domesticated pork, albeit with good flavor." She tasted the mushrooms and the sauce. She frowned, then tasted it again.

Helena tried not to grin.

"Red wine this time," Penelope stated, "but there is an underlying flavor I don't believe is authentic. In fact, the flavor is quite muddled." She went back for another bite of the second plate with the wild boar. "I have doubts that the wine is German in origin, but as you were forced to make do with available ingredients, I don't know if that should influence my decision. Still, the muddled flavor of the third makes me believe you used some kind of additive to mask ingredients."

Helena raised an eyebrow, still maintaining a calm outward demeanor, though she was bubbling with delight on the inside.

Penelope dabbed at the corner of her lips with a napkin. "Considering all these factors, I believe the second is the most authentic of the three."

"You're quite wrong," Helena pronounced. She stood and pointed at the third plate. "The muddled flavor in the third is, in fact, *quite* authentic! It comes from an overabundance of flour and butter in the sauce."

Penelope's eyes widened. "You weren't hiding anything in that sauce?"

"I easily might have. As you can see, I've much improved the sauce in my version," she said, flourishing her hand at the second dish.

"Yes, yours is superior. I suppose it proves once again that cleaner, more robust flavors can be achieved with the correct techniques—is that to be your proposal?"

Helena shook her head. "Nothing so trite, I assure you."

"From what I see, that is the natural conclusion—I would imagine Lady Rutland would agree."

Their headmistress approved every project before the girls could begin research in earnest. She'd approved Penelope's trip to the Americas and helped Helena find opportunities to consult with royalty.

Helena pursed her lips and started pacing down the length of the room.

"And the wine in your version?" Penelope asked.

"A Riesling grown in Alsace, but it was the closest my purveyor had that day. Would you believe, Penelope, that he dared question my desire for Germanic wine? He claims there is no demand for it." Helena rolled her eyes.

Penelope, who had never seen Germanic wines once in her travels through the Americas, but had often seen French and Spanish vintages, shrugged. "He may very well be correct, Helena."

Helena scoffed and turned back to face her friend. "The man has the palate of a candlestick maker. And so does the public if no one drinks German wine as he claims. I tell you, Pen, this country mainly consists of insular fools who believe nothing resides outside of Britain."

That had been Penelope's perception since her early days at the Royal Academy, but she'd never heard Helena say so. Penelope stood from her chair. "Perhaps you should come with me on my next expedition. I plan to meet my parents after graduation. We'll be sailing to the Pacific—"

"I shall give it some consideration, but I cannot imagine I would be at all suited to the climate. And I do so dislike sea voyages. And of course, I shall have so much work here once we graduate. I cannot believe you would forego the excitement of starting your vocation—of consulting with the queen and the nobility—just to go gallivanting with your parents."

When Penelope's father had encountered her mother while on a merchant trade expedition in the South Pacific, they'd fallen in love, and they'd soon married. Neither of their families had accepted the union. Though they'd returned to England to live when Penelope was an infant, they soon discovered that life was far more agreeable beyond British borders. When it came time for Penelope to train to become a Culinarian as she'd always dreamed, her parents agreed that they could never harm her future at the Royal Academy with their presence. They stayed abroad for that precise reason, and Penelope missed them dreadfully when she was at the Royal Academy. Knowing how much they wanted her to have everything didn't make it any easier. "Gallivanting" with them to faraway locales during the summer holidays, therefore, was time Penelope always looked forward to.

As it happened, Penelope had quite a fair complexion and medium brown hair in a shade reminiscent of steeped tea leaves— many shades lighter than her mother's deep raisin-brown hue. Penelope's hair also waved like her father's, and his hazel eye color had combined with her mother's nearly black irises to give Penelope brown eyes that lay precisely in the middle of both their shades. Because of her appearance, most people who met Penelope believed her to be an average English girl studying to be a Culinarian. Only her hooded eyes that tipped slightly downward at the inner corners lent a clue to her heritage, if someone knew what to look for.

It had taken a full two years before Penelope had even spoken of her mother's origin to Helena—due to some offhand remark Helena had unthinkingly made in Global Sourcing class about coconuts and "primeval little islands in the Pacific Ocean." After Penelope had told Helena about her parents, Helena had gone to considerable pains to say she'd meant no offense. Judging by this most recent comment, however, Penelope wondered if Helena had given the matter of her lineage any further thought since they'd last spoken of it, or if, indeed, it had escaped Helena's mind completely.

"Why, only last week," Helena continued, "Queen Charlotte sent me an urgent summons asking me to create a menu for Princess Adelaide's sixteenth-birthday celebration. Another opportunity you missed simply by being absent."

Penelope raised an eyebrow. "I thought Princess Adelaide was not at all well disposed toward you after the Italian meringue incident."

Helena shrugged. "Oh, she isn't. That Goose wouldn't know the difference between French, Swiss, and Italian meringue if it hit her in the nose, which it very nearly would have if the queen and Lady Rutland hadn't walked in."

Penelope coughed to stifle a laugh. "Then why did the queen ask for your consultation?"

"Oh, the queen quite likes me. Of course it's common knowledge how much she and the royal family revere Culinaria, but I confess I was surprised to see *how* passionate they are about the field. You know, Pen, I rather fancy Queen Charlotte wishes she could have been a Culinarian herself—if her royal responsibilities might have allowed it."

Penelope bit the inside of her cheek. "Imagine being *the queen* and not being able to pursue your passion. Though, I suppose we all have our limitations. Even the Queen of England."

Helena shook her head. "I don't agree. One can be anything one strives to be—if one strives hard enough."

Penelope did laugh at this. "You and I could strive to be the Queen of England every day from now until doomsday, but we'd never achieve it."

Helena rolled her eyes. "That's because *that* is a hereditary title. However, if we truly cared to, we could become prime minister. And do not tell me there has never been a female prime minister before. Twenty years ago there were no Culinarians either, and now look at us! It's only a matter of time."

"Your point is well taken," Penelope agreed. "Though you must admit that some people are more hindered by societal limitations than others."

"No doubt you are right. Yet I still say they needn't be. At any rate, I believe I was telling you about the queen and the princess."

Penelope waved her hand in the air. "Yes, yes. Do go on." She settled back down into the dining chair as Helena continued.

"After the success of Princess Adelaide's midsummer fête—the food for which I organized with only minimal supervision from Lady Rutland—I believe the queen thinks quite highly of my skill.

But the Goose told the queen she'd rather create the menu for her birthday herself than ask me again."

Penelope wondered at the wisdom of calling the crown princess *the Goose* but said nothing. Princess Adelaide loved food as much as her mother did, and indeed, had a reputation for maintaining an ever-rotating circle of friends composed only of Culinarians, Culinarians in training, and young gentlemen chefs. None of them seemed to stay particularly long in the inner circle, however. Whether this was because the Culinarians were frequently drawn away to consult with nobility across Europe, or because the gentlemen chefs often fell into advantageous marriages just by virtue of their proximity to the princess, or due to some other reason entirely, was not well understood by anyone except, perhaps, Princess Adelaide herself.

Helena paced to the far end of the table. "But then, last week, the royal secretary came to Cavendish Square three times in the hopes that I'd magically appear. I can only assume that the pressure must have become too much for her in the end." Helena let out a sigh. "But I wasn't at all surprised. That Goose thinks she has all the knowledge of a Culinarian but without any of the training. I suppose that's what happens when her parade of fawning Culinarians have more interest in being paid their fee than telling her the truth."

Penelope didn't bother to point out that many Culinarians lived on their fees alone. They'd all learned in Consultation Management class that a delicate balance existed between appeasing one's client and espousing perfect culinary principles. It had been one of the few classes where Penelope had edged past Helena for the top rank. "So you weren't here?"

"When? Oh, last week! I was in Bristol. Lady Rutland sent me to help the admiralty with their officers' banquet and ball for the new year. It was a pity you missed it, Pen." Helena stretched to her full height and waved her hands as though she might paint the picture in the air. "Imagine if you will, whole fish roasted to delicate firmness, their scales replaced by gold leaf, and sitting on beds of potato coins roasted in duck fat, surrounded by a silky seaweed salad. Then three-foot-high sculptures of tropical fruit inspired by naval voyages. The men had never seen the like."

"Sounds quite impressive. Lady Rutland did not accompany you?" Lady Rutland was one of the first and most celebrated Culinarians in Britain, but since she had become headmistress of the Royal Academy some years ago, she generally solely took on consultations during the summer and winter holidays. Only her best and brightest students were invited to assist her.

"She was there for the first two days, but she left on a commission for one of the royal dukes. I carried out her plans, and she returned at the end of the week to oversee the banquet. Her time has been spread as thinly as low-pectin preserves."

"But how good of her to consult for the admiralty. I cannot imagine the navy's budget compares to the Duchess of Marlborough's or to the palace's."

Helena laughed. "I'm certain you're correct, but I don't believe Lady Rutland cares a jot for the fee. She wishes to make the food the most awe-inspiring it can be, which I have to admire. It is her interest in satisfying everyone that I do not particularly agree with. I thought it would be fascinating to contrast the practicality of the navy with the whims of the aristocracy I've seen thus far. Instead, I learned the admiralty has an entirely different set of whims. Lady

Rutland took great pains to listen to all their demands and even changed some of her ideas despite knowing her judgment to be correct. I don't know that *I* would be so tolerant of clients who wouldn't come around to what's right"—she cleared her throat—"er, that is, to what I suggest. In the end."

Penelope politely ignored the slip. "As the princess did?"

Helena laughed. "She just grew bored with the planning, I'm certain. She has the attention span of a waterfowl, that one. Which is why I call her *the Goose*, as you might have inferred."

Penelope shook her head. "You might wish to take care, Helena. She *is* the future queen."

Helena waved her hand in the air. "Oh, I never call her that in mixed company."

Penelope raised an eyebrow. "Will you be planning her party, then?"

Helena let out a short breath. "Since I was in Bristol, they had to find someone else, and for some unfathomable reason, Lady Rutland referred them to Mabel Pilkington!"

"To Mabel?" Penelope let out a breath. "To be quite honest, I'd wondered if she'd even passed her exams last spring. She misplaced her saccharometer the day before the oenology test and then tried to talk me into loaning her mine."

Helena scoffed and moved around the table again to stand at Penelope's side. "And just how did she imagine *you* would take the exam without a saccharometer?"

"She claimed I was so advanced in my oenology that I wouldn't need it."

"What a halfwit. I can only infer she was the sole culinary student available and in town last week for Lady Rutland to refer. Gracious, if Princess Adelaide disliked me, can you imagine what she will think of Mabel?"

Penelope shook her head. "Poor Princess Adelaide."

Helena plucked a mushroom off one of the plates and popped it into her mouth. "It almost serves the Goose right. Though Mabel would have thought the lemon thyme you detected in that first dish was sumac, the princess will likely find her a willing sycophant. She won't even know how average Mabel's palate is. I have no sympathy for either of them."

"Do you ever wonder that I'm your only friend, Helena?" Penelope asked with a pointed stare.

Helena let out a breath. "Not at all. You're the only girl at the Royal Academy who isn't jealous of my abilities. So of course we're friends."

Penelope sighed.

"It *is* nice having you about, Pen. I'd forgotten what fun it is to challenge you." Helena tapped her chin, considering. She started walking down the length of the table once more. "But I wonder if you are correct about what Lady Rutland would say about the Jäger-schnitzel debate. Too commonplace by half. My project must have real significance; be something that could change our perceptions of food and society. And of course—"

"I beg your pardon, Lady Helena, but a young man is at the door."

Helena glanced back and saw the family butler, Pierce, standing just inside the door to the dining room. She blinked, wondering how he always seemed to appear out of nowhere.

In fact, Pierce had been standing there for some time waiting for Helena to take a breath. Finding none imminent, he'd resorted to interruption.

"What sort of young man?" Helena asked. "We aren't expecting a young man. Are we, Penelope?"

Penelope shook her head. "Not to my knowledge."

Helena waved her hand in the air. "There you are, we're expecting no one, Pierce."

"He claims he's here to see you on business, Lady Helena. I would have turned him away, but you do often see the oddest characters," stated Pierce.

"Is he a gentleman?" Helena asked.

The butler cleared his throat. "I should say not, by his manner of dress. But he smells faintly of bread, so I would hazard he's some sort of baker."

"Ah, interesting! Bakers, you know, Pen, often have palates that can discern varying strains of yeast, even if they haven't the knowledge to name them. It might be worth it to see how this fellow's palate compares to yours."

Penelope opened her mouth to protest.

"Just as an experiment, mind," continued Helena. "No use in letting all this Jägerschnitzel go to waste. And I do admit I have a certain degree of curiosity as to what sort of business he could refer to."

Penelope tilted her head. "As you like, but the next experiment should be of my choosing. In fact, I've half a mind to make a mole negro and see how many of the thirty odd ingredients you can decipher."

Helena inclined her head regally. "I welcome the challenge. We'll go down to the market after we see this fellow."

"*I'll* go to the market. You shan't have any more unfair advantage than I had."

"Oh, very well, *you'll* go. Bring the young man in, Pierce."

Pierce nodded. "As you wish, Lady Helena," he said in a tone that implied he wasn't happy about it.

"Do you often bring in people off the street to do tastings?" Penelope asked, angling her torso toward Helena.

"Not as a rule, but I *have* been using every opportunity to find inspiration for the most marvelous final project the Royal Academy has yet seen. The Jägerschnitzel idea came from a German immigrant I encountered on Oxford Street and—"

"Here is the young man, my lady," Pierce interrupted. Helena turned to the door as Penelope sat forward and sucked in a breath. Just preceding Pierce stood a young man with shaggy brown hair that waved and curled over his forehead in a fashion reminiscent of a mop. He stood slightly taller than Pierce, though he stooped as if to minimize his height. Then Helena's gaze dropped to his face. "You! You're the fellow from last night. What are you doing here?"

The boy straightened his spine. "Well . . . I . . ."

"Out with it, boy," Pierce said. Pierce was a rather judgmental person.

The boy frowned and took a step forward. "I've been thinking 'bout what you said last night."

"Have you, indeed?" replied Helena. "And you came to tell us your Salvadoran—I beg your pardon, *Peruvian*—pasties are now the toast of London?"

"Er—" Penelope began, debating whether it would be worth the time to correct Helena yet again.

"I ain't come to give away me recipes or bow at your feet. I come with a proposition," the young man said.

Pierce cleared his throat. "Really, boy, Lady Helena doesn't entertain prop—"

Helena held up a hand. "What sort of proposition?"

"Now you're talking," said the boy. Then he seemed to see Penelope for the first time. He touched the brim of his ratty hat and bowed his head. "Good day, miss."

Helena frowned, wondering why she hadn't gotten such a cordial greeting.

"Good day, Mr. . . . ." Penelope trailed off, prompting him to give his name.

"Little, miss. Elijah Little."

Penelope nodded to him. "How pleasant to see you again, Mr. Little. Now, perhaps you might tell us what your, er . . . proposition is for Lady Helena."

"Yes, sit down, and state your business," Helena said, gesturing to a chair.

Elijah looked at the chairs in front of the dining table, but didn't sit.

"Do as you're told, boy," Pierce said.

"Look here, I won't be ordered about by the likes of you," Elijah said, turning to Pierce. "I'll sit if I have a mind to and not before."

"Mr. Little," Penelope said, "would you care to rest your feet?"

She held her palm out to the chair across from hers.

Elijah looked at her, then down at the chair. "Thank you, I will, miss." He smiled at her—a slightly crooked yet nonetheless attractive smile, even Helena had to admit—and took the seat.

Helena rolled her eyes. She took the chair beside Penelope's. "Well, Mr. Little?"

Elijah narrowed his gaze. "You may be a hard one, but since you're not too proud to talk about giving lessons, I've come to have me some. I'm willing to pay, so you needn't turn up your nose neither."

Helena blinked rapidly. "Who says I give lessons?"

"*You* said last night. You said you could turn me into a proper gentleman chef. So here I am. Ready to pay, as I said." He pulled his trouser leg up, then crossed his ankle so it sat on his left knee.

For a moment, no one said a word. For another moment, Helena, Penelope, and Pierce all stared at the rather bedraggled young man sitting at the table so very matter-of-factly. Then Penelope let out a loud hoot. All heads turned to her.

She laughed again.

"What's so blasted amusing?" Helena demanded.

"You," Penelope said between giggles. "You absolutely said that to him."

"Here now," Elijah said, frowning, "I don't see what's so funny about it. I didn't come here to be laughed at. If you're gonna be impolite, I can take me bloomin' self elsewhere."

"Yes, do be quiet, Penelope, you're offending the poor fellow," Helena said.

Penelope schooled her features. "I beg your pardon, Mr. Little," she said. "I assure you, I wasn't laughing at you."

He gave a short nod, but his expression didn't soften.

Penelope leaned forward. "Gentlemen aren't paid to cook, you know. They are admired if they can, of course, and it gives them a more elevated stature in the marriage market, but they cannot use their culinary accomplishments to make a living as you do now."

"I know that, miss. I don't want to be no gentleman. I only want enough culinary skills so as I can work in a shop and maybe one day *own* me own pasty shop with an oven. I'm bone-weary baking for me neighbor Charlie during the day and selling me pasties at night."

"Well," Helena said, looking between Penelope and the boy, "how much do you propose to er . . . offer for these lessons?"

He shoved his hands into his trouser pockets. Onto the table he dumped two handfuls of coins. "This here is all I have in the world. I can pay this for me lodging"—he pushed forward a few silver coins—"but I should keep some to buy ingredients for me pasties." He pulled a few shillings away from the pile. "I'm willing to part with the rest for lessons from an almost Culinarian."

Helena leaned forward over the table and glanced at the remaining coins. "Good Lord, Pen, if you consider how much this fellow is willing to pay as a percentage of his means, it's incredible. It's the most flattering fee I've ever been offered!"

"It's the only fee you've ever been offered," Penelope pronounced.

Helena gave her a pointed look. "I'll have you know that Lady Rutland offered me a stipend to cover the cost of travel to Bristol and back."

Penelope nodded. "I would expect nothing less from Lady Rutland. Not only is she the *first* Culinarian, she remains the highest regarded. And she is generosity itself. You, however, are *not* a Culinarian yet."

Helena waved her hand about. "I soon shall be. One day I shall surpass Lady Rutland and so shall you. That is why she became a teacher, after all. To advance the field and teach girls to become Culinarians even more skillful than herself."

Penelope raised a brow. "So, you still believe you can turn Mr. Little into a culinary shop owner, as he wishes? In some ways, that requires an even more refined skill set than being a gentleman chef does."

Helena stood. "Of course I can turn this pie-peddling rogue into a shop owner—or any fellow alive, for that matter."

"Hey! I won't be called a—"

"You know, Helena," Penelope said, coming to her feet and extending a pacifying hand to Elijah, "it occurs to me that you may have found your final-year project. One actually difficult enough to prove you truly are as good as you claim." She tilted her head to the side when Helena said nothing. "Well?"

Helena brushed at the hair of her temple, though not a strand had moved. A smile spread across her face. "You know, Pen, you really do make life a dashed sight more interesting." She licked her lips, glanced at Elijah, and brought her fist down onto the table. "It's perfect! No one at the Royal Academy has attempted a final-year project such as this. When we succeed, my project shall become the stuff of legend! And this mud-trodden pasty of a person will be a croquembouche before I'm finished with him. Once we get him cleaned up, his hair cut, his grammar fixed, and some basic culinary technique embedded in his skull, he'll be beating ladies away with a walking stick—why, he could even marry a shipping magnate's daughter—or a countess's cousin!"

"Wait, I don't want none of that! I just want to cook better," Elijah stated. "I only want what I came here for, not the blasted moon."

Helena put her hands on her hips. "And what, if I may ask, is wrong with the moon?"

He stared at her. "The likes of me don't get the moon, and I ain't so simple as to think I will."

"With a little education you'll want even more than the moon, my boy." She threw her arm in the air. "You'll be wanting Venus or Saturn or—"

"Not me." He stood from the chair and looked at Penelope. "I've changed me mind. Thank you for your trouble, miss, but it ain't worth it. She's too balmy to abide."

Helena huffed out a breath. "So I'm mad, am I? Very well, back to the gutter with you. Enjoy hawking your barely above-average Peruvian pasties."

Elijah pulled a face and turned toward the door.

"Helena, do be reasonable," Penelope said, following her as she stalked toward the opposite end of the dining room. "He's not asking for any privileges."

"Indeed he isn't. He wants the very minimum, which I find to be abhorrent. If he wants to be more than he is, then he better get the education necessary—otherwise he will always be stuck exactly where he is now." She tilted her head toward him. "But far better to have what you understand than to reach for the moon and get nothing at all. Isn't that right, Mr. Little?"

He looked at her over his shoulder, a frown creating creases between his eyes.

Helena arched a dark brow. "I know what's going on in that little brain of yours, Mr. Little."

He folded his arms across his chest.

Penelope sighed.

"You're thinking this offer is too good to be true," Helena continued, "and you're right. It is. If you go through with it, you will be stuck with me and whatever I can teach you, and you *could* end up gaining everything you've ever dreamed of." Helena's eyes widened as the plan formed in her mind. She walked toward him. "At the end of the term, we'll take you to a culinary faire, where you will show off your talents. The gentlemen will envy you, and every lady and Culinarian in the place will find your food irresistible. You'll be able to open a shop of your choosing, with the financial backing of some of your newfound, fawning acolytes, and live an honorable, well-rounded life.

"If you do not accept this offer, you shall go back to whatever mold-covered, worm-ridden room you live in, spend a few blessed, euphoric weeks spending all the coins you've offered me, then return to your thankless, uneventful life and continue to be bone-weary for the rest of your days. How does that sound?"

Elijah eyed her, but said nothing. She'd closed most of the distance between them as she'd been talking, and they now stood within arm's length of each other. A muscle next to his left eye ticked.

"Really, Helena, does it occur to you that the young man may have feelings?" asked Penelope.

"Oh, I don't think so," Helena replied. "At least none we need worry about. Have you, Mr. Little?"

Elijah gave her a look that Helena believed proved her point.

Penelope exhaled and crossed the dining room until she stood by Helena's side. "I don't know that what you described was the best way to put the situation to him. This would be a *research project*—an attempt at seeing *if* you can transform him from what he is now into a shop owner. And there are no guarantees it will succeed."

Helena opened her palms. "That is what I said." She turned back to Elijah. "Indeed, this will be just as much a risk for me as for you. If my hypothesis fails, I'll be the laughingstock of the Royal Academy come graduation. But I know I can succeed if you work hard. If you do, we shall both reap the benefits. Can I put it more plainly?"

Elijah cleared his throat. "All right then."

Helena's green eyes lit up in triumph. She almost clapped her hands, but decided against it when she noticed Penelope's frown. Helena truly didn't know what Penelope had to frown about. This final project would solidify Helena's reputation as the greatest Culinarian ever to graduate from the Royal Academy. But Penelope often assigned far more importance to minor circumstances than she, so Helena clasped her hands behind her back and tried to regulate her smile.

Penelope stared at Elijah with a grave expression. "You must understand what you're getting yourself into. *Do you, Mr. Little?*"

He met her gaze. "Oh, I think so, miss. But I also ain't the kind of fool who turns down the chance to change me life."

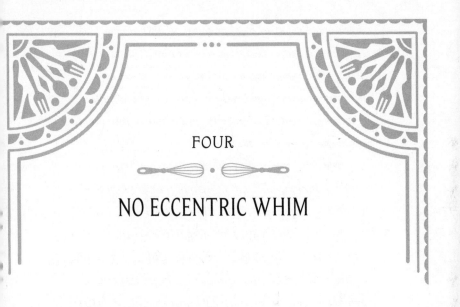

FOUR

NO ECCENTRIC WHIM

Number 9, Cavendish Square   *January 6, 1833*
Marylebone, London

My Dear Papa and Mama,
I was pleased to hear that your journey through the Alps did
not go awry and that you are now enjoying an interlude on
the banks of Lake Como. I daresay it shall give my brother a
chance to improve his Italian well before you arrive in Rome.
As you made no mention of his behavior in your letter, I do
hope that Roland has not hampered your enjoyment with
his annoying habits. I, for one, have found the last month a
welcome respite from his company, although I must confess
that the house occasionally felt quiet. Happily, Penelope's
arrival has kept me occupied.

    You will be pleased to learn that I have finally

determined what my final project shall be! I propose to transform a bedraggled street vendor into a culinary shop owner. This is a project unlike any other that has ever been attempted at the Royal Academy, and I am quite certain that Lady Rutland will find it both ambitious and containing higher social value.

Such an experiment will necessitate <u>total</u> immersion in the culinary world and, indeed, in the right society. As a result, I have housed one Mr. Elijah Little here at Cavendish Square. Pierce insisted the boy sleep in the servants' quarters instead of the guest rooms as I wished. I find this arrangement wholly unacceptable, as the fellow cannot possibly learn to better himself if he does not <u>live</u> in better accommodations than he is accustomed to.

I am certain you shall agree, as my entire culinary career depends on the success of this project. As such, I shall endeavor to change Pierce's mind until your approval arrives.

I am, as ever, your dutiful daughter,
Helena

Number 9, Cavendish Square   January 6, 1833
Marylebone, London

Dearest Nanay and Papa,
As I hope you know from my last letter, I am safely ensconced in Cavendish Square with Helena. Though the term begins next week, Helena had not yet determined upon a concept

*for her final project until this very day. The first evening I
arrived, we encountered a young street vendor at the Covent
Garden Market, and Helena has now taken it into her
head to transform him into a merchant. The young man
is well-meaning and clever from what I have seen and goes
by the name Elijah Little. He has some natural ability for
flavors (and quite interestingly, has a flair for making rather
authentic empanadas—they're not at all like yours, Nanay,
but they are very close to those we ate in the Americas), but
his education is woefully lacking, a situation Helena seeks
to remedy. Helena moved him into a room in the servants'
quarters, where he is watched closely by the butler, Pierce.
To turn a pasty hawker into a respectable fellow capable of
running his own shop, where he will have to court the favor
and patronage of the best circles in the gentry and nobility,
seems an extraordinarily massive undertaking. In truth, I do
not know if it will yield Helena the rewards she craves. Still,
if she can help Mr. Little in some small way, perhaps it will
be worth it.*

*At any rate, I am missing you both dreadfully and
trying not to consider how long it will be before I see you at
the end of the term.*

With all my love,
Penelope

*Post Script: Nanay, I attempted your pinakbet yesterday
as Helena was instructing the staff about Mr. Little and
getting him settled in his quarters, and though the end result*

was close to yours, I could not source bitter melon or dried shrimp paste. I did make a prawn stock, but I still found it lacking. Of course, pinakbet is never as good without you to share it with. Despite the modifications I was forced to make, I must say that Helena quite enjoyed it (though she was, upon first taste, somewhat confused by it). Papa, please send me a sketch of your current location when you next write.

Number 9, Cavendish Square   January 6, 1833
Marylebone, London

Dear Uncle Jonathan,
I've got me an apprenticeship with a Culinarian. It should be good for me, I think. I'll keep paying Mrs. Willet her rent to keep your room, but I'll be moving into Number 9, Cavendish Square, for a while. I dunno if this'll reach Barbados before you do, and I may be done with this apprenticeship before you return to London, but I'll leave a note for you at the room in Old Fish Street too.
    Elijah

"There you have it, Lady Rutland, my final-year project in a nutshell. Don't you agree it will have great social significance if I succeed?" Helena sat back in the spindly chair and beamed at Lady Rutland.

Her headmistress lifted a blue-and-white china teacup to her lips and sipped delicately, but she made no outward show of her thoughts. The tea service and a two-tiered tray of petit fours coated in daffodil yellow icing and candied white flowers sat on the table between them in Lady Rutland's private parlor at the Royal Academy. Lady Rutland had converted the old Hiller estate on the outskirts of North London into a state-of-the-art school for Culinarians, but she had kept many of the rooms cozy enough to feel like a home away from home. Helena had spent enough time in this room with Lady Rutland over the last three and a half years to know that the petit fours would be scrumptious regardless of the flavor, but her stomach buzzed with excitement and she didn't think she could get one down. Helena held her breath as she waited for Lady Rutland's judgment.

Her headmistress placed her cup on its saucer. "What does the young man's family think of all this?"

Helena paused. She vaguely remembered Penelope asking him that question, but Helena had attended little to his answer. "He has no family." Wasn't that what he'd said?

"And where shall he live, Helena? I cannot imagine your parents will approve having him in such close proximity to you girls. And of course, Miss Pickering's parents must be consulted as well."

"Penelope's parents have given her leave to do as she sees fit—as they do every term. But she wrote them a letter in any case. My own missive is already on its way. My parents want me to be the very best Culinarian I can be, and if you approve, Lady Rutland, they will not object. Penelope's parents will feel the same, I am certain."

Lady Rutland arched an eyebrow. "Even if that is so, Helena, have you considered the propriety of having a strange boy in your home? Even if it is only in service of your final-year project, you cannot very well disclose that to anyone. It would compromise the entire experiment."

"Oh." Helena waved her hand. "We shall tell people he is my distant relation or some such thing. Then there won't be anything improper in him living at Cavendish Square."

Lady Rutland shook her head. "That won't do, Helena. That would be elevating his status with familial ties—not by his own merit or what you could teach him. No, I'm afraid I don't quite see how this can work." She took another sip of her tea.

Helena's jaw dropped for a moment, but she recovered quickly. "Lady Rutland, there must be a way. Surely such outmoded notions of propriety have all but disappeared in the last fifteen years. A lady can hold a profession now! She should not be bound to the old ideas of having a chaperone present for every encounter with someone of the opposite sex."

Lady Rutland gave her a pointed look over the rim of her teacup. "Helena, whether you believe it or not, people of the older generation still firmly hold to those ideas. Some do not care for the parliamentary reforms of the last two decades, and some wish to return to what they consider a simpler time."

Helena cast her eyes at the ceiling. "A time when ladies could do nothing but marry and bear children?"

Lady Rutland nodded. "Just so, I'm afraid."

Helena let out an exasperated breath. The idiocy of some people frequently astonished her—to be more precise, the idiocy of *most* people. In Helena's opinion, the days of women being their husband or father's chattel could not disappear soon enough. "I don't care a fig for their opinions, Lady Rutland, and I can't fathom why you would. Those sorts of fools would not bother employing a Culinarian anyway."

Lady Rutland set her cup and saucer down and motioned to the teapot with one hand, asking Helena if she cared for more. Helena shook her head. Lady Rutland poured herself another cup. "You may find many of them employ Culinarians in a roundabout way, and you will be expected to acquiesce to their demands. And they may judge you by your behavior. Unfortunately, society has not changed so much that a lady's behavior doesn't affect her life. In truth, that is the case for everyone."

Though it set her back teeth clenching, Helena knew this to be true. "Very well, then the experiment must be kept secret from society. And the only way to do that is to keep Elijah Little in Number 9, Cavendish Square, until his training is complete. That will keep the experiment from being compromised, and keep our reputations intact."

"And if he is discovered?" Lady Rutland asked.

Helena frowned. "Our servants at Cavendish Square are extremely loyal, Lady Rutland, and not at all prone to gossip." Her father paid his staff well, and they were aware that their employment hinged, in no small measure, on their discretion. "But rest assured that I shall impress upon them the gravity of the situation."

"Yet things happen. You cannot control every eventuality, Helena."

Helena raised an eyebrow. She could bloody well try.

Lady Rutland tilted her head as she considered. "Pending your parents' approval of the scheme, I will agree to let you undertake the project."

Helena jumped to her feet. Her cup rattled on its saucer, but she barely noticed. "You shan't regret it, Lady Rutland! Just think what it could mean for the lower classes. Once I prove that this boy can be improved by the right teachings, it will mean anyone can do the same—with the correct training, of course."

"It is an ambitious undertaking," Lady Rutland pronounced.

"I should hope you would expect nothing less from me, by now," Helena said, unable—and unwilling—to contain what her detractors, had they been present, might label an unladylike grin.

"I do, however, wish to meet the young man, Helena."

"Ah yes." Helena tapped a finger to her chin. "Could you come to Cavendish Square? I don't think I should bring him here and risk compromising the endeavor."

Lady Rutland smiled. "And wouldn't it be difficult explaining this to your classmates?"

Helena wasn't about to admit it to Lady Rutland, but the last thing she wanted was any of her fellow fourth-years catching wind of how very epically clever her final-year project was bound to be. They'd only copy her if they could.

Helena sat and picked up a glossy petit four. "I simply believe that secrecy will be of the utmost concern if I wish to succeed." She lifted her chin and met Lady Rutland's gaze. "I have no intention of failing."

Lady Rutland nodded. A small smile bloomed at the corners of her lips. "I daresay this will be good for you, Helena."

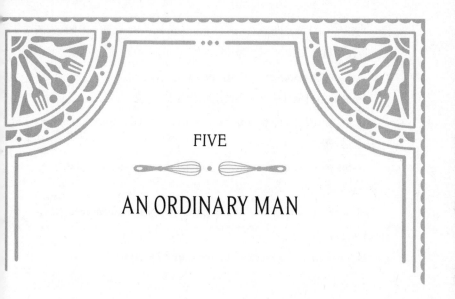

FIVE

AN ORDINARY MAN

"Are you quite certain this is an altogether clever idea, Helena?" Penelope asked.

Helena set the platter filled with an assortment of Elijah's empanadas on the dining table and looked at her friend. Elijah stood next to Penelope with crossed arms, wearing ill-fitting trousers, a loose shirt, and a dark waistcoat Helena had appropriated from her father's wardrobe. Elijah's hair still fell in unruly waves around his head, but at least now that he was clean, it didn't so much resemble a mop. Both Penelope and Elijah regarded Helena with equally dubious frowns.

"Lady Rutland wanted to meet Elijah in the flesh. She set it as a condition for the project—I couldn't very well refuse," Helena stated.

"What am I supposed ta say?" Elijah asked. He crossed his arms across his chest.

"Simply tell her the truth. Be yourself, as it were. It will be more than enough, I have no doubt."

"I won't be parading about," he stated.

Helena rolled her eyes. "No one's asking you to, you silly boy. But if you want me to be able to teach you all you'll need, we must have Lady Rutland's approval."

"And your parents' approval," Penelope interjected. "Don't forget that."

"I have not forgotten, Pen. But they will certainly agree. All we need is Lady Ru—"

"Lady Rutland, my lady," Pierce stated from the door.

Helena moved to greet Lady Rutland. Her puffed, wide gigot sleeves and similarly wide skirt filled the doorway. Her angular face reminded Elijah of nothing so much as a gray fox, and he frowned as she swept into the room. Elijah didn't know what he'd expected, but Lady Rutland was one of the most elegant ladies he'd ever seen. Elijah thought he'd seen quite a few cultured women—after all, they often congregated outside the night market after an evening's entertainment at the theater—but in truth he'd met very few of Lady Rutland's caliber in his life.

Earlier in the day, Penelope had told Elijah that Lady Rutland was a rare member of the aristocracy who cared little for the trappings of her rank. Her late husband, the Earl of Rutland, had died young, making her a wealthy widow at the age of twenty-nine. She'd spent years training with the very best chefs of Europe and advocating for women's causes. After the Freedom of Female Education Bill had passed, she'd secured the first charter to open a school to educate women in the culinary arts. She and her pupils had almost single-handedly made Culinaria into the most sought-after profession a lady could train and work for.

All these facts swirled in Elijah's mind, but as Lady Rutland assessed him from the top of his head to the toes of his quite dull boots, he couldn't help wondering how this smallish, unprepossessing person held the key to his future. But that was why he was going through this, wasn't it? So he could make his own future one day? He uncrossed his arms and then crossed them again as she eyed him.

Lady Rutland quirked an eyebrow. "So this is the young man you wish to help."

"Indeed, Lady Rutland," Helena said. "This is Elijah Little."

"Lady Helena tells me your family approves of this scheme, Mr. Little?"

Elijah nodded but said nothing.

Helena widened her eyes and gestured for him to speak.

He exhaled. "I only have me uncle and he's at sea. I sent him a letter, but he won't mind long as I keep paying rent at his lodging."

"Is your uncle your only family?"

"Me father died when I was little. Then me mother when I was twelve. Uncle Jonathan kept an eye on me after that."

Lady Rutland nodded. "Lady Helena told me you have a talent for interesting flavor combinations. I must say I *am* curious to taste some of your creations."

Elijah swallowed. Though Helena had prepared him for this eventuality, he now realized that his future could hinge on this single tasting. He reached for the platter of empanadas he'd baked earlier in the day. He'd also included a stuffed bread he'd developed on his own, a sour rye dough in the shape of a round parcel filled with pickled beef, caraway, and cabbage and topped with caramel-ized onions. He'd based the recipe on food his mother used to cook, and whenever he baked them for his customers, they always thought they were an interesting variation on British pasties. Elijah held the platter out to Lady Rutland.

She sat at the dining table and removed her knitted gloves. The rest of them sat as well. Elijah held his breath as Lady Rutland took one of his rye parcels and crunched into the dough, and the beef-and-cabbage mixture yielded under her teeth. She chewed. Once. Twice. Her eyes met his.

He shifted in his chair. His own stomach felt like he'd kneaded it as much as the rye dough.

Lady Rutland didn't speak. Instead, she pulled a corn empanada from the platter and took a bite. At Helena's insistence, he'd made the same ones the girls had tried at the night market. Lady Rutland placed the remainder on her plate next to the rye parcel. She dabbed at her lips with a napkin.

Elijah's throat had gone dry.

"Where do you get your recipes, Mr. Little?" Lady Rutland asked finally.

"All over," he hedged. "Keep me nose to the ground when it comes ta interesting preparations."

She tilted her head and gazed at him. Elijah got the impression she could read him, and he didn't particularly like it. "It's rather rem-iniscent of something I had in Warsaw. Have you ever been there?"

"Can't say as I have."

She nodded, then smiled. "And your Central American empana-das?" She turned to look at Penelope, who was sitting on her right side. "Helena tells me you found them quite authentic."

Penelope nodded. "From what I sampled on my travels, they are. Especially considering the ingredients Mr. Little could come by easily."

Lady Rutland regarded Penelope and then Elijah with a serene expression. "What an interesting fellow you are, Mr. Little. And what a range of flavors you have under your belt already. I suppose I must ask you why you wish to do this thing. Why would you wish to upend your life to let Lady Helena try this ambitious experiment?"

Elijah let out a breath. "I want to change me life. And I want to change for the better. Really, I ain't got nothing to lose."

Lady Rutland studied him for a few long moments. "Very well, young man." She turned to Helena. "I shall give my approval, as long as you meet my conditions."

"Of course, Lady Rutland," Helena said, leaning forward in her chair as a triumphant grin spread across her face.

"Since your parents' reply will not be forthcoming for some time, to maintain propriety, Mr. Little must stay in the servants' quarters. Preferably supervised by a male member of your household. Dare I hope that Pierce would be willing?"

Pierce stepped into the room from the hallway, where he had clearly been listening, and stood in the door. "By all means, my lady."

Helena rolled her eyes. "But, Lady Rutland, how can he learn the manners a shopkeeper needs to impress the gentry and nobility if he's living in the servants' wing?"

"I don't see how sleeping in the servants' quarters will preclude you from teaching him everything he needs to learn, Helena. In the absence of your parents, I must make some reasonable rules for this situation. You may, by all means, choose *not* to comply with my condition and devise a completely different final-year project if you so choose." She smiled.

"No, of course," Helena said, sitting back in her chair with only a hint of a grumble in her tone. "I'm happy to comply."

Lady Rutland nodded. "Well, Penelope, Mr. Little, do you also agree to these terms?"

Penelope bobbed her head. "To be sure. And I shall help however I possibly can."

Lady Rutland smiled. "I have no doubt, Penelope. Mr. Little?"

For the first time since her arrival, Elijah felt a smile spread across his own face. "Aye, ma'am. Let's get started."

SIX

NO TIME FOR A CHAT

"Now that the formalities have been dispensed with," Helena said with a grin of a kitten lapping a saucer of cream, "I believe we can commence your training, Mr. Little."

After Lady Rutland had departed, Helena, Penelope, and Elijah had reconvened in the kitchen. Elijah couldn't quite believe the modernity, cleanliness, and sheer scope of the place. This morning when Helena had brought him to the kitchen to bake for Lady Rutland, it had been all he could do not to stare at the room and every pristine feature within it.

Soon after Helena had expressed her dream to become Britain's foremost Culinarian, her father had renovated their kitchens at Number 9, Cavendish Square, and at the family estate in Wiltshire. The kitchen at Cavendish Square was a large, clean, open room with two long wooden worktables offset from each other in the center. Natural light poured in from high windows. A stove with more burners than Elijah had ever seen in one place, and which also housed two ovens underneath, took up the space of almost an entire wall.

A white marble–topped table stood in one corner for chocolate tempering and pastries that relied on cold butter. A massive fireplace, wide and tall enough for a large man to stand inside and fitted with multiple roasting spits, blazed at the opposite end of the room. Pots and pans of every size and shape gleamed from open shelving on another wall. Everything was absolutely state-of-the-art. It was, by far, the most impressive kitchen Elijah had ever seen, let alone cooked in.

Elijah's neighbor Charlie's kitchen, down at the end of Old Fish Street, had been cramped, dark, and almost always coated in a layer of flour and other ingredient remnants. This morning, after Elijah had pulled his filled breads and empanadas out of Helena's fancy oven, he'd given them a taste. He'd thought they'd lost a touch of flavor—such a clean, new oven had its downside, he supposed—but Lady Rutland hadn't seemed to notice.

Elijah glanced at the kitchen staff milling about, preparing elements of the evening meal. He wondered what they must think of Helena's plan—and of him.

Helena clapped her hands, startling Elijah into looking at her. "Don't worry about them. They have their tasks and we have ours. Besides, this is our side of the kitchen." She spread her arms and rested her palms on the wide, wooden table. "Papa designed it this way so I could cook without disturbing the staff. Now, to my mind, how one elevates ingredients into something sublime is the single most important measure of a Culinarian, so we shall begin there."

Elijah noticed the corner of Penelope's lips quirk upward. She angled her body slightly away from Helena's side and cast a quick smile at him across the table. He recognized the encouragement for what it was even as he glimpsed a hint of a dimple at the left side of her lips. Somehow, he hadn't noticed it before.

"To that end, Mr. Little," Helena continued, "today you shall turn the humble carrot into a delicacy pleasing to all the senses." With a flourish, she gestured to the oblong basket of carrots sitting in the center of the worktable. The wicker overflowed with carrots of all colors, shapes, and sizes. Purple carrots—both light and dark—white, yellow, green, varying shades of red, and finally the ubiquitous orange all stared back at Elijah. He wondered how Helena could think a carrot humble with such bounty at her fingertips. Even at the night market, he'd never seen such a variety.

"Your first task is to make something fantastic with the carrots of your choice and the ingredients available in the larder. But carrots, of course, must be the primary ingredient. We'll give you . . ." She tapped her chin. "One hour, I should say."

Elijah swallowed hard. He certainly couldn't make bread or pastries in an hour.

"Helena," Penelope said, turning toward her, "surely this is a task more suited to *after* you've given him some training."

"We might as well see what his skills are first, Pen. Then I can judge better what teaching he needs."

Penelope bit her lip. "I suppose that makes some sense."

"Of course it does," Helena said with a smile. "Now, are you ready, Mr. Little?"

He opened his mouth to say yes.

"Very good. Off you go!" She pointed at the small room adjoining the kitchen.

Slightly irked that she hadn't even let him answer, he hesitated, then walked into the larder, trying to disregard the thump of his heart and the inescapable truth that he had no idea what to make. He reminded himself that he wanted to succeed at this, and he knew one thing for sure: dithering wasn't going to get him anywhere. He took a breath and looked around the room. His gaze immediately fell on labeled jars of dried fruits of multiple varieties. He took the candied orange and lemon slices and then some tart cherries from the shelf before moving on. On other shelves he found flour, hazelnuts, and eggs.

He pored over the labels on the bags, jars, and ceramic crocks until he'd found ingredients he thought would go well, all while attempting to ignore the two girls' stares boring into his back. By the window to the kitchen garden, he discovered dried herbs and garlic hanging from cords and he pulled some off each. "You sure got everything a body could want," he commented as he dropped all his findings back on the worktable.

Helena's eyebrow arched. "Of course we do."

He shook his head as he rubbed the cloves of garlic between his palms to loosen the paper. "Most people don't have half so much. Got a knife I can use?"

Penelope pointed to a knife block behind him. She gave Helena an amused look as he took one with a long blade and set about cutting yellow and red carrots into chunks.

He popped a piece of the yellow carrot into his mouth and chewed. "Haven't had a yellow carrot before. Can't say as it tastes much different. Did get me hands on a bunch of purple ones once, though. The vendor wanted to unload them fast and I—"

"Mr. Little," Helena interrupted, "you have only forty-five minutes remaining. Perhaps you should stop talking and start cooking." She tapped her fingers on the tabletop.

Elijah opened and closed his mouth. He glanced at Penelope. Her lips pressed together in a slight grimace. He swallowed as his neck went hot. "Aye. Course." He pulled his attention away from them and focused on the ingredients in front of him. He could do this.

He did his best to pay them no notice, but every so often he'd catch a glimpse of Helena cringing out of the corner of his eye, or Penelope fiddling with her fingernails. He continued to cut carrots, smash garlic, and crumble the dried herbs between his hands. He turned his back to them as he pulled a pan from the open shelving and put it on the stove.

He began cooking in earnest, and when Helena called for him to put his dish on a plate, he grabbed the nearest platter he could find. It happened to be a deep wooden bowl. He set his food on the long table and took a step backward.

The girls inched close to the workbench and simultaneously bent over the bowl. Penelope bit her lip. Helena wrinkled her nose. Elijah huffed out a breath.

"Great gooseberries!" Helen exclaimed. "What did you do to them?"

Elijah felt his ears turn red. "I cooked 'em."

Penelope cleared her throat. "They are oddly cut, to be sure. But the use of color is . . . well-intentioned."

"You mean unappetizing," Helena stated.

Elijah peered into the bowl. The colors had bled together as the carrots cooked, turning the entire dish a violet-gray hue that he hadn't intended.

"Let's try it, shall we?" Penelope said, injecting cheer into her voice.

Elijah clamped his lips together.

Helena handed Penelope a fork. Penelope dug in first, spearing some of the soft mixture before bringing her fork to her lips. Elijah watched her expression morph from hesitancy to surprise. He wondered what that meant.

Helena bit into the motley mélange of carrots, predicting mushy mediocrity to meet her palate. But beneath her teeth, the carrots yielded less than she'd thought. Some of their texture remained. Elijah had spiced them with thyme, cumin, and mustard seeds in clever proportions so that no one spice overpowered the others. Toasted hazelnuts brought a crunch she hadn't expected, and the dried, tart cherries complemented the slight earthiness from the cumin while bringing the carrots' sweetness to the fore. It was—well, it was *good*. Not transcendent, but certainly worth eating. Helena looked at Penelope and knew from her hint of a smile that she felt the same.

"The taste is quite adequate," Helena pronounced.

"One might even say quite *nice*," Penelope said with a smile at Elijah.

He let out a breath, his features loosening as he returned Penelope's smile.

Helena pressed her lips together. Penelope was the kindest creature in the world, but surely if she gave the boy more praise than necessary, he would feel he had little to learn—which was patently *not* the case. "But your presentation is abysmal, the technique nonexistent, and if I start analyzing your knife skills, I will expound for the rest of the day," Helena said with a shake of her head.

He nodded, but the tension around his jaw returned. "Well, I'm here to learn, ain't I?"

She winced at his grammar. "Had you not wasted time with useless talk, I think the food would have been even better," she replied. "We really must start changing your speech patterns and accent as soon as may be. You'll never own the right kind of store speaking that way."

Elijah crossed his arms over his chest.

Penelope cleared her throat. "It really isn't fair, of course, but investors and culinary patrons will be more inclined to take you seriously the more refined your accent and speech sound."

Helena nodded. "Exactly. Listen to how Penelope and I converse and try to emulate it. It's really not difficult. But we'll go over the finer points if you don't pick it up. And"—she tapped a finger to her chin—"perhaps until you grow used to it, it would be better to listen more and speak less."

His eyes widened. "So I should keep me mouth shut?"

She forced herself not to roll her eyes. "That's not what I meant at all. I merely said you should *listen* more." In Helena's experience, men in general could hardly count listening as one of their strengths.

Her father and brother certainly fit in that category, as did most of the gentlemen she'd met. It seemed Elijah was no different. She really did feel sorry for the opposite sex at times. So many of them bordered on feeblemindedness. And if one aspect of human nature vexed Helena more than any other—though a great many irked her, to be sure—ignorance with a lack of desire to improve one's mind hovered at the top. Elijah Little, however, wished to elevate his skills and position—that, at least, stood in his favor.

He grumbled something inaudible under his breath. She opened her mouth to ask him to repeat it, but then he spoke in a clear voice. "Fine."

Helena nodded once. She turned to Penelope. "This shall be more work than I'd perhaps anticipated."

Penelope's eyes flitted between her and the boy across the table—uncertainly, Helena thought.

"Yet I have not lost heart," Helena assured her. She lifted her chin. "It will doubtless mean I shall have to endure a great many sacrifices, but it will be worth it when we succeed." She pointed to Elijah.

He gave her a wary look.

Helena rolled her shoulders back and straightened her spine. "I can see we'll have to start with the basics."

"One of the most essential skills any Culinarian must have is knife dexterity," Helena pronounced.

Elijah stepped back as Helena pulled knife after razor-sharp knife from a wooden block and set them side by side on the work-table. A long, thin-bladed one sat beside a thick, square one. Next to those rested a large knife with a triangular-shaped blade, smaller ones with medium-thick blades, and then an abundance of knives that fell somewhere in between. Elijah blinked at them.

Elijah had honed the knives in Charlie's kitchen every few days or so, but their blades were dented in multiple places and had lost their edges long ago. The honing helped a bit, but they were never what he'd call especially sharp. These knives looked like they could shave the top layer of skin off your knuckle with barely any friction. He swallowed. He could manage this. Besides, he'd cut himself before, and he likely would again. He wasn't going to let that possibility keep him from cooking.

"Judging by your carrot concoction yesterday," Helena continued, "we'll be devoting most of today to which knives are used for what. Then we'll teach you how to cut, chop, dice, mince, and slice. Ready?"

Elijah nodded. "Aye, ready." He glanced at Penelope. She gave him an encouraging smile. He was quickly growing to like her smile—probably more than he ought to. If any other girl had smiled at him so much, he would have thought something of it. But with her . . . he didn't rightly know why, but she seemed different somehow.

Helena lifted her chin. "Good. Now, these are the basic knives. In reality you only need to know how to use a handful of them—"

"Shouldn't he really know all of them?" Penelope interrupted.

Elijah had been wondering the same thing.

Helena clasped her hands behind her back. "I spent a great deal of time last night thinking this over, Pen. I can't teach—" She stopped herself midsentence.

Penelope raised an eyebrow. "You . . . *can't*?"

Elijah almost snorted. The word "can't" clearly didn't fit in Helena Higgins's mouth.

She wiggled her head, sending her black ringlets bobbing. "That is, Mr. Little shouldn't be *expected* to learn, in a matter of months, everything we were taught in three whole years at the Royal Academy. It would be too much for anyone."

Penelope nodded, apparently conceding the point.

Elijah ran his hand over the back of his neck. When she put it like that, the idea sounded a bit daft. But he hadn't expected it to be a wedge of cake neither.

Helena began pacing down the length of the table. "Thus, I shall teach him the basics that most amateurs who compete in culinary exhibitions to bring favor and patronage to their culinary businesses would know. For those amateur cooks starting with nothing, the exhibitions are the surest way of creating a reputation for oneself that can lead to financial backing and, of course, a seal of approbation from the nobility or landed gentry. So, shall we carry on?" Helena asked, coming back to the center of the table. She looked between Penelope and Elijah.

Penelope shrugged. "By all means."

Elijah didn't know how he felt about getting less of an education because of the time constraint. Still, she was probably right that learning three years' worth of a Culinarian education in a few months would be like trying to harvest honey with bare hands, so her plan made some sense.

Helena pointed at the smallest knife with an angular blade. "Now watch. The knives you'll need are the paring knife, which you'll use for small jobs such as topping strawberries or peeling or cutting apples, potatoes, or anything where fine detail work is needed." She picked up the paring knife and showed Elijah how to hold it properly.

With her other hand, she pointed at the way she'd positioned her thumb. "You see, a firm yet comfortable grip is a necessity. Now you try."

She gestured for him to come to the other side of the table to stand beside her, then pointed to the many knives laid out on the table. He took up the one lying on his left. The blade looked identical to hers except the handle had been carved from a different type of wood. He gripped it as she demonstrated.

"Good. Now . . ." She pulled a small basket of hothouse strawberries from where they'd been sitting behind her on a table by the window, and set it in front of them.

"Watch and learn how a strawberry is properly topped," she said, taking one from the basket.

She held the berry by its point with one hand and ran the tip of her knife in a circular motion under the strawberry's stem as she simultaneously rotated the berry in the opposite direction. Then she set down her knife on the table and plucked off the strawberry's top with three fingers.

"Like so. Then we can slice the berry into uniform pieces."

She set the berry top-side down on the table and demonstrated equally spaced cuts, which she fanned out into a tiny arch.

"Beauty often comes from precision, so precision is what you must aspire to. That is what impresses. Now you try."

Elijah set his chin with a determined nod. He held the knife as she had. He picked up a strawberry and made a fist around its tip, making sure not to hold it too tightly. He picked up the paring knife with his other hand and moved the tip of the knife toward the edge of the strawberry's stem.

Before he could cut anything, however, he heard Penelope suck in a breath.

He froze and looked up.

"If you plan to cut it that way, you will likely find your entire hand bloody by the end of the day," Helena pronounced. "If you hold the strawberry between the tips of your fingers as I showed you, you have far more control, *and* you minimize the amount of flesh you can possibly cut if your knife misses its mark." She demonstrated the correct way to hold the berry again, and Elijah copied her grip.

"Now watch once again as I top the berry. This is more in the wrist than anything else." She demonstrated the circular motion again, then gestured for him to try it. "Ensuring you keep your gaze firmly on what you are cutting is a further safeguard against cutting yourself. Soon you will have such a feel for the knife that such routine tasks will feel like second nature."

Elijah tried again with another berry, holding it between his thumb and first two fingers. This time when the tip of the knife punctured the strawberry, he twisted his wrist so it cut in a circle around the stem, but when he got halfway around the circle, his arm twisted at an unnatural angle, and he cut far more than he'd meant to.

He heard Penelope make a sound of alarm in her throat.

Helena shook her head. "No, you must rotate both hands at once. Like so." She showed him yet again, and yet again pointed for him to pick up another berry. This time, both of his wrists ended up at strange angles.

"Helena," Penelope tried to interject, "perhaps you should start him on something slightly simpler?"

Helena cast her gaze to the ceiling. "Pen, there's nothing much more basic than holding a strawberry correctly! Besides, he will need to understand this technique for a myriad of other tasks. What good will he be if he cannot even master the basics?"

Penelope looked at Elijah.

He felt his jaw flex, but he said nothing. He wasn't about to give Helena the satisfaction of hearing him complain.

Penelope worried at her lower lip. "Perhaps if you begin with—"

"Now, Pen, you must allow me to conduct this in my own way," Helena said. "You should be spending time on your own project, should you not? And I'm quite sure Mr. Little doesn't need your sympathy."

"Er . . ." Penelope threw another glance his way. "Indeed, I can always work on my project. The cuisine of the Americas covers a vast deal of territory, so Lady Rutland wants me to focus my study. I still have many notes and recipes from my travels to parse through, but I did think I could help—"

"You are kindness itself," Helena interrupted, "but I'm certain Mr. Little doesn't wish you to sacrifice your own career to help me teach him."

Elijah's neck heated—whether with anger, embarrassment, or both, he didn't know. But he forced his gaze to meet Penelope's. "Course not, miss. Don't worry 'bout me."

She let out a small exhale that he didn't think meant she was relieved to go. "I'll return in an hour or so."

Helena bounced on her toes. "Very good. He is sure to have

mastered strawberries by then."

Penelope's brown eyes lingered on his face a moment longer, and Elijah tried to give her the equivalent of one of her reassuring smiles. As she turned toward the hall, looked back at them once more, and slowly exited the kitchen, he was fairly certain he'd failed miserably.

❦

When Penelope returned to the kitchen after two hours of compiling her notes on the process of fermenting, drying, and roasting cacao and the subsequent processes for making chocolate, Elijah was rotating the tip of his knife around the eye of a sprouted potato. It popped out onto the workbench. In front of him, in a copper pot of water, sat a veritable mountain of potato cubes. Penelope stepped forward and fished a handful of pieces out of the water, noting they were of relatively equal size. "Mastered the potato and the strawberry in two hours, Mr. Little? I must say I'm impressed."

Elijah opened his mouth to reply, but Helena spoke first. "You should see the cubes at the bottom of the pot! They're extremely irregular. We quite gave up on strawberries—I'd hoped he'd find the potato easier to grasp—and he did, quite literally. I must own, Pen, I never gave any thought before today to the fact that smaller hands are more suited to delicate jobs such as strawberry hulling. By contrast, he had very little trouble using the same technique on potato eyes. I suppose that is why we ladies alone are permitted to become Culinarians."

Penelope bit the inside of her cheek. She'd been on the verge of suggesting Helena start him on potatoes before Helena had asked her to not interfere. "I'm not so certain. That implies that women are not suited to professions once reserved only for men, such as architecture or the law. But as we know, some of the brightest stars in both fields are now women."

Helena smiled, her catlike eyes tipping upward ever so slightly. "Well said, Pen. You might have become a great barrister yourself, you know."

Penelope didn't know if that was true—traveling with her parents had instilled a passion for food in her at a very young age. She thanked Helena for the compliment, even as she wondered if her friend might, on some level, wish that Penelope distinguish herself in another profession far removed from the culinary world. But then Penelope mentally shook herself. Very likely, Helena had meant the comment generously, even if Penelope had heard her say before that she thought the law an honorable, albeit inferior, profession for a person of any gender to pursue.

Gentlemen, of course, could support and distinguish themselves financially by the law, politics, in the military, or through any of the traditional professions that society had considered acceptable at the turn of the century. In practice, the Freedom of Female Education Bill had meant that women could pursue such professions themselves, but many gentlemen had voiced strong objections to the change, causing certain professions and emerging fields to be reserved for women alone.

Ironically, the newer fields such as Culinaria, Vehicular Ergonomica (carriage design and comfort), and Croaqua, a league of professional women athletes who traveled around the country playing croquet in specially designed shallow fountains at stately homes, had become the most sought-after (and envied) vocations—a fact neither Penelope nor Helena was bound to forget anytime soon.

"Perhaps you might try the technique on a strawberry again, Mr. Little?" Penelope asked, realizing he'd continued twisting the point of his knife around countless potato eyes as she and Helena had ignored him.

"Yes, might as well try again," Helena agreed.

Helena placed a rather large berry in front of him on the workbench. This time, Penelope watched as he picked it up by its point, then rotated each hand in opposite directions. Then, with the thumb and forefinger of his knife hand, he plucked the top off to reveal a perfectly hulled berry. He then set it on the bench, slowly cut it into equally spaced slices, and fanned them out on the table as Helena had originally shown him.

Penelope couldn't help a laugh from escaping. "Well done, Mr. Little!"

Elijah smirked and gave her a quick wink. "Thanks, miss."

"We'll have to disabuse you of winking at ladies, that's for certain," Helena cut in.

Elijah's face didn't so much fall as wiped itself clean of any hint of his thoughts. But Penelope noticed the change. Helena was correct, of course—learning manners and courtesy would be necessary if he wished to elevate his status—but did she have to be quite so blunt with him? It was only his first day, after all.

"At least you're starting to understand that precision is key," Helena continued.

"I believe that might deserve a break for tea," Penelope stated.

Elijah caught her eye, and she thought she saw some of his good humor returning to his face. Her spirits lifted at the thought.

"It's as good a time as any, I suppose," Helena agreed. "Well, you've managed to finish your first day of knife technique unscathed, Mr. Little. We'll see if you can stick to the pattern." She moved across the room to ask one of the servants to prepare them tea and cake.

Elijah glanced at Penelope again, made sure Helena's attention was still directed elsewhere, and winked once more.

Penelope shook her head at him, but she couldn't help a giggle from escaping nonetheless.

⌒∞⌒

"Moving on! Today we tackle onions!"

Elijah squared his shoulders, but Penelope almost groaned. "Are you quite sure onions are the best choice for his second day?"

"As I recall, Pen, we learned onions our first week at the Royal Academy," Helena said as she rolled the sleeves of her purple, green, and yellow checker-patterned day dress up to her elbows. The girls had been taught from their earliest days at the Royal Academy that functionality must take precedence over fashion when one was cooking. For this very reason, Culinarians had to fill their wardrobes with even more styles than the typical society lady.

Along with the fashions of the day, which currently favored wide, puffed gigot sleeves that flared around the arms, and wider skirts that flowed out from the waist, Culinarians also wore a variety of dresses in patterns and colors that hid stains, had much more practical, tight-fitting sleeves, and slimmer skirts. Pretty aprons of durable material were also *de rigueur*.

Penelope had always preferred shorter sleeves so she didn't have to spend time rolling up her sleeves in the kitchen, but Helena usually wore the first dress she pulled from her wardrobe. At least, she had when they roomed together at the Academy. Now that Helena had her maid to tend to her, Penelope supposed Julie must have chosen the dress. Helena finished with her sleeves and caught Penelope's eye. "Besides, this shall be the perfect opportunity to test my new invention—I believe I mentioned it to you in a letter?"

Penelope frowned. "I don't recall . . ."

"It is of no matter—I've only just come back from Mr. Shaw's workshop." She raised both eyebrows dramatically, pulled a box the size of her hand from her pocket, and brandished it in the air. "I give you . . . the Tear Stopper!"

Elijah stared at the box with a blank expression. When Helena neither opened the box nor said anything more, he finally asked, "What's that, then?"

"Presumably a device Helena has created to keep one from crying while cutting onions?" Penelope said with a tilt of her head.

"Correct as usual, Pen!" Helena replied. "Now we shall see just how effective it is." She set the box on the table, then crossed to the larder to retrieve a massive basket of onions before plunking it down in front of Elijah. His eyes widened.

"Doubtless you have chopped onions before to make your pasties," Helena said, "but perhaps you can guess what we shall be teaching you today?"

Elijah's brow furrowed.

"What did we work on yesterday?" she prompted.

"Uh . . ." He trailed off.

Helena's green eyes narrowed. "It starts with a *P*."

"Paring knives?" he ventured.

Penelope nodded.

Helena let out of breath. "Yes, but also . . ." She flipped a palm over, encouraging him to say more.

He frowned. "Potatoes?" he replied, though his tone held little confidence.

Penelope bit her lip so as not to laugh.

"Precision!" Helena said. "*Precision, precision, precision!*"

Elijah nodded. "Aye. Precision," he echoed.

"And *why* must cuts be precise and pieces be equal in shape and size?" Helena asked.

"So everything cooks evenly," he said with a glance at Penelope.

She smiled, and she thought he stood a little straighter.

"Correct," Helena said. "Now . . . " She took a brown-skinned onion from the basket and placed it in front of her on the table. Then she selected a medium chef's knife from the wooden block. "For onions, one generally has more control with a larger knife." She pointed for him to find one in the block. When he did, she nodded and showed him the correct way to hold it. Then she had him lay down the knife while she demonstrated.

"One can, of course, slice an onion into equal rings or semicircles with relative ease, but perhaps the most difficult cut to perfect is a diced onion where every square is equal."

Penelope briefly closed her eyes. Only Helena would begin with the most difficult cut first.

"One holds the onion with the root end up after slicing the top so that one has a flat surface to rest it on. Holding each side with a firm, arched grasp of your fingers, and placing the knife through the archway your hand makes, you cut the onion in half. You now have two sets of flat surfaces to place on the table as you cut, which is far safer, and obviously gives you more control as you make your cuts," she said, placing each onion half flat-side down.

"Now, here is where you will need to practice." She looked up, and Elijah nodded to show he was watching.

"On each side, you will slice toward the root end, but stop short of cutting through it. This ensures the onion rings stay intact while you cut."

She demonstrated what she meant. Each slice down into the onion was evenly spaced, the fingers of her guiding hand curled slightly to keep her fingertips safe, each cut stopping short of cutting through the root end.

"Next, you lay your hand flat against the top of the onion and make one or two horizontal cuts through—again stopping short of slicing the root end." She caught Elijah's gaze. "This is where many people balk, but if you pay attention to what you are doing, you should not cut yourself."

Elijah frowned, but he bobbed his head for her to continue.

"Finally, you cut down parallel to the root end, and as you see, you end up with dozens of perfectly equal onion cubes." She put her knife down and pointed for him to inspect the pieces.

He picked up a handful and sifted through them with his opposite hand.

"One doesn't expect yours to be so precise at the beginning, but this is the standard you must eventually realize," Helena pronounced.

He mumbled something affirmative, but Penelope thought he looked overwhelmed. She wet her lips. "Helena, perhaps to improve on yesterday's process, you should take Mr. Little through it again, step by step."

He shot her a grateful half smile.

"That is precisely what I intended, Pen," Helena said as though surprised they would imagine anything less of her.

Penelope watched as Helena directed Elijah to take an onion from the bushel. Helena took one herself and went through the procedure again. Elijah emulated her a step at a time until a pile of chopped onion pieces sat before him. Helena sorted through them with one hand, pointing out the size differences.

"Rough. Very rough. Still and all, not *terrible*," she concluded. "We'll do it together once more; then it'll be all about practice. Pen, oughtn't you take this opportunity to work on your project? We cannot monopolize all of Miss Pickering's time, can we, Mr. Little?"

He began to speak, but Helena talked over him, waving her hand in Penelope's direction. "Go on, Pen. I warrant he'll be chopping evenly in an hour or two with my expert guidance."

～⌘～

When Penelope stepped into the kitchen after an hour perusing the ceviche recipes she'd brought back with her and deciding which she wished to attempt that day, she caught sight of Elijah's face and gasped. His light brown eyes were red-rimmed, angry, and though he swiped at them with the back of his wrist, tears flowed freely. Hundreds of onion pieces littered the table. Helena stood a good distance away from where he chopped, arranging similar-sized pieces into piles. The box Helena had touted earlier in the day sat forgotten on the workbench.

"What happened to your 'Tear Stopper'?" Penelope asked.

They both looked up at her. Elijah swiped at his left eye and sniffled.

Helena's face registered confusion. "Ah!" she exclaimed after a moment. She moved to the box to reveal a pair of spectacles with oversized lenses. Extra glass had been welded onto the sides to almost wrap around the face. She brought them to Elijah's side of the table. "Try these," she said, placing them carefully on Elijah's nose and wrapping the frame around the back of his ears. They were clearly meant for Helena's smaller face, for they sat rather awkwardly.

"Good heavens, you look quite dreadful," Helena told Elijah, evidently noticing the state of his eyes for the first time. "These are far from a perfect fit, but they should make some difference."

He sniffed. "Thanks."

Helena turned to Penelope. "Do you remember our first week? Not a one of us could hold our tears, but I must say Mabel Pilkington looked the most ridiculous of us all."

"Helena—" Penelope began, not at all sure that Helena should be denigrating a classmate in front of Elijah.

"I can just remember her sniveling at Lady Rutland to let us take a break. What did she expect? That being a Culinarian would be like a summer day at Royal Ascot?"

This reference was lost on Elijah, and Penelope (who'd never actually attended Royal Ascot as she was usually abroad with her parents during the summer) had only a vague idea of what her friend meant by the comment.

"Er, Helena—" Penelope began.

"You're quite right, Pen, as Mr. Little is learning, being a Culinarian is not for the fainthearted," Helena stated, completely misreading Penelope's thoughts. "We had no such devices when we were learning." She gave Elijah a pointed look. "Now, why don't you show Miss Pickering how you fared at today's lesson."

Without a word, he pulled yet another onion from the basket and set about chopping it into a small dice. When he'd finished, Helena flourished a hand toward the pieces.

Penelope moved to inspect it. She ran her hand over the onions. Only a few pieces were larger than the rest. "Well done, Mr. Little," she said, looking up to meet his gaze. His brown eyes had stopped watering, but they were still red, and he looked a bit like a squished puppy with those oddly shaped spectacles on his head. She almost laughed, but instead offered him a sympathetic expression. She'd never seen a young man look both pathetic and adorable in equal measure.

"These things actually work," he said, gingerly touching the side of the glass near his temple.

"Of course they work," Helena stated. "Now. On to sauces!"

<hr />

Over the next week and the weeks that followed, the trio fell into a routine. Helena reserved most mornings for teaching Elijah new knife skills and basic techniques while perfecting ones he'd already learned, and each afternoon brought a different method of cooking. Each meal brought on a new sauce, each evening a new pastry or dessert. Within weeks, Elijah could cut, clean, and filet a fish properly, debone a duck or pheasant, truss a rack of ribs into a crown roast, and boil a lobster.

For the most part, Elijah stayed silent as he learned. Penelope spent the majority of each day working on her own project, but for much of that time, she tested recipes in the kitchen as Helena taught Elijah. Penelope offered an insight here or there, but mostly she let

Helena teach Elijah lesson after lesson.

Even as she went about her business, Penelope often thought she saw his patience slipping. His neck would turn red under his neckcloth, and sometimes she'd even observe the tips of his ears flush. The day Helena had taught Elijah to boil lobsters, Elijah had balked when the first one had tried to crawl out of the pot before he could secure the lid. Helena had shown him the other method of killing the lobster with a knife before putting it in the pot, but he'd hesitated for a half hour—during which Helena had grown so frustrated that she'd started railing about ignorance and idiocy and stalked out of the kitchen. Penelope had had to pick up the pieces with Elijah.

"I hope you don't take her ranting too seriously, Mr. Little," Penelope had said as Elijah let out an angry breath.

He ran his hand over the back of his neck. "Don't see how I can't. Even you have to admit, miss, that she's a tyrant."

Penelope had picked up the lobster he'd been hovering over with a chef's knife. Elijah had released it when Helena had left, and now it was crawling down the long, wooden worktable. "I know she can be difficult, but it's only because she is so passionate about food and Culinaria."

"Don't seem like she's got much understanding for anything *but* food," he stated. He put his knife down and rubbed his forehead.

Penelope nodded. She knew many girls at the Academy who felt the same way about Helena. Penelope had the dubious privilege of being the person they accosted to discuss their resentment when Helena flew off the handle or acted like they were slow-witted for not grasping a concept as quickly as she had. Penelope decided to tell Elijah more than she would have told her schoolmates. "Do you ever wonder why her parents and brother are not here at Cavendish Square with us?"

He eyed her. "S'pose I thought rich people travel if they can."

Penelope wobbled her head to indicate he was partly right. "Helena's parents wish to give their son and heir a more varied education than he could have in England. Once he was born, they let Helena do as she pleased without any real restraint. It's my belief"—she looked around to see that no servants stood too nearby, then lowered her voice—"that they don't particularly care what she does, so long as she doesn't disgrace them or the family name. That is why she wishes to distinguish herself so badly—if she becomes the most celebrated Culinarian of all, they will have to take notice. This, unfortunately, often keeps her from seeing other things—important things. Yet, I do think she cares."

Elijah's brow furrowed.

Penelope tried another tack. "She wants you to succeed, Mr. Little. If you succeed, she will as well."

He let out a big breath.

"And for what it's worth," Penelope continued, "I think you're making excellent progress—lobsters notwithstanding." She held up the lobster by its shell and twisted her wrist in the air to expose its belly and wriggling legs.

He pulled a face. Then his brown eyes met hers. "You really think I can do this? Not the"—he pointed his chin at the creature in her hand—"but this whole thing?" He looked behind him at the bustling kitchen.

She tilted her head to the side. "I most certainly do. You're going to be a fine shopkeeper one day. So long as you keep your wits and don't let mishaps get the better of you. Unexpected occurrences happen all the time, especially in the kitchen—the trick is to adapt, think of another solution, and make sure the food tastes delectable."

"I used to do that when I was baking pasties. Had to adapt to what was available, what I could afford. This just seems . . ." He trailed off. "Seems like everything has to be perfect here."

Penelope bit the inside of her cheek. Helena *did* demand perfection. "Eventually, you should strive for perfection. But at the present, you're still learning a number of techniques. When you began baking, did you instinctively know how long to leave your pasties in the oven? Or did you have to keep checking them to produce the perfect crust you wanted?"

He nodded as he considered. "It took time to get a feel for it."

"This is just the same. With each technique you learn, you're forming new instincts that you'll perfect with practice. In the meantime, try to remember how extremely capable you are."

That smirk of his that she'd noticed the night they'd met at the market materialized at the corner of his mouth. "Thanks, miss. That means a lot."

Her cheeks heated. She looked down at the lobster in her hand to keep from looking into his eyes. "Did you know that the lobster is an arthropod? That means that scientifically, it is closer to an insect than a bird or a mammal."

He looked at it again. "I'm not surprised," he grumbled.

"I imagine you'd have little compunction killing a cockroach," she ventured.

"Course not," he replied.

She shrugged a shoulder. "Perhaps if you think of the lobster as the cockroach of the sea, you will have less trouble."

"Wouldn't much like to see a cockroach that big."

She laughed. "Nor I. Come, I'll drop it in the water and you can put on the lid."

He exhaled again. "Right. Let's try it."

They moved to stand side by side in front of the pot of boiling water. Penelope held the lobster firmly in her right hand. Elijah stood with the pot lid in his. She looked at him. "I'll count to three. On two, I'll put it in the pot, and on three, you'll press the lid down tightly. Ready?"

"Aye." She watched his Adam's apple bob as he swallowed.

"One. Two. Three." Like clockwork, she dropped the lobster, and he rammed the lid onto the pot. They stared at it together for a moment. Then she turned to him. "You did it."

He let out a shaky breath. "Aye. My first boiled cockroach."

A chortle burst free from Penelope's throat. "Perhaps don't call it that when Helena returns."

Their eyes met and his uncertain frown fractured. His grin turned into a chuckle. Then they were both laughing without a care for the wide eyes of the kitchen staff.

SEVEN

THEY DON'T BOTHER ME

Elijah looked around as he entered through the stone archways of Leadenhall Market behind Helena and Penelope. They'd chosen Leadenhall precisely because Elijah had rarely hawked his wares there in the past and was less likely to know any of the vendors or hawkers. Still, he wondered if he might see someone familiar. Hawkers often roamed the city looking for the best selling spots, so he could easily come across someone who remembered him.

Helena was technically breaking Lady Rutland's rules by bringing him along today. But after so many weeks of staying cooped up inside the townhouse and only being allowed to venture out into the garden to walk or breathe the outside air (which felt bloody ridiculous when he was so used to traversing the markets and city streets every night), when Helena told him they were going to the market, he'd been so relieved to escape the house that he hadn't asked questions.

Helena had gifted Elijah her father's old trousers for the time being, but because Elijah's legs were longer than the marquess's, they sat rather low on Elijah's waist, which would have worried him more if she hadn't also gifted him a pair of braces to hold them up. He was well accustomed to cast-off clothes, but the quality of the marquess's trousers was so far beyond anything he'd ever worn that Elijah couldn't help thinking he looked like an acorn wrapped in gold leaf. The marquess's frock coat also drooped on Elijah's slimmer shoulders, and despite the state of his own ratty clothes, which Helena had refused to let him wear—"No one would ever believe we'd allow you to accompany us in such attire!"—he felt far more conspicuous in the marquess's ill-fitting garments than he ever had in his own. The girls had assured him that the clothes fit him well enough not to draw any undue attention.

Helena turned around to face Elijah and Penelope, the basket on her arm swinging outward. Penelope stopped, and Elijah stepped closer to them.

"I wish to acquire a few things for tomorrow's lessons, but I rather fancy I should keep them a surprise for now. Pen, you had quite a list of your own, I believe?"

Penelope's periwinkle-blue bonnet bobbed. "Perhaps Mr. Little should come with me." She looked up at him with a smile. "We'll see if we can find any achiote today."

He tilted his head toward her. "It ain't the easiest to find on the best of days. But maybe with enough ready money—"

"*Isn't,*" Helena corrected. "You really must make more of an effort with your grammar. Remember to pay attention to how *we* speak. That should help."

"I do," he ground out.

Helena raised a brow. "Then I don't know why you're still saying *ain't.*"

He clamped his mouth shut as heat rose at the back of his neck.

"But anyway, yes, you two go on," Helena continued. "If I don't find you when I'm finished, I'll meet you back here in an hour."

Penelope nodded in confirmation. Helena turned and hastened into the market.

Penelope looked up at him. "Shall we?"

He opened his mouth to tell her to lead the way, then shut it and gave her a short nod.

Her brown eyes widened a fraction. He realized they had an almost amber ring around the pupils. He looked away, casting his gaze into the stalls of the market. To their left, a cheese maker's apprentice handed samples of a blue-veined fromage to passersby.

The apprentice looked a bit younger than Elijah, but judging by the boy's thicker frame, he appeared better nourished. A few weeks ago, Elijah would have envied him. Apprenticeships were hard to come by—unless a lad had parents who could lay out enough money to get him a position. But boys like Elijah—with no money and no parents—lived on their wits, whatever wares a few shillings could buy, or the charity of others. Sometimes all three. Well, he'd gotten *himself* an apprenticeship of sorts. No use complaining that they didn't like the way he talked or dressed.

Penelope followed his line of sight to the cheesemonger's stall. "Shall we try a slice?"

He shrugged but started toward the boy handing out cheese.

"What do you have today?" Penelope asked as they approached.

"A Nottingham Stilton, miss. Made with the finest milk and cream," the boy said, holding out a piece to each of them with his silver tongs.

Penelope went quiet as she chewed.

Elijah popped it into his mouth, though blue-veined cheeses were never his favorites. The creaminess coupled with the earthy, bitter notes coated his tongue, and he wished for a piece of bread to diffuse the flavor.

He looked at Penelope, who favored the boy with a nod of approval. "A lovely grassiness behind the cream. And just the right amount of salt. I imagine it would go quite well as an accent to a broccoli bisque."

The boy nodded. "Oh yes, miss. Or with some lamb or beef."

Penelope looked at Elijah. "What do you think, Mr. Little?"

He looked at her, then at the boy, then settled his gaze back on her. She simply smiled and waited. He realized she wasn't going to let him get away without speaking again. "It's not really my taste, but I could see it going with mushrooms and horseradish. Maybe some leeks." He shrugged.

Penelope's smile widened. "Absolutely. Perhaps in some kind of flaky pastry case?"

He nodded. "Why not?"

She grinned. "More items to add to our list." She turned to the boy. "We'll take a wedge, please. About yea big." She gestured an approximate size with her hands.

The boy nodded and bent into the glass case to retrieve the wheel. He cut her a piece, then offered it for her inspection and nod of approval before he wrapped it in paper and twine.

Penelope paid the boy and put the cheese in her basket. As they moved away from the stall, Penelope gave Elijah an amused look. "You needn't be so worried about talking, you know."

He let out a breath. "Don't wish to offend, that's all."

"No one will be offended. Least of all, me," she said.

"No use speaking if I can't say it the way she wants."

Penelope raised a brow. "You'll soon get the hang of it. But in the meantime, you can talk to me if you wish to—in whatever way seems natural." She tilted her head up to catch his eye.

He couldn't help a smile from breaking through. "Thanks, miss. I appreciate it."

She smiled back. "That's settled, then. Now," she said, casting her head about, "let's see if we can't find that achiote."

They didn't find the achiote, but at one stall they found a plethora of fresh chili peppers of all different colors and sizes piled in large baskets fresh off the packet ships from Spain and the Kingdoms of Naples and Sicily. Penelope planned to use them in a number of recipes. Elijah had also spotted a stall selling spices where the owner kept a supply of dried chilies from the Americas.

"Can you believe he had ancho, pasilla, *and* mulato peppers?" Penelope said as they left the man's stall with a decidedly fuller basket. "I'll be able to make mole poblano for you and Helena! I had wanted to recreate a mole negro, but one must make do with the ingredients available. In any case, there's no possible way she'll be able to guess all three chilies."

He looked at her and opened his mouth to speak, both bemused and charmed by her excitement for the ingredients.

"Though, I grant that it might not be the most *fair* tasting," she continued. "I hope you don't think me ill-mannered. But Helena and I do this sort of thing quite often," she finished, clearly misinterpreting his expression.

"I don't think you could be ill-mannered if you tried, miss," he stated. Her face relaxed. "I was gonna say I can't wait to taste it."

"Oh." She bit her lower lip. "Well, that's splendid, then."

He smiled. "Except I think we've only gotten half of your list, and the clock tells me we've got a quarter hour before we're supposed to meet Lady Helena."

Penelope looked at the watch hanging from a chain around her waist. "Oh, you're quite right. Perhaps we might split up the list? Could you procure the rest of the produce?"

"Not a problem. I'll have it all in a swish of a cat's tail."

She bit her lip again, but he could tell she was trying not to smile as she tore off the rest of her list and handed it to him along with some coins. She thanked him and moved off in search of the meat she wanted. He scanned the list; she'd scratched out a few of the items with a pencil.

2 bundles fresh coriander

8–10 lemons or limes

4 Seville oranges

1–2 pounds chilies (if available)

8 onions (white or yellow)

6–8 plantains (if available)

2 pounds tomatillos (if available)

3 pounds tomatoes (if available)

Oranges and lemons should be easy to find, and he, luckily,

had hawked oranges and lemons frequently as a child. He knew just what to look for. He went in search of the nearest fruit stall and soon found one in the center of the market. The vendor's stall boasted a variety of citrus as well as apples, quinces, and dried figs and stone fruits.

Elijah inspected a lemon from the top of the pile. The thick and lumpy outside skin meant it would likely be less juicy. He rummaged around for the smaller ones and rolled a few in his hands.

"Lemons you're after?" a stout man called, stepping closer to Elijah.

Elijah held up three lemons in his hand. "I'll take these."

"The big ones are better—get more fer your money that way," the man said, picking up one of the lemons Elijah had moved to the side. He set about polishing it on his sleeve.

Elijah ignored the statement. The man probably took him for a rich nob who wouldn't necessarily know better. "Got any Seville oranges?"

The man's balding head dipped. "Over 'ere." He walked to a wide basket filled with lumpy-skinned yellowish oranges and handed one to Elijah.

Elijah squeezed it. The skin had a bit more give than he liked. "How long have you had them out?" Sevilles grew tougher and drier the longer they were kept in the ambient temperature, and he doubted Penelope would be happy with tough oranges. He wasn't about to bring her any if he could help it.

"Two days," the man replied, sifting through the basket to hand Elijah another. "They just arrived from Spain the other day."

Elijah frowned. This second one seemed even drier than the first. Elijah grabbed one himself, hoping some of them would be salvageable. "More like five days," he muttered, pinning the vendor with a pointed look.

The man narrowed his eyes. "What're you, an expert?"

"I know me oranges," Elijah shot back, just as he found two that would suffice.

The man scoffed as he looked Elijah up and down. "Took ye for a gentleman, in those clothes. But ye talk more like one of them orange-hawking Jew boys. Come ta think of it, ye probably are."

Elijah's entire body tensed as he met the man's glare. As though some imaginary smell offended him, the man's bulbous nose wrinkled and his nostrils flared wide as his lip curled upward. It was a look Elijah knew well—one he'd felt nearly every week of his childhood when he'd walk the streets with oranges or lemons or rhubarb and bring home whatever coins he made to his mama. She'd insisted he go to school, but he still hawked whatever he could in the mornings and evenings so they could eat better. Most of the boys hawking oranges and lemons in the city were Jewish like him, to the point where if you sold oranges or lemons, you were usually taken to be Jewish, whether you were or not. Elijah had quit selling them soon after his mother died to avoid the derisive looks and comments.

He'd always wondered what he could say to get people like this bald fool in front of him to shut his gob. But Elijah had never come up with anything that didn't make him angrier or regretful later, so rather than say a word, he dropped the oranges and lemons back into the nearest basket. He gave the sneering vendor a blank stare, turned on his heel, and ignored the man spitting the words "Dirty Jew" at his back.

Elijah clenched his teeth together and held his breath as he crossed the market in search of a different fruit stall. He wished he'd kept his bloody mouth shut about knowing his oranges.

EIGHT

A HABIT ONE CAN ALWAYS BREAK

"Now," Helena said, pointing to the kitchen windows, "as the weather is delightfully dry today, we shall teach you the different types of meringues. *Certain* people who claim to know everything any pre-Culinarian should know truly don't understand the very basic differences between the styles of meringues and their practical applications, but I have no intention of letting you be one of *those* people, Elijah." She paused as though waiting for Elijah to respond. On the other side of the table, Penelope rolled her eyes at Helena's thinly veiled jab at Princess Adelaide. When Elijah opened his mouth, Helena continued. "The most basic, and least stable of the meringues—at least until it is baked—is the French style, which we will be starting with today. Are you taking notes?" Helena asked him.

Elijah started at her abrupt question, for though he'd been listening, he'd yet to scribble anything on the paper before him. He immediately started writing "French Meringue" with his pencil in the smallest script he could. After the close shave at Leadenhall, Elijah had decided to learn everything he could as fast as he possibly could. Who knew when another such encounter might happen? He'd been lucky that the girls hadn't witnessed the bigoted vendor's comments that day. It would've only led to a bigger scene or, worse, questions. And if Helena didn't like Elijah's answers, he had little doubt he would've been sleeping back on Old Fish Street before day's end.

He wanted to make a success of this. He wanted his uncle to return to see him well on his way to owning a shop or a permanent stall.

Despite the hardships of the situation, Elijah was making progress. Even Penelope thought so, and she was one half of the two most brilliant girls he'd ever met. He now had sheaves of notes sitting in a pile in his room on more paper than he'd ever thought he'd keep—other than the few books his mother had left him. The amount of paper Helena had given him for his use had truly shocked him, having a knowledge as he did of what such quality paper cost. He'd known a number of families on Old Fish Street who worked at the paper mills.

But Helena and Penelope had insisted that he grow used to writing down recipes that worked well or were worth improving upon.

They'd also loaned him tomes on everything from menu planning and timing to more modern theories of flavor enhancement, which Helena now expected him to read in his spare time. In truth, he had very little leisure at all. Helena filled the entire day with lessons, and Elijah was often so exhausted by the time he climbed the stairs to the servants' quarters, crossed the hall past Pierce's open door, and said good night to Pierce's narrowed gaze, that he often sank into his bed and barely stirred until the sun rose.

Elijah spent most mornings reading the texts at a round tripod table in the library downstairs and taking notes on dishes or techniques he'd like to try. At Penelope's urging, he'd also started making a list of anything he didn't understand, and often she would explain or point him toward other books she thought might help.

All this he'd usually accomplished before breakfast, when Helena would appear in the dining room. She didn't always eat much, but she seemed to thrive on variety, and if the kitchen staff didn't provide it, she'd often complain to Pierce or whichever footman was at hand, then disappear into the kitchen to make something herself. By the time she emerged from the kitchen with some beautiful platter, Elijah and Penelope would have finished eating, and Helena would throw up her hands good-naturedly, eat a small helping, then offer the remainder to the servants.

The abundance of food and ingredients at Number 9, Cavendish Square, still amazed Elijah. They didn't even have to sell any of it to recoup what they paid on ingredients! He'd always thought it far better to be independent—to try to make a go of it on his own rather than enter into service—but the servants at Cavendish Square ate like kings and queens, as far as Elijah could see.

"To make French meringue, we begin by—" Helena continued, breaking Elijah out of his thoughts, but as he looked up, Pierce entered the kitchen and cleared his throat.

Helena turned. "Yes, what is it, Pierce?"

"The post, Lady Helena. There is something from Italy," he said.

"Ah, very good. It must be from Papa! I'll read it now." Helena reached for the letter.

"I thought you might, my lady," Pierce intoned.

Instead of leaving the kitchen, he hovered in the doorway and eyed Elijah as though the letter's contents would expel Elijah from the townhouse within the hour. Elijah kept his face free of emotion, but he shifted his weight between his feet. He felt Penelope's gaze shoot toward him from the other end of the table.

"Hah!" Helena exclaimed.

"What does he say?" Penelope asked.

"Precisely what I thought he would," Helena replied, triumph evident in the glee in her voice. "They trust my judgment on every particular!" She held the letter out to Pierce—practically dancing as she did so—and he stepped forward to peruse it. "Lady Rutland has their consent, as I knew she would, and Mr. Little will move into the guest quarters as I wished."

Elijah's eyes widened. He threw a shocked glance at Pierce.

The butler's mouth gaped open. "But, Lady H—"

"You see what the marquess says, Pierce. My parents trust me above all." The smile playing at the corner of her lips was not malicious so much as knowing. As though she'd expected this all along—as though getting her way was a circumstance she was not only used to, but a foregone conclusion.

Elijah tried to imagine what it must be like to live life with the confidence that all would turn out to your own benefit. He rubbed his hand over the back of his neck. It must be bloody nice. He glanced up at Penelope, wondering what she thought of Helena moving him into a guest room, despite Lady Rutland's conditions, but she said nothing and only offered him a one-shoulder shrug. Not for the first time, Elijah wondered what went on in her head.

He hadn't really felt right asking her anything that wasn't food-related, but more and more, he found himself curious about what she thought of Helena's opinions or behavior. What Penelope had told him that day about Helena's parents didn't seem to completely line up with how Helena was acting now. She seemed glad that her parents let her do as she pleased, not irked that they weren't here paying attention to her. Was it all bluster?

Maybe he should put something like *How do I get a life where I get everything I want like Helena Higgins?* on his list of questions about things he didn't understand. On the other hand, he didn't truly believe such a life was possible for the likes of him. Too many barriers stood in his way. Even if he could hide, or learn to mask some of them, there were some things that, if revealed, others would never look past.

⌒∞⌒

Elijah followed Pierce's stiff frame down the stairs from the servants' quarters onto the first floor. Down at the very end of a short hall, Pierce opened a thick wooden door and, with one swipe of his forefinger, motioned for Elijah to enter.

The bedchamber that greeted him was almost double the size of his uncle's lodgings in Old Fish Street. Elijah had thought the room he'd been sleeping in upstairs rather grand because it was clean and the bed lump-free, but this room with its wide four-poster bed, large wardrobe that matched the bed's dark wood, and spindly-legged writing desk and chair tucked in a corner by the window was nothing short of opulent. Elijah dropped his scruffy bag in front of the wardrobe and moved to look out the window.

A circular park in the center of Cavendish Square with gravel pathways and lush green grass beckoned. What a difference from the muck and cinders clinging on to Old Fish Street. He looked back into the bedroom, noting the intricate design of the paper on the walls, the crown molding around the impeccably clean ceilings. What a place for *he*—Elijah Little—to be sleeping and living in. He looked to Pierce. His lined face sported a hint of a frown, but that was nothing new.

"You shall be expected to keep everything exactly as it is now," Pierce said.

Elijah nodded. "Course, Mr. Pierce."

"I shall know if it is not," Pierce added.

"I'll watch me—myself," Elijah said, expecting nothing less from the butler by now.

Pierce turned to leave, then seemed to think better of it. "I don't mind saying that I believe Lady Helena is making a mistake by allowing you to stay here, boy. Be absolutely certain you do not abuse her trust. Footmen shall be posted by the stairs."

Meaning if he tried to go near the girls' chambers on the opposite side of the stairwell, he would be seen. Elijah tried to smile to reassure the butler. "Mayhap you should sleep in the room next door to be really sure, Mr. Pierce." Elijah gestured to the left with his thumb.

"I cannot sleep in the guest quarters, boy," Pierce replied, his eyes wide with outrage.

Elijah shrugged. "Suit yourself."

Pierce scowled. "I shall speak to Lady Helena." He shut the door as he left.

Elijah let out a breath and looked around the room again. He wasn't about to do something foolish enough to get himself evicted from the house before his lessons were through. As galling as Pierce's frowns and insinuations that Elijah always hovered on the cusp of some bad behavior felt, if sleeping next door gave the butler some peace of mind, so be it.

Elijah went to his bag and started to untie the lacing. He rummaged around until his fingertips brushed a familiar metal cylinder. He pulled it out of the bag and stared at the mezuzah his parents had brought with them to England when they'd left Bavaria to escape the registration law. As part of the anti-Jewish restrictions in their region, the local government enforced how many Jews they allowed to marry in a given year. If one could not obtain a license, one couldn't start a family.

Elijah's parents had thought they'd have a better life in Britain with more freedom to live as they pleased. But Elijah's father had died when he was still a small boy, and before Elijah's mama had passed, he'd never thought to ask her if life actually *had* turned out better for them here. Elijah suspected it hadn't.

The brass mezuzah was neither ornate nor particularly eye-catching—in fact, the metal had acquired a dark, tarnished patina over the years—but it was one of his parents' few belongings Elijah had taken pains to keep safe. The mezuzah had hung in the doorway of their lodgings until the day his mother died and his uncle Jonathan had taken him to Old Fish Street. By that time, his uncle had changed his last name from Levin to Little. He hadn't wanted his brother's mezuzah hanging on his door, proclaiming their religion and heritage to all the world. So Elijah had kept it with his own belongings. And every so often, he would take it out, look at the handwritten parchment scroll within, think of his parents, and remember what they'd left behind to create a better life.

Sometimes he wondered if they watched him in some way. He looked around the room once more. If they were watching, he hoped they'd be proud of him. He was doing what he could to improve his own lot in life.

A knock came through the door. Elijah pressed his fingers to his parents' mezuzah and brought the fingers to his lips. Then he tucked it back into his bag and cinched it closed. When he pulled the door open, Penelope's tentative smile greeted him.

"Hello," he said, smiling back.

"I just wanted to enquire as to what you think of your new room." She peered around him, and he stepped aside. "Oh, how charming! You must have a delightful view of the square."

He let out a breath. "Whole lot different than what I'm used to. Wanna see?" He gestured to the window with one arm.

Penelope took a step forward, then hesitated at the threshold. "I would, but it's not—well . . . *proper* for a lady to enter a gentleman's private room."

He let out a short laugh. "I ain't a gentleman."

"You're *not* a gentleman. *Yet*," she corrected.

He sighed. "I'm *not*." Then he frowned. "Whaddya mean *yet*?"

"Well . . ." Her eyes brightened. "Gentleman or not, today you truly begin to live as a gentleman would"—she opened her hand to indicate the new room—"so Helena has decided to begin your lessons into *behaving* as a gentleman. Which will, of course, benefit you immensely when you are looking for the right patrons for your shop."

"Bloody hell," he muttered, running his hand over the back of his neck.

"I heard that," Penelope said. "To begin, a gentleman never swears in a lady's presence."

Elijah raised his brows. "What if swearing's the only thing that'll do?"

Penelope shook her head. "A true gentleman keeps it to himself. Gentlemen do swear around each other, but never in front of a lady."

He sighed. "Fine. Not in front of a lady."

She smiled. "Now, perhaps you might escort me down to the dining room, Mr. Little? I believe Lady Helena has some interesting things in store this afternoon."

He nodded and closed the door behind him. Penelope showed him how to offer a lady his arm, and they made their way to the dining room, where three places had been set with more cutlery than Elijah had ever seen at a table for a single meal. He gulped.

"Ah, you're here," Helena stated. She moved a small fork a fraction of an inch as Elijah and Penelope walked in.

"We've gone over a bit of this at other meals, of course, but it occurred to me that we'd better work on formal table manners sooner rather than later."

"What'll I need this for?" he asked, unable to help himself. "How many formal meals will I be eating?"

Helena exhaled slowly, clearly annoyed at his question, but he wasn't sure he cared. "If you wish to attract the kind of patron who will invest in you, your shop, and your cuisine, you must know not only how to converse with the right sort of people, but how to *dine* with them as well."

He pulled a face but had to admit that sounded reasonable.

Helena pointed at the two places across from each other. "You two sit there. At formal meals, one usually waits for the hostess to sit before taking one's own chair." She sat at the head of the table, and Elijah and Penelope took their seats on either side of her.

Elijah put his hands on the table, then leaned over the utensils. Three forks of varying sizes sat to the left of the plate; on its right side, three knives, two spoons, and another fork stared back at him. Another smaller plate and knife rested diagonal to the main plate in front of him, as did another fork and spoon set perpendicular to the other utensils. A bevy of glasses of differing shapes and heights waited beyond the cutlery, as if daring him to make a mistake.

"Sit up straight," Penelope whispered across the table. "And don't worry—it's not as hard as it looks."

He sat straighter, but let out a breath.

"Yes, one should never hunch over one's food," Helena agreed. "Put your hands in your lap if you don't know what to do with them, but when you eat, your elbows should be bent with your hands level to your knife and fork. Your napkin"—she pointed to his—"should be placed on your lap after you sit." She demonstrated, and he mimicked the action.

She nodded. "Everything else could not be simpler, really. A good table should not be set with utensils one will not be using, so there's no need to guess what's what as long as you work your way closer to the plate with each course. Really, it would be far more difficult if we were still conducting meals à la française, don't you agree, Pen? We were still quite young when dining à la russe came into fashion, but I do recall how different it all was whenever I was allowed to eat with Papa and Mama."

The old way of eating, à la française, was still fashionable amongst the older set who enjoyed having many dishes all at once, and with those who preferred to carve roasts at the table, but the rise and subsequent prominence of Culinarians in society had led to a fundamental shift in the way the upper and middle classes ate formal evening meals. Culinarians had traveled the world for inspiration, and the Russian habit of eating meals in many courses had returned to Britain with them. Rather than show off one's wealth with more dishes than an assembled party could comfortably eat, one now impressed others with the caliber of Culinarian one could hire, as evidenced by the quality and ingenuity of their dishes.

As Penelope had spent little time in England before entering the Royal Academy, her childhood memories consisted less of dinner parties and more of eating at coaching houses, in hotels, and on packet ships with her parents, so she ignored Helena's musings and turned to Elijah.

"The only utensil that might seem slightly counterintuitive is the fork on your right," Penelope said. She put her index finger on the fork in question.

"Yes, that's the oyster fork," Helena said. "It may not always be there, of course, but one can distinguish it by its small size."

Elijah made a mental note of the oyster fork. "What're these for?" he asked, pointing at the little plate and blunt knife.

"That's your bread plate and butter knife," Helena replied. "The fork and spoon next to it are for dessert. You've used them at previous meals with us, if I recall."

"That don't mean I rightly knew what they were for," he muttered under his breath. Usually he copied whatever utensils the girls picked up when they all ate at the table together.

"The footmen will pour the beverages into their appropriate glasses, so you needn't worry there," Penelope said.

"But when in doubt, just remember to work your way inward with each course," Helena said.

He let out a breath. "Think I can do that."

"Remember your pronouns, Elijah," Helena admonished.

He raised his brows. She'd told him that before, but he didn't even know *which* exact pronoun he'd left out.

"*I* think I can do that," she said in that tone she used when she wanted him to repeat something her way.

"Oh, right," he said, then repeated the sentence correctly.

She wobbled her head from side to side, only half pleased. "You are making progress with your accent. It's just the words now. At any rate, let's get you sounding and acting like a gentleman first and then you can play with the language. And for the love of perfect pastry, just keep your thoughts to yourself when you're not certain how to say them correctly."

Elijah clenched his jaw to keep from saying what he wanted. Sometimes she could be so damned *insulting*. Yes, far better to say it in his mind—no more swearing around the ladies.

"He does need to practice, Helena," Penelope said.

"Yes, of course, Pen," Helena said with wide eyes. "That's what he *is* doing."

Every so often, Elijah wondered if she misunderstood Penelope on purpose. He looked at Penelope to gauge her reaction. She gave Elijah a tight smile. In that moment, he thought Penelope might be wondering the same thing. And for some reason, the idea gave him some small degree of comfort.

Number 9, Cavendish Square   *February 28, 1833*
Marylebone, London

Dearest Nanay and Papa,
I very much hope you are both well. You may be interested to hear that Helena's parents have given their most hearty approval to Helena's project and to Mr. Elijah Little. Their letter arrived a few days ago, much to Helena's joy. Helena's butler, Pierce, was less pleased, but he cannot gainsay the marquess. Pierce has, however, taken great pains to ensure everything is being done with all propriety.

Mr. Little has shown great promise in his studies over the last weeks, and I continue to find his food better with every passing day. Helena, as you might surmise, is something of a taskmaster, but Mr. Little rarely bats an eye at her demeanor—even at times when I find her unreasonable.

I believe more and more that Helena's project will

have wide-spreading implications for expanding culinary education if we can give Mr. Little all he needs to be successful.

He has already mastered (or become quite proficient at) a number of skills and techniques such as braises, fricassees, roasting, searing, and sautéing. He was already well versed in pie and pastry making, so teaching him laminated pastry and more difficult cakes and confectionary has proceeded much faster than I anticipated. (I suspect Helena feels the same, though she always pretends to be nonplussed at his progress.) His knowledge and interest in the dishes of other cultures also continues to surprise me. His empanadas, it seems, were only the tip of the bavarois. He makes a delightful curry after the East Indian style, and his fried plantains (both the sweet maduros and the crispy double-fried green ones) have become my new favorite snack before our evening meal. You would love them, Nanay, I am certain.

Nanay, I've also taught him most of the rice dishes in my repertoire (as Helena continues to find rice to be rather lowly—though she eats risotto and paella readily enough when they're on the table), and although he was surprised when I first showed him plain, unadulterated rice as you make it, he soon gobbled it up and has been experimenting with more Eastern-inspired rice dishes and desserts and puddings ever since. I taught him your bibingka recipe and he's been extrapolating from there. I also had to teach him how to properly open a coconut as his method was more than a trifle alarming to watch. He has started using dairy milk instead of coconut on many occasions, however, to save time, which I cannot fault him for since his studies do keep him occupied most of the day. Perhaps one day there will be a stall at the market selling ready-made coconut milk—in fact, maybe I should suggest it to some of the vendors!

At any rate, Elijah has progressed so well that Helena has planned that he shall cook for her grandmother, the Dowager Countess of Rexborough, in the next week or so. This will, of course, be his first attempt cooking for anyone in society, so Helena shall help him prepare a menu, but all the cooking will be his own. We have begun going over proper manners and etiquette, but we continue to help him refine his speech, so this will be nothing if not a challenge. Yet we both feel he is up to the task. I shall write again to apprise you of our progress and let you know how Lady Rexborough reacts to our charge.

All my love to you both,
Penelope

P.S. My own project continues well.

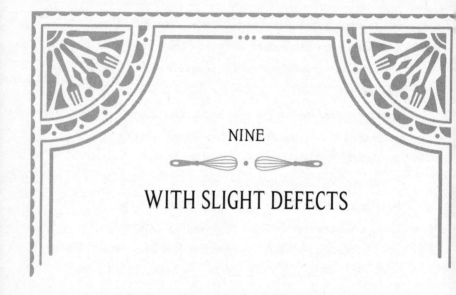

NINE

WITH SLIGHT DEFECTS

Cobbled streets bustling with horses and carriages expanded into open roads of dirt and gravel as Helena's coach and four carried Elijah, Penelope, and Helena out of London. Though Elijah had seen the black-lacquered coach sitting out in the mews behind Number 9, Cavendish Square, nothing had prepared him for the luxury inside the vehicle. The plush dark velvet cushions had been stuffed in ways to conform to the body, including two bolsters protruding on either side of his head. A person could even sleep without his skull lolling uncomfortably. Footstools had popped out from a compartment under the seats when Helena pulled a lever. She'd shown Penelope where to find her own, and the girls had contentedly settled their shorter legs on top of the cushioned stands. Elijah had almost gaped.

"Elijah, will you open the compartment above your head?" Helena asked as they hit a rut and the carriage wobbled on its struts.

Elijah looked up and realized the ceiling housed a flat

compartment with a metal latch. He pulled the latch and the panel opened, stopping a few inches above his head.

"Would you hand me one of the back bolsters?" Helena asked.

He frowned, but reached up to rummage around. Small cushions of different sizes idled in the compartment, waiting to be used. He pulled out a few, and she pointed at the longer, rectangular one. He gave it to her.

"Thanks. Do you care for one, Pen?"

Penelope shook her head.

"Take one for yourself, if you wish, Mr. Little," Helena said as she placed the pillow behind her back and wiggled her torso to get comfortable.

"Did your father hire a design consultant to customize the carriage?" Penelope asked. "Or is this one of the newer models?"

"This one he bought ready-made for me," Helena replied. "He took his pride and joy—which he built from scratch with a design consultant—to the Continent. You wouldn't believe how very comfortable it is, Pen. One can barely feel the road at all. And besides the footrests that come out from under the seats, it has a table that comes out of the floor and a small icebox for storing food. Oh, he's prodigiously proud of it," she pronounced with a smile.

"He must be," Penelope agreed.

"Mama was skeptical at first, but when he told her it would be perfect for her comfort as they traveled the Continent, she relented," Helena said.

"Do you ever wish you went with them?" Penelope asked, her gaze still as she looked out the window.

Helena made a moue with her lips for comic effect. "And miss all this? Are you mad?" She laughed quite genuinely. "I could not have neglected our final term. My parents should have planned accordingly!" She rolled her eyes. "But parents are such bothersome creatures."

Penelope said nothing, and Elijah looked away, thinking that was all well and good for someone who still *had* her parents. He stuffed a flat, circular cushion behind his back and returned the remaining pillow to its compartment. He couldn't even imagine a carriage with more luxuries than this one, let alone parents with so much wealth, they could gift a vehicle like this to their seventeen-year-old daughter.

Not that he was going to complain about sitting in it while he could. No, he could easily get used to such a life if he let himself. Of course, *he'd* never be so rich that all he had to worry about was his own comfort. He ran his hand down the fine fabric of the marquess's old trousers to rest his hand on his knee. He hoped today would go well. He'd never cooked an entire meal for a dowager countess before.

Elijah exhaled and looked out the window.

They were reaching the city's edge, and at the crossroads stood a group of boys waving goods in the air. None of them were above the age of twelve, by the looks of them, and they wielded everything from paper and sealing wax to pocket mirrors, sweet cakes, and the ubiquitous oranges and lemons. Their cries carried into the carriage, and Elijah looked at Penelope, who peered at them with an unreadable expression, and then at Helena, who ignored them. Elijah fiddled with the coins in his pocket. Despite not selling any pasties since he'd moved into Number 9, Cavendish Square, he'd had very few—if any—expenses, and as a result, his store of coins had barely depleted.

"Think—*I* think," he corrected himself, "I'll buy something."

Penelope raised her eyebrows. "Shall I knock to stop the carriage, Helena?"

"Why, in heaven's name?" Helena asked with wide eyes.

Penelope frowned and looked at Elijah. "Mr. Little wishes to make a purchase."

Helena let out a breath. "I meant why would you want to buy something from those urchins?"

Elijah shrugged, not wanting to reveal why he wanted to help the boys. She wouldn't understand how it felt to stand on the street hawking goods or food. She wouldn't understand how it felt to have insults hurled at you. And she sure as hell wouldn't understand hoping you made enough for a satisfying meal. "I feel like a sweet cake and an orange," he stated.

"You really should be mentally preparing yourself for what you'll have to do when we arrive. Besides, you can make far superior sweet cakes yourself," she argued, "and I'm sure Grandmama will have oranges if you really care for one."

"I'd rather have some now," he said, frustration building in his chest.

"I'll have one too," Penelope said.

His gaze shot to hers. She raised a brow and knocked on the door of the carriage to get the driver to stop.

"Oh, very well," Helena said. "But those Jewish hawkers won't leave you alone after you've bought something, you know." She settled back into her seat as the coach rolled to a stop.

Elijah took a series of deep breaths as his face reddened. He purposely avoided the girls' eyes and opened the window.

Half a dozen voices assailed him, all telling him the merits of their products. He pointed to the boy selling oranges. "Three of your juiciest, lad."

The boy's round cheeks puffed out as he smiled. "Course, sir!"

Elijah let out a bark of laughter at the boy's use of "sir." He'd never been called "sir" in his life, but then, he supposed he would have called anyone driving about in such a fancy carriage "sir" too.

The boy stepped close to the window and handed Elijah three oranges. Elijah squeezed them, and finding them as promising as he'd hoped, he winked at the boy and handed him more coins than the fruit was worth. "Keep the change," he said.

The boy's cheeks puffed outward again. "Thank ye kindly, sir!"

Elijah smiled back. It hadn't been too long since he'd been just like this boy.

The other youths now wanted a turn, and Elijah bought something small from each of them (giving them all slightly more money than their items were worth), plus the two sweet cakes for him and Penelope. Feeling a bit like a fraud yet glad he could be generous to boys like himself for once, he let the boys thank him, then told the coachman to drive on.

He sat back against the soft cushions with his purchases, which consisted of a penknife, a comb, a pencil, a pocket mirror, and the food. He handed Penelope her sweet cake and orange, and she took them with thanks and a smile. He offered Helena the third orange, and though her green eyes narrowed for a second, she accepted it.

"Thank you," she said as though she wished she didn't have to say anything.

"You're *quite* welcome," he replied, his spirits somewhat brighter. He chomped into the sweet cake, enjoying the soft dough and the crackle of the sugary glaze.

Helena began peeling her orange. "But I was right. You now have far more items than you'd planned."

He swallowed down the cake and cleared his throat. "Those lads do what they can to eat. Just like most people." Not *her*, though. She never had to worry about food—or rather, the lack of it. "I can use all these things," he said, "and they get—*have* a bit more to live on."

Helena shrugged as she placed pieces of orange peel into a hand-kerchief on her lap. "I suppose so. But you really shouldn't be so softhearted. After all, you can't help everyone."

"Helena," Penelope said, "have you forgotten where and how we met Mr. Little?"

"Of course I haven't, but I'm also not teaching what I know about Culinaria to *every* young pasty hawker from the night market. Besides, Elijah isn't like *those* people who pester every person who leaves London." Helena popped an orange segment into her mouth.

Penelope frowned, but said no more. Instead, she started eating her sweet cake with small, slow bites.

Elijah clenched his jaw as he used the penknife to slice a shallow cut around his orange's equator. He caught Helena's eye. "I think you're right. Some people really can't be helped."

"There, you see, Pen, he agrees!" Helena said. She bit into another orange segment and smiled, perfectly oblivious to the fact that he'd been talking about her.

Elijah placed a final silver dome over his last uncovered dish. He cast his eye across the elegant platters and tried to breathe.

"Now, recall only to speak when spoken to," Helena said. "Your speech continues to improve, but keep any discourse that is not food-related to a minimum. Are you paying attention, Mr. Little?"

In point of fact, Elijah had been thinking that his food was growing cold. He'd been more than a little overawed as they'd driven up the tree-shielded road that opened to reveal Helena's grandmother's imposing dower house with a grand Palladian facade, and even more so when he'd seen the vast kitchen, which was nearly double the size of the kitchen at Number 9, Cavendish Square. After Helena and Penelope had left him in the kitchen to greet Lady Rexborough, it had taken Elijah a good ten minutes to tamp his nerves into submission and start preparing the beautiful ingredients waiting for him. And now Helena wanted him to consider his speech and manners while the food grew colder.

"Speak when spoken to," he parroted. He had no intention of doing anything else.

"Perhaps we should bring the food to the conservatory," Penelope said.

Elijah thanked her with a look and picked up the largest platter.

"I'll lead the way," Helena said, picking up two dishes that supplemented the meal. "Mr. Little will follow me, and Miss Pickering will bring up the rear. George, Jerome," she said to the two footmen lingering by the door, "you shall bring the rest." The dowager still clung to the older tradition of dining a la française—*especially* when she was in the country, Helena claimed—so they had decided to present all the dishes at once.

Helena led the small procession out of the kitchen via the kitchen garden and through a series of paths lined by manicured shrubberies. Elijah had only seen parts of the kitchen garden from the windows, and he hadn't expected grounds so perfectly trimmed at every corner. How many gardeners did the lady have? Sweat began to form at the back of his neck, making his neckcloth stick to his skin.

Finally, they reached a glass structure that sat cleverly hidden out of view from the main house. Elijah swallowed as he followed Helena into the conservatory. The humidity hit him first, and sweat suffused the starch of his new neckcloth to run down his back. A round card table stood in the center of the room with all its leaves extended. At the table sat a dignified older lady with silver hair twisted at the top of her head in a series of coils. She wore a fashionably wide-sleeved salmon-colored day dress and a polite expression. He didn't see much resemblance between the dowager and her granddaughter—except the stately air that seemed to emanate off them like an expensive scent.

"Grandmama, may I present Mr. Elijah Little?" Helena asked as they approached the table.

The lady inclined her head forward slightly.

"Mr. Little, my grandmother, the Dowager Countess of Rexborough," Helena stated.

"A great pleasure, my lady," Elijah said, bowing his head as the girls had taught him.

"I've heard much of you from my granddaughter, Mr. Little."

Helena had said she'd written her grandmother about the project and that this would be his first practice using the techniques he'd learned, but beyond that, Elijah wondered what exactly Helena had told her about him. He didn't dare ask.

"You're most welcome," the dowager continued. "Do please tell us what you've prepared."

Elijah nodded and placed his silver platter in the center of the table. Remembering Helena's instructions to present with some flair, he removed the silver cloche with a flourish of his arm, feeling very silly as he did so. "Roasted pork leg in an Italian style with a fricassee of chanterelle mushrooms."

The dowager raised the lorgnette hanging from her neck to her eyes and leaned in to inspect the dish. "Smells delightful. I suppose that is one of our pigs from the farm?"

He looked at Helena. "I believe so, my lady."

Helena placed her dishes down on the table, and Penelope and the footmen followed suit. "What luck that we should come just as your pigs were ready, Grandmama. I know how much you prize them. We had planned a leg of lamb roast, but when I saw your beautiful pork, I knew we had to adapt the menu accordingly," Helena said.

Elijah cleared his throat, hoping for the best.

"Do tell us what everything else is, young man," the dowager said with a smile for Helena.

"Of course, ma'am," Elijah replied. Remembering the correct way to say everything still took quite a bit of effort, so he spoke slowly. "To continue with the Italianate theme, I've prepared braised artichokes with basil sauce, risotto with courgettes and green grape tomatoes, salad of cos leaves dressed with anchovies and olive oil, yeasted fritters coated in parmesan cheese and wrapped in prosciutto, and a cold melon soup." As he spoke each dish's name, he removed the silver coverings, and each time, the dowager's gaze roved over the food with the assistance of her lorgnette. Finally he came to the last plate. "And prosecco-soaked apricots with pyramid creams." He held his breath. He'd said it all correctly. He glimpsed Penelope smiling broadly in the corner of his eye. Even Helena wore a satisfied expression.

The dowager gave him a slow nod. "Most impressive. Shall we?"

The girls joined her at the table. Elijah remained standing to carve the pork leg as the footmen carried the other dishes around the table for the ladies to serve themselves. Elijah portioned each of them a generous slice of pork, making sure every serving had a piece of crispy skin, and ladled the drippings over the meat. When he finally sat to eat, he suppressed the exhale he wished he could express. He'd never been so bloody nervous giving people his food in his entire life.

It was an utterly humbling and foreign feeling, and he didn't know what should be so different about cooking now. Well, he *did* know—there had never been so much at stake before. He supposed he should thank Helena for teaching him how to eat at a formal table. He'd certainly never thought he'd be eating across from a dowager countess one day. He took a gulp of his elderflower cordial, then ate a mouthful of risotto. It had stiffened up a bit more than he would have liked, but the flavor came through. He started for the artichokes next.

"These prosciutto-wrapped fritters are delectable," the dowager remarked. "I could eat the whole platter."

He closed his eyes briefly, relieved he'd gotten them right.

"And they go so well with the cold melon soup. Have you tried dipping them?" Penelope asked, shooting a smile Elijah's way.

"Yes, a lovely combination," said the dowager.

"That was of his own devising, Grandmama," Helena said. Elijah nearly choked on the praise, rare as it was coming from Helena. "I told him to pair it with sliced melon, but he—" She stopped midsentence, chewing as a frown materialized on her face.

Sweat pooled at the back of Elijah's neck again as her eyes met his.

"Did you taste the pork?" Helena asked.

His stomach plummeted. He hadn't—*couldn't* make himself.

"The roast—not the prosciutto fritters," she clarified when he didn't speak.

Dread swelled within him as Penelope and the dowager each cut a bite of the sliced pork leg. He watched in horror as their expressions changed from confusion to distaste to embarrassment.

His throat went dry. This was the moment he'd known would eventually come. They'd surely guess his secret now. Why he hadn't tasted the pork—and *only* the pork. Then they'd throw him back to London on his arse.

"It is somewhat overseasoned," the dowager said. She reached for her glass of wine.

"Somewhat?" Helena said. "It's practically a salt lick!"

"Did you taste it, Mr. Little?" Penelope asked in her usually generous way.

His gut twisted. He didn't want to lie to her after all her kindnesses. He opened his mouth to reply.

"He clearly didn't," Helena broke in, her voice rising in both pitch and volume. "His palate isn't so far off that he wouldn't have tasted *this* amount of salt. Besides," she said, quickly tasting a bit of her salad and a forkful of risotto, "everything else is reasonably seasoned. Don't you agree?" She looked back and forth between her grandmother and Penelope, who both nodded.

"As I said, the fritters and melon soup are quite clever," the dowager said. "Perhaps you might tell us how you thought of melon soup, Mr. Little."

"I—I—" He stood and bowed at the dowager, unable to take any more of her pitying looks, Penelope's baffled frown, or Helena's heated glare. "Thank you for your hospitality, ma'am. I must return to the kitchen and clean up my mess." And with that, he hightailed it out of the conservatory. A blanket of mortification settled over him, setting his ears and neck aflame. If they were about to realize who he was, they might as well do it when he was out of the room. Far better not to hear the recriminations—and any slurs if they were coming— until they were back in the carriage and away from the dowager and her footmen. Elijah loosened his cravat and took a fortifying breath of the clean country air. If he was going to be humiliated, he'd rather be humiliated in private.

⁂

"He's a proud one, my dear," Helena's grandmother said after Elijah had disappeared.

"I don't know what he has to be proud about after that performance," Helena stated, dabbing at her lips with a napkin.

"Now be fair, Helena," Penelope said. "Everything else was quite good."

"*Good*, my dear Pen, is simply not good enough. How could he do something so careless as to not *taste* everything?"

Penelope sighed, having no answer to this. Still, it wasn't like Elijah not to taste his food. Had he merely forgotten in the bustle of preparing so many dishes? Or was there something else at work?

"I'm beastly sorry he wasted your beautiful pork, Grandmama. Such a shame."

"Do not worry, Helena. It is of no real consequence," the dowager reassured her. "One cannot learn without making a few mistakes here and there."

Helena scoffed. She was attempting to hide it, but Penelope could see Helena was almost as embarrassed as Elijah.

Penelope pressed her lips together. Things hadn't turned out perfectly, but she had to agree with the dowager. Mistakes were how one learned. Helena, however, had little tolerance for anybody's mistakes. Penelope had certainly observed this failing of Helena's many times during their years together at the Royal Academy, but never had it shone in such stark relief as it had during the last months with Elijah. Penelope puffed out a breath. It was a wonder Elijah hadn't forgotten to taste *more* components, considering the immense pressure he was under.

"I hope *you* have not made a mistake by taking on this young man, my dear," the dowager continued. "He has talent, but his presentation lacks showmanship. His manners are brusque, and his food lacks finesse."

Penelope thought this assessment unfair. After all, Elijah had only had a little over two months to learn many of the things she and Helena had learned in three years—and manners and a more refined speech besides. Still, she voiced none of these thoughts as she hardly thought the dowager would regard them.

"I am all too aware, Grandmama," Helena replied, exhaling. She straightened in her seat. "He shall simply have to work harder."

TEN

HURRICANES HARDLY HAPPEN

The next morning, Penelope rose early as she usually did and went in search of Elijah. Helena had spent the entire carriage ride from Berkshire back to Cavendish Square telling Elijah every detail (no matter how minute) of what he'd done incorrectly at her grandmother's house. Penelope had thought it all a bit much, but when she'd tried to say so, Helena had replied that he couldn't improve if he didn't know what needed improvement. Elijah had kept his mouth shut as he stared out the carriage window, and when they'd finally arrived, he'd disappeared into his room without a word.

As the cold day had dawned, Penelope woke knowing she wanted to speak to him before Helena could. She knocked first at his chamber door, but met only silence. After peering into the library and finding it empty, she ventured into the kitchen. He stood in front of the stove melting something over a bain-marie as the kitchen staff stoked the fires and kneaded bread. It was still early yet for the staff to be preparing breakfast in earnest, so only a few people milled about.

Penelope issued a "Good morning" to the room as a whole. The kitchen maids responded in kind and bobbed curtsies as she crossed the room to stand at Elijah's side. It hadn't escaped her notice that his reply had been nearly inaudible. "Some kind of custard?"

"Had an idea for a frozen meringue chocolate cream—thought I might fold some mint leaves into it," he said without looking at her.

"It might be more intense of a flavor if you infused the mint leaves into the custard," she replied, craning her neck to peer into the bowl sitting over the pot of simmering water. A thin chocolate concoction coated the bowl. "It doesn't appear that your custard has thickened yet. We could go into the garden and pick some mint before it does."

He gave the mixture one last stir with his wooden spoon before taking the bain-marie off the heat and setting it on the nearest wooden table. "After you, Miss Pickering," he said, gesturing to the door to the garden.

She bit the inside of her cheek at his new formality. They'd been correcting his manners and teaching him the accepted forms of address for weeks, yet now that he'd gotten it right, a part of her missed that free and easy way he had before. She wondered if he was regretting the whole experiment.

Though it was still early spring and the kitchen garden at Number 9, Cavendish Square, could not rival the vast one at Helena's grandmother's house, within its compact, boxwood-lined borders grew all manner of herbs, which had mostly died back or gone to ground over the winter; four espaliered apple trees; and new spring vegetables starting to sprout. Carrots and parsnip tops poked their heads out of the dirt in one square bed, small cabbages and miniature lettuce heads in another. Penelope walked toward the pots covered in protective cloths where she knew certain herbs like the mint sat. Elijah's footfalls crunched in the small gravel behind her.

"I'm sorry about yesterday," she said. "Perhaps we should have helped you more?"

When he didn't answer, she turned back to face him. He merely shrugged, not meeting her gaze.

Penelope wet her lips. This quiet, expressionless young man before her seemed like a shadow of his former self—real, yet somehow neither crisp nor tangible. Like a thing with little animus of his own. And that thought frightened her. For if she and Helena had done this to him, they certainly hadn't put him on the path to a better life. They may well have done the opposite. "I think the reason Helena was so irate was because she knows—as much as *I* know—that you pride yourself on flavor. Did . . ." She paused. "Did your nerves overcome you?"

He ran his hand over the back of his neck. "No. It weren't—*wasn't* that."

Penelope looked down at her clasped hands. "Do you still wish to continue here? With us? Because I can see why you wouldn't—"

"No. I do. I just . . ." He trailed off when she caught his eye. "I dunno." He bent to pull aside the protective cloth, and started sifting through the mint stalks to find the best ones.

Penelope cleared her throat. "Because if you *truly* do, I've resolved to take a greater role in your education." She'd come to the conclusion late last night. Helena's endless harping during the carriage ride home and his obvious dejection at how the day had gone plainly meant something in the arrangement had to alter. Penelope thought this the best solution. "I believe I could assist you in the areas where Helena . . ." *Cannot. Or perhaps* will *not,* she thought. But instead she said, ". . . is less observant." His brows rose at this, but he didn't speak. "But if that's something you'd prefer, we must be honest with each other. Helena has already taken a risk with this project. And if I help you more, I'll necessarily have to take time from my own project to get you where you need to be."

She clamped her mouth shut then, worried she'd sounded patronizing, but she'd told him the truth. She'd determined that her project would show how European influences had come together with the native food traditions and crops of Central America to create a new (and utterly delicious) cuisine. Penelope still had a great deal of historical research yet to do, recipes to try, and even a few experts on Spanish and Portuguese cuisine to contact (and consult if possible), but she couldn't shake the feeling that helping Elijah succeed would be just as important as all the work she had yet to complete.

He straightened with the mint sprigs now gathered in a bundle. "You can't let your project suffer just to help me, miss. I wouldn't feel right about it."

Penelope appreciated the thought, of course, but she shook her head. "Nonsense. I can manage both. Besides, if you truly want my assistance, I could find a way to teach you while integrating it with my own project. Luckily, you're already interested in the food of the Americas, I believe?"

Elijah ran his free hand through his hair. "Course I am, but . . .

do you think anyone else will be? People always seemed to like eating me—my—pasties when I put different flavors in. But will those flavors *impress* the sort of people you want me to rub elbows with?"

"Of course they will! Why wouldn't they?"

"I dunno, miss. Some people don't like things to be different than they're used to."

An expression that Penelope couldn't put a name to drifted over Elijah's features. The tension in his jaw pointed to some worry that seemed to go beyond people he didn't know not liking his food. "Let me tell you something, Mr. Little. You are correct—undoubtedly—but you must not let those worries keep you from being yourself. Very few of my instructors at the Royal Academy hold much interest in dishes that hail from beyond Europe, so I found the ones who did and learned from them. I furthered my own study, and I'm one of the top students at the Royal Academy as a result."

"We ain't exactly the same," he stated, though he wouldn't meet her eyes.

"I've had different opportunities, if that's what you mean. To be sure. But look at what you've done already—what you've accomplished already. I may be better off than you in some ways, but I've fought for every inch of it—my parents have as well."

He gave her a look that might as well have said he didn't believe her.

She exhaled. "My mother—my *nanay*—comes from an island in the Pacific Ocean called Panay—part of the Philippine Islands. My papa was the third son of a baronet with no fortune of his own, so he went to sea on a private scouting expedition. That's when he met her. They fell in love, and he brought her back to England. They tried to live here after I was born, but the prejudice against their marriage was too great. When I was still a young girl, they decided to leave England. We've traveled abroad ever since, exploring different countries."

Elijah seemed to be taking this in. His eyes roamed over her face, as though looking for signs of her mixed lineage. She'd endured such scrutiny before, but coming from him, it didn't feel like she was being judged. Then his eyes locked on hers. "Are other countries more accepting?"

She let out a sigh, as much from relief that he didn't seem inclined to immediately shun her as to the answer to his question. "Some places are, but we do not have a permanent home. The three of us simply travel from place to place. Before starting at the Royal Academy, I don't think I ever stayed in one location for more than a few months at a time. My parents don't return to England so as to not jeopardize my chances to become a great Culinarian."

"And nobody knows?"

She couldn't read his expression. "My father's family ignores my existence. In general, I don't make a great secret of who my nanay is, but since I do look rather like my papa, it rarely comes up in conversation. Helena knows, as does Lady Rutland, of course." Penelope started down the garden path toward a bed of curly-leafed cabbages still glistening with morning dew.

He followed. "Yet you don't tell everyone you meet," he said, almost to himself.

Penelope frowned. Did he think she should? But how could she possibly manage that? And why would she? Another thought flashed through her. Could he . . . She turned to face him. "Elijah, why didn't you taste that pork? Please, just tell—"

"I don't eat it." His brown eyes met hers, and she knew why he'd been hiding. For the very same reason she didn't tell everyone where her nanay came from. "I never have."

"So you're . . ."

He let out a breath. Then he stretched his shoulders back. "I'm Jewish."

Penelope licked her lips, not quite knowing what to say. She didn't know much about Judaism, but she, like everyone else, knew that not eating pork had been used as a way to identify Jews for centuries. In their Ethnography of Cuisines seminar in their second year at the Royal Academy, they'd learned that the prevalence of pork in Spanish cuisine had been adopted in the middle ages as a way to root out "hidden" Jews or those who had converted to Christianity but still clung to their Jewish traditions. People who were never seen eating pork became suspects—and victims—of the Inquisition.

Penelope's mother had always claimed her family had some Spanish ancestor from when the Spanish had occupied the islands, and Penelope recalled feeling disappointed (and a bit disgusted) during the seminar as she realized she might have some connection to a people who had changed their food traditions to persecute others.

But this explained why Elijah had certain gaps in his cooking. Why the prosciutto—which had come from Helena's storeroom— had tasted fine, but the pork leg they'd left him to prepare had been inedible. And then, there'd been the lobster day. "What about shellfish? You've eaten cockles and prawns with us. But the lobster—I don't actually recall you having a bite of it."

He ran his free hand through the hair at his left temple, causing the waves to sit in an awkward pattern. "Being Jewish where I grew up meant eating what you could. *When* you could. Shrimp and winkles and cockles ain't—aren't—my choice meal, but I eat 'em if I got ta."

"Have to," she corrected reflexively.

"Have to," he muttered.

"So you'll eat those, but not pork?" she asked, genuinely confused at the distinction.

He shifted his weight from one foot to the other. "I just never have. So it felt—odd. Same with the lobster. I work on Shabbat—Sabbath, you'd call it—sometimes too, though me mother didn't let me. Me uncle took me in after she died, and he'd changed his name so he could get work as an able seaman. So I thought I might too. No use having people look at you sideways just because your last name's Levin. Having folks single you out for how different you are ain't the best feeling. Which I guess you know, miss."

She nodded slowly. She did know what it was like to be treated differently from everyone else once they discovered you weren't what they thought you were. But in actuality, Penelope didn't know many—if any—Jewish people. She knew certain people disliked the Jewish London magnates for their pursuit of wealth, and that many considered the poor Jews of the street who eked out a living as peddlers and old-clothes men a blight on society—conveniently ignoring the fact that there was an equal, if not greater, number of Christian poor doing the same.

She also knew that the English held a contradictory dislike of and simultaneous captivation with anything they considered foreign.

Her father had told her stories of how isolated England had been during the wars with Napoleon, and only now in their Charlottian age was this suspicion the British had harbored for different cultures changing into a mild fascination. Some members of society—in the younger generation especially—believed other cultures were actually worth emulating. Times were changing. Slowly.

Of course her experiences hadn't been exactly the same as Elijah's, but she doubted they were so dissimilar either. She let out a breath and it fogged in the cool morning air. "Enough of this 'miss' nonsense," she stated. She stuck out her hand. "I'm 'Penelope' from now on."

He eyed her and her outstretched hand. Then the corner of his lips kicked upward. He took her hand in a solid grip and shook it once. An inexplicable warmth traveled through her palm and into her arm. Her hand must have grown more chilled in the morning air than she'd thought. "Friends call me 'Elijah.'"

She smiled at him, unable to help herself. "Well, my friend"— she pointed to the mint in his hand—"I believe we have custard to infuse. And you have someone to tell about your dietary requirements."

His smirk faded. "It's not the easiest thing to bring up."

"Well, the pork conversation yesterday might have been the most logical time."

He let out a breath. "Aye. That woulda gone over well. Soon as people know you're different, they think less of you."

She raised her brows. "I don't think less of you."

"That's cuz you're—you. You heard what she said about those

boys on the road yesterday. She thinks people like me are beneath her. Which ain't surprising—I knew it that night we met."

Penelope bit her lip, unable to deny what Helena had said about the boys hawking their wares. She realized now why Elijah had seemed so distant after that exchange yesterday. How could it *not* affect him? She would have been just as angry if Helena had said such a thing about someone of mixed heritage like herself or someone from the Philippine Islands like her nanay.

But the fact remained that Helena *was* her friend, and she had taken Elijah in to help him better himself. Helena had done much the same for Penelope their first day at the Academy. She still remembered feeling alone and wholly out of place among so many girls who had grown up in the midst of society. All Penelope had known of London society was what her papa had told her and what she'd read in books.

But when she'd walked into the room she'd be sharing with Helena and two other girls, Helena had bounded up to her with an outstretched hand. Her enthusiasm for Culinaria had been unmistakable, and had matched Penelope's. They'd talked about food so much, their roommates soon found excuses to leave their company. She and Helena had become fast friends, and they'd been that way ever since. They'd supported each other through all of their years at the Academy, and though she'd watched Helena alienate person after person, Penelope had stood by her because she knew Helena never *intended* anyone ill. She simply wanted others to take Culinaria as seriously as she. Surely that was why she had spent last night berating Elijah? Once Elijah told Helena he was Jewish, she would likely react just as she had when Penelope had explained her lineage, and they would all move on.

"She decided to help you, Elijah. She can't really think you're beneath her."

Elijah scoffed. "Course she can. She's probably not thought herself anything less than extraordinary for more than an hour in her entire life. And why would she? She has everything!"

Penelope shook her head. "Helena may seem to have everything, but you must know by now that much of her demeanor is bluster. I *do* think she has a good heart—I would not be her friend otherwise. When I told her of my *nanay*, it didn't seem to matter to her, and she treated me the same." She blinked as she realized he was staring at her. "What?"

"I was thinking that *you're* the one with the good heart."

"Oh," she said, his statement catching her off guard.

"Course, I figured that the night we all met at the market. Glad I was right."

She didn't quite know what to say to that. "Well, I'm glad we met that night. I can always use a new friend."

"Aye. Friends are hard to come by." His lips quirked up into that smile she'd thought rather rakish when he'd first sold her his empanadas, but which she was now coming to understand was quite genuine.

"There you two are," a voice called from the back door.

Penelope whipped her head away from Elijah's smile to see Helena standing in the kitchen doorway with one hand on her waist.

"Well? Do you plan to stand there all day? We have work to do!"

Penelope cleared her throat. "Helena, I was just talking with Mr.

Little about my taking a greater role in his education. I can devote the mornings before breakfast to teaching him more international cuisine and to strengthening anything else he's struggling with. You can continue the rest of the day with anything you had planned, of course," Penelope said, walking back toward the house.

Helena frowned. "What of your own project, Pen?"

Penelope waved a hand in the air. "I have it all under control, I assure you."

Helena tapped her foot as they approached. "Well . . . to be candid, that suits me quite well. I have any number of tasks I attend to before breakfast, so if it's of no inconvenience—"

"None whatsoever," Penelope stated with a look at Elijah, who now stood behind her on the gravel path.

"Well. Good. I'll see you at breakfast, then. I have correspondence to finish." She swiveled in the doorway, then turned back. "See that you work on the pork roast with him at some point, Pen."

Penelope made a noncommittal noise in her throat, then looked back at Elijah with wide eyes. When she realized he wasn't going to speak, she turned toward Helena, but her friend had already disappeared into the house.

She raised her brows at him. "*That* would have been the perfect opportunity to tell her."

He narrowed his eyes. "She really don't seem the type to *not* care."

Penelope tilted her head and gave him what she hoped was an encouraging smile. "Doesn't. And you'll never know until you try."

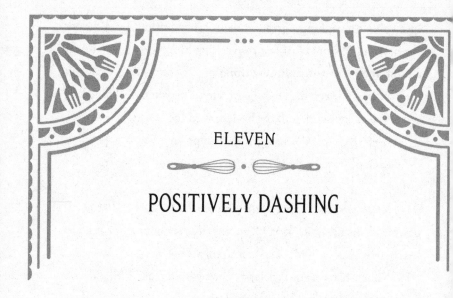

ELEVEN

POSITIVELY DASHING

In the days and weeks that followed, Penelope and Elijah met every morning in the kitchen, setting up at their designated table well out of the way of the kitchen staff preparing breakfast. Bit by bit, the pair covered the topics Helena held little interest in, starting with an overview of the different gastronomies within East and Southern Asia, North Africa, Persia, and the Ottoman Empire, and then progressing to the practical techniques used in each cuisine. They also, of course, went through what Penelope had learned in the United States and Central America.

Helena, meanwhile, compiled her notes on Elijah's development or dealt with her correspondence. Elijah's progress increased to a rapid clip with Penelope there to listen and adjust Helena's analytic teaching style that expected Elijah to memorize facts, ratios, and recipes, to a style Penelope thought more palatable to how her new friend learned. Instead of focusing on specific tasks and actions,

Penelope gave him enough information to help him achieve broader goals creatively. She also began coaching Elijah on his presentation skills, showing him various ways to make food look more inviting and then letting him improvise. Elijah could soon create everything from small garnishes like radish roses to chocolate leaves and curls to feathered sauces in geometrical designs. All helped make his platters into something even more special.

"The difference between a good plate of food and a transporting plate comes from making the dish a true *experience*," Penelope said one day as they were taking a salt and herb–encrusted mackerel out of the oven. They'd gone over the general principles of salt crusting together, and then she'd given Elijah the latitude to decide what he wanted to try it with; she'd answered any questions he had along the way. "Remember that the first thing anyone does is eat with their eyes. Before the diner even takes a single bite, what they see, hear, and smell is what will often entice them to eat—or to partake of some other dish if they have the opportunity. For the ultimate, transcendent food experience, the mind must be engaged on multiple levels. *That* is the way to keep your food from being *better* than common. *That*..." She trailed off as she realized Elijah seemed to be studying her instead of the fish. He'd set it down on the workbench, but turned away from it with a smile she couldn't read.

"What is it?" she asked, wondering if she had something on her face.

"I'd never thought of it that way," he replied.

Penelope raised her brows. "Hasn't Helena said something to that effect?" It seemed such an obvious sentiment to her that the idea of Helena never telling him something similar—something *so* integral to his future success—took her aback.

"She mentioned using all the senses, but the way she put it . . ." He frowned, then cleared his throat. "I suppose the way you said it just made me think. To do something special, it can't just taste and look good. It's really gotta surprise people."

"Got to," she corrected. "But yes. That's it exactly."

He nodded. "Seems to me that goes for other things in life too."

She tilted her head. "How so?"

"I mean what ya said about a person's mind being engaged on many levels. Seems like any really amazing experience would have to be cuz of that."

Penelope considered. "I think you're very likely right."

"Not that I have much experience with anything 'amazing' myself, mind," he said with a self-deprecating laugh.

She thought of some of the things she'd experienced with her parents—climbing the Mayan pyramids of the Yucatan Peninsula, riding a camel outside of Marrakesh, watching stars shoot across the sky as the three of them slept outside—they were all memories she cherished. She couldn't recall each of them with all her senses. Yet now, if she tried, she could remember the bite of the wind against her cheeks as she scaled the pyramid's steps, the pungent smell of the dusty camel, and her excitement and her nanay's delighted hoot when the first of many stars blazed through the summer sky while her papa tried to follow them with his spyglass. Yes, Elijah *was* right. Engaging all of the senses and the brain applied to much more than food.

"You must have some wonderful experience you recall, Elijah. Otherwise, how did you draw such a clever conclusion?"

He shrugged and turned back to face the fish. "I ain't had—"

"You *haven't*," she corrected gently.

He nodded. "I haven't had too many good times. But, I was thinking of this." He gestured with one hand at the kitchen.

"Today?" she asked.

"Aye, today. And most of the days since I came here." He wouldn't meet her eyes.

Penelope's chest tightened. She couldn't imagine what his life had been like before, but the thought that this time with them was generally the only thing he could recall challenging him enough to even *approximate* an extraordinary experience both saddened her and strengthened her resolve.

She put her hands on her hips. "Well, my friend, this is only the beginning. I can see that there are great things on your horizon."

He gave her a half smirk. "You see that, do you? How, if I might ask?"

She nodded once. "In my crystal ball."

He stared at her for a moment. Then he laughed. The warm sound of it washed over Penelope, and she realized that it was probably the first time she'd ever heard him laugh. She was growing quite accustomed to his smiles—that grin that usually began at the left side of his face— but his laugh? She couldn't recall him ever laughing before. No, now that she thought of it, he had laughed before, but some self-imposed restraint always seemed to hold him back. But just now, she had been able to make him forget his worries, if only for the moment.

"What else does it tell you?" he asked.

She couldn't help her lips from curling up into a smile of her own. "That that mackerel isn't going to jump off the platter into our mouths without help."

He shook his head, but she could see that he was trying not to laugh again.

She adopted a serious expression as she handed him a knife and serving fork. "So, how would you present this to the queen in a way that would make it into more than simply a well-cooked fish dish?"

"Well," he said, his brow furrowing as he looked down at the fish piled high with herbaceous salt, "I would think a bit of theater might be in order?"

Penelope raised her eyebrows. "Yes? In what way?"

"What about a series of pedestals in shallow pools of water? Each pedestal could have a different dish on it to complement the salted mackerel, which could be in the center of the pool?"

Penelope let out a low breath. "That sounds spectacular. How wide would the pool be?"

"Not so wide that the food couldn't be reached." He spread his arms out to approximate a width. "I suppose it might depend on the size of the table it'd be served on."

Penelope nodded, pleased with his progress.

"Perhaps it could even be a pool of salt water with sea creatures?" he mused, almost to himself.

"Sea creatures?"

"Nothing large, mind. Mussels, starfish, some big shells if one could come by them." He turned to catch her gaze. "What do you think?"

The earnest appeal in his light brown eyes flustered Penelope just as her growing pride at how quickly he was progressing made her want to clap her hands with joy. "I think the queen would find it glorious."

He smiled at her again, but this time it was a different smile.

Something altogether more pensive. Penelope wondered, not for the first time that day, what he was thinking. "You would have to taste any shellfish, I'm afraid—especially for the queen."

He nodded. "I've eaten it before, as I said."

She exhaled. "I still don't know what to do about the"—she looked around the room at the kitchen staff and decided not to mention the pork issue aloud—"the other," she settled for.

He raised his eyebrows, then let out a sigh. "It's not just that it's a thing that's expected of me. If I saw it like that, I think I could let it go once in a while—like I do with some of the other things I told you about. It's just . . ." He exhaled again and looked at her. "Poor as my parents were, they never ate it. Even when food was scarce, we always found something else. It likely sounds foolish, but holding onto that feels like holding on to some part of them."

"That's not foolish," Penelope stated. She couldn't even imagine what she would do if she'd lost her parents at such a young age as he had. "I think your parents would be proud of you for honoring their traditions."

"I dunno," he said, looking down. He shuffled his feet. "I ain't— I'm not exactly perfect at it. But I hope they would be." He cleared his throat, and Penelope felt the strongest urge to comfort him. Unfortunately, she had never had a boy as a friend before, and for a moment, an appropriate way to go about it baffled her.

Finally, Penelope settled on saying, "None of us is perfect. But if I've learned anything about you during these last months, it's that you always do your very best, Elijah Little."

He glanced up at her with surprise in his eyes—and something more. Something she couldn't name, but it made her cheeks heat nonetheless. She clumsily changed the subject.

"Was it nice growing up with other people like you? Forgive me for asking, but I never knew anyone like me when I was younger—someone who was a part of two worlds and yet neither world fully. My nanay's family didn't accept my parents' marriage either, so she is the only connection I have to her island."

He eyed her, and Penelope again wondered what he was thinking. "I never thought of it," he eventually said. "It weren't—*wasn't* easy having people call you names just for being born. But"—he ran a hand over the back of his neck, and she didn't have the heart to remind him not to—"I suppose it would've been worse to go through it without anyone else like me around."

She nodded, torn between wanting to say more and not wanting the staff to overhear. "I do still think you should tell Helena."

"Tell her what?" Helena asked as she walked into the kitchen.

Penelope looked at Elijah, then back to Helena. "I was . . ." Her eyes shot toward Elijah once more, but seeing he had little intention of speaking, she said, ". . . saying he should tell you his brilliant idea for a culinary presentation fit for the queen."

"Indeed?" Helena prompted.

He nodded and proceeded to describe his ideas to highlight the salt-encrusted mackerel, embellishing it even more now for Helena's approval.

"It's very similar to what I did with Lady Rutland for the Admiralty," Helena pronounced when he'd finished. "Very good, Mr. Little."

He bowed his head in a somewhat formal gesture.

"In fact," Helena said, "I think you're more than ready to try your skills in public." She handed Penelope the letter she'd been holding in one hand. "Lady Rutland writes that there is a culinary faire at the end of the week. It's the perfect opportunity!"

Penelope read the letter quickly. "It would be ideal, but do you think you're ready, Elijah?"

"Of course he is," Helena answered before he could open his mouth. "He's improved by leaps and bounds in the last weeks. Besides, he'll have to appear in public eventually, and there's no better time than the present."

Penelope glanced at Elijah.

He looked at the fish in front of him. "What would I have to do?"

"This particular faire is to be a preliminary event for those wishing to qualify for the Royal Culinary Exhibition that will be held in honor of Princess Adelaide. Each participant creates a menu and prepares it, and the guests in attendance will taste and judge their favorites amongst the amateurs, gentlemen chefs, and Culinarians. The top two winners in each category shall cook at the Royal Exhibition along with others invited from different countries," Helena said, nearly bouncing on the tips of her toes.

Penelope thought she heard Elijah gulp.

"No one expects you to be perfect, Elijah," Penelope said. "And we'll help you."

"Yes, yes, of course we will," Helena agreed. "We'll start practicing after breakfast. I have every confidence that we can teach him all he'll need."

"What, er—category will I be in?" Elijah asked.

"Gentleman chef, of course," Helena exclaimed, just as Penelope said, "Amateur."

Both girls looked at each other and then at Elijah, whose head swiveled back and forth between them.

"We've been training you to act like a gentleman, Mr. Little, and your first foray on the culinary stage should be as such," Helena stated.

"Helena, as we've discussed before, he doesn't wish to be a gentleman," Penelope said. "Even if he could pass for a gentleman chef now—"

"They don't look up a fellow's genealogy in *Burke's Peerage*, Pen. I said from the beginning that with the right training he could pass for a gentleman, and it's even truer now." Helena gestured at him with one hand.

His torso stiffened, but Penelope had noticed that lately he'd been listening to Helena's admonitions that he use his height to full advantage. Yes, with the aloof bearing he usually adopted around Helena, he could easily pass as a gentleman, but that was beside the point. "I agree," Penelope said, "*but* he cannot make a living from food if he's a gentleman. If he enters in the gentleman chef category, and he does well at this faire, everyone will know him as a gentleman—a new potential catch on the marriage mart—not as an amateur cook who hopes to catch a patron's or investor's interest."

"I don't see why that should be so," Helena replied. "These culinary class distinctions shall soon fall by the wayside—indeed, in a few years, they'll be practically antique! Tell me this, Pen: Why shouldn't a gentleman own a shop, or marry well, or do neither, or *both*, if he so chooses? For that matter, why shouldn't a Covent Garden pasty hawker do the same?"

Penelope made a noise in her throat. She, too, thought Elijah should achieve everything he wanted, but social constraints didn't disappear just because Helena wished them to. "It's not done, Helena, you know that."

"Poppycock! What we're doing now hasn't been done either, but it hasn't stopped us—or Mr. Little—from trying. I don't see what's to stop him from being whatever he wishes." She smiled broadly at both of them, and Penelope couldn't deny that her zeal was catching. "Let us also consider the following," Helena continued. She started pacing the length of the worktable. "Currently, gentlemen chefs don't own culinary shops because they perceive that engaging in trade would somehow lower their standing in society—an arcane way of thinking left over from the Georgian age. But, for someone like Mr. Little, becoming a member of either class would mean a marked improvement in his quality of life. We must also recognize that it is far more difficult to climb in society than it is to fall down a rung—that is why we have partaken in this experiment, is it not?" She paused and looked at them for confirmation.

Elijah nodded. Penelope drew in a breath, heartened to know that Helena hadn't lost sight of why they had started all this.

Satisfied, Helena pressed the pads of her fingers together. "Therefore, I still say that Mr. Little might as well give himself a greater range of opportunities. And in my humble estimation, the gentleman chef category will do just that."

Penelope threw a glance at Elijah, but his brow was furrowed. She clasped her hands together. "She's right. You shouldn't let outdated social norms keep you from what you want. It would be doing yourself a disservice."

His brown eyes met hers, and though he said nothing, she

thought he understood what she meant. His origin shouldn't stop him from reaching for the stars or even the moon—if he wanted it.

"Times are changing, my friends," Helena pronounced with a self-assured smile. "And *we're* going to change them."

⌒∞⌒

Elijah resisted the urge to run his hands through his newly shorn hair. The girls had insisted that a gentleman must look the part as well as act the part, so Helena had brought a barber to Cavendish Square. The man had cut the sides of Elijah's hair far shorter than he'd ever bothered to cut it himself, and he was still growing accustomed to his new appearance.

Helena had called it "a vast improvement," and Penelope had told him he looked very fine, which had given him some peace of mind, but he still wasn't sure why the top should be so much longer than the sides. Still, Elijah did recall seeing other high-class gentlemen walking about Covent Garden with similar styles, so he supposed it must be the fashion among certain people. There wasn't much he could do about it now, in any case.

Helena had also summoned a tailor, who had taken Elijah's measurements and promised to return in two days' time with at least one set of garments to fit on Elijah's frame. Helena had tried to pay for it all in her own high-handed way, but when Elijah had balked, Penelope had persuaded Helena to let him pay what he could, and Helena had relented. It bothered him that he couldn't afford the new wardrobe with his own savings, but Helena had reminded him the clothes would be a necessity in his new life.

He glanced at Helena out of the corner of his eye. They stood on opposite sides of the parlor, waiting in awkward silence for the tailor to arrive and begin the fitting. Penelope had remained in the kitchen to finish nixtamalizing corn for the tamales she planned to show him how to make, but she'd promised to come to the parlor as soon as she'd finished. He realized that over the last weeks, she'd become a welcome safeguard between him and Helena. After the day at Helena's grandmother's, he'd initially been surprised that Helena hadn't guessed the reason why he hadn't tasted the pork, but it had slowly dawned on him that she saw what she wanted to see.

He thought it very strange for someone so clever to outright miss (or ignore?) so many circumstances around her, but once he'd made the conclusion, all evidence seemed to confirm it. The only other inference he could draw (and the one he would have believed more if Penelope hadn't tried to convince him of Helena's good qualities) was that Helena simply wanted everything her way and was willing to turn a blind eye to the whole lot—society's rules, the feelings of the people around her, and even common sense—to achieve her own ends.

Helena was brilliant, *that* no one could deny, but he knew she wouldn't have reacted to his ancestry as Penelope had that day in the kitchen garden. Of course, Penelope hadn't guessed that he was Jewish either, but she'd clearly known he was hiding something. If Helena had suspected something similar, he'd probably never know. He certainly had no mind to ask her. Helena might have grown accustomed to the idea of Penelope's parents, and even said condescendingly nice things about some of Penelope's mother's recipes, but he had little doubt that being Jewish would be an entirely different matter.

Though England had no special laws against Jews like the ones existing in other European countries, Jewish people didn't have the same rights as other English citizens. They could be kept from voting, couldn't attend Oxford or Cambridge, couldn't enter government service or sit in the House of Commons, and weren't allowed to train for the law. But more disturbing than these restrictions was the constant worry that simply walking down the street one day might lead to an encounter with someone threatening to force pork down your throat, or robbing, beating, or even murdering you—just for being Jewish.

Elijah had certainly received threats and taunts aplenty in his day. (He doubted there was a boy hawking wares in London who hadn't.) But the intolerance that always set his head spinning and brought a raw lump to his throat was seeing people's reactions when they heard the word "Jew." In the eyes of many, the word itself was linked to vulgarity, degradation, and a cunning nature, all of which they considered contemptible. But Elijah only understood this in a very general sense. Had he known their reasoning, it wouldn't have lessened the damage these people had done to his heart or spirit throughout his childhood.

Elijah had never known how to combat it, so he'd gone about his life trying his best to ignore it. Yet, there was no escaping the censure if you had a Jewish name or looked as those people expected Jews to look. Despite whatever Penelope thought, Helena's comments about the boys hawking at the crossroad said, in no uncertain terms, that she held preconceived notions about people like him. That was why many of the children he'd gone to school with now hid their religion, practiced in less than traditional ways as he did, or forsook Judaism altogether. Though the charity school's goal was to teach poor Jewish children the rudiments of reading, writing, Hebrew, and arithmetic in the hopes they could elevate themselves into trades other than hawking or peddling, in London, Jews couldn't operate retail shops of their own due to the prejudice among the city merchants—something Elijah hadn't exactly mentioned to Penelope (though it was hardly a secret).

There were, of course, ways and means around some of the exclusions. Certain Jews claimed to be wholesale merchants and called their establishments "warehouses," yet still sold their goods or services to people retail if they came in off the street. Wealthier Jews often registered their property in a Christian friend's or employee's name. But these relatively effective blinds weren't achievable for poor street vendors like Elijah without any wealth, influence, or connections. But perhaps if he succeeded at this culinary faire . . .

Elijah had meant what he'd said the day he'd bought the goods from the boys by the side of the road. Some people couldn't be helped; their minds were set and they'd never change their views. He'd crossed paths with enough persecutors in his life to know the truth of that statement. Yet, he was also learning that some people, like Penelope, asked questions and truly wanted to discuss the answers.

He still believed more people existed in the world who didn't ask questions—and not because they didn't know to ask them. No, they didn't ask because they only wanted the answers they'd created in their minds. Elijah was fairly certain Helena belonged in the latter category.

He eyed her profile. For once, she wasn't moving about like a whirlwind or telling him what to do. She simply gazed into the fire as he stood by a window facing the square. In that moment, part of him wondered if Penelope was right about her. Though he trusted

Penelope's judgment more than anyone else he knew, he could also see that she thought the best of people—almost to a fault. He didn't like keeping his identity out of sight, but what had Helena herself counseled him to do? Give himself all the opportunities he could. If that meant shielding his upbringing from her, that's what he would do. Becoming a gentleman chef or a shopkeeper would mean hiding his true self in any case. And it had all been Helena's idea.

Pierce opened the parlor door, and the bespectacled tailor followed him inside. "Mr. Benjamin, Lady Helena," Pierce said.

Helena stepped away from the fireplace to greet the man. "How do you do, Mr. Benjamin. I trust you were able to create something for Mr. Little?"

The tailor bowed his head and lifted the handled box he carried at his side. "Yes, my lady. I believe it will meet your standards." He looked at Elijah. "Perhaps Mr. Little would be so good as to try it on?"

"Yes, indeed," Helena said, moving toward the door. "I shall return shortly and see how it fits. Come along, Pierce. I wished to speak to you about—"

Pierce closed the door behind them, leaving Elijah with the tailor. Mr. Benjamin offered some everyday pleasantries as he set his box down and pulled out a light gray coat, trousers, and blue waistcoat. Like the marquess's clothing, they all looked far too fine for the likes of Elijah, but he shunted those thoughts to the side and tried them on. The trousers fit well, but the waistcoat gaped a little under his arms.

"Ah, not to worry, Mr. Little," Mr. Benjamin said. He began pinning the fabric until it sat flush against Elijah's torso. "How's that?" he asked over the rims of his spectacles.

Elijah, who had never had any kind of custom garment made for him, didn't really know what he should say. "It seems to fit."

Mr. Benjamin touched the top of his balding head. "Can you move?"

Elijah frowned, then moved his arms about in an arc. He was fairly certain he looked ridiculous. The waistcoat was tighter than the marquess's castoffs, but it felt normal otherwise.

"Hmm . . . I see. Perhaps if I . . ." Mr. Benjamin adjusted the fabric at one side and rearranged the pins. "Try moving now."

Elijah swung his arms. He raised his brows. "It's definitely easier now."

The man smiled. "I thought so. Let's see how we did with the coat."

Elijah threaded his arms through the fabric. The tailor tsked in his throat and immediately started pinning. Elijah stood as still as possible to keep from getting poked.

"You know, I was wondering why you looked so familiar the other day when we met, young man," Mr. Benjamin said through the pins he held between his teeth.

Elijah tensed and got a pin in his shoulder. "Ouch!"

"My apologies. Try to hold still, Mr. Little."

Elijah let out a breath.

"But, in fact, you reminded me of a friend I had when I lived near Duke's Place. Man by the name of Moishe Levin. He supplied me with buttons and thread when I was just starting."

Elijah felt the blood drain from his face. His papa. This man had known him—unless there was some other Moishe Levin in London. "When was this?"

"Oh, more than ten years gone now."

Elijah swallowed. His father had died twelve years ago.

Mr. Benjamin continued. "Moishe used to say that like his name-sake, he was a stranger in a strange land, but unlike his namesake, he was not slow of speech—he spoke quite quickly, you see—at least in Yiddish. Ah yes, I very much enjoyed his sense of humor. An altogether optimistic and contented fellow he was. I miss him to this day."

Though sometimes Elijah thought he barely remembered his father, his uncle had often told him stories of him—including some of his favorite little jokes. There could be no coincidence. Mr. Benjamin had known his papa. Elijah's chest tightened, and he swallowed back the lump rising in his throat. "What happened to him?"

The tailor circled back to scrutinize the other side of the coat. "Ah, a sad story it is. He peddled goods of many types. At times he left London to sell his wares. Men overtook him on the road and stole all his goods and money. They beat him very badly. He made his way back to London to his wife and child, but died soon after."

Elijah's fist clenched. Some of his memories had faded, but he remembered his papa's bloodied face. He remembered how he'd held Elijah's small hand in his larger, battered one as he'd told Elijah he loved him for the last time. And he remembered his mama's tears flowing down her cheeks.

Mr. Benjamin stood and caught Elijah's watery gaze. "You look much like him. And like your mama."

Elijah gulped back the tears. He didn't want to feel the pain; the lingering void that his parents' absence had created within him always lurked, waiting to swallow him whole if he let it. He looked around the room and then down at his new clothes. "I don't know what I'm doing here. I haven't done any wrong to get here, but I just wanted to have a better life—make them proud if I could. But I—"

Mr. Benjamin put up his hands. "Wait a minute, young man. I don't go looking into people's pots and kettles. *A mentsh trakht un Got lakht.* Do you know what that means?"

Elijah and his uncle rarely spoke Yiddish anymore, and Elijah had forgotten a great deal, but he thought he remembered that saying. "Man plans and God laughs."

The tailor nodded. "We all do what we must to have the life we want. Of course, things don't always turn out the way we like. But we try. If you *don't* try, I think God laughs anyway."

Elijah blew out a deep breath. "That's what I always thought too."

"And besides that, I think if Moishe were here, he would tell you what I tell my customers. *Di pave zol nit hobn di sheyne federn, volt zikh keyner af ir nit umgekukt.* If the peacock didn't have beautiful feathers, no one would pay attention to it."

Elijah chuckled, grateful for the sentiment, regardless of whether his papa would have actually said it. "Thank you. I—" He broke off as someone knocked. He told whoever it was to come in, and the door opened.

Penelope peeked her head into the room. The curls framing her face looked somewhat disheveled, as though she'd had to push them out of her eyes multiple times as she bent over the worktable. She still wore her apron with a colorful floral pattern. "I'm not too late, am I?" she asked. He shook his head, then watched her eyes widen as they landed on him. "You look . . ." Her eyes roved over him once more. She seemed to be struggling for words. "You look every inch a gentleman, Mr. Little."

He smiled then, relaxing. He didn't even mind the pin partially poking into his arm when she grinned at him like that. He wished they were alone so they could talk freely, but then Penelope's eyes darted away from his face to his chest, and then to Mr. Benjamin.

"Mr. Benjamin, you've done yourself proud," Penelope continued. "I cannot wait to see the rest of the wardrobe."

Mr. Benjamin smiled at her. "It's a pleasure to clothe someone like Mr. Little." He looked at Elijah, and Elijah sent him silent thanks. Of course, it wouldn't have mattered what the tailor told Penelope about Elijah or his parents, since she already knew the truth, but Mr. Benjamin didn't know that.

"Oh, let's see!" Helena exclaimed, swirling into the room through the open door. She looked Elijah up and down once, then tilted her head toward Mr. Benjamin. "I don't know that I would have paired the blue waistcoat with the light gray. However, one cannot deny that it suits him very well indeed."

This was high praise coming from her, and Elijah tried to take it as such, but Penelope gaped at her, wide-eyed. "Helena, he looks quite marvelous!"

The tailor regarded Elijah over the rims of his spectacles with raised brows, amusement painted in the lines around his mouth.

And though Elijah pretended to watch the girls discussing their opinions about the cut of the coat and the length of his cuffs, rather than meet his papa's friend's eyes, he couldn't stop a grin from overtaking his face.

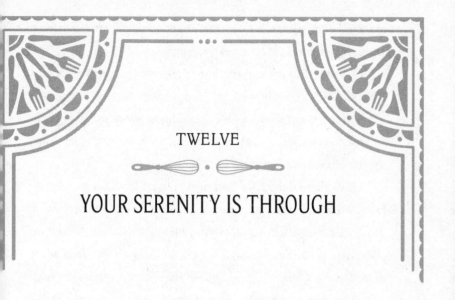

TWELVE

YOUR SERENITY IS THROUGH

Elijah kept his mouth shut and his eyes open as he followed Helena and Penelope through fluted Ionic columns and under the porticoed entrance to the Pantheon on Oxford Street. The Pantheon had once been assembly rooms and later a theater, but the Grand Saloon now functioned as a bazaar four days a week and as an exhibition hall for functions like culinary faires on the remaining days.

He followed the girls through the vestibule and hallway until they reached the Grand Saloon, which was almost as wide as it was long. The room seemed almost entirely lit from two ranges of long, curved windows in the semicircular ceiling, which Elijah guessed to be fifty or sixty feet high. On either side of the room, counters and tables, which housed the bazaar, had been taken over by the day's competitors. People from many walks of life milled through the saloon. Some were competitors carrying crates of food or dishes to their designated table; some were attendees who'd arrived early to assess the food and pick their early favorites.

Halfway through the room, the girls stopped at a U-shaped table and set down their baskets laden with the food Elijah had spent all morning preparing. He placed his heavy crate full of plates and platters on the table as Helena directed her footmen to lay down the rest of the food and utensils.

Elijah glanced to his left and right. The table to his right already brimmed with small plates crowned with colorful concoctions. A young man only slightly older than Elijah was spooning food onto plate after plate. Even though his tall hat and burgundy coat lay draped over a chair behind the table, the fellow continuously used a cloth to wipe his hands—presumably to protect the rest of his garments.

Elijah took stock of his own hands before smoothing down the lapel of his first new coat. Mr. Benjamin had brought the completed garments back to Cavendish Square a couple of days ago and guaranteed the rest of the wardrobe would soon be completed. He'd wished Elijah luck and had reiterated his promise to Helena about discretion. Helena had made confidentiality a stipulation of his employment. After all, the experiment couldn't be compromised by loose lips. The tailor had also given Elijah a meaningful look and extended an invitation to one day visit him in his workshop. Elijah had thanked him again. Once this was all over, he fully intended to do just that. Besides his uncle, Elijah didn't know anyone else who'd known his papa and, painful though it may be, it would be good to speak of him.

It felt strange—or perhaps, *fitting*?—to have met someone who'd known his parents just as he was about to start this new challenge, but as Mr. Benjamin had so rightly said: Man plans and God laughs. Elijah just hoped God wasn't laughing too hard.

Helena had reminded him in the carriage ride over that today would be the makings of his new life. Elijah exhaled and looked down to ensure that his waistcoat was still buttoned properly. It looked just the same as it had in the carriage—he was worrying needlessly.

He took a steadying breath. As he looked up, his gaze alighted on three strolling sailors pointing at food, and Elijah thought of his uncle Jonathan. A part of him wondered what he'd think seeing Elijah all kitted out like this, competing as a gentleman. He hoped he'd be proud.

"Woolgathering?" Penelope asked, stepping close to him.

He blinked and turned his attention to her oval face. Her kind smile had become one of the highlights of his days, especially in these last weeks. "I can't quite believe I'm here," he admitted. He glanced at Helena to be sure she hadn't heard, but she was directing the footmen to start placing plates in alternating sizes for more visual interest.

"Don't be nervous," Penelope said. "Your menu will more than impress the people and the judges. My crystal ball told me so." She winked, then looked around to be sure no one had seen her.

He couldn't help but laugh at the absurdity of *her* trying to appear ladylike just as he was pretending to be a gentleman. Down the aisle to their left, clashing plates drew his attention as one of his gentlemen competitors, decked out in an immaculate brown coat and trousers, set about unloading his food onto his table in a haphazard manner. The chap looked familiar, though Elijah couldn't place him.

"Are you two planning to stand there chattering all day?" Helena said loudly.

Elijah moved to take the food from the crates, and started placing each element on the small plates that members of the public would eat from and judge. Each attendee who paid the entrance fee received tokens and could choose their two favorite competitors in each category by dropping their tokens into the glass jar sitting at the corner of every participant's table. Elijah eyed his jar and suppressed the urge to rub the back of his neck. Whatever happened happened. All he could control was the food—and try to be sure he acted and spoke like the gentleman the girls had taught him to be.

Silently, he placed element after element where it should sit on each plate. Every so often Helena would tell him how much time remained before the tasting began, but Elijah kept his head down and nodded so she knew he was listening. He'd learned over the last few months that Helena not only didn't need much more of a response than that—she didn't particularly care for one.

Penelope, of course, couldn't be more different. In all these months, she'd never implied that his opinion counted for less than hers or Helena's. He wondered if this came from her childhood. Having parents from such different backgrounds who cared for her, and each other, and the fact that she'd never settled in any one place, must have given Penelope a wider view of the world. He might have envied Penelope for all that—if she didn't also happen to be one of the most interesting, bighearted, and clever people he'd ever met.

He glanced up at her. She stood watching him in a flattering green dress and bonnet near the edge of his table. She gave him one of her sunniest smiles, and he returned it. He finished placing the last purple potato pancake on the final plate—a nod to his heritage he was certain Helena would overlook—and stepped back to survey the portions.

Helena reminded him to wipe any drips or spots from the plates' edges, and he nodded, staying silent despite the fact that he'd already been looking at which plates needed attention. He finished wiping the sides of the last plate, scrutinized his hands for any residual sauce, then stepped back to survey his menu.

Multiple plates full of colorful elements stared back at him. Beet-cured salmon sliced thinly, sitting atop Andean purple potatoes made into a crispy cake, crowned with a tiny salad of arugula, edible flowers, and passion-fruit-pickled shallot rings, which could all be picked up and eaten in one bite, was his nod to both the South American flavors Penelope had been teaching him and his own Jewish traditions. Next he'd created a Lapsang souchong tea–smoked pigeon breast with a tamarind sauce in a flaky, herbed pastry cup (a refined version of one of his pasties), and for dessert, a chili and cinnamon–infused chocolate bon bon filled with a horchata liquid caramel. He knew the flavors were what he'd wanted, but he'd worried they wouldn't be elevated enough for the competition.

Luckily, Penelope had backed the menu and even defended it to Helena when she'd tried to veto some of the harder-to-obtain ingredients such as tamarind.

"Well, we'd better step away so as not to influence anyone's opinion," Helena said, interrupting his thoughts. "It all looks just as you practiced, so we shall see what the public thinks."

"If they don't eat it up—pun intended," Penelope replied with a smile at him, "then I shall be very much surprised."

"Good luck, Mr. Little," Helena said. "The gong shall ring momentarily."

He clasped his hands behind his back. "Thank you."

Helena moved away to inspect the tables close by.

Penelope took a step toward him. "Are you quite well?" she asked in a low tone. "You look a bit pale."

He cleared his throat. "I'm not certain I know what I'm doing, to be honest." He smoothed the front of his coat again.

Penelope tilted the crown of her light green bonnet toward him. "Elijah, you will be stupendous. You have prepared for this. You look every bit the gentleman. Your food is everything it should be. Now, all you need remember is that saucy charm you had when we met at the night market. *That* fellow wouldn't take no for an answer, and *this* fellow"—she gestured to him with both hands, then folded them together in front of her—"knows how to project a gentleman's courtesy and self-assurance to entice people to taste his food and drop their token into his jar. You have all those qualities within you. You simply have to remember you do."

When she put it that way, it wasn't so daunting—or so different from selling pasties at the market. And maybe she was right. He didn't have to be a pasty hawker or a gentleman. Maybe he could actually use the best parts of both. He let out a breath and then stood straighter. "You're right. Thank you, Miss Pickering," he said, bowing at the neck as they'd taught him. He still didn't quite dare to call her Penelope as she'd asked him to, partly because their friendship still felt tentative, and partly because they were in public, but she didn't take it amiss.

"You are more than welcome, Mr. Little," she said with that sweet smile of hers and a small curtsy. "We'll see you later," she whispered. She then turned to follow Helena.

He watched her petite form for a moment before taking another deep breath to steady his pulse. He practiced a few phrases under his breath. It'd been a long stretch since he'd talked to customers. These people weren't exactly customers, but as Penelope said, they weren't far off. "Good day, madam. Would you care to sample a bon bon? Good afternoon, sir. Might I interest you in a potato cake with beet-cured salmon? Perhaps you'd care for smoked pigeon in flaky pastry instead?" He exhaled. He could do this. Or maybe he should say something like—

The gong sounded. He abandoned all other thoughts and pasted a pleasant smile on his face as the first group of attendees approached his table.

⌒◯⌒

Helena nodded at the young gentleman in the booth and glanced back toward Elijah's table to see if she could spot Penelope. Penelope's light green confection of a dress with its wide puffed sleeves trimmed with forest-green bows should be easy to find in this crowd. Helena took a plate of what appeared to be an éclair filled with some sort of curried chicken from the gentleman's table.

The crunch from the top of the choux pastry contrasted well enough with the coconut-milk yellow curry inside. "Adequate spicing in the curry," she said as the gentleman looked at her expectantly. She pointed to a series of sliced green tomatoes sitting atop circle-shaped disks of polenta. "Are those tomatoes a green variety or are they underripe?"

"The latter," the young man said with an easy smile. "I pickled them. The polenta I coated in rice flour before twice frying them."

Helena raised an eyebrow before placing the tomato-crowned polenta in her mouth. The sourness of the tomatoes almost made her cheeks pucker, but she kept her countenance admirably, if she did say so herself. If all of Elijah's competition made such basic mistakes, she didn't see how he could fail—unless, that was, he and Penelope spent the entire competition whispering together.

Helena had never been one to put much store on introspection, but even she couldn't deny that the friendship that'd been developing between Penelope and Elijah ever since the disastrous day at her grandmama's house irked her to some—very *small*, mind you—degree. The reason behind these sentiments was, as yet, something Helena could put neither face nor name to. Though an outsider might have called it the stirrings of jealousy, or perhaps the fear of losing one's only friend, Helena had never had cause to feel either of those emotions in her young life—at least not in any *demonstrable* way—and therefore had little context to put a name to such things.

She did wonder why Elijah seemed so able to talk to Penelope and not to her. But, on the other hand, Pen was dashed easy to talk to.

"Next time, you might consider a bit of honey in your pickling liquid for something so sour to start," she told the young man. No need to embarrass the fellow, after all.

His cool response was lost on Helena, however, as Penelope called her name.

"There you are," Penelope said. "You disappeared so quickly." She looked at the plates before them. "This looks promising."

"Try the green tomatoes," Helena said, unable to help herself.

Penelope picked up a plate, then put the polenta into her mouth. Her eyebrows rose as she chewed. "I did not realize they were pickled," she said when she'd finished. She caught the eye of the young man behind the table. "I quite enjoyed that level of sourness. It reminds me of something I've come across in Philippine cooking or even in Persian dishes. In both cultures, sour elements are venerated."

The young man's easy smile returned. "I confess, I've not had any dishes from the Philippine Islands, but I was aware of the Persian proclivity for sour foods. Your friend rightly pointed out that some sweetness to balance the sour would not be unwelcome." He glanced at Helena.

Penelope nodded. "We are taught that balance is key. But I still quite enjoy a good sour pickle every so often."

The young man's dark blue eyes widened with interest. "Are you Culinarians, then?"

"We're in our final year at the Royal Academy of Culinaria Artisticus," Helena said.

"I must say," the young man said, tilting his head at Penelope, "you look deuced familiar." He cleared his throat. "I beg your pardon, *quite* familiar. Have we met before?"

Helena forced herself not to roll her eyes at his impudence, but Penelope's face lit up. "Yes! It was a rainy evening across from Covent Garden. You were there with your mother and sister, as I recall."

"Hah!" he exclaimed, whacking the table. Some of his plates rattled together. "The Culinarian who'd just returned from the Americas! Might I beg a formal introduction?"

Penelope obliged, introducing first herself and then Helena. Helena had no interest in being introduced, but made an effort to remain polite for her friend's sake. As much as she abhorred the outdated dictates of Georgian society, she almost wished that a gentleman still had to ask a mutual acquaintance for an introduction to a lady. If this person before them had been forced to do so, she and Pen could have been on the other side of the Grand Saloon by the time he returned.

"Freddie Eynsford-Hill, at your service, ladies," the young man said with a bow.

"Do you compete often, Mr. Eynsford-Hill?" Penelope asked, taking his dessert offering, a sugared fruit gelée topped with a piped soft meringue kiss.

"When the fancy strikes, Miss Pickering. I've always enjoyed partaking in the culinary arts, but I don't practice as much as I ought to."

That explained his less-than-stellar offerings, Helena thought.

"Practice is essential," Penelope said, but she popped his dessert into her mouth regardless. Her brown eyes widened. She smiled as she finished chewing. "Rosehip gelée?"

He gave her a wide smile. "With a hint of lemon verbena."

She nodded. "I thought so. What an original pairing. It goes quite well with the sweetness of the meringue." She pulled one of her tokens from her pocket and dropped it into the jar at the corner of his table.

"You are too kind, Miss Pickering," he said, bowing his head to her again.

Penelope clasped her hands in front of her. "Not at all, Mr. Eynsford-Hill. I quite enjoyed it."

Helena cleared her throat, annoyed Penelope had awarded one of her precious tokens to someone who had just admitted how little he practiced. "Good luck, Mr. Eynsford-Hill." She moved away before he could answer, but she could still hear him thanking Penelope for her comments and professing his hope that they would meet again.

Helena clenched her teeth. What would a culinary dabbler like that want with Penelope? To be sure, Pen's expertise would ensure her success after they graduated—a fact even that dimwitted fellow could discern. Some gentlemen competed for the lark of it, while some did it to attract a wealthy or well-positioned lady with her own professional prospects. This Freddie Eynsford-Hill very much struck Helena as part of the latter cohort.

She rolled her eyes as she surveyed a few amateur competitors' tables and determined them not worth stopping at. Hopefully, Penelope was clever enough to see through such a character. Besides, it would do her no good to marry before she could establish herself in the world.

Helena, for her part, had little interest in marrying anyone. Perhaps when she had secured her position as the preeminent Culinarian in England, she would consider it, but until then, the idea held little appeal. Luckily, her brother, Roland, would inherit the majority of her father's holdings, and moreover, she would be well provided for if, by some chance, she couldn't support herself on her own Culinarian income. She wondered what Penelope had planned for the future. In point of fact, she'd never asked her.

It was in the midst of such musings that an unwelcome voice called Helena's name. She stopped short, then wished she hadn't as Mabel Pilkington barreled into her from behind. Helena let out an "Ooof" as Mabel muttered apologies.

Helena turned. "Do have a care, Mabel. The crowd is not so thick that you need tread upon me."

Mabel's pin curls bounced about her head as she wobbled it from side to side. "I hardly did so for my own amusement, I assure you. Are you here with Penelope?"

"Yes, she's about somewhere." Helena looked around, hoping Penelope might appear to keep Mabel at bay. "Ah, there she is, by Lady Hartley's table." Helena pointed at a Culinarian known for her flair for Scandinavian cuisine. "Why don't we—"

"I'm sorry you could not attend Princess Adelaide's birthday feast," Mabel interrupted. "You'll be happy to hear it was a great success."

Mabel must have been dying to tell her this. Helena put on her most tolerant smile. "Of course it was." The Goose wouldn't know good food if it hit her in the face. "I'm certain Princess Adelaide must feel indebted to you."

Mabel let out a small laugh. "The princess is graciousness itself. Indeed, she has asked me to consult again for the Royal Exhibition."

This brought Helena up short. Had Mabel truly made such a good impression on the Goose that she would ask Mabel to return to the palace for an occasion of such international significance as the Royal Exhibition?

"Indeed?"

"It's quite an honor, of course. And Lady Rutland says I may use it as part of my final project." She tilted her head to the side, and her curls bounced again. "What is your project, Helena?"

"Now, now, Mabel, I mean it to be a surprise. But I *can* say it is of great social import." Helena's lips twitched as Mabel's eyebrows knit together.

"I'm certain Lady Rutland would expect nothing less of you, dear Helena. I'm certain we *all* do."

Helena gave her an arch smile.

"I, however, am content to be the princess's helper and confidant," Mabel said with a little sigh.

"Confidant?" Helena repeated, unable to stop herself, though she wished it unsaid the next moment.

"Oh, to be sure. In fact"—she looked around as if afraid of being overheard—"I have it on the best authority that the Royal Exhibition will be of even greater consequence to the fate of the nation this year."

Helena narrowed her eyes. "And why is that?" she asked, not at all believing it.

Mabel lifted her chin. "I really shouldn't say more."

Helena scoffed. This was all some charade Mabel had concocted to sound important. "Because there *is* nothing more, I daresay."

Mabel huffed. "Very well, but you mustn't tell anyone else."

Helena rolled her eyes. "As you wish."

"Princess Adelaide will choose her husband-to-be at the Royal

Exhibition. Princes and noblemen from around the world will be showcasing their culinary skills to impress her. At the end of it all, she will choose her favorite, and *he* will become her betrothed!"

Helena's mouth dropped open. Mabel began to preen, and Helena clamped it shut. Everyone knew how much Queen Charlotte and the entire royal family revered and promoted Culinaria as one of Britain's greatest strengths. They had often sent Culinarians on diplomatic tours abroad to build bridges through a shared love of food. By promoting cooperation, collaboration, and experimentation across cuisines, other political divides had broken down.

Diplomacy, rather than colonization, had become the government's overarching policy, and Britain had gained more allies than it had lost because of it. The Royal Exhibition was the embodiment of all these Charlottian values—both a place for countries to send their best culinary stars to compete for recognition, and an opportunity to obtain coveted British Royal Seals of Patronage. Helena had never had more than a passing interest in politics, but if Queen Charlotte was allowing the Goose to choose a husband from among the competitors, diplomatic relations abroad must be better than ever before. Because, if what Mabel had said was indeed true, the Princess could, in theory, marry a commoner if she thought his food impressive enough.

"What a pity you could not consult for Princess Adelaide's birthday," Mabel continued with wide eyes. "You might now be in the princess's confidence yourself." Mabel was clearly enjoying having something to lord over Helena for once in her life, but Helena's thoughts were elsewhere—with a new scheme that would prove once and for all that she was a legend the likes of which the Royal

Academy of Culinaria Artisticus had never seen before.

She made a hasty excuse to Mabel and headed back to Elijah's table. Lady Rutland stood there with a number of other Culinarians. Members of the public also milled about the table, taking plates, eating, and above all, *smiling*. Elijah smiled too, conversing with the people, albeit in very short, technically correct sentences, as they asked him about ingredients and preparations.

Helena looked at the jar at the corner of the table. It stood nearly three-quarters of the way full of tokens. Helena glanced at the watch pinned to her dress. Only a quarter hour remained before the final tally, which was probably for the best as Elijah would soon be out of plates. She moved to the corner of the table and tasted the smoked pigeon. The pastry melted in her mouth. Just as she'd taught him. She grinned at Lady Rutland and dropped her tokens into Elijah's jar.

Lady Rutland moved through the people to stand by Helena. "The young man is most impressive. Would you not agree, Helena?"

"I believe I would, Lady Rutland," Helena replied with a small curtsy. "Though, perhaps the pigeon could use a dash more salt."

A pair of young ladies standing beside her let out offended huffs. "More salt? Are you mad?" said the first girl.

"It's delectable just as it is," the other agreed, giving Elijah a wave, and giggling when he bowed in their direction with that slightly crooked smile of his.

"The tamarind sauce was something of a revelation, I'd say," Lady Rutland stated loudly.

A number of people agreed and dropped tokens into the jar before moving to the next booth.

"And I couldn't help noticing the American influences in the dishes," Lady Rutland continued as Penelope walked up to the opposite side of the booth and greeted the other Culinarians. Penelope took one of the last bon bons from a plate and closed her eyes as she chewed.

"What made you go in such a direction, Mr. Little?" Lady Rutland asked.

His gaze shot to Penelope, then back to Lady Rutland. "I suppose I was inspired."

Lady Rutland smiled. Then she took Helena aside, a little way off from the booth. "I would be quite astonished if he should not win one of the spots today. Which means, as you know, he'll be cooking for the royal family. I would be very certain he knows what's expected."

Helena nodded. "Of course, Lady Rutland."

"His speech did falter a few times, but I doubt anyone else noticed. His food is very good, and that can cover a multitude of flaws. If he does well at the Royal Exhibition, I believe we can safely say your project will have been a success."

Helena let out a breath. "Thank you, Lady Rutland." Her eyes flew to the jar of tokens again, her mind brimming with thoughts of turning Elijah into a gentleman chef so perfect even the Goose couldn't overlook him. What a triumph it would be to eventually tell Mabel and all of the other horrid girls at school how she'd pulled one over on that brat of a princess. Helena let out a self-satisfied breath as she watched a lady and a gentleman argue over the last of Elijah's bon bons, and sweet scenarios materialized in her mind.

THIRTEEN

HEARTBEATS SPEED UP

"My goodness, how handsome you look," Penelope exclaimed as Elijah came to the bottom of the stairway at Cavendish Square in his brand-new formal tailcoat and trousers. "You shall be the toast of the Royal Exhibition. And the ball, I daresay."

"It's awfully grand," Elijah said sheepishly. He still couldn't quite believe he'd been one of the two finalists in the gentleman chef category at the culinary faire, let alone the fact that he now had to compete at the Royal Exhibition. He smoothed the front lapel of his coat even though one of the footmen had pressed it perfectly. This black coat, trousers, and silk cream-colored waistcoat were by far the most elegant of all the clothes Mr. Benjamin had delivered.

"Everyone *must* be grand for the ball," Helena stated behind him. She walked off the end of the steps and stood next to Penelope in the foyer. "I fancy the assembly will consider him very fine. Now, come along to the drawing room," she said, sweeping the bell skirt of her dusky-rose day dress into Penelope as she turned to walk down the hall.

When the trio entered the drawing room, Pierce and two footmen were in the midst of moving chairs and a table to the sides of the room. The sofa already sat against the wall.

"Ah, very good, Pierce," Helena said. "Mr. Little, it occurs to me that now that we have your clothes and manners sorted, and of course we continue to practice your dishes for the Royal Exhibition, there is still one thing lacking."

"Dancing!" Penelope clapped her hands together, surprising both Elijah and Helena with her excitement. "Of course, you *must* dance at the ball that closes the exhibition," Penelope stated. "Do you—er—know how to waltz, Elijah?"

He looked back and forth at them with wide eyes, then looked behind him at the door. "No."

"Of course he doesn't," Helena said. "That's why we're going to teach him."

Pierce cleared his throat in a way that Penelope and Elijah both understood to mean he disapproved.

"That will be all, Pierce. Thank you," Helena said. "Do avail yourself of my propolis-and-elderberry tincture in the stillroom for your throat."

Pierce grumbled in the affirmative and left the room with the footmen in tow.

Elijah's eyes followed them; he wondered if he could excuse himself and simply not return, but he knew Helena would only hound him. He glanced Penelope's way, and she caught his eye. Her lips quivered in an effort to suppress a giggle. Her eyes darted at Pierce's back. Elijah smirked, realizing it was rather funny.

At least she was here to make it all a bit more palatable. He snuck a look at her without moving his head, noting how the mustard-yellow swirl print of her day dress complemented her brown eyes, the way she stood with her small shoulders back, the pretty curve of her chin as she smiled.

"Eventually, of course, you shall have to learn all the dances," Helena said, cutting into his thoughts, "but as we have only a matter of weeks before the exhibition and the ball that concludes it, I suggest we focus our time on the waltz and the minuet as those are most often danced at court. Of course, a gentleman generally still asks for dances, so you should be able to only ask for waltzes and minuets."

"There is the royal privilege, however," Penelope said.

"Indeed," Helena agreed. "The queen and the princesses may ask a gentleman to dance—usually through an intermediary—but I happen to know that the Goo—that is, *Princess* Adelaide has a particular penchant for waltzes. Thus, that is where we shall begin."

"Why would the princess want to dance with me?" Elijah asked. "She'll have her pick of gentlemen."

Helena raised her chin. "One *never* knows, does one? And as we've discussed before, you should give yourself every opportunity you can. What would you do if Princess Adelaide *did* ask you and you'd never danced a waltz in your life? Insult her by saying no? Tell her you cannot dance?"

He shrugged, annoyed that her logic seemed sound . . . as usual. "I hadn't thought about it."

"Precisely. Now, you watch as Penelope and I demonstrate. The first thing you must know is that a gentleman must lead the dance. *And* one learns a waltz by counting to three. Like so . . ."

Helena and Penelope clasped hands and moved in a circle as Helena counted to three. "You see? One, two, three. One, two, three. It's quite simple. You merely step like this over and over to the beat of the music," Helena said. "Now you try."

He stared at her for a moment. When she didn't elaborate, he felt his pulse jump. "By myself?"

"No, of course not," Helena replied. "I shall play while you and Penelope dance." She turned to Penelope. "I'm sorry, Pen, but as I recall, you do not play the pianoforte so well as you cook."

Penelope laughed. "Very true."

Helena pulled Elijah by the arm until he stood facing Penelope. "Now, take her right hand with your left hand. Her other hand rests on your shoulder or holds the train of her dress. In this case, Pen has no train."

Penelope and Elijah clasped hands, and Penelope rested her other hand on his shoulder.

"Your right hand then sits at her back or her waist so you can guide her where you wish to lead," Helena continued.

Slowly, almost haltingly, Elijah placed his hand on the yellow sash around Penelope's waist. As his gaze met her brown eyes, he realized that the only time they'd actually touched had been the day they'd shaken hands in the kitchen garden. But as it had that cold morning, her hand, soft and small, but strong, felt good in his—almost as though it belonged there. The thought had him grimacing at himself just as the scent of her—some flower distillation he couldn't ever distinguish—made him wish to step farther back just so he wasn't tempted to move closer.

She smiled up at him then, and he almost released her altogether. "There's no need to glower so."

He let out a breath. "Right. Sorry." He attempted to smile, but he was sure it came out looking rather pained.

She squeezed his hand to reassure him. "Don't worry, I'm not a porcelain doll."

He blinked, unsure of her meaning.

"You can hold me a bit tighter. I shan't break."

He cleared his throat, and clasped her waist in a surer grip. She said nothing, but the air around them seemed to thicken as she peered up at him through her lashes.

Helena sat at the pianoforte and began playing a waltz.

"You can start with your right foot and I'll follow," Penelope said, dropping her eyes level with the cravat at his neck. "One, two, three. One, two, three," she repeated to the beats of the music.

He chanted with her in his head a few times, then stepped toward her with his right foot as she'd said, but instead of following, she also stepped back with her right foot, and his knee hit her in the leg.

"Ooof." She laughed.

He released her immediately. "I'm sorry," he said, unsure what had gone wrong.

She shook her head. "No, I misspoke. You begin with your left foot and I will step back with my right. I've never had to teach a boy to dance." She laughed again—somewhat nervously, he thought, which calmed him somehow.

"Try again!" Helena called from the piano.

"We'll count together," Penelope said, holding out her hands to show she was ready.

He grasped her hand and waist again and followed her count. "One, two, three . . ."

This time they managed a half rotation before she trod on his foot. "Oh dear, I'm so sorry."

He let out a laugh this time. "We may both be bruised by the time this is over."

She giggled and looked up at him with a twinkle in those brown eyes of hers, the almost-amber rings around her pupils captivating him as they had the first time he'd noticed them months ago. "I do hope not." Then her smile seemed to fade as she held his gaze a second longer than he'd expected. The moment seemed to stretch.

"Go on, go on," Helena said from the pianoforte.

Penelope blinked and looked down. "One, two, three . . ."

He mentally shook his head at himself as he tightened his hold on her waist. "One, two, three . . ."

This time they completed a full rotation without injuring each other, and Penelope looked up at him again with a brilliant smile.

"You've got it," Penelope said. "Now you have to lead me in wider circles. Obviously in a ballroom there will be more people, so you'd keep an eye on everyone else as well as your partner. Shall we attempt moving about the room?"

"It's worth a try," he replied. They started again, and Elijah decided it was better if he didn't look at her. He could pay attention to his feet and the room very well if he didn't look into those eyes or let his mind linger on that hint of a dimple that appeared at the left of her lips when she smiled at him.

"Beg your pardon, my lady." Pierce's voice rang out from the doorway, and Elijah stopped short, causing Penelope to collide with his chest in what he imagined Pierce would consider an unseemly manner.

Helena stopped playing. "What is it, Pierce?"

Elijah looked down at Penelope. "Are you all right?"

She met his gaze, though she did not move away from him. He could feel the heat radiating from her. "Yes. Thank you."

He smiled, feeling for the first time that maybe he affected her as she did him. He took a step back but didn't release her hand.

"What's that coxcomb doing here?" Helena asked, and Elijah realized he'd missed whatever Pierce had said.

"He claims he's here to call on Miss Pickering."

"Great galloping gammon! Of all the . . ." Helena rolled her eyes. "Pen, do you wish to see Mr. Freddie Eynsford-Hill?"

Penelope blinked and gently released Elijah's hand. He took another step away from her. Who was Freddie Eynsford-Hill?

"Oh. I . . . I had no notion that he'd actually call so soon. He did ask my permission to call when we met at the faire, but . . ." She looked at Elijah and then at Helena. "No. We are otherwise engaged at present." She turned to Pierce. "Please tell him I am out today."

"Very good, miss," Pierce said. He disappeared down the hall.

"Shall we continue?" Penelope asked. She held out her right hand to Elijah. Elijah took her hand but did not catch her eye again.

"Why you'd *allow* him to call is a mystery to me," Helena said, shaking her head at the pianoforte. "He wasn't even good enough to win one of the spots to the Royal Exhibition. Which is almost a shame. Mr. Little would have out-cooked him soundly had he been chosen as the other gentleman chef."

"He's not as talented as Elijah, to be sure," Penelope said, trying to catch his eye, "but he was pleasant."

"Pleasant indeed." Helena sniffed. She began playing again.

Elijah started guiding Penelope around the room once more, staunchly refusing to look her in the eye. What madness had made him think she might feel anything for him but friendship? She was a true lady and she deserved a *true* gentleman. Not someone merely pretending. Certainly not a poor fellow like him, whose future was unclear. Unless . . .

If he won one of the top spots at the Royal Exhibition, he would be set for life. Helena had told him the first-place winner received a knighthood and the queen's Royal Seal of Patronage, which was similar to a Royal Warrant of Appointment, but imparted more prestige. The second-prize winner would be awarded the Order of British Culinary Artists and another Royal Seal of Patronage, this time awarded by the Princess of Wales, and the third prize would be a Royal Seal from the prince consort.

Elijah didn't have much interest in titles and the like, but he'd be more than happy if he could somehow secure a Royal Seal. With a Royal Seal of Patronage, no one would dare deny him the chance to have a business. If he could win a Royal Seal, patrons and investors would come to him with their pocketbooks open. Even those prejudiced London merchants who kept Jews from opening retail businesses wouldn't be able to stop him. And then, just maybe, Penelope would think of him as more than a boy from the streets who she and Helena had elevated through a culinary education.

Maybe then he'd have something real to offer Penelope—if she wanted it.

Elijah clenched and unclenched his jaw. He ventured a glance at Penelope's face.

"Well, my friend," she said, "I believe any lady would be delighted to dance with such an accomplished gentleman. I truly believe that by the time the Royal Exhibition comes around, you will have nothing to worry about." The faint dimple appeared at the left side of her mouth again, and Elijah dragged his gaze away. He sincerely hoped she was right.

FOURTEEN

IT HAS BEGUN

"**M**onstrous monkfish, Helena, I don't think I've ever been so worried in my life!" Penelope exclaimed as they walked onto the great lawn of Hampton Court Palace, where the first day of the Royal Culinary Exhibition would soon begin. Thankfully, the weather seemed ready to comply with royal wishes, for the sun peeked out from behind a smattering of white clouds. Only a slight breeze filled the air with the scents of early summer blooms and freshly prepared food from the tents laid out facing each other upon the wide paths extending out through the Great Fountain Garden.

"What about before our final exam on Culinary Chemistry last year?" Helena asked as she scanned the lawn for Elijah's tent.

Penelope had removed her gloves in the carriage and now wrung them in her hands. "Not even then. Though I grant you that was a different test. But we were *prepared*. There's so much more we could have taught Elijah. Why didn't we—"

"Pen." Helena stopped in the middle of the path to look at her. "For one thing, you had better stop calling him 'Elijah' in public. I am not at all certain when you adopted the habit—"

Penelope played with the pendant hanging from her neck. "Well, I—"

"—but," Helena continued, not really interested in the answer, "recall that, for the sake of the experiment, Lady Rutland has stipulated that no one must know of Mr. Little's connection to either of us. He must succeed on his own merits."

"Yes, I do recall," Penelope said. "I shall take care to be formal in mixed company. Just as I did at the faire."

Helena nodded once. "And secondly, we have spent the last weeks working with him eighteen hours a day. Unless you wished to prepare him for twenty hours a day, or wanted to forego sleep altogether, I do not see what more we could have done. I barely saw you work on your own project in the last week or so." Helena raised her brows at her friend and started walking again.

"I did do a little," Penelope replied as they passed the tent of a Russian count decked out in his full military regalia. "I just . . . it was far more important that Elijah be as ready as he was able."

Helena arched a brow. If Penelope wasn't careful, she'd end up falling short of her usual second place in the class come graduation. She could even end up below Mabel Pilkington, what with the new opportunities Lady Rutland had given her. And how would Penelope ever be able to live down such ignominy? "Lady Rutland will want our final reports by the end of the month, you know." Helena walked purposely past the other English gentleman chef preparing his tent. He and Elijah had nearly tied for their number of tokens at the culinary faire. Helena had tasted his food, and as far as she was concerned, this Curtis Loewe had more style than culinary talent, which definitely gave Elijah an advantage.

Penelope let out a breath. "I'm well aware of that, Helena."

"I simply thought it bore repeating. Ah, there he is!" They made their way to Elijah's tent, which sat in the shadow of one of the historic pyramidal yew trees a little ways off from the Great Fountain itself.

Helena observed that the sight of Elijah plating his dishes in his new blue frock coat, without a hint of distress on his face or in his bearing, seemed to relieve Penelope's anxiety on his behalf. She greeted him with a smile.

"How goes everything?" Penelope asked him.

"Well enough," he replied with a reassuring nod at them. "There was some confusion about which tent was mine. A count from Liechtenstein seemed to want it, but they placated him with a tent closer to the palace."

"I wish we could have helped you set up and plate," Penelope said as Elijah continued to add colorful elements to small dish after dish.

"We could hardly have explained that this time around," Helena stated. "Besides, Mr. Little must appear to be a gentleman chef like any other in Britain. We cannot help what foreign princes and nobility do, but if anyone thinks Mr. Little to be the protégé of a Culinarian who hasn't *technically* graduated yet, he'll have a smaller chance of succeeding." There would also be less of a chance that the Goose would think well of him, but Helena kept this thought to herself.

Penelope found herself noting, with no real surprise, that Helena had left Penelope's own contribution out of the equation. She exhaled. "I know all that to be true, but it doesn't keep me from wishing to be of use."

Elijah looked up from his plating to smile at her, and Penelope's stomach fluttered in the most inexplicable way. It had been doing something similar since Elijah had left Cavendish Square in the morning with two footmen, his food, and crates of plates and utensils, but now that she'd seen him settled and all but ready for judging, she should feel better. Instead, if anything, she felt jumpier than ever. She tried not to think about how his new, perfectly tailored coat and waistcoat somehow made him look even taller than he'd always seemed, and how the haircut the barber had given him before the faire showed off the squareness of his jaw in a way she hadn't expected. Instead, she cast her gaze away from Elijah to survey his nearest competition.

The gentleman in the tent across from Elijah's looked just as busy, arranging his puffed flatbread in a conical basket for attendees to take as they passed his booth. His kilt and fine, well-tailored coat pegged him as a Scottish lord or gentleman. His dish appeared to be some sort of game bird. It could taste impressive, but so far, the Scot's presentation did not appear to be anything special.

At least there Elijah would best him. Each day of the exhibition would present a different challenge that each competitor must rise to. During the three days of competition, the finalists would eventually be narrowed to the three best chefs and amateur cooks, all of whom would receive the coveted Royal Seals of Patronage. The prestige of showing well at the exhibition could not be underestimated, for a Royal Seal benefitted the amateurs and gentlemen chefs who won them in countless ways. Amateurs who secured a Royal Seal often used their success to start a food establishment or company. Gentlemen saw their prospects in society soar. Foreign competitors could achieve recognition for their country or their businesses. And though the Culinarians competing could not be chosen as the three finalists because they had already risen to the pinnacle of their profession, even they benefitted from having another opportunity to showcase their skills to royalty and the attending nobility from multiple countries.

Penelope glanced at the gentlemen and nobles in the other tents nearby, and wondered again at the wisdom of entering Elijah as a gentleman. If he did well—as she had every confidence he would—he would become society's darling overnight. If he won first or second place, he would be known forevermore as Sir Elijah Little or Elijah Little, Order of British Culinary Artists, one of the most eligible gentlemen in London. But was that what he wanted?

With such notoriety, he could marry a rich widow or a high-dowried daughter of the landed gentry and be set for life, but then he'd likely never own a shop as he'd once hoped. Most society ladies wouldn't want their husband creating and *selling* food to make a living. Some things had changed, but gentlemen's professions hadn't altered that much. Then again, maybe if Elijah found someone who cared for him as much as his culinary mastery, she would support whatever he truly wished to do.

Penelope swallowed. A lump had lodged in her throat, and she couldn't for the life of her guess why. She turned back to Elijah, watching as he wiped the edges of his plates until they gleamed. One lock of his hair—a varicolored brown that reminded her of a star anise pod in the sunlight—curled at his left temple under the brim of his tall hat.

No matter what happened today, he deserved the best of everything, and she aimed to see that he got it.

"Well, you seem to have everything well in hand," Helena said to Elijah. "The opening ceremony shall begin soon, so close up your tent, and we'll see you by the podium."

Elijah nodded, and Helena set off down the path back toward the palace.

"Good luck, Elijah," Penelope said. "Not that you'll need it." She gave him a bright smile to reassure herself as much as him.

"Not with you here, I won't," he replied.

She almost expected him to wink at her as he once did at the night market, but instead he held her gaze with those rich, hazelnut-hued eyes of his. Her stomach flipped. Ever since Penelope had first tasted Padrón peppers a few years ago, she had loved the uncertainty in knowing there would likely be one or two in a bunch that would hit your palate with a fiery heat you weren't prepared for. You ate the spicy Padrón's neighboring peppers one by one, luring your mouth into a false sense of security. Until, of course, a spice-concealing Padrón forced your eyes to widen and your breath to hitch. At that moment, as though a fiery Padrón had just burst over her tongue, Penelope's eyes opened.

꩜

"Welcome, one and all, to the Royal Culinary Exhibition!"

Elijah swallowed as Lady Rutland, who'd also be acting as the mistress of ceremonies, held out her arms in an expansive gesture.

She stood at an elevated podium in the center of the wide pathway separating the grand façade of the palace from the Great Fountain Garden. Elijah couldn't help feeling in awe of the whole scene. Hampton Court had to be the largest, most imposing structure he'd ever laid eyes on with its Tudor redbrick towers stretching into the sky, and its grandiose, symmetrical baroque façade spreading out on either side of Lady Rutland behind the podium. Elijah hadn't even stepped inside the palace yet, but if the expansive gardens around them were anything to judge by, the palace's interior must be nothing short of extravagant. The gardens alone had made him gawk when he'd arrived, and he'd only seen a small portion of them so far.

He glanced around at the crowd of competitors and attendees and wondered if any of them felt as overwhelmed at the grandeur as he. Elijah noted the princes and lords who stood as though this was their due. Only a few people—possibly the amateur cooks, for he recognized at least one as a winner from the culinary faire—fidgeted with their hands or fussed with their clothes. Perhaps like him, this day would make or break them.

"I'm heartened to see so many innovative cooks, chefs, and Culinarians from all over the world here with us today in the shadow of Hampton Court," Lady Rutland continued with a smile, "which, as some of you know, was the favorite palace of one of Britain's most infamous, food-loving monarchs, Henry VIII."

Some of the crowd laughed.

Lady Rutland carried on. "Food, of course, has evolved a great deal since King Henry's day, and most especially in the last ten years, as evidenced by this exhibition. Our first year, we had seven competitors from throughout Britain and Europe. Today, we are privileged to welcome twenty-four culinary faire winners from Great Britain alone, as well as delegates from thirty-five countries, all of whom come from vastly different food cultures."

The crowd clapped. Elijah glanced at the ladies and gentlemen who'd journeyed from countries halfway across the world. Next to him, a brown-skinned man decked out in the regalia of a kingdom Elijah didn't have the knowledge to identify murmured something to his companion. He then saw Elijah watching and inclined his head in Elijah's direction. Elijah gave him a slight bow, wondering if that was the correct protocol where he was from. Not knowing the man's rank or title, Elijah decided to err on the side of paying more regard than less. The man bowed back and Elijah relaxed somewhat.

"As you know," Lady Rutland said, "all competitors are welcome to exhibit their dishes of choice in their exhibition tents, regardless of whether they place in the top twenty after today's blind tasting or not. Those in the top twenty will go on to cook and present tomorrow, from which only ten will emerge to compete on the final day. I am certain you all wish to start the blind tasting, but first I have the pleasure of introducing this year's special judge. Princess Adelaide, would you care to say a few words?"

The entire crowd started clapping as a girl with very light brown ringlets wearing a gown made from blue satin trimmed with lace ascended the few stairs to stand next to Lady Rutland at the podium. Elijah realized she'd been standing behind the podium the whole time, watching the proceedings, and he'd been too absorbed in the spectacle to notice. He stood about fifty feet away, in the middle of the crowd, but he could see that she was approximately Helena's height. The princess had a long, almost angular face, a pert chin, and a pretty smile.

"Welcome to you all. Lady Rutland has said everything I would have said, but with far more savoir faire. I shall only add that we are not only honored that so many of you have journeyed such great distances to exhibit, but we are privileged to taste your diverse culinary creations as well. Narrowing the competition to only twenty of you shall be no easy task, and I am very grateful that Lady Rutland and my father, Prince Leopold, shall be adding the benefit of their palates and experience to today's blind tasting. Thank you all." The princess offered a serene smile, and the audience clapped.

She stepped back and began down the stairs. Lady Rutland took her place at the podium. "Princess Adelaide, Prince Leopold, and I shall now retreat to the palace to await your dishes. Please return to your tents. Footmen will convey your prepared dish to the tasting room and give you a number so that you may later identify if your dish ranked in the top twenty. Good luck!"

Elijah exhaled and started back toward his tent. It had begun. When he arrived at the tent, a footman in red-and-gold-braided livery already stood waiting. "Very efficient," Elijah remarked.

"Thank you, sir," the footman replied with a bow.

Elijah's breath hitched. He wondered if he'd ever get used to being called "sir." Other than the boy hawking oranges on the road, no one had addressed him with any kind of reverential honorific before. The servants at Cavendish Square certainly didn't, but he supposed that was because they'd known him when he was still that hawker roaming the streets with his pasties. But *this* fellow didn't know where Elijah had come from. To him, Elijah really *was* the gentleman he was pretending to be. Elijah walked into his tent and verified that his platter for the blind tasting looked just as he wanted. Like the food for the culinary faire, today's food had to be prepared off-site and brought to the palace for assembly, which essentially meant it needed to be served at ambient temperature. At least one of the elements also had to feature the British strawberry, which was apparently one of the princess's favorite foods and very much in season.

Elijah had roasted duck confit legs in toasted, ground coriander, cumin, and chili; he'd paired it with a strawberry and pink peppercorn gastrique sauce drizzled overtop and dotted on the platter. He'd baked walnut, ramp, and queso fresco financiers in small round molds and topped each of them with a strawberry flower. He'd colored more of his homemade queso fresco—one of Penelope's recipes—with beet powder, which he'd molded into spheres, dotted with nigella seeds, and topped with strawberry stems to approximate the look of strawberries while adding a creamy element to the dish. To punctuate the strawberry-patch appearance further and add another contrast, he'd scattered pickled half-ripe strawberry cubes, more strawberry blossoms, and tiny, fragrant yellow and red alpine strawberries across the plate. Shards of sumptuous, crispy duck skin finished the dish.

It looked like a small garden on the plate, and the girls had loved the concept when he'd thought of it. They'd both given their ideas as to how the presentation could be improved, and in the end, he'd taken some of each of their tweaks and trusted his own judgment on others.

He exhaled and gave the platter one more look before covering it with its silver cloche and taking it outside to the waiting footman. "Please take care with it," he said, trying not to sound nervous.

"Of course, sir," the footman agreed. He bowed and set off toward the palace with Elijah's dish.

Elijah took a bracing breath. It was out of his hands now.

⚬

An hour or so later, Helena and Penelope had made a tour of two-thirds of the competitors' tents, and for her part, Helena had little doubt that Elijah had a great chance of placing in the top twenty. Penelope had especially enjoyed the elegant food from the Spanish count, as well as the offerings of a female amateur from Wales who had made tiny towers of Welsh cakes with strawberries folded into them, which she'd paired with strawberry-glazed Welsh lamb chops.

Helena, however, thought Elijah's competition came from the Duke of Transylvania's strong technical skills and bold flavors, which he'd shown in a complex rabbit dish with multiple contrasting elements. There were a few others who Helena thought Lady Rutland would praise, but Helena also knew what that Goose of a princess counted as impeccable cuisine, and she felt quite certain Elijah's dish could not help but impress.

Helena looked at her watch as Penelope stopped at the Sardinian delegation's tent to sample some kind of multicolored terrine. Perhaps they should stop by Elijah's tent and see what sort of reception he was getting. Surely enough time had passed that they could now do so without suspicion.

"Ah, Helena!"

Helena clenched her back teeth at the sound of Mabel's voice.

How did the girl always seem to appear when least expected?

As usual, Helena had been far too engrossed in her own thoughts to see Mabel waving at her from down the path.

"What a delightful day for it, don't you think?" Mabel asked as she approached.

"Yes, quite," Helena replied. "I should have thought you inside assisting with the tasting, Mabel."

Mabel gave a tiny shrug. "My part is done for the day. Princess Adelaide would have had me present, but Lady Rutland is such a stickler for rules, as you know. Only she, Prince Leopold, and the princess may be present in the tasting room, and the footmen were allotted competitors at random, etcetera, etcetera. Everything must be eminently fair and equal. Did you know that certain royal delegations tried to bribe footmen beforehand in previous years? Such scandalous behavior!" Mabel held her hand to her chest as though she were truly shocked.

Helena tried not to roll her eyes. "Yes, of course I knew, Mabel. Lady Rutland condemned it at great length last year in her Modern Culinary Presentation seminar."

Mabel fluttered her hand in Helena's direction. "Oh yes, of course. What a memory you have, Helena. We girls always used to comment on it—some of them are quite envious, you know."

"So I gathered," Helena said, looking at Penelope to catch her eye. Helena knew the girls at the Royal Academy envied her for many things, but she suspected her memory to be the smallest source of their ire. A good memory certainly helped in one's studies, but far more important for success was actually paying attention, which many of the girls at the Royal Academy, including Mabel, seemed to find exceedingly difficult.

Her very first term at the Royal Academy, Helena had discovered that most of the girls wanted to be Culinarians, yes, but they also became distracted by the most inane things, such as the attractive undergardener, the newest fashion in mantelets, or the house party they'd be attending when the term ended. Helena firmly believed then, and firmly continued to believe, that one could not become one of the best Culinarians in the nation by focusing on frivolous pursuits unrelated to food. It was one of the reasons she and Penelope had become friends. *Penelope* never allowed herself to become overly preoccupied with the mundanities of everyday life. At least, that's what Helena had always thought—until recently.

Helena's eyes widened as the unmistakable profile of Freddie Eynsford-Hill approached Penelope while she continued to converse with the gentleman at the Sardinian tent. How had that popinjay gotten an invitation to the exhibition? He hadn't even placed at the faire!

Mabel followed Helena's gaze with some curiosity. "Ah, there's Penelope and Mr. Eynsford-Hill. Do you know him?"

Helena pulled her attention back to Mabel. "He's a recent acquaintance. *You* know him?"

"Oh yes!" Mabel said, throwing a hand out to touch Helena's arm.

Helena grimaced. She disliked people touching her when it wasn't warranted, and disliked it from Mabel on principle.

Mabel continued, oblivious to Helena's discomfort. "The Eynsford-Hills are great friends of my family. Freddie was somewhat flighty when he was younger, but he's not a bad catch overall."

That clinched it. If Mabel Pilkington thought Freddie a catch, he had to be as inane as Helena surmised. They both watched as Freddie said something and Penelope laughed.

"Penelope could do worse, I should think," Mabel pronounced.

Helena rolled her eyes. "Mabel, Penelope has no intention of marrying. Certainly not any time before we become Culinarians," she stated firmly.

Mabel raised her eyebrows. "Has she said so?"

Helena wobbled her head from side to side, irritated they were having such a ridiculous conversation. "She doesn't need to. I know it to be true."

"Indeed, many Culinarians marry. And marry well. One could certainly do both if one wished to. Recall the Duchess of Audrey— one of the best Culinarians and now a duchess!"

Helena scoffed. "The Duchess of Audrey rarely consults any-more. All she does is raise her passel of children in the country. She gave up all her training to sit at home."

Mabel shrugged. "That may have been *her* choice. And who's to say she isn't happy?"

Helena pressed her lips together. She hated to concede any point to Mabel Pilkington, though even Helena had to imagine it was pos-sible. She didn't know the duchess, however, so she could not say for certain. She wondered now if Mabel had decided to be a Culinarian simply to make a good match. If so, Helena held her in even lower esteem than she had before. What a waste of time and training! "I still say an education—in any profession—is reprehensible to waste."

Mabel's airy laugh set Helena's teeth on edge. "Ah, Helena, not everyone is so independent as you! To some, making a fine match may elevate them and their status immeasurably. It would certainly do so for Penelope."

Helena's eyes narrowed. "Just what do you mean by that remark?"

Mabel wet her lips, then glanced around her as if to make sure no one overheard her. "Penelope's birth, of course."

Helena gave her a cold look. "What about her birth?"

"Not that there's anything wrong about it, I daresay," Mabel whispered. "But her parents' marriage does make Penelope's position in society rather precarious. The right husband could make all that go away, as it were. Secure her standing."

Helena swallowed. She threw a glance at Penelope, who was still speaking animatedly with Freddie Eynsford-Hill. To Helena's knowledge, only she and Lady Rutland knew that Penelope's mother was from the Philippine Islands. How had Mabel learned of it? "What makes you think there is anything about Penelope's origin that society would censure?"

Mabel twirled a ringlet around her finger. "Well, Dora Smith-Smythe overheard some of the teachers discussing it. Apparently, Penelope's father stole her mother away from some savage island. That's why they never return to England."

Helena could hardly believe it. Not only was this offensively embellished story circulating around the Royal Academy, but if Mabel and Dora Smith-Smythe had heard it, they'd likely repeated it to everyone they knew. Helena rarely gave Penelope's parents any thought, but all those awful girls at school could have been speculating about Penelope's origins for months, spinning the truth of it out of all proportion. Meanwhile, she and Penelope had been quietly going about their days working on their final projects at Cavendish Square.

Helena stretched to her full height, ignoring the fact that Mabel still stood a good few inches taller, and stared her down. "That is patently false, Mabel Pilkington. I know Penelope's parents. You can tell Dora Smith-Smythe to stop spreading vicious lies, and I will thank you to do likewise."

Mabel blinked a few times in succession. "Are you quite sure it's all untrue?"

The denial had left her mouth of its own accord. Before Helena could consider the consequences. This was generally the natural state of affairs when it came to the inner workings of Helena's mind, but on this occasion, a pinprick of doubt wended its way into her consciousness. These qualms, as unformed as they were, however, did not stop her from forging on in the same direction.

"*Quite* sure. And what's more, I fully intend to speak to Lady Rutland and ferret out which teachers are spreading gossip."

Mabel nodded. "I've always liked Penelope, as you know. And I wasn't at all certain I believed it. She is so fair-skinned, after all."

"And what has that to do with anything?" Helena snapped.

Mabel waved a hand in the air. "Oh, let's change the subject. Here comes dear Penelope now."

"Hello, Mabel," Penelope said as she approached with Freddie in tow.

"Good day, Penelope," Mabel returned, a smile firmly affixed to her lips.

Helena clenched her jaw. If not for Penelope, Helena would have stalked away, but she couldn't leave Penelope with Mabel now.

"I believe you both know Mr. Eynsford-Hill?" Penelope said.

He bowed at Mabel and Helena and they bobbed curtsies.

"Sorry you didn't qualify to compete, Mr. Eynsford-Hill," Helena stated, not really caring that she didn't sound sorry in the slightest.

"Not at all, Lady Helena," he replied with a good-natured smile. "This would have been far too much pressure for a chap like me." He gestured around at the tents. "I'm vastly contented to taste all the delights and converse with such charming would-be Culinarians as you ladies. It makes me feel as though I'm on the cutting edge of Culinaria just to know you all before you become society's leading ladies."

Mabel and Penelope laughed at his compliment. Helena pressed her lips together.

"Mr. Eynsford-Hill offered to walk through the rest of the exhibition with us, Helena," Penelope said.

Helena gritted her teeth, but didn't speak. At the moment, she felt unequal to the task of finding something polite to say.

"Would you care to join us as well, Mabel?" Penelope asked.

Mabel's smile lit up. "It'd be a pleasure. I happen to—"

"I'm certain we wouldn't wish to incommode someone so busy as yourself," Helena cut in, shooting Penelope a glare.

"You are all thoughtfulness, Helena," Mabel replied. "But I was going to say that I happily have the rest of the day to myself. At least until the results of the blind tasting have been announced. Then I must return to Lady Rutland's side to discuss preparations for tomorrow."

"Excellent!" Penelope proclaimed in her genial way, and the

four of them set off to sample the rest of the exhibition.

Resentful of being forced into the company of a young man clearly after her best friend's talent and a two-faced girl spreading mean-spirited rumors about said best friend (who appeared blissfully oblivious to it all), Helena pulled up the rear as they tasted bread after bread, pastries from half the countries in Europe, smoked meats of every type, and vegetables prepared in more ways than she could count. All while she kept herself from retching as Freddie plied his charms (in other words, flirted like mad) with Penelope, who seemed nothing so much as flattered, if her smiles were any judge. Mabel and Freddie did indeed have a rapport, and at Mabel's request, between bites he told them of his sister's adventures at the Royal Academy of Commoditas & Design, which bored Helena to no end.

Finally, Helena saw Elijah's tent and took the lead, walking at a brisk pace to force them to follow. A middle-aged lady and gentleman and two ladies her grandmama's age loitered by Elijah's tent, tasting and talking. Elijah appeared composed as he spoke to them. A hint of a smile made him appear approachable, which was something they'd practiced in the last few weeks. He seemed to be handling himself well.

Helena stepped into the empty space between the couple and the older ladies. "Good afternoon, Mr. Little. How nice to see you again. We've come to sample your dish." She gestured widely at the group behind her.

Elijah inclined his head in their direction. "Good day, Lady Helena, Miss Pickering."

"Allow me to introduce you all," Helena replied, and performed the introductions before Mabel or Freddie could say or do anything awkward.

"Good show on making it here today," Freddie said. "I was at the faire as well, but clearly the best man won! Your duck looks delicious."

"Very decent of you to say so," Elijah said. He handed each of them a plate with the elements he'd created carefully arranged. They all took forks from the basket on the table.

"So you're one of the English gentlemen chefs," Mabel mused. "Is that when you met Helena and Penelope?" She inspected the pink queso fresco in the shape of a strawberry and popped it into her mouth. "My goodness! This is delightful. Is it a mild chevre?"

"It's a queso fresco—a fresh cow's-milk cheese from Mexico," Elijah said.

"And you made it yourself?" Mabel asked.

He inclined his head. "Of course."

"I've never even heard of it," commented Freddie. "But it goes very well with the spiced duck. Have you all heard of it?" he asked the three girls.

Penelope and Helena nodded just as Mabel said, "Penelope has a particular interest in the Americas, do you not?"

Penelope made an affirmative noise, but looked like she didn't quite know what to say.

"How did you come by the recipe, Mr. Little?" Helena asked to move attention away from Penelope. They had rehearsed his answers to questions like this.

"My uncle is a great traveler, Lady Helena," Elijah began. "He sends me recipes from every port, and I replicate them whenever I can."

"I must say, the financiers are my favorite," Penelope said, giving him a smile. "Ramps and walnuts and cheese—always a clever combination."

Helena exhaled. Penelope was so transparent with her praise, Helena half expected her to wink at Elijah and ruin the entire enterprise.

Elijah, meanwhile, could not seem to keep his gaze from Penelope, even as he bowed his head in thanks to the couple to their left who had loudly agreed with Penelope's assessment, wished him luck, and moved on to the next tent.

"My favorite element must be the pickled strawberries," Freddie piped up, "though, I do tend to savor sour foods a tad more than perhaps I should."

Penelope laughed and turned back to face Freddie. "Oh yes! I still contend that your pickled green tomatoes at the faire were unique and quite enjoyable. Though, they were, perhaps, not everybody's pot of tea. I imagine that might be why you didn't place in the top two."

Freddie grinned at her, and Helena thought this had to be his most brazen attempt yet to exert all his (truly limited) powers of pleasing to beguile her friend. She hoped Penelope wasn't falling for it, but he had already extracted a compliment and further encouragement from Penelope's generous mind. What more might he accomplish if she gave him the chance?

"You are too kind, Miss Pickering," he said. "But it is my lot in life to be well loved by some and disregarded by others. I have made my own peace with it, but I do hope you shall become one of the former group." Freddie leaned slightly closer to her.

Penelope laughed him off and refused to meet his eyes or anyone else's, but Helena watched Elijah's affable smile melt away, and what's more, she noted Mabel seeing it as well.

"Mr. Little, why don't you tell us how you determined on adding pink peppercorns to the strawberry gastrique," Helena said to draw his attention and Mabel's.

Elijah looked up at her in that way he sometimes did when he was thinking of something else, and she pressed her lips together, hoping it would get him to focus.

"You really do have a flair for interesting flavor pairings, Mr. Little," Mabel said, stepping closer to the table. "You must have been cooking quite a while."

Elijah smiled at her, but it did not quite meet his eyes. "Since I was a child, Miss Pilkington. My mother taught me before she died. She had a gift for cooking well, though she never measured anything."

"I'm so sorry for your loss," Mabel said. "She must have taught you a great deal. Your technique is almost as strong as a Culinarian's."

Penelope looked at Helena. Mabel was fishing. Helena didn't bat an eye.

"I studied a fair bit on my own after she passed, and with my uncle's help, I was able to learn more flavor combinations. One can do anything with enough practice, I believe," Elijah replied.

"And raw talent, I daresay," Mabel said.

Elijah laughed. "With such praise from three Culinarians-to-be, in the midst of such strong competition, I must weigh this day a success, no matter the outcome. Thank you, Miss Pilkington."

Helena watched as Mabel's narrowed eyes and arch smile flew away on the breeze. She even fluttered her eyelashes at Elijah. Sometimes Helena couldn't believe how silly girls her own age could be, but so much the better if it led to success today.

"Not at all, Mr. Little," Mabel said. "I do think Princess Adelaide will very much enjoy how you've featured the strawberry with such reverence—"

A liveried footman cleared his throat, and they all turned to look at him as he handed Elijah a piece of paper. "The list, sir."

Elijah nodded and took it from him. "Thank you."

The footman bowed and moved to the next tent. Helena held her breath as her eyes darted from the dozen other royal footmen handing out lists, to Penelope biting her lip, to Elijah's deceptively calm visage as his eyes tracked down the row of numbers. Then his eyes stopped. He took a deep breath. Then another.

He looked at Penelope. Then Helena. No one said a word.

Freddie broke the silence. "Well, man, are you on it?"

Helena glared daggers at him, annoyed that he'd said something when she and Penelope had to hold their tongues and keep to the pretense that they only knew Elijah as a casual acquaintance.

Elijah exhaled, then emitted a strangled laugh. He caught Penelope's gaze and smiled slowly. "Indeed, I am."

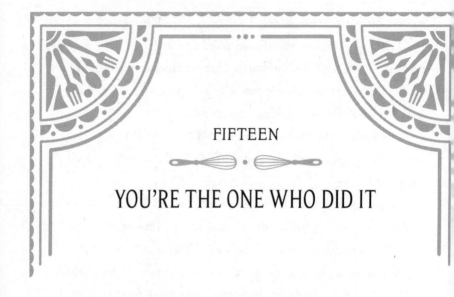

FIFTEEN

YOU'RE THE ONE WHO DID IT

"What a day! What a triumph!" Helena crowed in response to Pierce's greeting as they all dragged themselves into the townhouse that night. "I'm certain you'll be pleased to hear that Mr. Little placed in the top twenty, Pierce, and that all your griping these past months was for naught!"

Pierce's eyes widened, but he took Penelope's and Helena's cloaks and directed the footmen who'd accompanied Elijah to the exhibition to take the crates of plates and utensils back to the kitchen for washing. "Well done, Lady Helena. I never doubted your eventual success," Pierce stated. "Perhaps you'd care for a celebratory refreshment?" he asked the three of them.

"No food, Pierce, I am stuffed," Helena said as she removed her bonnet with a wide smile. Then she looked at Elijah and Penelope. "On second thought, let's open a bottle of champagne. Such successes deserve a special bottle. I'm certain my parents would agree.

In the drawing room, perhaps, Pierce?"

"I just so happened to have a bottle chilled and waiting, Lady Helena," he replied. "Just in case." He inclined his head to Elijah, who stood a trifle straighter. Penelope had seen, time and again, how Pierce seemed to consider Elijah beneath Helena's notice, but her spirits lifted with the knowledge that Pierce had had some faith in Elijah's abilities in the end.

Helena laughed. "You sly fellow. Despite your objections, you had confidence after all."

"I merely know you succeed in whatever you put your mind to, Lady Helena," Pierce said.

Penelope blew out a breath and tried to give Elijah a reassuring smile as some consolation for Pierce's comment, but Elijah wouldn't look at her.

Helena cast her gaze at the ceiling. "So I do." Another merry laugh bubbled out of her. "Come along and have a glass with us, Pierce." She started toward the drawing room.

"Just one for me, Helena," Penelope said. "I'm quite exhausted from the events of the day, but I do wish to celebrate properly." She cast another glance at Elijah. She thought he looked tired as well, and he had to cook on the morrow. He needed all the rest he could get.

"As you wish, Pen," Helena said. They reached the drawing room, and Helena headed straight toward the champagne bottle and ice bucket. Penelope flopped down on the settee, and Elijah moved to stand near the mantelpiece, where he stared into the low flames. Pierce held the glasses as Helena popped the cork and began to pour.

"We could have celebrated at the exhibition had not that

dreadful Mabel been following us about. And that *ridiculous* Freddie whatsit-whatsit." Helena rolled her eyes. "I do wish you weren't so blasted polite sometimes, Pen."

Penelope looked up, surprised. "I couldn't very well *not* ask Mabel when I'd already agreed to let Mr. Eynsford-Hill accompany us."

Helena let out an exaggerated sigh. "Perhaps not, but I don't see why you agreed to let him walk with us either. Even if you are considering marriage in the future, as Mabel seems to believe, you could do far better than Mr. Pickled Green Tomatoes. I, for one, don't see why you would give up your freedom or your brilliant career to have a man hanging on your culinary coattails, but—"

"Helena," Penelope interrupted, "this is supposed to be a celebration—not an analysis of my marriage prospects. Thank you, Pierce." She took her champagne glass from Pierce's outstretched arm, and ventured a glance at Elijah's back as she took a sip. He turned slightly as Pierce offered him a glass, but did not look in her direction. She wondered what he was thinking about.

"Well, you are quite right, Pen," Helena agreed. "Here's your glass, Pierce." He nodded and took it from her. Helena held up her glass. "To victory! This one-time crushed cabbage leaf"—she gestured to Elijah—"is now one Mr. Elijah Little, gentleman. A gentleman chef of the first order, cooking for royalty! Today in the top twenty, tomorrow in the top ten, and after that, well in the running to marry none other than Princess Adelaide herself! From cabbage to croquembouche, just as I planned! Cheers!"

Penelope's grip tightened on the glass. Her eyes shot to Elijah and then to Helena. Helena merely sipped her champagne and sighed contentedly. After a long moment of silence, she seemed to feel Penelope's and Elijah's stares.

"Well? Drink up! Aren't you pleased?"

Penelope shook her head. "What do you mean 'marry Princess Adelaide'?"

Helena fluttered her free hand in the air. "Ha! That is the best part of all! Mabel told me at the faire that Princess Adelaide plans to choose her husband-to-be from the finalists of the exhibition! Of course, we all know how much the royal family honors culinary talent, but even I could not have predicted this! All Mr. Little has to do is cook well tomorrow—and I have little doubt of that, since the dish shall be made from tomorrow's catch of the day, and we know how well he does with fish—and he will automatically be under consideration by the palace to be the next crown prince of Britain!"

Penelope felt her mouth drop open as she watched Helena bounce on her toes and sip more of her champagne. "Can you imagine the Goose's face when she realizes that he learned all his skill from me?" Helena continued. "Or Mabel's face? How I shall laugh!" She dropped into the nearest chair, oblivious to the shock permeating the room.

Elijah was the first to recover enough to attempt speech. "I—I can't *marry* the princess," he said, blinking rapidly.

"Don't be silly," Helena scoffed. "If she's willing to marry whoever makes it to the top three, *you* certainly have no reason to object." She took another sip of champagne and smoothed the printed muslin of her skirt.

Penelope cleared her throat as she watched Elijah's mouth open and close. "Perhaps Elijah doesn't *wish* to marry Princess Adelaide," she stated. She felt his gaze shoot toward her.

"Don't be ridiculous, Pen." Helena sniffed. "It's simply his fear talking. The *same* fear that almost kept him from doing all this that first day he called here asking for lessons."

Penelope opened her mouth to refute this, but Helena continued before she could.

"And why *wouldn't* he wish to marry the princess? He'd be well and truly set for the rest of his life. He'd never have to go back to hawking pasties or working *in any capacity* if he didn't wish to. He could cook for the mere pleasure of it, as many gentlemen do."

"I've not even *met* her," Elijah said in a tone of voice Penelope hadn't heard him use before. A muscle flexed in his cheek.

"Oh, if it's *her* you object to, I wouldn't worry. She may be a goose, but she's only sixteen, after all. She could improve with age, much like this vintage." She sipped again and smiled. "Besides, you shall meet her tomorrow, I have no doubt," Helena stated. She stifled a yawn with the back of her hand. "In the meantime, we should all get some rest. You have one of the earlier cooking spots, and you'll want to arrive at the palace with plenty of time to grow acclimated to the space." She pushed herself up from the chair. "Thank you for thinking of the champagne, Pierce. You may finish it if you'd like."

He nodded. "Thank you, my lady. And sincerest congratulations on your success."

"Thank you, Pierce," Helena said, looking supremely pleased with herself.

Pierce bowed his graying head and took the bucket and its contents with him as he left the room. Helena downed the remaining champagne in her glass and set it on a side table. "You two look completely done in for the evening. I'll see you in the morning."

A cold heaviness had settled in Penelope's stomach. "Helena," she said, getting to her feet, "you should have told us about this scheme to catch Princess Adelaide's eye before now. Elijah had a right to know what he was getting himself into today. He has a true chance to make it into the final three, and what if Princess Adelaide does like him above the others? He couldn't refuse her hand. If he did, he would offend the entire royal family and more than half the nobility and gentry, and then where would he be? Back where he started, except infamous as well."

Helena exhaled. "But what fellow in his right mind would refuse the Crown Princess of Britain? No matter her faults? In any case, had I told you both, it simply would have added to your anxiety. As it stands, Mr. Little cooked his best, and it worked in his favor. Think of how nervous you were this afternoon, Pen, and only imagine how it would have been compounded had you known what I knew."

Penelope pressed her lips together, realizing the truth of the assessment, yet not appeased. Helena should have consulted him—it was *his* future, after all. She looked at Elijah, but his face betrayed none of his thoughts. She willed him to speak—to tell Helena some of what went on in that enigmatic mind of his, but she also knew from experience that he would likely say nothing more.

"Now, I do believe you are simply tired, Pen," Helena continued. "You'll see in the morning that I was quite right to keep it from you both. I shall say good night. Elijah, please extinguish the candles on your way upstairs." She left the room, and Penelope let out an exasperated breath. Yes, she was tired, but she also knew she'd feel the same in the morning. Perhaps, after a night's rest, *Helena* would be more inclined to hear the truth of how heavy-handed she'd acted.

Penelope tried to give Elijah a look she hoped would cheer him. "You did so well today. I was exceedingly proud of you. And I hope you know you needn't do anything you don't wish to do."

He bowed his head. "Thank you for everything, Penelope. I could not have done this without you."

She started, realizing this was the first time he'd actually called her "Penelope" despite all the weeks that'd passed since they'd started calling each other friends. The tones of his warm tenor had seemed to linger on the syllables of her name, as if to give them some extra meaning. Could it be that he . . . ?

But then Penelope's mind floundered. Her understanding of her growing feelings for him was still so new. She'd spent the carriage ride back to Cavendish Square sneaking glances at Elijah in her peripheral vision, but as yet, she had little idea of what she should do. In the carriage, she'd come to the eventual conclusion that his presence might be clouding her judgment. Penelope had hoped some solitude and the light of day would bring her some insights. Thus, instead of putting any of her thoughts into words, she said, "I doubt that. You are one of the most capable people I've ever met. *And* you have more talent in your right hand than most of the people at that exhibition. No matter what happens tomorrow, no one can take that away from you." She smiled at him then, hoping he'd take her words to heart.

He smiled back, but she thought he looked somewhat sad. The smile certainly hadn't reached his eyes. She stretched out her arm, took his hand, and squeezed it in hers. "Good night, Elijah."

He looked down at her small hand clutching his larger one, and

Penelope had the most inexplicable urge to flee before his eyes could lock on hers. She pulled her hand back and hastened from the room, pausing for only one heart-pounding moment as he whispered, "Good night . . . Penelope."

∝∞⌐

After Penelope left, Elijah stared into the fire, watching the embers flicker and wane. A smorgasbord of emotions churned in his gullet, yet he didn't know which to think or act upon. Anxiety for tomorrow, despair that his hopes for Penelope might have been thwarted by a congenial gentleman before Elijah could fully prove himself, confusion about how she felt, fear he wouldn't cook well, and sheer exhaustion from the day's events all pressed in on him, but the anger—yes, the anger was perhaps the chief among them, overriding all.

He hadn't done all this—*any* of this—to be trapped into something he didn't want. He'd endured months of training and Helena's high-handedness to change *his* life and pay back his uncle for taking him in. Well, he'd changed his life all right. If he cooked well tomorrow, he'd be under consideration as a *husband* for the crown princess. The thought was bloody ridiculous, yet Helena had said it as if it were a casual lark. It would be a joke she could play on the princess—another experiment. Only this experiment gambled with the rest of his life.

If he made it to the top three as he'd meant to try for, and Princess Adelaide did take an interest in him, he couldn't turn her down without suffering serious repercussions to his future. And if he didn't try for the top three spots, he'd have nothing tangible to offer Penelope. Of course, Penelope might be more interested in a true gentleman like Freddie Eynsford-Hill. He was clearly interested in her.

Elijah's hand itched to hurl his glass into the fire. It would have made him feel better, but then he'd have to tidy it, and Pierce would've asked where the glass had gone and given him a supercilious glare when Elijah told him he'd broken it. It didn't seem worth the trouble. Instead, he set down the glass on the mantel, and ran both his hands through his hair. A growl reverberated out of his throat. What right did Helena have to put him in this position? What right did she have to play God when it suited her? Elijah's nails bit into his palms. She had the rights of a wealthy, aristocratic lady with every resource at her disposal—even parents so permissive and trusting that they'd let her bring a strange boy they hadn't even met into their home.

But the worst of it wasn't Helena's luck or even her behavior. The worst was that she would never consider him her equal. He was just a pawn to her. Even after today when *he'd* done everything possible to prove he could be the gentleman they'd trained him to be, she could only congratulate herself. Nevermind that Elijah felt like he'd scraped himself inside and out with a knife and doused himself in salt and vinegar like he would a piece of tripe to clean off all impurities. To her, he was that unclean piece of flesh and would always remain so.

"Oh, you're still here, Elijah."

Speak of the devil. Elijah turned from the fire as Helena walked into the room in a burgundy dressing gown and slippers. "I would have thought you'd gone to bed by now, but since you're here, have you seen my reticule? I wished to go over some of the notes I took on your competitors before bed. There was an Austrian count who baked some fascinating strawberry and seaweed pastries that I rather wished to experiment with. I suppose we'll see tomorrow if he made the top twenty, but—"

"It's over there," Elijah interrupted. He pointed at the side table where she'd set down her champagne.

Helena blinked. "Ah! So it is." She moved to get it, then pulled her palm-sized notebook out of the bag. "I daresay this shall come in handy once we discover whom your real competition is tomorrow."

Elijah clenched his jaw but said nothing.

Helena started to the door. "Don't stay up too late. You don't want to be too tired to make a good impression on the princess."

Heat flashed through him. "I am perfectly capable of determining when to sleep."

Helena stopped short and looked at him. "While I'm certain that is generally true, you have never taken part in a multiday culinary competition. And, to be perfectly honest, you don't always seem to *know* what is actually good for you."

He stepped away from the fire as he stared at her. "And *you* know what's best for me, I suppose."

She peered at him, all wide-eyed innocence. "I have been right more often than not, as I recall."

He ran his hand over the back of his neck. "So I am to keep my mouth shut, go to bed, and be your puppet in some juvenile game where you humiliate the crown princess, Mabel Pilkington, and me? Ah yes, it's a fine joke."

Helena's posture stiffened. "Elijah, you forget yourself. I think you are far more fatigued than you realize. You should—"

"Yes, I am tired. But I'm also thinking clearly for the first time in months." He took a step toward her. "You wanted to turn me into a gentleman. I didn't want to be one, but you insisted. And now, after today—after *your* triumph, as you refer to it—I am one. As you said yourself, that means I can do what *I* wish. And *I*, Lady Helena, have no wish to settle scores for you or play to your vanity or any other damn thing! I thank you for the training that you *and* Miss Pickering provided, and for the opportunities, but I shall be going my own way from this moment on."

For a few seconds Helena said nothing. In Elijah's mind, his anger had eclipsed everything until now. The silence grew. Helena sniffed. Then she did the last thing he'd expected her to do. She laughed.

"Hah! You do surprise me, Elijah. But I must say, you'll need opinions to appeal to Queen Charlotte. She rather likes people who speak their minds. I can't say for certain what the princess finds appealing, but I shall appeal to Mabel's self-importance—"

"You're not listening," Elijah interrupted, his pulse jumping. "I *cannot* marry the princess." He enunciated each word, hoping that would make some sort of impact.

Helena cast her gaze to the ceiling. "Very well, why do you say you can't marry the princess?"

Elijah let out a deep breath. He was going to have to tell her. Otherwise she would never relent. He shook his head, then looked her in the eye. "I'm Jewish."

Helena blinked. Then blinked again harder. "What?"

"You heard me," he ground out.

"What do you mean *you're Jewish*?" Helena said, clearly shocked into a rare bout of stupidity.

"Jewish. A Jew. Not Christian. Take your pick," he replied, growing hotter under his coat as his anger flared.

"But you . . ." She trailed off. "That's why you didn't taste the pork roast!" She shook her head, turned to pace across the room, only to wheel around to face him again. "Why didn't you say something?" she demanded.

"I don't see why I should have to," he shot back. "Yet somehow, I knew it would make a difference."

"Of course it makes a blasted difference! You should never have . . . I would *never* have . . ." She turned away again.

His chest tightened. "What? Taught me? Turned me into a gentleman? Just because I'm Jewish?"

Helena threw her arms in the air. "I certainly wouldn't have groomed you to marry the princess! King George wasn't even allowed to legally marry Maria Fitzherbert because she was a Catholic. I cannot imagine they'd allow Princess Adelaide to marry a Jew. I mean"—she paused and leveled a glare at him—"I don't believe you can even own a shop in the city of London! Isn't there a law against it?"

He shook his head. "It's not a law. The merchants don't allow it. Because they're prejudiced. Not for any reason beyond that. And there are ways around it—"

She snorted. "Ways around it?! Ways that doubtless rely on money or influence. Of which you have neither. How can someone like you reasonably expect to—"

His entire body tensed. "What do you mean someone *like* me?" His shoulders ached with the effort to keep calm. He reminded himself that this was nothing he hadn't dealt with before. She'd acted just as he'd expected she would—no, worse—but he'd had enough.

"Someone like you," she sputtered. "You know what I mean."

He crossed the room to close the distance between them. "I know very well what you mean. You've thought me worthless since the moment we met. I'm sure this only confirms it for you."

Helena raised her chin to look straight at him. "If I thought you worthless, I would not have spent months giving you the benefit of my expertise."

He shook his head. "You did this—took me on—so you could get top honors on your precious project. Don't pretend it was about me."

She crossed her arms in front of her. "I cannot believe you have the gall to reproach me when you have lied from the start about the very nature of who you are!"

He let out a scornful laugh. "Would you expect me to do otherwise when you've acted this way—"

"I trusted you in my home. The least you could do is be honest—"

"When I watch you dismiss Penelope's mother's recipes or change the subject when she mentions her parents?" His pulse raced, but he would have his say for once. "After a week in your company, I could tell that you had no tolerance for anyone different from *you*. The only reason Penelope remains your friend is because she sees the good in everyone—including you. And you treat her heritage— something that is a great part of her—as something to be overlooked or left unspoken. If you have any doubt about why I kept my own background and beliefs to myself, realize that *you* are the reason." Elijah's pulse thrummed in his ears as he stalked out of the room, too full of ire to spare Helena another glance.

SIXTEEN

WITHOUT YOU

Penelope pinned the last few free strands of her hair into the coil at the crown of her head and inspected her coiffure in the looking glass. Helena's maid, Julie, probably could have done something more intricate, but Penelope had grown used to attending to her own hair during her travels and their days at the Royal Academy. The previous day's events had drained Penelope enough that she'd slept later than she'd intended, so she'd decided not to ring the bell for Julie, as she would likely already be attending to Helena by now.

Last night, Penelope's muddled mind had been no match for sleep's beckoning grasp, and she had fallen into a dreamless slumber. She hoped Elijah had slept as soundly as she had. She played with the curls framing her face so they sat at a more flattering angle, then let out an exasperated breath at her fussing. Despite Penelope's wishful thinking, the morning had not served her a silver platter of sage stratagems to handle her blossoming feelings for Elijah. Standing from the dressing table, she opened the closet to look for her lavender bonnet.

She wanted to get downstairs before Elijah left for the exhibition. He hadn't looked quite himself last night, and she hoped to reassure him that he would be fine. He also had to know that he needn't worry about Helena's plans. In reality, Helena couldn't—and indeed, *shouldn't*—make him do anything (let alone marry someone) he didn't want to. And, as for those troublesome *feelings* Penelope was harboring, she would let Elijah's behavior be her guide. At the moment, she didn't know what else she could do.

A screech reverberated through the walls. Penelope's back stiffened. She rushed to her bedroom door and pulled it open.

"What do you mean, 'he's gone'?!" Helena's shout rang out. "Pen-elll-opeee!"

Penelope stepped into the hall. "What's happened?"

Helena stood on the landing to the staircase with her hands on her hips and her black curls cascading down her shoulders. She'd clearly been in the process of dressing. Julie hovered behind her, hooking the back of her day dress, as Pierce stood awkwardly averting his gaze at the floor.

"Pen! That ingrate has disappeared," Helena barked.

It took a moment for understanding to dawn. "Elijah?" Penelope asked.

"Yes, of course, *Elijah*. That puffed-up three-day-old baked good with delusions of grandeur. He's supposed to be downstairs preparing to leave for the exhibition, but Pierce tells me he's nowhere to be found." She threw her hands up in the air, causing Julie to pause in her attentions. "Do hurry, Julie," Helena admonished her.

Penelope exhaled, feeling her own patience melting like butter on a hot crumpet. "Isn't it possible Elijah left earlier than expected for the exhibition? He seemed rather distressed last night."

Helena scoffed. "*Distressed*, you call it? That ungrateful wretch has been lying to us for months, and he had the unmitigated impudence to tell me—"

"I take it he told you about his religion," Penelope interrupted, feeling more and more frustrated with Helena by the second.

Helena opened and closed her mouth like a tuna. "You knew?"

Penelope nodded through clenched teeth.

"And *you* kept it from me?"

Penelope lifted her chin. "It wasn't for *me* to tell you. He needed to do so in his own time."

"But you let me carry on with his training knowing who he was? I would never have guessed it of you, Pen," Helena said, shaking her head.

"You never cared *who* he was, Helena. Only what he could do. *I* asked him questions—Lady Rutland and Pierce asked him questions. Not *you*." Penelope folded her arms in front of her. "*You* didn't care anything about who he was until this very moment. And even now, I don't believe you care a jot for what makes Elijah tick—what makes him who he is—you only care how all this affects your plans. How it affects *you*. Can you deny it?"

Helena's green eyes narrowed. "I wanted him to be the best he could be! And I'd almost accomplished it!"

Penelope's chest tightened. "You really can make everything about yourself, can't you? How *your* plans are ruined, how *you* triumphed yesterday. Have you ever thought how worried he must have been all these months, learning a new way of life and living with the fear that if you discovered he was Jewish, you might change your mind? Or act exactly as you are doing now?" She let out a mirthless laugh. "Perhaps you imagine that telling someone you are different is the simplest thing in the world, but you are mistaken, Helena. My parents live abroad to save me from gossip, so you've not seen how we are treated when we're together, or how people behave toward me once they know my lineage, but I shall tell you now that it is painful. And unfair. And I don't think you have the slightest inkling—"

"Hah! You think I don't know?! There you are mistaken! Just as you are to be kind to Mabel," Helena huffed. "She was spreading rumors about your parents only yesterday. Saying your father kidnapped your mother from a savage island or some such rot. And I—*I* was the one who told her it was all lies, but who knows who else she's told. And I fully intend to convey to Lady Rutland that Mabel and Dora Smith-Smythe have been circulating such falsehoods. I won't have those horrid girls treating you like some kind of pariah—"

"Wait!" Penelope cut her off, wanting to make sense of Helena's words. "Did you tell her my mother *is* from the Philippine Islands?"

Helena shook her head emphatically. "Of course not. I denied the whole story. I won't have the likes of Mabel Pilkington ruining your social standing before you've even graduated."

Penelope drew in a slow, steady breath. She met Helena's gaze. "Why didn't you tell her the truth? *I've* never hidden who I am. And I never told *you* to hide my parentage. And you don't counter a lie with another lie. You counter it with the truth. That my parents love each other and care for me."

Helena threw up her arms. "That doesn't mean everyone won't act differently toward you if they know!"

"Yes! Exactly! Can't you see that it's the same for Elijah!?"

Helena froze. Then her lips flattened into a thin line. She started to shake her head. "I was only thinking of your reputation—"

"You know what I think, Helena?" Penelope continued, unwilling to hear any more of her narrow-minded excuses. "I think you were worried Mabel and the girls would treat *you* differently if they knew your only friend was of mixed race. I think your anger at Elijah isn't because he didn't *tell* you he's Jewish—it's because he *is* Jewish. He and I both heard what you said about those young hawkers on the outskirts of London, and it caused Elijah no small share of pain, I assure you."

Helena shook her head. "I don't even recall *what* I said, but I'm certain I didn't mean to offend anyone."

"Yes, that's what I told Elijah at the time. That's what I've always told people. That you don't *mean* to cause offense. The blatant truth, however, is that though you may not mean to, you *do*. And no matter how you try to justify it, it's wrong. What you said about Elijah's people was not only an egregious generalization, it was cruel."

"I couldn't have guessed he was—"

"It doesn't matter if you knew or not. From your behavior today, I can only conclude that a part of you must *believe* those things you said and implied. It was foolish of me to pretend otherwise, because you *always* speak your mind. So I am also to blame. I've watched you belittle Elijah from the start of all this." She waved a hand at Pierce. "We've *all* watched, in fact. And I've said very little because"—she shook her head at herself—"I don't even really know why, except I thought you were doing all this for a greater good. To make one person's life better in the hopes that it might help others in the future." She took in a heavy breath to steady herself.

"But I was wrong. You only ever do anything to benefit yourself. Now, you can stand here and rail at Elijah for the rest of the morning, even though I have never known him to be ungrateful for a single moment since he's been here, but I certainly won't stand by and listen." Penelope gave them all a glance, took in Helena's scowl, Julie's wide eyes, and Pierce's discomfort, and strode down the hall to Elijah's room.

She opened the door and shut it behind her, not caring a whit for what Pierce or any of them thought. After taking a series of steadying breaths, Penelope shook out her arms at her sides. She couldn't recall ever being so angry at *anyone*, let alone Helena, since leaving childhood behind. Penelope had always been a good-natured child, quick to trust, and happy when basking in her parents' attentions. However, her travels had taught her that people of all credos and colors lived both happily and unhappily at times. The world was never so fair as it ought to be, yet she'd never seen much value in extremes. Penelope liked to consider herself levelheaded on most occasions, and generally prone to offer people the benefit of the doubt, but in this, Helena was simply out of order.

As Elijah had known she would be. The unshakable feeling that Penelope had misjudged the very character of her best friend and facilitated Helena's ill-treatment of Elijah gnawed at her conscience. She should have done more—*said* more—to check Helena. And now it might be too late.

She scanned the tidy guest room. Everything that might have

been Elijah's appeared to be gone. She opened the closet to see if he'd left any clothes. Only half of his new wardrobe remained. She smoothed her hand over one of the white cotton shirts, then closed the closet. She moved to the window. It overlooked Cavendish Square and the circular green park in its center.

Penelope wondered what Elijah must have thought waking up to the activity of the square every day. It had to have been so different from where he'd grown up. She sighed, wishing she'd asked him more. But they'd been in Helena's company or in observation distance of the servants more often than not, and she'd always tried to keep from talking about anything he might not want everyone to know.

Penelope turned away from the window, and a number of books and papers on a small writing desk caught her eye. They were mostly culinary history books and cookbooks from the library, but a stack of paper had been folded and sealed with a bit of wax. She turned over the bundle and saw "Miss Penelope Pickering" written in Elijah's careful hand. She sat at the table and broke the seal.

Number 9, Cavendish Square   *June 3, 1833*

Dear Penelope,
Forgive me for leaving Cavendish Square without saying
farewell, but the events of last evening made me believe it
would be best to depart before the house stirred. I'm sure
Lady Helena will tell you that I told her of my origins and
beliefs. As I suspected, she did not take it well. Whether she
decides to tell anyone or not, I still mean to compete today.

Penelope sighed, relieved to know where he was. He'd run through the next sentence with his pen a number of times, but after studying the pieces of the words she could see, Penelope found she could decipher most of it.

—though I must say that I do so for myself alone

Penelope didn't quite know what to make of that sentiment or why he'd tried to hide it. She continued reading.

Despite whatever Lady Helena says, I have no intention of trying to marry the princess, though I shall cook my best today, as I feel I owe you—and myself—this much. I told you I couldn't have gotten this far without you. I said it because it is true. I also say this knowing you have sacrificed a great deal of time from your own project to help me. Though I've told you before how very grateful I am, I hope that I may finally begin to repay your efforts.

After many months, I received a letter from my uncle with the enclosed recipes. He collected them on his current voyage through the West Indies and into the Americas, and I hope they will add to your project in some small way. I hope also that you will allow me to read your final project once you have finished it, and that my absence from Cavendish Square will allow you more time to focus on your own work and graduate from the Royal Academy with every honor you rightly deserve. I know a gentleman should never put a lady in an awkward position, but I do wish to state that despite

the drills, late nights, difficulties, and disagreements of the
last months, and this final (probably inevitable) row with
Lady Helena, I would do it over again, as I wouldn't trade
the privilege of your friendship for anything. If you ever need
anything at all, I hope you won't hesitate to call on me.

> *Yours,*
> *Elijah*

Penelope's gaze lingered over the last words and his signature. They'd put him through all the trials of Hades these last months, but he still would do it again. For *her* friendship. Penelope licked her lips. Her throat had gone dry.

She shuffled through the recipes behind Elijah's letter. Everything from tostadas to grilled fish, and a surprising preponderance of roasted goat variations, that Elijah's uncle had collected from Mexico, Central America, and Brazil were there, all written out in Elijah's hand. At the end, he'd even included his recipes for empanadas from a variety of different countries.

Penelope ran her fingertips over the ink of the last recipe. *Salvadoran Empanadas.* She didn't know when he'd found the time to copy all these recipes out for her—he'd certainly had very little free time in the last few weeks as they'd prepared for the exhibition.

She, meanwhile, had allowed Helena to treat him more like an experiment than a person. Penelope had tried to teach him in other ways and supplement what she had plainly seen Helena couldn't or wouldn't provide him in the way of sympathy or understanding, but if this morning had taught Penelope anything, it was that by taking more of Elijah's education on herself, she'd allowed Helena to believe her own methods were working—that she could continue to treat him like a recalcitrant child instead of a boy their own age who simply hadn't been blessed with the same opportunities.

In reality, Penelope had done Elijah a great disservice, and all he wanted to do was thank her for it. Her stomach churned. He deserved so much better. He truly was one of the most talented cooks she'd ever met and he *merited* recognition. And a true culinary education—not second-rate schooling from two girls who thought they knew everything though they weren't *actually* Culinarians yet. Penelope, it seemed, didn't even truly know her best friend. She never thought Helena would react in such a bigoted—yes, *bigoted* was the right word, though Penelope hated to admit it—way to Elijah's admission, let alone pretend that Penelope wasn't the child of a mixed union. But she had. And that spoke volumes. Penelope folded the letter and recipes. She needed to apologize to Elijah.

Penelope glanced at the clock ticking over the mantelpiece. If she left now, she might still be able to reach Hampton Court before Elijah began cooking.

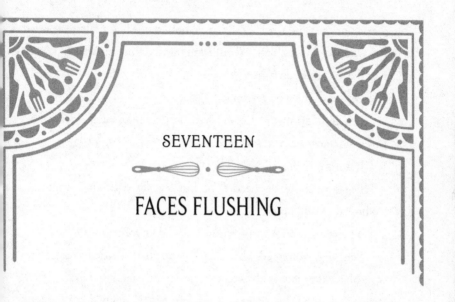

SEVENTEEN

FACES FLUSHING

Penelope hurried through the garden at Hampton Court and made her way to the back entrance of the palace where Elijah and his fellow competitors were supposed to meet. Hiring a boat to take her down the Thames had taken far longer than she anticipated, and she now had little hope that Elijah had not yet gone into the palace kitchen. She strode to the back entrance all the same, looking around the grounds in case he happened to be milling about with the attendees and other exhibitors. Diverse smells and sounds wafted through the air toward her, but she ignored them all.

Finally, she spotted a group of people waiting by the palace door. Penelope wended her way through them, scanning for Elijah, but he wasn't among them.

"Pardon me," she said to a tall lady with olive skin. The woman wore a beautifully ornate apron embroidered in multicolored thread. Under normal circumstances, Penelope might have asked about the apron's origins and whether she could obtain one herself, but she was too worried about Elijah. "Would you mind telling me which designated cook time you have?"

"Eleven," the woman replied.

Penelope grimaced. Elijah's had been at ten, which meant he was inside now as she'd suspected.

"And you?" the lady asked her.

Penelope shook her head. "Oh, I believe my friend just went in. I'd hoped to catch him."

The woman raised an eyebrow but said no more.

Penelope wondered what that meant, then decided she didn't care. She was perfectly allowed to have a male friend.

The door to the palace opened, and Mabel stepped out with a piece of paper and a pencil in hand. "Good morning!" she greeted them. "I shall be confirming all competitors for the eleven and noon cooking spots. Please tell me your names, and—oh hello, Penelope," she said once she caught sight of Penelope's waving hand. "I'm afraid this entrance is for cooking competitors only."

"Yes, I know, Mabel. I was looking for El—Mr. Little. Did he go in?"

Mabel tilted her head. "Why, yes. He's preparing now with the other ten o'clocks."

Penelope bit her lower lip. "Very good. I shall see you later, no doubt. Good luck to you all," she said with an apologetic look at the people waiting. She turned to go.

"Penelope," Mabel said, "certain choice people are being allowed to watch the tastings from the Minstrels' Gallery. If you'd like, I could ask Lady Rutland if you may be admitted." She arched her brows.

Penelope hesitated. If she agreed, would Mabel wish for a favor in return? Normally Penelope wouldn't have been concerned, but if Mabel truly was spreading ugly rumors about Penelope's parents—and for all her faults, Penelope didn't think Helena would lie about such a thing—Penelope had no wish to be in debt to such a person. On the other hand, she'd never known Mabel to be vindictive. Silly, yes. Quick to brag about any small thing, yes. Perhaps this was simply Mabel's way of showing her standing with Lady Rutland and here at the palace. If so, there was little point in not taking advantage of her self-importance.

Penelope smiled. "Thank you, Mabel. I should like that very much."

Mabel pulled delicately at her gloves as a satisfied smile played at her lips. "Just wait a moment while I take note of each competitor."

Penelope nodded, and Mabel proceeded to ask everyone's name and mark their presence on her list. "You may return a quarter hour before your call time, and I shall escort you into the kitchens. Feel free to sample the exhibition booths until then." The people murmured their assent and wandered off. Mabel motioned for Penelope to follow her inside.

They entered a paneled hall and Penelope, who had never been inside Hampton Court before, immediately felt as though she was following in the (very literal) footsteps of the Tudors. She exhaled, thinking how glad she was to be living in a time when women were more than just playthings for a man to toy with. Then her mind flitted to Elijah. His people wouldn't even have been tolerated in England when Hampton Court had been built. Society had come a long way since the sixteenth century, but clearly not far enough. Helena's recent behavior was proof enough of that.

"I just knew Princess Adelaide would enjoy Mr. Little's dish yesterday," Mabel said, half turning back to Penelope to see her reaction.

"You were right, it seems," Penelope agreed, still lost in thought.

Mabel paused, as though waiting for more of an answer. "He is a most impressive young man, wouldn't you agree?"

Penelope's ears perked up. She recognized fishing when she heard it. She considered how much she should say. "His diligence is admirable."

Penelope didn't really think that would appease Mabel's curiosity, but she was still surprised when it brought Mabel directly to the point.

"Have you known him long?"

Luckily, Penelope and Helena had rehearsed answers to this question if it happened to come up.

"I believe it was sometime in the winter. We came across him buying verjus at Smithfield's Purveyors, and Helena and I were both so intrigued that a young man would have any interest in verjus that we struck up a conversation. We saw him again at the culinary faire."

"Ah! How fortunate that you happened to meet again," Mabel said.

"As you know, the culinary world is still a small one." Penelope hoped she was being convincing enough—she really was no actress.

"Oh indeed," Mabel agreed. "Finding a young man of fine birth and standing who also has a palate of great discernment is almost like trying to find a sesame seed in a sack of flour."

"I suppose so," Penelope replied, wondering what Mabel was driving at. Could she somehow have guessed who Elijah really was?

Mabel turned to face Penelope again. "Princess Adelaide has *often* said so."

Penelope blinked. "Has she?"

Mabel briefly closed her eyes as she nodded, as though she were divulging a great secret. "Oh yes."

"I daresay it must be even more difficult for someone in the princess's position," Penelope said tentatively.

"Indeed it is. Which is why . . . I wonder if you might tell me if you think Mr. Little to be all those things. Would you"—she gave a little shrug—"vouch for him, as it were?"

Penelope bit the inside of her cheek. Mabel was asking her about Elijah so she could relay the information to the princess. Of course, Princess Adelaide hadn't even met Elijah yet, but he must have impressed Mabel enough yesterday for her to be interested in him on the princess's behalf. Whether Mabel would have the opportunity to tell Princess Adelaide anything before today's judging began, Penelope could not guess, but she also knew that no matter the consequences, she had only one answer to Mabel's question.

She looked Mabel in the eye. "I would indeed vouch for him. He is everything a gentleman chef should be." And in her heart, she knew it to be true.

Elijah concentrated on folding his shirtsleeves to his elbows as Lady Rutland explained today's rules and procedures to him and his two competitors from where she stood behind a long wooden table. The royal kitchen at Hampton Court was so grand and so spotless that Elijah found it difficult not to stare at his surroundings.

When Queen Charlotte had taken the throne, she had distanced herself from her mad grandfather George III and her highly unpopular father by adopting new traditions that still hearkened back to an older time. Though Hampton Court had fallen out of favor as a royal residence in the reign of Queen Charlotte's great-grandfather, she had reinstated its importance as a summer palace. Part of that effort had fallen to the Royal Culinary Exhibition, and the queen soon decided to renovate the old Tudor kitchens into a massive kitchen more modern and grand than even her father's Great Kitchen at the Royal Pavilion in Brighton.

The new Glorious Kitchen at Hampton Court boasted everything from a state-of-the-art ventilation system, high windows to let light in, an elaborate ceiling decorated with painted copper vegetables, an unending supply of water, the latest in steam-heating technology, a massive fireplace with automatic roasting spits, and the longest stove Elijah had ever seen, which sat against an entire wall.

Had Elijah thought too much about the circumstances that had brought him here, to this kitchen more magnificent than any place he'd ever imagined cooking, he might have fled the room, so instead he thought of Penelope. How she'd spent long hours teaching him when she should have worked on her own project. Of that partial dimple that appeared at the side of her mouth when she was happy.

If she had read his letter and what she must think of him. The latter thought made his throat go dry, so he centered his gaze on Lady Rutland.

"As you all know," Lady Rutland said, "you are tasked with creating a dish fit for a queen—using today's fresh catch. Queen Charlotte, of course, shall be judging today along with Princess Adelaide and myself." Lady Rutland gestured to a selection of whole fish, clams, oysters, cockles, lobster, and langoustine sitting on ice on the wooden table before her. "You may use whatever you choose from what's here, as well as any ingredient in the larder." She pointed to a large, well-lit room to Elijah's left. From his vantage, it looked as well stocked as the house at Cavendish Square, if not more so, which he'd expected. Still, it was an entirely different matter to actually have the abundance that royalty could command at one's fingertips.

"You shall have a quarter of an hour to plan and determine which ingredients you'll need. You'll then have three quarters of an hour to cook and plate your dish, and at the end of the hour, a few minutes to collect yourself before a footman escorts you to the Great Hall to present yourself and your dish to the tasting panel. You may produce one large platter to be shared and portion it yourself at judging, or three separate plates with identical portions. Cooking and judging shall be staggered, so please choose a token to determine in which order you'll be cooking."

Lady Rutland held out a small, blue velvet bag with both hands. Elijah glanced at his competitors, and stepped forward until he stood before Lady Rutland.

Elijah and the other man, a nobleman from the Grand Duchy of Tuscany who appeared to be in his late twenties, both bowed to let the lady competitor choose first. When they had given their names to Mabel, the lady—a stout woman with hair beginning to gray—had said she was from Wales, which meant she had to be either a Culinarian or an amateur cook. Judging by her age, Elijah thought she must be the latter. His suspicions were further confirmed when Lady Rutland gave no outward appearance of knowing her as the woman pulled a wooden token from the bag.

The Tuscan went next, giving a little bow to Lady Rutland. He smiled at his token as he inspected it.

Elijah gave Lady Rutland a nod as he pulled out the last token. A faint smile tugged at the corner of her lips, but she did not speak.

One side of the token was blank, but when Elijah flipped it over, the number 3 stared back at him. Elijah exhaled. He'd hoped to cook second, but third had to be better than being the first to cook.

"Who shall be going first?" Lady Rutland asked.

The Tuscan raised his token in the air.

Lady Rutland nodded. "And second?"

The Welsh lady raised hers.

"And Mr. Little shall go third," Lady Rutland said with a glance at him.

Elijah inclined his head.

"Very good," Lady Rutland said. "You all have a quarter hour starting now to choose your seafood and ingredients. Comte," she addressed the Tuscan, "I shall tell you when to begin cooking, but in the meantime, you may all choose your seafood."

They approached the table. The comte immediately grabbed as many clams as he could from the ice, along with two squid. Elijah had his eye on the sea bass, which he took quickly, careful of the spiky dorsal fin, so as not to cut himself. Someone had gutted and cleaned the fish, and Elijah sent silent thanks to whoever they were. Cleaning the fish would have severely eaten into his time. The lady took two of the dabs and started snatching the cockles. Elijah wanted to do something fried or sautéed, as well as a ceviche if they had the right ingredients in the larder, so he made the decision to take some oysters as well and drop everything at his cooking station before heading to the larder. If his competition chose everything else, which he doubted, his bass was large enough to feed three people well, even with all the ideas flying through his mind.

The larder was indeed larger than the one at Cavendish Square. In actuality it was double the size of his uncle's room on Old Fish Street. Elijah took a deep breath and concentrated on the task at hand. Baskets of fruits and vegetables lined the shelves, as did bags of flour, salt, sugar, and small jars of spices in triplicate. Fresh herbs sat in jars of water, and dried herbs hung in bundles from a rack on the ceiling.

Elijah first looked for citrus, onions, and chili peppers for the basis of his ceviche. To his relief, he found not only lemons but Seville oranges and Persian limes. He took some of each. Onions were there in abundance, as he would have guessed, and he gathered a few red onions and a dried bulb of garlic. The store of chilies was sparser, but they had amassed a small variety. Elijah pulled one of each to test for heat. He was also surprised, but eager, to see a bushel of plantains, brown coconuts, and one pineapple, which he seized quickly, just as he wondered if each slot of competitors was supplied one pineapple or if he'd taken the only one. He also pulled a variety of herbs, some small, thin-skinned potatoes, and a jar of mustard seeds before heading back to his worktable to drop everything.

"You have seven minutes remaining to take what you wish from the fish table and larder," Lady Rutland announced. "You may return for more supplies while you are cooking, but you shall have to make do with whatever remains at that time. I highly suggest you get all you need now—especially those of you cooking second and third."

Elijah glanced back at the fish table, considering what more he might need. Had he more time, he might have cured salmon or trout. He considered salt-crusting a mackerel as he'd practiced with Penelope, but thought cracking the salt crust for the judges might prove a messy prospect that could go either way. He returned to the fish table and took a small cod that he thought he could fashion into some kind of fritter.

The rest of the shellfish had been picked over by his competitors, but other than the oysters, which he thought he might bake, he didn't much care. Despite what he'd told Penelope about eating shellfish when necessary, he didn't seek it out. The times he'd eaten it—usually when it was the cheapest thing at the market or one of the fishmongers had an abundance they wanted to get rid of—he'd always felt a lingering sense of guilt, even if his overriding instinct was that neither God nor his parents would want him to starve. Of course, who could ever say what God wanted, but Elijah had gotten here, for better or worse, and he could cook well without compromising himself or his traditions. He pushed last night's scene with Helena from his mind, and decided to leave out the oysters altogether.

"Two minutes remaining," Lady Rutland called.

Elijah returned to the larder and picked a rye loaf, butter, eggs, bell peppers, and one of Penelope's favorite chili powders—chili de árbol—from the spices. He didn't know what she'd think after hearing whatever Helena had told her about the night before, but he would make a dish worthy of her today. After that, he'd worry about tomorrow, the rest of his life, and what in the world he planned to do about it.

⁂

Penelope leaned forward in her chair to peer out the open doorway of the Minstrels' Gallery to where Lady Rutland, Queen Charlotte, and Princess Adelaide sat behind a long table running down the center of the Great Hall. Mrs. Rowlands from Wales had just presented whole roasted dabs and a cockle sauce with individual-sized Welsh leek-and-onion cakes. Fried leeks arranged in a decorative pattern completed the platter. Queen Charlotte had been polite and gracious as Penelope had always seen her be, but Lady Rutland and Princess Adelaide had mentioned that the cockles in the sauce were a tad too chewy for their liking.

The panel seemed more united in their opinion of the Comte di Fratini, who had presented first. He cut a fine figure with his dark, curly hair and impeccably tailored green frock coat. Now knowing what Helena had said about Princess Adelaide choosing a husband from the finalists, Penelope had tried to gauge the princess's reaction to the comte's charms and food.

Princess Adelaide hadn't shown him any particular favor, but she had seemed to enjoy his freshly made pasta colored with squid ink and peppered throughout with clams, mussels, more squid, and roasted fennel. White wine finished the sauce, and he'd topped the entire dish with fried squid tentacles coated in rice flour and lightly dusted with fennel pollen. The princess's face had transformed from a mask of politeness into one of surprise as she'd taken a bite and then gone back for more. Penelope would wager that the comte had a good chance of advancing to tomorrow.

"Mr. Elijah Little of London," a steward announced.

Penelope held her breath as two liveried footmen with plates entered the room followed by Elijah. Though he mustn't have gotten much sleep, he looked like the most dapper of gentlemen chefs. He walked into the Great Hall without a hint of trepidation, standing straight as they'd taught him, his jawline parallel to the floor. He had come so far from the scraggly, slouched young man with a mop of wavy hair and a tray of empanadas. His height was an advantage she'd often heard Helena reminding him to utilize, and as much as the thought of Helena harping on Elijah set Penelope's pulse pounding, she couldn't deny that Elijah heeding this point made him look like he belonged in this grand palace.

He'd worn his ash-gray coat and tan trousers today, and the coat—which had been one of her choices and not Helena's—was still perfectly pressed and clean, from what she could see. Perhaps he wasn't a count or a prince, but he looked every bit what a princess's consort should. Elegant. Restrained. Handsome. Now only his cooking remained. The footmen set the plates in front of the queen, Lady Rutland, and Princess Adelaide.

"Good morning, Mr. Little," Queen Charlotte said with a serene smile.

Elijah bowed from the neck as they'd shown him. "Your Majesty."

Penelope held her breath again, but if Elijah felt overawed, he certainly didn't betray it. The queen wore an exquisite day dress of cornflower-blue silk with wide, translucent silk net sleeves. Her auburn hair had been twisted into an intricate loop at the crown of her head and woven through with a bejeweled chain.

She peered down her straight, rather prominent nose at Elijah. "You are most welcome. I imagine you know my daughter and Lady Rutland even if you've not met," the queen said.

Elijah nodded at both women. "Your Royal Highness. Lady Rutland. It is an honor to be cooking for such distinguished ladies."

Penelope thought she saw Lady Rutland smile. The princess presented a neutral expression that was almost a copy of the queen's, except for the dark, perceptive eyes and high cheekbones that she'd inherited from her father.

"Would you be so good as to tell us what you've prepared?" the queen asked, motioning for the footmen to remove the silver cloches from the plates.

Elijah stood a bit straighter. "Today I've prepared a dish I'm calling 'Sea Bass of Three.' The first is a citrus ceviche with yellow chilies and a hint of preserved lemon, to be eaten with plantain crisps on the left of your plate."

Even from her vantage, Penelope could see Elijah had molded the ceviche into a vague fish shape that pointed to the center of the plate.

"Next, in the center, is a pan-sautéed fillet of sea bass coated in chili de árbol, and paprika potatoes sliced and arranged to resemble fish scales," Elijah continued.

Penelope's mouth watered at the sight of the fillet, which looked perfectly crisp and very much resembled a small fish. It again seemed to point to the third and final part of the dish, thanks to the way he'd arranged it all.

"And for the final phase, you have a sea-bass-and-cod fritter with fresh coriander leaves, serrano chilies, and a pineapple, chili, and lime foam."

The queen and the princess nodded and started to eat the ceviche.

"Will you explain what you've done with the samphire?" Lady Rutland asked, pointing to the green seaweed that resembled very thin asparagus spears.

"The samphire is meant to symbolize the sea, just as the pineapple foam is meant to suggest sea foam. I sautéed the samphire in a spiced butter," Elijah replied.

Penelope grinned from her seat behind the Minstrels' Gallery's open door. He'd almost made it look like the fish (especially the potato-scaled fillet in the center) was still swimming in the sea. From what she could see, he'd dotted the foam in strategic places on the plate, including near the ceviche, so one could take a bite with a plantain crisp and the foam, or try it plain.

"Is this 'ceviche' as you call it—is it cooked?" Princess Adelaide asked.

Penelope had been paying so much attention to Elijah, she'd forgotten to watch Princess Adelaide. Penelope's eyes snapped to her now, but from where she sat, she could really only see part of the princess's profile.

"Not cooked so much as marinated in citrus juice, which cures the fish while maintaining the soft texture," Elijah said.

"I don't think I've had something like this before," the princess said. She looked at Lady Rutland. "Have you, Lady Rutland?"

"It is rarely seen in Britain and Europe, but I have had occasion to try it," Lady Rutland said as she delicately chewed. "I believe it hails from the Americas, does it not, Mr. Little?"

Elijah paused for a moment. Then Penelope saw him start to smile for the first time since entering the hall. "Yes, Lady Rutland. I do tend to draw inspiration from their cuisine."

Lady Rutland nodded, adopting a smile of her own.

Penelope bit her lip. She hoped her influence wouldn't go against Elijah in the judging. Of course, Lady Rutland was the only one who knew that Helena and Penelope had taught him, and she didn't think Lady Rutland would ruin his chances in the competition. It would go against everything they'd set out to do. But if Lady Rutland thought he couldn't cook for himself . . . Penelope shook her head. That was absurd. No one had been in that kitchen helping Elijah today. And he'd had an interest in the Americas long before he and Penelope had met—Lady Rutland had even tasted his empanadas.

"I especially love the fritter," Princess Adelaide said. "It's so very light."

"I could eat three more," said the queen with a laugh.

Elijah's grin widened. "Thank you, Your Majesty."

"The pineapple foam sounded strange, but it accompanies everything so well," the princess went on. "And the whimsy of the potato scales and the samphire—quite clever. Would not you agree, Mama?"

The queen nodded. "Very well done, Mr. Little."

Penelope wanted to jump from her seat, but she clapped a hand to her mouth as her toes danced beneath her skirt. She looked at Elijah, wishing she could catch his attention.

"Yes indeed," Princess Adelaide concurred. She gave Elijah an inviting smile. Penelope's chest constricted. "Thank you for a delightful dish."

Elijah murmured his thanks and bowed to the room. As he walked out with his head high, Penelope watched Princess Adelaide whisper something to the queen and then sit back in her chair with a short giggle. The princess's gaze darted to the doorway Elijah had disappeared through before she began filling out the scorecard that the steward handed her.

Penelope swallowed twice. Her pulse beat a quick tattoo, and she didn't think it wholly because of her excitement for how well Elijah had done on his first day cooking for the monarch. She had to see him. With one last glance at the princess busily writing, Penelope picked up her reticule and hurried out of the gallery.

⁓⁓

Penelope caught sight of Elijah as he exited the palace door. She'd been waiting some way off to ensure none of the competitors would ask her any questions, but now she hurried forward so Elijah couldn't help but see her.

"El—" She caught herself. "Mr. Little," she called.

His eyes met hers as he moved through the small group waiting to be confirmed for their time slot.

She didn't know what to make of his smile, for it came and went in the blink of an eye.

"Miss Pickering," he said as though they were only common acquaintances, "good morning."

Though it was exactly what he should have said, Penelope wished they weren't in front of so many prying eyes so they could speak properly. She tried to angle her neck back toward the podium where Lady Rutland had spoken yesterday, hoping he'd catch her hint.

Elijah inclined his head, and they moved away from the group. Once they were out of earshot, Penelope spoke. "You were so wonderful just now! Mabel and Lady Rutland let me watch from the gallery. The potato scales on the fillet looked beautiful, and the pineapple chili foam was so clever—you must show me how you did it—and most importantly, they were *all* impressed. Even the queen. You were—" She broke off as that bold grin of his washed over his face. Then she laughed. "You were simply . . . magnificent. I wish I could have tasted it all."

He raised a brow. "I just so happen to have saved the last fritter for you." He put his hand under the lapel of his coat, reaching for his breast pocket.

"Wait," Penelope said, "did you really?" She hoped he hadn't ruined the fabric, but also couldn't decide if it mattered.

He laughed at the look on her face, which was a mixture of hope and disapproval. "I'm afraid not," he said, holding open his empty hand. She giggled, glad he was in good spirits, yet rather disappointed not to try the fritter just the same.

"I didn't know if I would see you today," he said. "Otherwise I would have saved you a few. As it is, though, I'll be happy to make them for you anytime you wish."

Penelope blinked at him. The way he'd said it seemed to imply something more than just as two friends who cooked together. It seemed to imply something more than gratitude or gentlemanly conduct. It just seemed . . . more. But maybe she was imagining it? She wet her lips.

"I'm so sorry about last night. Helena had no excuse to say what she did to you, Elijah. I wish I'd been there. I would have told her so. But—" Penelope took a deep breath and tried to meet his rich brown eyes. "I have failed you in all the ways that count. I should have told her—so many times—to leave you be or to be kinder or—"

"I never blamed you," Elijah cut in. "I asked for this, and *I* said yes to the scheme even with an idea of the difficulties involved. I knew she would react badly to who I am. I believe I mentioned as much." He shrugged.

Penelope swallowed against the thickness in her throat. "You were right." She shook her head at herself. "I always thought she took my parents' marriage so well. But yesterday she told Mabel that anything she'd heard about them was a lie. Instead of saying there was nothing immoral or wrong about their marriage, Helena lied. I cannot believe I ever thought her anything but ashamed of my origin. Or that she'd feel any different about you. I just—" She sighed and looked into Elijah's eyes. "I thought she was my friend."

A line materialized on his brow. "You see the best in people.

Nothing wrong with that."

Penelope certainly didn't feel that way at the moment. "Thank you so much for the recipes. They are perfect."

His eyes warmed.

"When did you have the time to copy them out?"

He fiddled with one of the buttons of his coat, avoiding her gaze. "I made time. Will they help?"

"Of course they shall. It was so thoughtful of you. I—" She didn't know what else to say, so she took a deep breath and beamed at him. "I appreciate it more than I can say."

His eyes captured hers, and she found she couldn't look away.

"And I appreciate everything you've done for me," he said. "You never treated me like a Jewish street peddler. You treated me like a gentleman even before I knew how to talk or act like one." His smile curved up in that familiar grin, and Penelope realized for the very first time—and with shocking force—that she wanted him to kiss her. The thought left her slightly breathless.

"She, on the other hand, treats gentlemen like street peddlers," he finished, turning half of Penelope's thoughts away from kisses and back to Helena.

She sighed. "I rather think the point is that everyone should be treated the same, don't you?"

His brow furrowed as he considered. "That's not the world we live in. Certainly not anywhere I've ever seen."

"Nor I, but that was what I thought Helena's project would prove. That your success would mean others could follow in your footsteps. Not only in food, but in every field." She bit her lip.

He looked around them. "Perhaps I can use all this to start a permanent stall at the night market." He raised his brows, clearly trying to lighten the tone of the conversation. "Should be able to make a killing with those fritters, don't you think?"

Penelope laughed. "I don't believe I should venture a professional opinion before I've tried them."

He inclined his head toward her. "Very wise."

"But in all seriousness, the queen *and* the princess found them delectable. I very much doubt that a distinguished gentleman chef such as yourself will find it necessary to work at the night market again. You could do any number of things now. Of course, if you *want* to return to the night market, you could. Have you given any thought as to what you'd like to do?" The unspoken implication of *now that Helena couldn't influence him* escaped neither of them.

Elijah watched Penelope carefully. "Can you really believe that someone like me can get all he wants?"

She raised her chin. "I can and I do."

He took a deep breath. "I don't really belong anywhere now. I can't go back to my uncle's lodgings at Old Fish Street. No one'll recognize me. And if I tell them what I did, I'll be like some sort of oddity."

Penelope wrung her hands together as a lump rose in her throat.

"I haven't decided what I'm going to do after all this," Elijah continued. "But, there is something I've been thinking about. I—"

"Little, good chap! Miss Pickering!" Freddie Eynsford-Hill's jolly greeting, which he'd shouted from some yards away, brought Elijah's speech to a halt.

Penelope bit her lip, wondering what he'd been about to say. She gave Mr. Eynsford-Hill a little wave as he bounded over to them.

"How'd it pan out?" Freddie asked Elijah after they'd all dispensed with the necessary pleasantries. He laughed. "Pun intended."

"Not at all bad," Elijah replied.

"Actually, he was a triumph," Penelope cut in. "Mabel and Lady Rutland let me watch the first-round judging from the Minstrels' Gallery. Queen Charlotte and Princess Adelaide were *most* impressed."

Elijah looked rather embarrassed, but Freddie clapped him on the shoulder. "You don't say? Good show, old boy."

Elijah murmured his thanks.

"Do you exhibit at the tent again?" Freddie asked.

Elijah shook his head. "Only those not chosen for the top twenty exhibit in their tents today."

"Excellent," Freddie said. "Then we can find some luncheon together. You didn't get to sample the other tents' offerings yesterday, and I'm sure Miss Pickering must be in want of some delicacy or other after watching the judging. What say you both?" His openness and enthusiasm for food that, of course, Penelope and Elijah both shared made it difficult to refuse him.

Even though they both would have preferred to continue their private conversation, Penelope was too polite to say so, and Elijah's state of mind hovered somewhere between annoyance at Freddie's presence and a desire to keep the two of them from being alone together. So the trio set out to sample the delicacies of the Persian tent, with two of the three wondering if the day was about to take a turn for the worse.

Later that afternoon, Helena approached the back entrance of Hampton Court where she knew the competitors had been told to wait. She'd been battling with a headache since her discussion with Penelope that morning and had almost decided to stay at Cavendish Square for the rest of the day. Her apprehension that Elijah would throw away everything she had gifted him had dragged her into the carriage and out of London to the exhibition. She'd known she'd arrive long after Elijah's cooking time, but even if he hadn't appeared to cook, at least she would be able to explain why to Lady Rutland.

"Hello, Mabel," Helena said once Mabel stepped outside with her list in hand.

Mabel arched a brow. "Helena. I take it you and Penelope came separately."

Helena rightly concluded this to mean Mabel had already seen Penelope. "I had more work to attend to on my project. Might I see Lady Rutland?"

Mabel sniffed. "She is quite busy, you know."

"I only need a moment."

"If this is about our conversation yesterday, then surely it can wait until later," Mabel said.

Helena blinked as she realized Mabel was worried she was about to tell Lady Rutland about Mabel spreading rumors about Penelope. "It's to do with my project," Helena said. "I need her counsel. If you'd be so kind, Mabel." It irked Helena to appeal to Mabel's vanity, but if it worked . . .

Mabel exhaled. "Very well. She may have *a* moment between time slots. I must confirm everyone is here first, however."

Helena pressed her lips together to keep from smirking, and waited as Mabel took the competitors' names. Mabel then ushered Helena inside, took her to a small sitting room with serviceable furniture, and told her to wait. After ten minutes or so, during which Helena's headache came and went at unpredictable intervals, Lady Rutland walked in.

"Helena, I'm afraid I must be brief. Mabel said you needed to speak about your project."

Helena nodded. "Thank you, Lady Rutland. I wanted to ask you if Mr. Little cooked this morning?"

Lady Rutland's eyebrows rose. "He did indeed. Quite well, as a matter of fact. Had you reason to doubt it?"

Helena tried to smile. "Not really. Last night he seemed a trifle disinclined to continue in the competition, so I merely thought to ask—"

"Why was he disinclined?"

Helena debated whether or not to tell Lady Rutland what she knew about the princess choosing a husband from amongst the finalists. She realized it would reflect worse on Mabel's loose tongue than on her, so she decided to forge ahead. "Mabel told me Princess Adelaide would be choosing a husband from the top ten competitors. I told Mr. Little I thought he could become a finalist. He—he wasn't particularly interested."

Lady Rutland exhaled. "Mabel should not have divulged that information. I will speak with her. However, it shall be common knowledge by the end of the day when the finalists are announced. You, on the other hand, should have come to me for confirmation before telling Mr. Little."

Helena nodded. "I also must tell you that Mabel and Dora Smith-Smythe have been spreading vicious rumors about Penelope's parentage. Mabel claimed Dora heard a professor talking about it. I told her I fully intended to come to you with the information." At the moment, Helena didn't care a fig if she'd implied to Mabel that she wouldn't say anything just yet.

Lady Rutland frowned. "How is Penelope?"

Helena bit the inside of her cheek. "She tried to kill the messenger, I'm afraid. I told her I denied everything to Mabel, but she berated *me*. She said I should have told Mabel the truth—as though Mabel wouldn't have exaggerated even the truth out of proportion and ruined Penelope's future prospects, in any case. Penelope said I couldn't understand what she or Elijah must live with—"

"And you think you can understand the difficulties of a young street hawker with no money or connections and those of a girl of mixed race whose parents have chosen to stay out of England to protect her?" Lady Rutland asked.

Helena wobbled her head, then promptly stopped when it intensified the throbbing on the left side. "I don't see why not."

Lady Rutland arched a brow. "In your years at the Royal Academy, I've known you to be a student capable of everything one might challenge you with Culinarily. However, you have never been able to adapt well to anyone who challenged *you* as a person. Mr. Little and Penelope have other trials in their lives that you will never face."

"That doesn't mean they cannot rise above them," Helena argued.

"Indeed, that was the objective of your project, was it not?"

Helena couldn't deny it.

"It appears to me as though Mr. Little has accomplished every goal you had for him. The queen and Princess Adelaide were quite impressed with his food and presentation, and I—"

"Yes, but he—" Helena tried to interrupt.

"Helena, you wished to graduate from the Royal Academy with honors, and *he* has accomplished that for you. I suggest that this be the end of the experiment. If Mr. Little advances today, he must decide whether or not to compete. And you should not attempt to influence him further. Is that quite clear?" Lady Rutland tilted her chin down and regarded Helena with a steady gaze.

Helena nodded. She could go about her life now without the worries of having to teach that lying empanada peddler anything else. It should be a freeing prospect. Why, then, had the pounding in her head doubled?

⚮

"I say, this custard tart has cardamom. I quite like it, though," Freddie said, putting the rest of it in his mouth. "What do you think, Miss Pickering?" he asked between bites.

"It's utterly decadent," Penelope said, giving one of the gentlemen from the Portuguese delegation a smile. "So brave of you to play with the traditional pastéis de nata."

Elijah crunched into the soft custard and perfectly flaky pastry beneath as the Portuguese gentleman gave Penelope a flirtatious wink. As luscious as the tart had tasted a moment prior, any trace of the sugary custard's flavor evaporated as Elijah watched the interaction. He looked away, remembering the days when he might have done the same without a second thought. But not now. *English* gentlemen didn't *do* such things.

"Shall we, Miss Pickering?" Freddie said, offering Penelope his arm.

"Yes, I believe the Croatian tent is next," Elijah stated, also offering his arm. Penelope and Helena had taught him a great deal about being an English gentleman, but he had learned quite a bit from Freddie Eynsford-Hill during the last couple of hours. Many of those things only made Elijah more self-conscious. Freddie had an ease of manner Elijah didn't know if he'd ever master in this new guise. Lord knew he'd had it before—he'd used it to great advantage at the night market—but now he felt like it had been thrown onto the rubbish heap with his ratty clothes.

Freddie's food knowledge was nothing like his own, but Freddie didn't need it. No one treated him as anything less than a gentleman, and no one—perhaps excepting Helena—ever would. He could cook when the feeling struck him, court any lady he pleased, do as he pleased, and no one would ever question him. Life would always come easy for Freddie Eynsford-Hill. And it was becoming abundantly clear from all the interest he'd paid Penelope this afternoon that Freddie believed his attentions to her would easily bring him the outcome he wished.

Penelope looked at them both, thanked the Portuguese gentleman, and took their arms. Elijah felt the pressure of her small, warm hand resting on his coat and thought back to the day she'd taught him to dance. She'd been so patient and sweet. As she always was. He looked down at the top of her lavender bonnet and wished he'd had the chance to tell her how he felt before Freddie had appeared. He'd hoped, rather than thought, that she'd understand his letter and gift for what it was. That when he'd said last night that he couldn't marry the princess, somehow Penelope would understand it was because he cared for *her*. He'd almost thought he'd seen that recognition in her face today. But then Freddie had interrupted them.

Freddie and Penelope spoke to the ladies at the Croatian booth, asking questions about their food, and finally taking some plates. Penelope handed one to Elijah, but he put up his hand to refuse. They'd been eating all afternoon, and though he still remembered the days when he had more appetite than food to eat, his hunger had just deserted him. He watched Freddie watching Penelope take small, delicate bites, an expression of interest evident in his countenance. As though she were some puzzle to decipher.

Penelope closed her eyes and made a sound in the back of her throat, something she often did when she truly enjoyed a flavor. Elijah had thought it endearing when he'd first noticed it, and he'd made rather a habit of trying to elicit the response during the last few weeks. But espying Freddie Eynsford-Hill observe her in that manner brought out some protective instinct Elijah didn't know he had. He cleared his throat loudly, and when Freddie glanced in his direction, Elijah gave him a knowing look.

Freddie shrugged in a careless way. He handed back his plate to the Croatian lady and pulled out a pocket watch. "I wonder when they'll announce the finalists," he said.

"I believe the last cooking time is four o'clock," Penelope said.

"It's almost five now. Must be soon." Freddie put his watch away. "Will you both be attending tomorrow's ball?"

Penelope started toward the next booth. "Yes. I'm quite looking forward to it." She looked back at Elijah, and he couldn't help but smile.

"Capital. Might I engage you for the first two dances, Miss Pickering?" Freddie asked.

The question squashed into Elijah like a rotten tomato. Why hadn't he thought to ask her? Perhaps because he hadn't even known he could ask for such a thing. He clenched his jaw. He certainly didn't remember the girls ever mentioning it.

Penelope looked at Freddie, then at Elijah. She seemed to hesitate. Then she gave Freddie a sweet smile. "Of course, Mr. Eynsford-Hill. I'd be delighted."

Her answer washed over Elijah with icy precision. What had he expected? For Freddie Eynsford-Hill, everything came easy. And Freddie had given Elijah an easy dose of reality. The hope Elijah had felt earlier when he'd seen Penelope waiting for him at the back of the palace faded into a slow, pulsing ache somewhere under his ribs. As he watched Freddie incline his head toward Penelope with a self-satisfied grin, Elijah considered, and not for the first time, what in hell he could do about it.

Penelope would have much preferred for Elijah to ask her to save the first two dances for him tomorrow evening. She did find Mr. Eynsford-Hill pleasant enough; he had a friendly, open manner and had been very attentive. Still, Penelope stole a glimpse at Elijah from beneath her lashes, wondering if he might ask her to reserve a different dance, but he refused to meet her gaze.

"Ah, there's Lady Helena," Freddie remarked.

Penelope's eyes shot forward. Sure enough, Helena marched toward them, a grimace etched across her usually carefree face. Penelope pressed her lips together and angled her body away from her. At least with Mr. Eynsford-Hill here, Helena couldn't create a scene. Penelope glanced at Elijah, but his face was an impassive mask.

Helena greeted them as she approached.

"Hello, Helena," Penelope said, unable to keep the frost from her voice. "You've missed a thoroughly pleasant afternoon." Though this wasn't strictly true since Penelope would have thought it more pleasant with only Elijah's company, she couldn't help herself from saying it.

Helena's gaze flicked from Elijah to Freddie. "How unfortunate. Excuse me, gentlemen, but might I have a word with Miss Pickering in private?"

Elijah's jaw shifted, but Freddie quickly gave his assent. "Of course. We'll move toward the tents closer to the podium. I imagine they'll be announcing the finalists soon. Come along, Little," he said to Elijah. Freddie touched the brim of his tall hat in the girls' direction and moved away.

Elijah said nothing, but he raised a brow at Penelope. She gave him a small nod, hoping it conveyed that she didn't wish him to be bothered with anything Helena might say. For once, Penelope had no intention of yielding. "I'll see you by the podium," Penelope told him. A line appeared between Elijah's brows, but he followed Freddie down the path.

"What is it, Helena?" Penelope asked once Elijah and Freddie were out of earshot.

Helena's green eyes looked anywhere but at her. "I may . . . I *might* have overreacted."

"Oh, really?" Sarcasm colored each syllable.

Helena straightened her spine. "I suppose I was just so surprised.

Elijah kept growing more and more skilled. With his talent, I thought I could make him into whatever I tried to. And I almost did. I think I was just angry that I'd wasted my time. And yours."

Penelope let out a breath. "You didn't waste your time. Elijah is not a waste—of anything! He's a person! With thoughts. And feelings. With experiences and ambitions all his own. Can't you see that?"

Helena sighed.

When she didn't reply, Penelope shook her head. "He should be whatever *he* wants. Not what you want, Helena. Thanks to us, he doesn't know where he belongs now. That's our fault."

Helena scoffed. "He went into this with his eyes open. More than we did, I believe. I certainly wouldn't have taken him on if I knew he couldn't rise to the heights of society—"

"Helena," Penelope cut in as an angry blush crept up her neck, "if you say that one more time, our friendship, such as it is, is over. Rising to society's heights was never Elijah's aim. All *he* wanted was a permanent stall at the market or a small shop—something modest that would allow him greater security. *You*, however, wanted to make him into some sort of luminary gentleman chef whom all of society would flock to. Despite my qualms, you argued that having Elijah compete as a gentleman would give him more opportunities, but all you wanted was the glory of telling the world that you turned a pasty hawker into a gentleman chef. And now that you find that Elijah's religion might be an obstacle in his way as far as society is concerned, you continue to diminish him."

Helena opened her mouth to protest, but Penelope didn't believe she could endure one more of Helena's skewed opinions about the truth of what had happened—what she'd done. "That young man can do anything he sets his mind to. He's proven that. Some of us have to fight every step of the way. Elijah more than most. So perhaps you might put your own petty assumptions aside and do something to actually build him up rather than blame him for *your* shortcomings and the faults in our society. I'll be leaving the town-house this evening."

Helena's mouth opened and closed. "You're leaving?"

Penelope gave a short nod. "I think it's best."

Helena raised her chin. "Very well. I don't need either of you. I much prefer to have the house to myself."

The heat suffusing Penelope's neck rushed to her ears. "You'll be quite happy, then." A horn sounded from the palace. They must be about to announce the top ten finalists. Penelope dragged in a steadying breath. "I hope you find that your self-conceit was worth the only friends you had."

She turned on her heel, unable to see Helena's reaction. As she hurried toward the gathering crowd, she spotted Elijah and Freddie. Lady Rutland had already announced a few names, and some people clapped others on the back and shook hands. Penelope made her way through the people until she stood by Elijah's side.

He raised his brows at her, then turned his gaze back to Lady Rutland at the podium. "What did she want?"

Penelope wet her lips. The warmth in her head had dissipated somewhat, but her pulse still jounced at an alarming rate. "Nothing of consequence. I told her I'd be leaving Cavendish Square tonight."

He looked down at her then, his forehead creased with concern. "Where will you go?"

"To a hotel, I imagine. Or perhaps there's a suitable inn near the palace."

"I—uh. I took a room at the Hungry Hare this morning," he replied. "They likely have another. We could inquire after—"

"Mr. Elijah Little of London," Lady Rutland's voice rang out over the crowd.

Elijah's eyes widened. Penelope's hand flew to her lips. Elijah looked toward the podium at Lady Rutland, who was already calling the next name. His gaze shot back to Penelope.

She laughed as she shook her head at the shock written on his handsome face. Then he laughed himself, his hazelnut-brown eyes still large—as though he didn't quite believe it.

"Jolly good show!" Freddie said on his other side. He offered Elijah his hand to shake.

A few others standing behind them also offered congratulations. Elijah thanked everyone with a self-deprecating smile, then turned back to Penelope.

"I told you," she said. "If you do well tomorrow, you can do anything you please." Unless Princess Adelaide took a liking to him, a small voice in her head screamed. If he turned the princess down, as he'd clearly stated he wanted to do last night, then his prospects would evaporate.

He exhaled and moved his hand to the back of his head as if to rub the back of his neck, then he seemed to remember his gentlemanly training and settled for smoothing the collar of his coat.

Lady Rutland finished the list with the Tuscan count, who turned and bowed to the entire crowd with a flourish. "Thank you to everyone who cooked today," Lady Rutland said. "You made this extremely difficult by showing your ability to improvise unique dishes. Now, Queen Charlotte has another announcement."

The crowd hummed as Queen Charlotte took the podium.

"Thank you, Lady Rutland, and everyone who has spent so much time and effort to bring this exhibition about. We are, of course, honored to taste everyone's dishes and delicacies. Those cooking tomorrow shall do so in the order their names were called, and then be brought into the King's Eating Room, where they shall present us with one dish they feel most represents who they are." She paused and looked out at the crowd. "At the ball tomorrow evening, my daughter, Princess Adelaide, will then choose, from among the top three male competitors, her future husband."

A collective gasp ran through the crowd. For a moment, silence reigned. Then, as astonishment turned to understanding, the mass of people began to clap. Heads cast around to take in the lucky ten again. Penelope watched Elijah's eyes cloud over.

"Good luck to you all," Queen Charlotte pronounced. The crowd applauded again as she left the podium.

"Well, I'll be bound! You could win the princess," Freddie said as the crowd dispersed.

"I'm sure she'll pick some foreign noble," Elijah said, not sounding convinced.

"You have just as good a chance as they," Freddie said, looking at Penelope for confirmation.

She met Elijah's eyes. "Yes. You absolutely do." It was true. And despite Helena's scheming, society's conventions, Elijah's background, and the overpowering feeling of warmth that appeared whenever she knew he was near, Penelope concluded that none of it

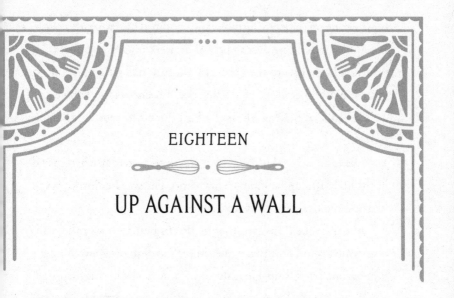

EIGHTEEN

UP AGAINST A WALL

Elijah spent most of the night staring at the ceiling of his room at the Hungry Hare. The exposed, dark beams were not so elegant as the plaster and ornate crown molding in his room at Number 9, Cavendish Square, nor as decrepit as the water-spotted ceiling of his uncle's dingy room on Old Fish Street, but they felt more real than anything had in quite a while. He supposed he should be grateful to Helena for not letting him pay for much of anything at Cavendish Square. His barely depleted savings had allowed him to secure the room for a few days.

He'd set his parents' mezuzah on the dressing table the night before, and his eyes strayed across the room to it now. He wondered if he'd have to return to Old Fish Street after all when his money ran out. Whether Mrs. Willet recognized him or not, perhaps it wouldn't matter. He barely recognized himself anymore.

Elijah swung himself out of bed, poured some water into the

bowl sitting on the dressing table, and scrubbed his face with a cloth. A round mirror hung over a chest of drawers, and he peered into it, brushing his hair with the hairbrush the girls had gifted him, along with a small toilette set. He looked over his cheeks for stubble and decided to shave. After all, he had a princess to win, he thought bitterly.

His mind strayed to Penelope's reactions yesterday when they'd heard Lady Rutland announce his name. The way her joyous laugh had hovered in the air. Her brilliant smile.

But then she'd insisted that he do his best to marry the princess, which could only mean one thing. She didn't feel anything for him beyond friendship. He really didn't know why he was surprised. She'd never said—or even done—anything demonstrable to make him think otherwise. Most of the girls he'd known who'd liked him had made their interest obvious.

Yet Penelope Pickering came from a different class, even as she belonged in a class all her own. She was unlike anyone he'd ever met: clever, ambitious, yet always thinking of others. She was special, and he'd deluded himself into thinking that meant she'd express her possible interest in him differently than other girls.

He swallowed hard, trying to quash the tightness in his throat as he finished dressing. He glanced at the mezuzah again, then on an impulse, placed it in the pocket of his coat. He wanted a piece of his parents with him on such a day.

Elijah left the Hungry Hare to walk the mile or so to Hampton Court. He tried to concentrate on what kind of dish he wished to create later, but his thoughts kept flashing to Penelope. After the announcement, she'd hired a carriage to take her back to London, and though he'd offered to go with her to help relocate her things, she'd insisted that he needed rest and that she would see him before his cooking time. He wondered if Helena had talked her into staying at Cavendish Square in the end. Penelope had never given him a real answer as to what Helena had wanted.

Then a thought struck him. What if Helena had convinced Penelope that he should try to marry Princess Adelaide? Could that be why Penelope had changed her mind and told him as much, despite knowing he didn't want to marry the princess? Of course, Helena had claimed Princess Adelaide couldn't marry a Jew, but what if Helena's pettiness had overridden that instinct? Or, worse, what if she planned to reveal who he was to show the princess that she was "the Goose" Helena had often claimed?

He ran his hand over the back of his neck, knowing it wasn't what a gentleman would do, but also not much caring. Would Helena be so mean-spirited? It wouldn't be particularly shrewd to antagonize the future queen of England. If Helena prided herself on anything, it was how much smarter she was than everyone else.

But as much as she liked to pretend she was a great lady and soon to be the most amazing Culinarian who'd ever lived, she *also* always believed she was right. Elijah kicked at a pebble in the road. He knew that fact all too well after so many months. He also knew that he'd better find out, once and for all, what she was after.

❧

Gravel crunched under Helena's slippers as she stepped out of her carriage and nodded at the royal footman who'd helped her down. She didn't quite know why she'd bothered coming to the palace today, except that Lady Rutland would expect it of her.

Helena, of course, was never one for self-reflection, but even she couldn't deny feeling something akin to low spirits—a phenomenon she'd rarely ever experienced. Penelope had departed Cavendish Square the night before without speaking a word to her. Helena had gone to bed with her head still pounding.

This morning, Pierce had informed her that Penelope had decamped to a nearby hotel. Though Helena had told herself it didn't matter—for surely Pen would soon come to her senses—she hadn't been prepared for how remarkably quiet the townhouse would feel with Penelope and Elijah gone. Helena had never really noticed how their presence seemed to lighten the breakfast table. Or how they'd always been filling the kitchen with discussion or laughter. Or how they simply *listened* when she wanted to examine a particular dish or technique. Helena had never really *thought* about any of those things. She certainly hadn't thought of how she'd miss them when they were gone. She'd been so immersed in turning Elijah into the best gentleman chef he could be and getting top honors on her project that she hadn't considered what would happen when it was over.

When Helena's brother, Roland, had been born, Helena had already spent seven years as her parents' only child and heir. They had doted on her in their quiescent way. But with Roland's birth, any expectations Helena's parents had originally had for her essentially receded to the back of their minds. They now had their male heir and more than enough resources to settle on Helena when she came of age. Thus, short of embarrassing them, Helena could have done anything she wanted (with only a few minor objections from her mother, who was easily persuadable by Helena's father).

Her grandmother had taken Helena to a local culinary faire

when she was eight or nine, and Helena had spoken to the visiting Culinarian. Helena had admired how the lady had a life of her own, independent of any parents or spouse, and from then on, Helena had resolved to become the best Culinarian of her generation.

It didn't bother her that it meant alienating all the silly girls at the Royal Academy—it was difficult to befriend those who were jealous of you—or that it meant having to stay in England to complete her studies while her parents gave Roland what they called a "Continental education." And even Lady Rutland's dressing down yesterday had irked Helena far less than Lady Rutland had clearly hoped it would.

What *did* vex Helena—though she still couldn't quite admit it to herself—were the things Elijah and Penelope had accused her of. She hadn't really thought either of them jealous of her—they'd certainly shown very little indication of jealousy during the last six months—which meant she couldn't dismiss their opinions out of hand as she might those of anyone else her age. And more to the contrary, she'd considered them friends.

Helena had always thought of Penelope as the only girl who understood her, so the thought that Penelope was reconsidering their friendship was no small matter. Elijah had lied to her, to be sure, but Helena also couldn't ignore the fact that she might *not* have taken him on as a pupil had she known the full extent of his origin. Meanwhile, she had been trying to prove that *anyone* could be a lady or gentleman with the right training and education. Which she had, in essence, done.

Helena frowned as she skirted the Pond Gardens on her way to the exhibition tents. She was willing to allow that she might not have been completely fair to Elijah. He'd never complained, even when Penelope had told Helena that she should let him rest. He'd done the work—*all* the work—when most would have whined (like some of the girls at the Royal Academy had) or simply given up. Helena couldn't fault him for that.

In reality, Elijah had impressed her at almost every turn. That had to be part of the reason she'd kept pushing him to reach greater heights. It couldn't be wholly for her own glory as Penelope had said. Could it?

These were the thoughts clouding Helena's mind when Elijah spotted her leaving the Privy Garden to turn toward the Great Fountain Garden, where he stood. She frowned as he strode toward her, unsure, for perhaps the first time, what she would say to him.

Elijah spoke first. "Hello."

"Hello," she said back, noting that he'd worn his burgundy tailcoat and gray-and-black-striped trousers for the occasion—not what she'd have chosen, but a pairing that complemented him regardless.

For a moment, neither of them said another word. Elijah straightened his spine, though he already towered over her by nearly a foot. "Do you plan to tell them who I am? The last thing I need is that hanging over my head while I cook today."

Helena contemplated this statement, realizing that she hadn't made up her mind one way or the other. That in itself felt oddly unsettling for someone as decisive as she. Even more startling was the way Elijah's eyes flashed as if ready to do battle. As if she was some foe to be vanquished.

"I'm glad you've decided to cook. Do you plan to pursue Princess Adelaide?" she asked.

His jaw worked. "Did you convince Penelope that I should?"

This brought Helena up short. She hadn't had any time to, but why would he care if she had? "Did she say you should?"

He let out a breath. "This is useless," he muttered. "Tell me once and for all, and then let us be done. Do you intend to sabotage me in any way?"

Though she'd been contemplating doing just that only yesterday, being confronted with it in such a stark manner made her wish to deny it. Yet her respect for him grew; he was no longer the ragamuffin they'd met at Covent Garden in January. "Lady Rutland has deemed my project a success, and I must say I agree with her. You *are* a gentleman chef cooking for royalty now."

His jaw shifted. "Do you recall the day you berated me for not eating the pork roast? I would have abandoned this 'experiment' of yours soon after if not for Miss Pickering. So when you consider how much of a success 'your project' is, you may wish to give her some share of the praise."

Helena raised a brow. She'd known Penelope had taken on more of his training than she should have, considering she had her own project to finish, but she hadn't realized he would have quit if not for Pen. "The project is done now. You may—and *should*—do as you please. But I rather like this new pillar of strength you've adopted into your disposition. I'd wager most of the ladies in London will find it irresistible—even Princess Adelaide."

He turned away.

Helena followed after him. "But it doesn't matter what I think," she said at his back.

He wheeled around to face her. "For once we agree. But this disposition, as you call it"—he gestured toward himself with one hand—"won't matter once people find out I'm Jewish. If they all behave like you did, all the training you gave me to become a gentleman chef won't mean much."

The ribbons of Helena's bonnet started to chafe at her neck. "I—I might have put it to you better. I was surprised. I . . ." She'd almost said she hadn't meant to offend him, but then she'd recalled what Penelope had said yesterday. Whether Helena meant to offend or not, she *did*. What did it say about her that she simply hadn't cared until now?

Helena took in his fine clothes and tall hat again. "I don't suppose everyone would react as I did," she settled on. Some of them might, but very possibly, some of them wouldn't. Penelope hadn't.

Elijah looked away from her, disdain written in the planes of his jaw and forehead.

Helena itched to adjust the bow at her neck. "What does Penelope say?" she asked.

He caught her gaze.

Helena blinked, unnerved by his pained stare.

"She said I could do whatever I wanted after today."

Helena had said the same thing before.

"Then she said I should try to marry the princess. After she talked to *you* yesterday."

Helena frowned. Penelope certainly hadn't seemed to want him to marry Princess Adelaide when they'd spoken. But clearly the point bothered Elijah. The question was why? He and Penelope had obviously grown closer during the last months, but was there something more?

"I shan't sabotage you," Helena said. "I *still* think you shouldn't have lied," she continued, "but I think I see why you did. You've worked hard to get here, and I won't keep anyone from seeing how well you, Elijah Little, gentleman chef, can cook."

The tension in his forehead and jaw melted away like lemon ice in a warm vessel. He nodded once. "If you see Penelope, tell her I'm looking for her." He strode away, leaving Helena to wonder if Penelope had been hiding more from her than she'd thought.

⚭

Elijah's fingers tapped against the side of his leg as he stood at his designated worktable in the Glorious Kitchen. A royal steward stood at the front of the room where Lady Rutland had been yesterday. The table of fish and seafood had been replaced with a table brimming with meat, fowl, and game of almost every type. The steward eyed his pocket watch.

Elijah kept his gaze firmly on the man, even as his mind strayed to Penelope. He'd seen nary a hint of her outside the palace, even though she'd said she would be here before his cooking time. He should have accompanied her to Cavendish Square. That's what a real gentleman would have done, despite her protests. He reminded himself that Penelope was well versed in traveling alone. She'd likely run into a delay on her way here.

And, regardless of the reason for her absence, she had told him to try to marry the princess.

The more Elijah thought about yesterday, the more he thought Penelope would probably marry Freddie Eynsford-Hill. She certainly hadn't bothered to discourage his attentions. And, though Elijah and Penelope were friends, once she married someone far removed from his sphere, he'd never see her again.

Which should be all he needed to know. She didn't care about him beyond their friendship. And he had to find a way to live with it.

"You may begin, Mr. Little," the steward said, closing his watch. "You have one hour to cook."

Elijah nodded and moved to the table to choose his ingredients. He'd spent a good portion of the night trying to think of what would impress the royals, but he hadn't settled on much beyond what he'd already done. He almost wished the challenge had been to create an entire meal or something grander than simply one dish.

A single dish to express who he was. Somehow it wasn't enough.

Yet, who was he really? He stared at the food on the table, not really seeing any of it as he recalled Penelope saying he would make a wonderful prince consort. Unfortunately, Elijah didn't actually believe her. He nervously smoothed his hand down the front of his coat, and his palm ran over his parents' mezuzah, sitting almost forgotten in his pocket. His hand stilled over it.

The steward looked at him with narrowed eyes, no doubt wondering why he simply stood there squandering his hour. Elijah had seen that slightly suspicious look from people his whole life—people who had more money, or more standing, or people who just didn't like his people. He'd thought that reinventing himself would mean he'd have to endure that look less and less. But the truth was that he'd have to endure that look no matter what. This new world of the upper classes brought a different scrutiny. People would always want to know who he was—where he came from. And if he didn't come to terms with that now, he'd be hiding from it his entire life.

He let out a breath and met the steward's pinched expression. "How much time left?"

The fellow looked at his watch. "Fifty-one minutes and thirty seconds," he said doubtfully.

"Well," Elijah said, thinking of all the timed drills Helena and Penelope had put him through during the last few weeks, "it's fortunate that I'm used to working under pressure."

∽∽∽

As Elijah and two liveried footmen holding his cloche-covered dishes approached the King's Eating Room, two more footmen simultaneously pulled open the doors.

Elijah inhaled through his nose and out through his mouth as the footmen holding his food entered the room. He followed, noting the dark wood–paneled walls covered in tapestries and paintings. In front of him, a rectangular table set for four sat in front of three tall windows. The King's Eating Room was not as grand or as large as he'd imagined, yet he still had to swallow at the sudden dryness in his throat as he stepped up to the long table to face Queen Charlotte, Prince Leopold, Princess Adelaide, and Lady Rutland. The queen and Lady Rutland smiled at him benignly, but the princess and her father showed no outward emotions. The footmen delivered the plates to the judges.

"Hello again, Mr. Little," the queen said.

Elijah bowed. "Your Majesty."

"Do tell us what you've prepared."

The footmen removed the cloches to reveal his final dish.

Elijah pulled in a deep breath. "Today I've prepared roasted quail spiced with sumac, coriander, and chili, atop sweet corn cachapas, which, as you see, are griddle cakes made from corn. I've also battered and fried fresh courgette blossoms stuffed with farmer's cheese." Elijah swallowed again. It was a deceptively simple dish. The cachapas were perhaps the least complicated, and possibly something royalty might find rather humble, but his uncle Jonathan had gotten the recipe on a voyage that had put in at a port in Venezuela long ago, and Elijah had perfected it over the years whenever he could get enough sweet corn.

Princess Adelaide eyed the dish, as though surprised it didn't look more elaborate. She looked up at him with a quizzical expression.

He kept his gaze steady. He'd always thought that food was a great equalizer, for whatever someone's creed or race or religion, every person had to eat to survive. This exhibition seemed to confirm his belief. The Royal Exhibition was showcasing the different cultures and cuisines of over thirty countries, and from what Elijah had seen, everyone was welcome, no matter where they hailed from in the world. Elijah's first instinct had been to make something from his food culture, something that would subtly—or perhaps, not so subtly—say, *I'm Jewish and there shouldn't be anything wrong with that.*

Since he'd been old enough to understand the slurs hurled at him on the streets of London, he'd worried that strangers would define him by their prejudiced perceptions of his people. His uncle's example had given Elijah the excuse he'd wanted as a young boy to distance himself from the beliefs, traditions, and habits that made him conspicuous. Yet he was no longer that scared boy his uncle had taken in or that brash soul relying on his wits and the coin he made at the night market. He was now someone altogether different.

And as much as he'd wanted to escape the pain that came with thinking of them, he'd realized that what his parents had endured would never leave him. Still, in the kitchen today as Elijah had started pulling the ingredients he'd need for potato pancakes, he'd considered the truth that although his background had shaped him, and would continue to, it wasn't *all* he was. He didn't need to define himself wholly by it any more than he wanted others to. The food of the Americas was what he enjoyed cooking. The flavors excited him, and even at the night market, he'd always loved seeing people's reactions when he'd sold them something they hadn't tasted before. So he'd kept to his pancake idea, but started mixing his corn batter instead. Really, what were cachapas but latkes by another name?

The queen and prince consort were already taking a bite of their quail.

"The spicing in the quail is quite straightforward, yet effective," Lady Rutland mused.

"I would concur," the prince said, nodding as he cut into the squash blossom.

"I very much like the courgette sauce accompaniment," the queen said. "Such a light texture with a delightful piquancy—perfect for summer."

"Thank you, ma'am," Elijah replied.

He watched the princess's face as she bit into the cachapa. At first, she showed little reaction. Then she cut into the squash blossom and paired it with another piece of the cachapa. Her eyes widened, almost imperceptibly. She took another bite. Then she dipped her last bit of squash blossom, speared on top of cachapa, into one of the light green dollops of courgette sauce he'd dotted on the plate. She lifted her eyes to meet his.

"What's inside the squash blossoms besides cheese? Onions?"

"Simply salt, Your Highness," he replied.

She tilted her head to one side. "Amazing. The batter was so light and crisp. I would never imagine a blossom could have so much flavor." A slow smile stole over her face.

"Nor I," agreed the prince, favoring Elijah with his keen gaze. "However, one might ask why you decided to veer from your usual course and make every element so simple—relatively speaking."

Elijah had been anticipating some question like this. "You asked me to show myself on a plate. Sometimes things that appear simple are actually quite complex. And sometimes the most complex-seeming things truly have little substance. On occasion, the ingredients must speak for themselves," he replied, feeling for all the world like whatever happened later, he'd done himself proud.

Princess Adelaide raised a brow. "How intriguing."

NINETEEN

IF YOU'RE IN LOVE . . .

Penelope stepped into the Great Hall at Hampton Court Palace in her best gown, a bright sunflower-yellow silk confection with imitation-pearl beads arranged in a leaf pattern on the skirt, a white silk sash that emphasized her waist, and short, puffed sleeves that sat at the very edges of her shoulders. The pearl eardrops and seed pearl necklace her parents had given her for her sixteenth birthday complemented the gown well. Penelope had pinned most of her thick brown locks into a twisted braid sitting at the crown of her head, and she'd spent far too much time arranging the curls at the front of her face until the effect satisfied her. It felt nice to dress up for a change, even if the fun of discussing her dress or hairstyle with Helena couldn't happen. She glanced around the room to see if Helena had arrived but didn't spot her. Perhaps it was just as well; Penelope still didn't particularly wish to talk with her.

She moved farther into the ballroom. Hundreds of beeswax

candles lit the moldings and carvings of the ornate hammer-beam ceiling, as well as the richly detailed Brussels tapestries that ran down the length of each side of the hall. Penelope had only seen them from afar when she'd been sitting in the Minstrels' Gallery yesterday. Now a stage stood in front of the gallery, and ten dishes covered with silver cloches took pride of place on the table at the front of the dais. Small paper cards that had been labeled with the numbers one through ten sat in front of the plates, facing the guests. Two liveried footmen stood guard on either side of the table as light string music emanated from the gallery behind them.

Penelope wondered which of the ten dishes was Elijah's. She cast her head about to spot his tall figure, but she didn't see him either. She hoped the day had gone well for him. She'd meant to speak with him before he cooked, but moving all her things to a hotel near Cavendish Square had proved more time-consuming than she'd anticipated, even with the housemaid Pierce had sent to accompany her. The girl had gone back to Cavendish Square directly after ensuring Penelope could secure an accommodation, and Penelope had been so exhausted that she'd fallen asleep and hadn't awoken until a hotel maid knocked on the door with her breakfast.

Even then, Penelope had stayed abed far later than normal. Really, there wasn't much to wake for. Elijah wouldn't be downstairs waiting for her. Helena wouldn't be there to fuss about the breakfast spread. Their little threesome had made Number 9, Cavendish Square, into a home for a few short months, and now it was over. Elijah would marry the princess—or barring that, could easily find some other lady of high social standing who could use her connections to get him a shop of his own. Penelope had no connections to speak of (unless one considered her father's estranged family, which she didn't).

Elijah would be far better off with someone who could help him socially. Eventually, he would marry and their friendship would have to end. Penelope swallowed at the tight feeling in her throat.

Helena, meanwhile, would go on to graduate at the top of their class and begin her illustrious career. Penelope would begin hers. They'd grow apart—especially once they were in competition for the same consultations.

Penelope had always thought to further her education abroad. That, at least, would distinguish her from Helena and allow her to see her parents. Yes, she'd had a plan, and she should stick to it. Nevermind that a tall, brown-eyed young man with wavy hair and a smirk she found adorable would be so far away. Nevermind that she wouldn't be able to laugh with him or test recipes with him. Nevermind that they'd never be shoulder to shoulder in a kitchen or across a worktable from each other. Nevermind that those thoughts made her want to sink into bed and pull the coverlet over her head like a little girl—or that the thoughts elicited a strange pain in her palm that she'd never felt before. No.

Elijah deserved the best the world had to give. He deserved not only to reach for the moon, as Helena put it—he deserved to grasp it.

And Penelope's plan, such as it was, was still valid. As she had been readying herself to leave the hotel for Hampton Court, a letter had arrived from her parents, forwarded from Cavendish Square. They still intended to meet her in Liverpool after her graduation, and from there, they would take her on the tour of the Pacific that she'd long been asking for. The trip they'd promised her as a reward for enduring all her schooling alone—for being the independent young lady they were so proud of. For being the first Culinarian of mixed race to graduate from the Royal Academy of Culinaria Artisticus.

The voyage was what she'd wanted; to succeed where no one like her had yet been able to had been something she'd worked toward and planned for years. And she had almost accomplished it. Why, then, did she feel like something essential was missing? She closed her eyes and let out a sigh.

These thoughts had gnawed at her all morning, and she'd decided to wait until closer to the evening ball before leaving London. She'd spent the afternoon cross-referencing the recipes Elijah had gifted her with her few books on the cuisines of the Americas, while doing her level best not to think of him. As she'd taken notes for her project, she'd come to the conclusion that she really was woefully behind, and that preparing Elijah for the exhibition had eaten a good deal of time that she should have spent writing and researching.

But as she stared at the ten silver-covered plates in the Great Hall illuminated by the flickering candlelight, then nodded at the footman warning her to not touch anything, and finally glimpsed Elijah as he entered at the opposite end of the long hall with his head high, she realized that had she to do it over again, she still wouldn't have left his education solely in Helena's hands.

After glancing around the room, Elijah caught sight of her. As he made his way across the hall, Penelope found herself grinning from ear to ear. He wore the same formal black tailcoat and trousers, cream-colored waistcoat, and eggshell cravat he'd put on the day they'd taught him to dance, and in the glow of hundreds of candles, he looked even more handsome than he had then. The Great Hall had been filling as she'd been woolgathering, and Elijah had to sidestep people and offer polite replies to others as he strode toward her. Penelope left the table to meet him halfway, but she had been watching Elijah's progress so intently, she didn't notice Freddie Eynsford-Hill until he spoke.

"Miss Pickering, you're looking quite lovely this evening," he said, bowing.

Penelope half turned. "Mr. Eynsford-Hill. I didn't see you there."

He raised a good-natured brow. "Didn't mean to startle you."

She shook her head to indicate it was of no consequence. She looked back at Elijah, but he had disappeared. She craned her neck, hoping to find him in the crowd.

"Are you quite well, Miss Pickering?" Freddie asked.

"Yes, thank you," Penelope replied, wondering where Elijah could have gone. But instead of seeing him as she peered around the hall, her gaze fell on Helena stepping into the room in a greenish-blue gown with blue-and-white bows adorning each sleeve.

Penelope turned away before she could tell if Helena saw her.

"You were missed at the exhibition tents today," Freddie said.

"That's very kind," Penelope replied. "I had to complete more work on my final project."

He nodded. "I do so admire your interest in the foods of the Americas. I imagine you'll garner great renown in the culinary world. Though I think it may take longer for American flavors to trickle down and be interesting to some in the older generation like my mama." He let out a short laugh.

Penelope raised her brows. "Yes, I do recall that she seemed to think me rather strange for having traveled there."

"The mater is a bit old-fashioned," he said, shaking his head. "Isn't too fond of anything foreign, if you take my meaning."

Penelope pursed her lips. She was about to question him further when the music stopped. A hush fell over the crowd, and everyone dropped into quick bows and curtsies as Queen Charlotte entered on the arm of Prince Leopold.

The pair made a fine couple as always, she bedecked in jewels and a gown threaded with strands of silver that shone in the candlelight, he still fit and handsome in middle age. Princess Adelaide followed in a blush-pink gown with intricately pleated puffed sleeves, a full skirt, and a bodice that echoed the pleats of the sleeves. Her light brown hair had been pinned aloft in a sophisticated style. A delicate tiara of pink sapphires and diamonds finished the look.

A princess had to appear her best on the night she announced her future husband, Penelope supposed. The royal family crossed by her to approach the stage, and the queen stepped beside the table with the silver-covered dishes. The prince and Princess Adelaide stood slightly behind her as the footmen retreated to the back of the dais. One motioned for the musicians behind the gallery to stop playing.

The music came to an end, and the queen spoke. "Welcome, everyone, to our final event of the Royal Culinary Exhibition."

The guests clapped.

The queen's serene smile remained in place until the applause faded. "We have so enjoyed tasting all of your delicacies from Britain and around the world. You have made the judging especially difficult this year with your superior culinary skills and techniques, and it has been our honor to consume every morsel." She smiled again and looked back at the princess. "Princess Adelaide, as you know, shall soon announce her choice of future husband and reveal the names and rankings of the finalists whose dishes line this table."

The crowd murmured to each other. Penelope surveyed the room again for Elijah.

"First, however, my daughter wishes to dance with three of the finalists. Let the ball begin!"

The musicians struck up a waltz, drowning out the rumbling excitement of the crowd. Then, out of the corner of her eye, Penelope saw Elijah. A footman escorted him through the guests all the way up to the edge of the dais. He bowed to the queen, the prince, and the princess. Penelope swallowed down the lump in her throat as Elijah offered Princess Adelaide his arm, and she stepped forward to take it. And before Penelope knew it, the young man she'd taught to dance was waltzing with the Crown Princess of Britain.

⁂

Elijah held his breath as he led Princess Adelaide into the middle of the Great Hall. What was he doing here? Every eye in the room centered on him and the princess. A cold wave of nausea washed over him; he forced himself to breathe. All he'd wanted was to gain enough knowledge to be able to own a stall at the market, or a shop, or even a warehouse if that's what he had to call it. He hadn't wanted to be singled out by the whole of society. But he was here. And he'd damned well make the best of it.

He turned to face the princess and held out his hand for her to grasp as the girls had shown him. Princess Adelaide clasped his hand lightly and rested her other on his shoulder. She offered a slight smile, and he did his utmost to return it while counting the beats of the music and starting them in a small circle. He concentrated on counting until others joined the dance. As people began to swirl around them, he swallowed.

Then he wondered if the princess expected him to talk. She'd singled him out by having him dance with her first, so he was evidently in the running for her hand. Bloody hell, *her hand*! Elijah cleared his throat. The idea that he might have to marry someone he'd barely exchanged words with was a staggering prospect. He knew arranged marriages occurred in all stratas of society, including among the traditionalists in his own community, but it was an extraordinary thing to now literally be dancing face-to-face with.

"You are a man of few words, I think, Mr. Little," the princess remarked.

He looked down at her. "It's one of many faults, I'm afraid," he said, hoping he wasn't being too obvious in his ambivalence to this possible betrothal.

She arched a brow. "Most gentlemen are not so quick to discuss the defects of their character. At least not around me."

He let out a mirthless laugh. "Most gentlemen have a healthy admiration for their own self-worth."

"But not you?" she asked, tilting her head up at him.

This brought him up short. He'd always wanted to elevate himself—in part to show the people who had denigrated him for being poor or being Jewish that they were small-minded—and that their perceptions of him could not keep him down. Yet he continued to carry their taunts in his mind. He still, somehow, considered himself beneath them. He *must* still think that. Why else would he keep hiding who he was? What kind of simpleton disparaged himself to a pretty and powerful princess who held him in contention for her hand? He let out a breath.

That wasn't the whole of it, of course. As attractive and apparently insightful as Princess Adelaide was, she was not Penelope.

Penelope. When her eyes had met his across the Great Hall, he'd thought . . . but then Freddie Eynsford-Hill had found her, reminding Elijah yet again of the type of gentleman Penelope should be courted by: the kind of gentleman Elijah would never be. But, in that thinking, Elijah was only knocking himself down again.

He swallowed against the tightness in his throat. By not telling Penelope how he felt, by not letting her make up her own mind, he was essentially admitting that everything people had said about him was true. He'd told Helena how wrong she'd been to say he couldn't achieve what he wanted because of who he was, but he hadn't been able to see until this moment that he'd been telling himself the same thing.

"Princess," he said, "you've just made me realize that I *am* inclined to think ill of myself." His heart started a fierce drumbeat in his chest. He had to talk to Penelope.

"I don't see why you should," she replied. "Your food has been consistently strong in every round. I don't wish to sound flippant about it, but you are in the top three for good reason, Mr. Little."

"That's generous of you to say. I—"

"Not at all. It is the truth, I assure you." She smiled at him, and Elijah smiled back, unsure how to reply. He was beginning to quite like Princess Adelaide; despite everything Helena had said about her, she seemed plain-speaking, and not at all like a "goose." Should he tell her of his background? It seemed the fair thing to do. Then she could make up her own mind as Penelope should.

At that moment, Penelope swirled past them in Freddie's arms. They were talking animatedly. Elijah's stomach dropped. The princess let out a little noise of alarm as Elijah almost led them into another couple. The other gentleman narrowly avoided them, but he glared at Elijah as they passed.

Elijah murmured his apologies, then concentrated on the dance.

"Do you know her?" the princess asked. When he feigned ignorance, she clarified. "The girl dancing with Mr. Eynsford-Hill?"

"Er . . . yes. She's one of Lady Rutland's pupils. She'll be graduating from the Royal Academy this month," he said.

"Has she a name?" The princess tilted her chin down.

Elijah swallowed. "Miss Penelope Pickering."

The princess's brows rose. "So *that's* Miss Pickering. Mabel Pilkington has mentioned her." She angled her head toward the edge of the room. "Isn't she a good friend of Lady Helena Higgins?"

Elijah glanced where the princess had indicated. Helena stood in a greenish-blue gown, talking with some matrons. "I believe so."

"Well," the princess said, "there's no accounting for taste. Still, Mabel tells me Miss Pickering has always been amiable to her. Do you know her well?"

Elijah met the princess's astute gaze. "She is the kindest lady I have the honor to know."

He didn't know what he'd expected, but the princess smiled at him enigmatically. "I'm gratified to hear you agree with Mabel."

The waltz ended, and Elijah had the presence of mind to bow before the Duke of Transylvania appeared to claim the princess for the next dance.

"Thank you for the dance, Mr. Little," the princess said as she took the duke's arm. "I've appreciated your candor as much as your food."

Elijah thanked her, not at all certain whether he'd just made a jumble of everything or not.

⟨∞⟩

Moments earlier, Penelope and Freddie's conversation had been no less jumbled than Elijah's thoughts as he'd spied them dancing.

As it happened, the sight of Elijah leading Princess Adelaide around the floor had produced pangs of jealousy in Penelope that made her pulse race in a most unpleasant manner. She would have left the ballroom entirely except Freddie had asked her to dance, and she didn't know how to refuse him without being rude. Yet his comments about his mother disliking anything foreign played in the back of her mind, so when he said, "Isn't it strange how some people speculate the most ridiculous things once someone becomes society's focus?" Penelope's gaze snapped from the princess and Elijah to search Freddie's expression.

He, in fact, was looking over her head. "Mabel had some fool theory that Mr. Little was not actually who he claims to be."

As though her entire body had been plunged into an ice bath, Penelope tensed. "Did she indeed?" She attempted to keep her voice calm.

Freddie chuckled and caught her eye. "She believes him to not actually be English at all! Of course, Mabel has always been one for gossip. She even intimated to me that *your* family had some sort of scandal in the past."

Penelope clenched her back teeth. "It was actually more of a disagreement than a scandal."

"What a load of tomfoolery—I knew she'd exaggerated!" He shook his head. "What was the disagreement, if I may ask?"

Penelope raised her brows. She should have confronted Mabel herself the other day. At least now she could set the record straight. "My father's family disagreed with his choice to marry the daughter of a Philippine chieftain. Her family disagreed with her choice to marry an Englishman. But they are quite happy nonetheless. I shall join them in a few weeks. We're taking a voyage to the Pacific after I graduate from the Royal Academy. I'm very much looking forward to learning more about the cuisine."

Freddie had gone silent as he continued to lead her around the floor. She had some inkling of what he must be thinking, though. That she looked so white. What his mother would say. That her origin could affect his standing. She decided to tread further.

"Rumors are indeed ridiculous things. One's perceptions can alter so completely because of them."

He nodded his agreement, but he said nothing.

"Did Mabel exaggerate?" she prompted.

That seemed to catch him off guard. He cleared his throat. "I suppose she did."

Penelope tsked. "I wonder how exaggerated the rumor I heard about you is."

He frowned.

Penelope schooled her features into a polite smile. "I had heard that you had little money of your own, and that you were rather looking for a Culinarian wife."

His brow clouded further as he refused to meet her gaze.

"Of course, you'd hardly want a Culinarian wife with a scandal—no matter how slight—in her past. It would make her social standing all the more precarious, I daresay. And yours, by extension, of course. But rumors, as you know, do not often tell the entire story—if they tell the correct story at all."

Freddie made an agreeable noise in his throat, but she knew she'd dealt him a blow. "Out of curiosity, why did Mabel think Mr. Little wasn't English?"

"Er . . . something about English gentlemen not having the patience to learn such culinary technique."

Penelope hummed. "Interesting. Well, to my knowledge, Mr. Little is as English as you, Mr. Eynsford-Hill. You may tell Mabel so."

This effectively ended any further communication from Freddie for the remainder of the dance. When the musicians played the final chords of the waltz, and Freddie escorted her to the edge of the room, making some excuse to leave, Penelope couldn't feel anything but glad. He'd been friendly enough since they'd met, but she felt nothing for him.

"He's certainly latched onto you like a leech."

Penelope didn't have to turn to know Helena stood by her side with narrowed green eyes. "Yes, well, I doubt he shall be a problem from here on out."

Helena stepped to face her. "Never say you gave him the chop, so to speak. You seemed so charmed by him."

Penelope raised her brows. "You simply assumed so, Helena. You never actually asked me what I thought."

Helena bit her lower lip. "You're right, Pen. I've—I've been doing too much of that lately."

"You have."

Helena looked away, then exhaled and brought her gaze back to meet Penelope's. "I've been a selfish creature. I cannot say even now how much of what I did was for Mr. Little's benefit or for my own."

"That is only part of the problem," Penelope stated.

Helena nodded slowly. "I suppose I don't often think of how others feel, though I assure you, it does happen. I shouldn't have lied to Mabel. Or said what I did to Elijah. You were quite right: I underestimated him from the start, and when he kept surpassing almost every measure I set, I thought he really should aim for the top. Whether he *actually* wanted it didn't influence my thinking. I suppose I thought I knew better."

Penelope shook her head. "Then you should tell *him* so. You *always* think you know better than everyone else. I can count on one hand the number of times you asked Elijah what he thought—or *wanted*."

Helena sighed. "That's true. I did let my vanity take over, Pen. But—" She paused as if she wished to say more.

Unbeknownst to Penelope, Helena had wanted to say that she'd grown accustomed to having Penelope and Elijah at Cavendish Square. That she wished they would both return and somehow let her make amends for her behavior, but instead she said, "Elijah was looking for you today. We both were. He said you told him to try to marry the princess after all."

Penelope did not meet Helena's look, but she nodded.

"Did you also counsel him to continue hiding his ancestry?"

"Of course I didn't, Helena," Penelope snapped, narrowing her eyes at her.

"I only wonder because I don't see how he could possibly marry Princess Adelaide unless he changed his religion or—"

"As you are so fond of saying, Helena, times are changing."

Helena arched her brows. "Even *I* don't know that they've changed that much."

"Well, as we've already established, you don't know everything, do you?" Penelope shot back. She lifted her chin. "There is no written law prohibiting anyone in the royal line of succession from marrying someone Jewish."

Helena opened and closed her mouth. "But no monarch or monarch-to-be can marry a Catholic without losing their place in the succession. King George couldn't—"

"And Mr. Little, as you know, is not Catholic."

Helena held her tongue for a good three seconds. Pen could be correct. She vaguely recalled that the law preventing heirs in the line of succession from marrying Catholics had been created because of centuries of wars and revolutions between Catholics and Protestants. There might not be any rule or law mentioning Jews at all. Which meant Elijah wouldn't necessarily be removed from consideration just because of his religion. She wet her lips. What she'd said to Elijah had been even more harmful than she'd realized—on multiple levels. "In the interest of considering people's feelings, Elijah did seem disturbed by the fact that you'd changed your tune," Helena said. "I think he thought I put you up to it."

Penelope rolled her eyes. "I'll speak to him."

"No—I didn't mean to say that it bothered me," Helena tried to clarify, "only that he—"

"Good evening," Elijah said over Helena's head.

Helena turned, but not before she saw Penelope's face light up. Behind Elijah, couples swirled about the dance floor to the music, and candles illuminated the room in a flickering glow, but Penelope only looked at him.

"Hello, Mr. Little," Penelope said. "Fancy seeing you here."

He centered his smile on Penelope, then nodded at Helena. "Lady Helena."

"Good evening, Mr. Little," she replied. "I must say that you cut a fine figure on the dance floor—many remarked on it."

He let out a breath and nodded his thanks. Then his gaze returned to Penelope. "I had superior dance instruction."

Helena thought Penelope's cheeks pinked.

"In fact, I wanted to see if you might dance the next with me, Miss Pickering," he continued.

"I'd be happy to," Penelope said quickly.

"Why wait for the next?" Helena asked. "There's no time like the present."

They both peered at her, and Helena gave them an awkward smile as she remembered what Pen had said about asking their opinions. "Only if you so choose, of course."

Elijah looked back at Penelope. "Well, Miss Pickering? Ladies' choice."

"In that case, absolutely, Mr. Little." She gave Helena a hint of a smile before taking Elijah's arm and letting him whisk her into the waltz.

Helena bit the inside of her cheek as she watched them whirl around the Great Hall, recalling the day they'd taught him to dance. A lump formed in her throat as all the long evenings of cooking, laughing, and eating played through her mind. Those two people waltzing were truly Helena's only friends in the world, and she'd lost them through her own actions. She'd acted abominably again and again and they'd forgiven her—until she'd said and done the unforgivable.

She followed their faces as they looked into each other's eyes and laughed. As Pen's upturned cheeks blushed to a rosy glow. As Elijah grinned at her with not only contentment, but *happiness*.

The suspicion she'd harbored all day pivoted to recognition with the clarity of a perfect consommé. They were in love.

Little wonder Elijah had refused to marry the princess; little wonder Penelope had said everything she had. Did they know it themselves? Helena frowned. She may have lost their friendship, but she would do what she could to ensure their happiness. The question was: What?

⌒∞⌒

Elijah swept Penelope in an oblong circle across the Great Hall, wishing for all the world that he could suspend the moment in time. Her eyes drifted closed, as though she trusted him to lead her anywhere, and in his heart, he knew he had to tell her now. "Penelope, I—"

Her brown eyes opened, the amber rings surrounding her pupils centering on him with a questioning look.

"Do you know how much I care for you?" There. He'd said it. He held his breath.

Her mouth opened, then closed, but she did not smile. "Our friendship is dear to me too."

He exhaled. "That's not what I mean. Why did you tell me to try to marry the princess? Do you truly wish me to?"

Penelope bit her lower lip. "Because you deserve the best in life. All of it. Not a girl who can't bring you the connections you'll need. Not a girl who didn't stand up for you time and again." She closed her eyes briefly. "You *should* marry Princess Adelaide. She clearly respects you and your work. And you would be crown prince. Despite what Helena told you, no laws or rules exist preventing the princess from marrying someone of your heritage or beliefs. I sent a letter to my father's solicitor last night, asking him in a very general way if there were any such laws, and he confirmed there are no legal barriers. Imagine all the things you could do. You could help so many; you could help your own people."

He shook his head. Even if that were true, it didn't change how he felt. "I don't—"

"Besides, once graduation is over, I'll be meeting my parents in Liverpool. We're going to the Pacific as we always planned."

Numbness enveloped Elijah's head and chest. That had to be that. She didn't care for him. Why else would she go so far away? Why else would she insist that he deserved to marry Princess Adelaide? His legs felt leaden as he guided her through the rest of the waltz. He'd tried. And she'd made her choice.

Penelope had read many books and watched countless plays and operas where the heroines and heroes spoke of broken hearts, but not until this moment did she truly understand what they meant. Her chest felt heavy, as though she couldn't quite breathe right, and her palm pulsed with that same strange pain that had been bothering her all day. She flexed and unflexed her hand by the side of the skirt of her gown, hoping that would make it dissipate.

Elijah had bowed to her as the dance ended, with that resigned frown she knew well, and disappeared into the crowd. When he'd told her how he felt, her heart had screamed that she felt the same. But her head.

Her head had told her that he needed better than her. And her mouth had parroted it. She took a deep breath to calm her pulse. Then another. She stretched her hand open again. Nothing changed.

She considered asking a footman for a glass of water or a cordial, but all the beverages carried on silver platters were likely alcoholic, and she doubted they'd help calm her. She'd just decided to go in search of the ladies' retiring room when the third waltz ended and the last gentleman escorted Princess Adelaide back to the dais. He was Mr. McAndrews, one of the Scottish gentlemen chefs. So only one foreign nobleman and two gentlemen were in the running. Penelope still thought Elijah's odds no lesser than before.

Princess Adelaide cleared her throat and moved to stand behind the dish sitting in tenth position on the table. "I thank you all, once again, for your indulgence and your artistry. As we have seen over the last few days, you are truly the best in the world. As you know, the field of Culinaria is ever growing, expanding, and changing. And tonight we came here to honor those of you on the forefront of such change."

She clapped for the crowd and they reciprocated.

"If the finalists would approach the table, I shall reveal the dishes in descending order."

Penelope swallowed as the ten finalists moved toward the stage. The princess lifted the first silver cloche away and handed it to a waiting footman. "Pork roulade with figs, pancetta, walnuts, and a sherry and basil vinaigrette, by the Prince of Westphalia."

The crowd pushed closer to the dais to see the food as they clapped for the prince. He looked slightly put out to have come in tenth, but he bowed to the princess. She continued on, and one by one, two lady amateurs, two gentlemen chefs, and two foreign princes' dishes were revealed until only the final three dishes remained covered with silver domes.

Penelope peered at Elijah. He stood tall and steady, looking straight ahead, ignoring her and the crowd. Her stomach fluttered, and she wondered if he felt as nervous as she.

The princess pulled the third cloche. "Veal saddle with chanterelle-and-cashew cream sauce, salt-roasted beetroot, and wilted sorrel by the Duke of Transylvania."

The crowd gasped. The princess, it seemed, had decided to marry a commoner. Penelope held her breath.

"And in second—"

"Wait!"

All eyes in the room flew to the two young men standing before the princess. For a moment, no one seemed to know which of them had spoken. But Penelope knew. She would have recognized that warm tenor of his even if she were blindfolded.

"Princess, if I may speak?" Elijah asked.

Princess Adelaide nodded slowly. "Of course, Mr. Little."

He looked behind him at the crowd, then seemed to think better of it. He stepped up to the dais. "Princess, Your Majesties"—he nodded to the queen and prince sitting in ornate chairs at the back of the stage—"I beg your forgiveness, but I am not what I seem, and regardless of your choice, you should know the truth."

Princess Adelaide arched an eyebrow. "Go on."

Penelope's fingers went cold.

"I am not a true gentleman chef," Elijah said as he held his head high. "I am, in fact, J—"

"He may not be a gentleman by birth, but he is certainly a gentleman chef by deed," interrupted a voice from the crowd.

All eyes turned as Helena pushed her way through to the edge of the dais.

Princess Adelaide lifted her chin. "Lady Helena." The trace of ice in her tone was unmistakable.

Helena dropped into a low curtsy. "Your Highness."

Penelope gaped at Helena's newfound deference, just as her heart threatened to thrum out of control.

"You have something to say, Lady Helena," the princess prompted.

Helena kept her expression carefully neutral. "Yes, Your Highness. If I may."

The princess glanced back at her parents seated on the dais behind her, then nodded for Helena to continue.

Helena looked at Elijah and raised her brows, almost as though asking for his permission to speak. His forehead tightened, but—almost indiscernibly—he inclined his head. Helena forged on. "I'm afraid this is all my fault." She gestured to Elijah with one hand. "I wanted to see if I could teach this young man to be a gentleman chef—along with everything that entailed. People counseled me against it. Even Mr. Little questioned the wisdom of the arrangement, but I wanted to prove that regardless of one's birth or social status, with enough training, anyone could raise themselves to culinary heights. But"—she paused and took a breath—"though my initial intentions were good, my approach proved flawed. My conceit got in the way of seeing what was truly important, and I hurt people I care for."

Her eyes flicked to Penelope.

The princess followed her gaze. Penelope bit the inside of her cheek.

Helena then looked at Elijah, who stood, unflinching, on the edge of the stage. "Mr. Little's hard work and persistence brought him here," Helena continued. "And though he never asked to be a gentleman chef, it is my firm assertion that he is one nonetheless. *That* is the truth."

A small smile appeared at the corner of Elijah's mouth.

The princess's sharp eyes contemplated Elijah and Helena. Then she angled her head to the side. "Thank you for your candor, Lady Helena." For a few moments, the princess said nothing. The room seemed to hold a collective breath. She peered out at the crowd and then, finally, spoke.

"I certainly agree with your assessment of Mr. Little's standing as a gentleman chef, regardless of his birth. In fact, Lady Rutland informed us of your project after the blind tasting."

Some in the crowd gasped. Penelope looked to Lady Rutland, who stood at the left of the dais, a tranquil smile playing upon her lips.

The princess put up a hand for silence. "One cannot choose a future crown prince and partner in life without possessing all the pertinent information."

Helena, of course, had expected her to do just that, and her mouth formed a small "o" before she schooled her features. "We had no desire to mislead you, Your Highness. I *know* Mr. Little didn't—"

"Yes, Lady Helena, I've surmised as much," Princess Adelaide interrupted. She turned to Elijah. "The fact that you advanced to the second round with your innovative flavors and superlative technique intrigued us all, and I was most keen to see you cook again. No matter how you came to the competition, in our estimation, you are a gentleman indeed, Mr. Little."

Elijah bowed. "Thank you, Your Highness. But I—"

The princess gave a little laugh. "Perhaps, before anyone else wishes to make yet another confession, you might allow me to reveal the last two dishes. Mr. Little, if you care to discuss anything afterward, I will be more than happy to oblige."

Penelope's breath caught. What could that mean?

Elijah nodded and stepped down off the dais.

Princess Adelaide smiled at the crowd again. "Perhaps some of you noticed the royal coat of arms on the cloche of dish two." She rotated the remaining two silver domes on their plates so they faced outward. As she'd said, the second dish displayed a lion and unicorn holding each side of a shield, etched into the silver cloche. "The royal arms indicates that my future husband did not create today's winning dish."

A buzz filled the air as people whispered to their immediate neighbors. Penelope thought her heart would jump from her chest.

The princess lifted both domes simultaneously. The crowd fell silent. Penelope gasped. Helena beamed. Elijah laughed, and the fellow next to Elijah grinned so widely his face could barely contain it.

"In first place is Mr. Elijah Little and his spiced quail, stuffed squash blossom, and corn cachapa," Princess Adelaide pronounced. "A dish that exemplified the very epitome of letting one's ingredients speak for themselves. Much in the same way that Mr. Little so bravely attempted just moments ago. I would hope his courage would also extend to following his instincts. Wherever they may lead him." Murmurs of approval rippled through the guests. "Which means that Mr. Leslie McAndrews of Scotland shall, in fact, be the next crown prince of England if he so chooses." She smiled widely at Mr. McAndrews, and he stepped upon the stage to kneel before her and kiss her hand.

The crowd erupted into applause, and whatever affirmations Mr. McAndrews offered were lost in the din, but judging by the princess's happy smile, they were exactly what they should have been. She soon recollected herself, and like a true princess should, gestured for Elijah to come up to the dais. Elijah approached and offered Mr. McAndrews his hand, which he shook as the queen and prince stepped forward. The prince also shook Mr. McAndrews's hand.

The queen addressed the crowd. "We could not be more

delighted with Princess Adelaide's choice. Thank you all for being present to witness her joy." She turned to Elijah. "Mr. Little, as the winner of this year's Royal Exhibition, we take great pleasure in knowing you shall soon become Sir Elijah Little, knight of the realm."

The crowd clapped again. Elijah bowed his head, clearly overwhelmed. "However, in the meantime," the queen continued, "we hereby present you with the Order of the Peacock, which is, of course, the highest honor we present to Culinarians and chefs of great worth."

Elijah's face slackened with shock.

"Huzzah!" Helena called loudly. Penelope almost laughed at her breach of decorum. But her happiness for Elijah bubbled over, and she started loudly applauding. Others joined as the queen directed Elijah to stand facing the crowd. She pinned a medal in the shape of a peacock on the lapel of his coat, then joined the applause herself. That grin of Elijah's that began at the corner of his mouth overtook his face as his gaze found Penelope's. She bit her lip and continued to clap.

The queen signaled to the musicians in the gallery, and another dance began. Mr. McAndrews escorted a happy Princess Adelaide onto the floor.

Up on the dais, Elijah touched the enamel-and-gold peacock pinned to his chest, feeling too astounded to say much of anything coherent. What could a fellow say in such a situation? "My humble thanks, Your Majesty," was the best he could manage.

The queen tilted her auburn head. "You have a great future ahead of you, Mr. Little," she stated. "And no matter your ancestry or circumstances in life, I think you shall find that this"—she gestured to the medal—"shall open almost every door you could wish." She gave him a knowing smile.

Elijah blinked. They'd known all along that he was Jewish. Then he realized how ridiculous he'd been. Of course the queen wouldn't let her daughter—the future ruler—marry someone without full knowledge of his background.

"I daresay you would have made as creditable a son-in-law as Mr. McAndrews," the queen continued. "But my daughter seemed to think your heart lay elsewhere."

He let out a breath. Had his feelings for Penelope been so obvious even to the princess?

"Though, at the time, I wondered if Miss Pilkington might have overstated the situation to my daughter, I now think her most astute."

Elijah followed the queen's eyeline. Penelope stared at him, wringing her hands, her brown eyes shining.

"Perhaps Miss Pickering might care for a dance," the queen pronounced. Before Elijah could thank her again, Prince Leopold claimed the queen's hand, and they stepped off the dais to join the whirling couples.

Elijah looked down at the medal again. He'd never have guessed that things would turn out this way. He put one hand in his pocket and gripped his parents' mezuzah, glad he'd transferred it into his evening clothes. Could his parents ever have dreamed this for him? That he'd have a future brighter than *he'd* ever imagined. He gave a short laugh and briefly cast his gaze upward as though they might be watching. Yes, he felt quite certain that they had.

Still, one thing was missing. He may have the moon and even Venus and Saturn in his grasp, but what use was any of it without the sun? Without her?

He stepped down off the dais toward her, thanking those who offered their congratulations, but never losing sight of her. Finally, they stood face-to-face.

"I couldn't believe you made the cachapas," she said. "But then, I could because it's part of who you are—and the kind of food you love to cook. That took such courage."

He shook his head. "Not so much, really. Some might call it foolish. To make a simple griddle cake for royalty."

"I doubt they would say that now," she said, pointing at the medal. "But I meant what you almost told everyone. About yourself."

He gave a self-deprecating laugh. "They already knew, as it turns out. I suppose I owe Lady Helena something for trying to protect me."

Penelope exhaled. "I rather think it was the least she could do after everything."

He inclined his head to show he agreed. "Though she finally recognized your worth. And in that, I can't ever fault her."

Penelope looked up at him through her lashes.

"I asked you the wrong question earlier," he stated.

She bit her lower lip but said nothing.

"Do you, Penelope Pickering, care for me?"

She let out a deep breath. "I . . . Elijah. You deserve—"

He put up a hand to stop her. "No more of that. Penelope, let me be as blunt as I would have been before we started all this—before *gentlemanly* conduct changed my manners and behavior."

She raised her brows.

"You've been the sunshine of my days. Could it be that I'm yours?"

She exhaled. Then looked at the ceiling. Then chewed her lip.

"Am I?" he prompted, his pulse hammering in his throat.

Finally, she met his gaze. "You are." Her cheeks flushed. "But my parentage will only bring you down, Elijah. And I could not do that to you. My parents are happy, yes, but they're also isolated from their homelands. They're isolated from me. Love is not always easy."

"Of course it isn't," he said. "What is?"

Penelope wet her lips, considering. "Very little, I suppose."

He took her small hands in his, not caring if people looked. "I'll take the chance if you will. If I've learned anything from all this, it's that you can always cook up a course of action for a dish, a meal, or even your life, yet things will never turn out quite as you expect. Sometimes they turn out far better."

A grin spread across her face. Her stomach fluttered as his eyes searched hers.

"And to be quite clear, the queen has advised me that this Order of the Peacock means doors will open for me."

She let out a nervous laugh. "Well, of course! It's the highest honor one can receive. And with your knighthood and Royal Seal of Patronage, you can truly create whatever future you wish."

He squeezed her hands. "Penelope, I don't know if I can do—"

"Nonsense, Elijah. You can do anything you put your mind to. Haven't you proven that?" she asked.

He smirked at her. "Thank you for your belief in me. I wouldn't be here without it. But, I was trying to say I don't think I can do . . . without you."

She let out a slow sigh as she peeked up at his earnest face. She didn't trust herself to speak.

"So if you wish to travel to the Pacific, the Americas, the Indian Ocean, or the ends of the earth, I want to be by your side." He took a deep breath. "If you'll let me."

She looked down at his hands enveloping hers. Funny how they seemed to warm her from the inside out—how they seemed to belong there. Her throat had gone dry, so she swallowed before peering up into his hazelnut-brown eyes again. "I believe I might be persuadable. If . . ."

His eyebrows raised, and her heart swelled at the hope on his face.

"You might favor me with another waltz? I know I don't have the royal privilege, but . . ."

"Well," he said as that adorable smile she loved spread across his handsome face. "Shall we dance, Miss Pickering?" The shadows she'd seen in his eyes and the planes of his jaw earlier that evening—and so often over the course of the last months—slipped away. For the first time, his happiness shone from him, eclipsing all else, and the effect was so brilliant, her own joy shimmered up out of her into a laugh.

Penelope grasped his offered hand with hers and rested her left hand on his shoulder. His hand settled on her waist, and she tilted her head back to beam at him. She somehow had the feeling that her heart had expanded and grown like the lightest of soufflés. "If it's with you, Elijah, I could dance all night."

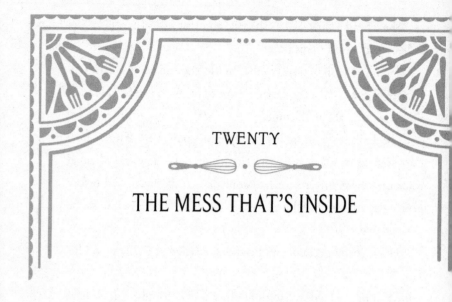

TWENTY

THE MESS THAT'S INSIDE

Helena trudged into the kitchen of Number 9, Cavendish Square, in the wee hours of the morning, the skirts of her ball gown brushing against either side of the open door. This was the only time of day when the kitchen stood like a silent sentinel, waiting for the people to return and prepare for the day. Helena had been known to come down to the kitchen to try a recipe if some new idea occurred to her in the middle of the night, so the staff had left a small fire burning in the massive fireplace.

Helena rather liked coming into the kitchen when everyone slept. It meant she had the room to herself. And there was no one to get in her way. No one talking when she was trying to concentrate.

Of course, there was no one to taste with either. No one to pose ideas to or offer tweaks if they thought of them. No one to laugh with. Helena looked about the room. The kitchen staff had cleaned every surface and pot. Nothing remained of her days spent cooking with Penelope and Elijah. Helena ran her palm over the wooden worktable, thinking of them dancing at the ball, joy written in the curves of their faces. Her heart had swelled for them as she watched Elijah lead Pen around the Great Hall to the beats of the waltz. Even if they never forgave her, she felt sure they'd found happiness tonight.

She would miss them both, but at least she had tried to make amends. Elijah would be knighted and Penelope would graduate with top honors, and the two of them could do whatever they pleased. With the queen's patronage, much of society would welcome Elijah, regardless of his background. Helena should have guessed Lady Rutland would have told the royal family about Elijah, especially after her conversation with Lady Rutland yesterday.

Helena blushed at the thought that, once the queen had learned the truth, she'd been more open to the idea of Elijah marrying Princess Adelaide than Helena had. This indisputable fact clearly said something about Helena—and her prejudices. Helena had always known she often rubbed people the wrong way, but before the last two days, it had never occurred to her that the fault might lie at her feet. For the first time in her life, Helena realized that there was something within her she truly didn't like. And she needed to change it.

Yet, recognizing a *need* to alter one's perceptions and the act of truly altering them are no small matters. And at that hour, all alone in the kitchen, Helena felt more flummoxed than she rarely had before when presented with a challenge. So she did the one thing that always comforted her when circumstances had perplexed her in the past. She decided to cook.

She walked into the larder and scanned the containers, jars, and sacks. Her eyes alighted on two brown coconuts Penelope had acquired from one of her favorite stalls at the night market. She picked one up and rolled it between her hands. Then she saw the block of semi-dark, bittersweet chocolate Elijah was always chopping chunks off of to create frozen delicacies or bon bons. She took the chocolate and then grabbed the flour and golden sugar. She juggled them all in her arms as she made her way back to the worktable. She placed each item neatly on the table—though the coconut did try to roll—then went back to get eggs and butter. She stopped at the knife block on her return and pulled out the square cleaver.

Helena surveyed the ingredients before her. Yes, she knew what she wanted to make. She gripped the coconut in her palm and started knocking it with her cleaver in a series of whacks around its equator. She'd only done it once at school, but she'd watched Penelope enough times to feel confident of the method. She even recalled watching Penelope teach Elijah how to hold a coconut correctly to keep from chopping his fingers off.

Despite herself, she smiled at the thought, remembering his struggles learning how to cut strawberries, hard squash, and mangoes. But once he'd perfected his knife skills, he'd excelled. She stopped thwacking the coconut and inspected the cracked shell. A few more should do it. When it split open, she set down her knife, held the coconut over a bowl to catch the water inside, and used both hands to open it the rest of the way.

A throat cleared in the doorway. Helena glanced up. Penelope and Elijah stepped into the kitchen. Penelope still wore her traveling cloak, and Elijah held his tall hat in his hand. Their finery looked out of place in the kitchen, but as Helena looked down at her gown, the front of which was now spattered with shards of coconut husk and shell, she realized she must look much the same. Penelope and Elijah walked toward her.

"What are you making?" Penelope asked.

Helena's eyes drifted between them as they stopped across from her on the opposite side of the table. "Chocolate coconut empanadas."

Penelope arched a brow.

"In honor of the most accomplished gentleman chef and soon-to-be Culinarian I know."

They traded glances, but Helena didn't know what to make of the silent exchange. "I owe you an apology, Mr. Little," Helena continued. "I should never have said—or thought—what I did. Or put you in that impossible situation. I understand if you cannot forgive me, but . . ." She trailed off, momentarily unsure what more she could say without offending them further. "But I wish to offer my sincerest congratulations. On *all* your triumphs. It couldn't have happened to a finer fellow. I truly believe that."

He met her anxious gaze with his steady one. "Thank you, Lady Helena."

"And"—she looked at each of them again—"I hope you'll be exceedingly, fiercely happy together—no one deserves it more."

"Thank you, Helena," Penelope said. She looked up at Elijah with an adoring smile. "I rather think we shall."

Elijah grinned back at her, then looked at Helena. "Did I ever tell you my secret for the perfect sweet empanada dough?"

Helena bit the inside of her cheek. "I'm certain I never thought to ask."

He unbuttoned his elegant tailcoat and yanked his arms out of the sleeves. Then he draped it on the other table and began rolling up the sleeves of his shirt. "It's a good thing I happen to have a free moment to teach you," he stated.

Penelope took off her cloak and retrieved a spoon, a paring knife, and one of the aprons hanging from a peg near the door. "And I'm quite certain you barely recall the best way to extract the meat from that coconut. Do you deny it?"

Helena swallowed down the tightness that had inexplicably appeared in the back of her throat. She shook her head.

Penelope nodded once as she tied on the apron. "Just as I thought. It's fortunate Pierce was still awake to let us in."

Elijah went for a bowl and began measuring the flour.

Helena opened and closed her mouth. "But . . . do you really wish to help me? I've been so awful to you both."

Penelope let out a sigh. "Of course we do, you goose."

At first, shock ran through Helena at the moniker, but then she started laughing. Penelope giggled. Even Elijah let out a snort of laughter and tried to cover it with a cough.

Helena bit her lip. "I deserved that. I promise to do my utmost not to act too high-handed in future."

"And to ask for our opinions," Penelope said, handing her the spoon.

Helena nodded, almost bouncing on her toes. "I give my word to you both." She set down the spoon and ran around the table to pull Penelope into a quick embrace. She felt her friend stiffen in surprise, but then her arms came around Helena, returning her impulsive hug. Helena felt a bit ridiculous, but she also thought it important Pen knew how she felt. Helena stepped back and turned to Elijah.

She offered him her hand to shake. His face registered shock for the second time that evening, but he took it, and Helena gave him a brilliant smile.

"I hope you know you are always welcome to come back here to stay. For as long as you'd like," she said.

"Thank you, Helena," Penelope said. "I already told the hotel to send my things here on the morrow." She glanced at Elijah.

"And I picked up my bag from the Hungry Hare after we left the ball. Now," he said, assuming a serious expression, "these empanadas aren't going to make themselves, are they?"

Helena swallowed as she felt tears gathering in the corners of her eyes. She shook her head at herself to keep them from falling. Then she stretched to her full height, swallowed once more, and beamed at her friends. "As usual, Mr. Little, you are quite right."

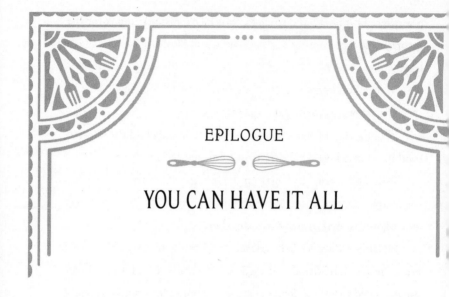

YOU CAN HAVE IT ALL

A few weeks later, Penelope, Elijah, and Helena stood by the railing of the ship that would take them and Penelope's parents down the Atlantic around the Cape of Good Hope to Australia and then on to Borneo, and as far as the Philippine Islands. Penelope and Helena still planned to return to England in a year or so and take their places in society as Britain's preeminent Culinarians, and Elijah wanted to use his knighthood and Order of the Peacock to secure investors for a grand food hall selling delicacies from throughout the world, but they'd all agreed there was plenty of time for that. Today, Penelope was simply ecstatic to be with her parents, her best friend, and her love. She grinned at Elijah and took his hand, not caring if the ship's crew noted it or not.

He squeezed her hand in his. "I wish my uncle could have seen us off," he said. His uncle Jonathan had returned to England only a week ago. Elijah had gone to see him and explained what had happened while he was at sea. His uncle had told Elijah his parents would have been proud to know their son had become such a fine gentleman—let alone a knight and recipient of some fancy Order of the Peacock. He'd also given Elijah more recipes he'd collected on his voyage.

Elijah and Penelope planned to try them together as soon as they could secure the use of a kitchen. Elijah had been reluctant to leave England just as his uncle Jonathan returned, but they were well used to letter writing by now.

He'd also visited Mr. Benjamin before they'd left. The tailor had taken one look at Elijah's medal and said, "What did I tell you about the peacock, young man? True, you were a *mentsh* before, but now you're a *mentsh* even the queen respects. But he who has not tasted the bitter does not taste the sweet. Be sure you enjoy the sweet. Moishe would want you to." Then they'd spent two hours reminiscing about Elijah's parents.

Helena's parents had proved more of an issue. They'd returned to Number 9, Cavendish Square, mere days before Helena and Penelope's graduation from the Royal Academy to find that the daughter they hadn't seen in months now wished to travel abroad with her friends. At first, Helena's mother had railed against the scheme, but neither she nor her husband could ignore the change in Helena that had occurred in their absence. Some of her selfishness, which they'd often lamented to each other, but had done little to curb, had disappeared. Her ambition had always surprised them, considering she would be well provided for on their deaths, and her ambition remained, yet it was no longer for herself alone. She now wanted her friends to succeed as well and talked of it often, which her parents considered an improvement in her character. An improvement that they concluded must be due to Penelope and Elijah's influence.

In the end, Helena's parents had relented and allowed their daughter to tour with the Pickerings, especially when Lady Rutland lent her opinion that a wider view of the world could only improve Helena's disposition and culinary breadth. As the marquess had always been of such an opinion himself, and had liberally applied such principles to his son and heir, the annoyance that Helena had only now come around to the idea of expanding her horizons abroad just as her family had returned to England soon waned, and Helena got her way—as she often did, it must be said.

As Lady Rutland had promised, Helena received top marks on her final project. After the exhibition, Lady Rutland had called Helena back to the Royal Academy, where she'd given her credit for defending Elijah. Lady Rutland hoped that Helena's project would, indeed, change how much importance society placed on an individual's birth. Elijah, at least, had proven one could elevate their status with education and hard work. Society wouldn't change overnight, but she did think Elijah's success could be an important step in the right direction.

At their graduation, Lady Rutland had surprised everyone with the announcement that Miss Penelope Pickering had achieved the Young Culinarian of the Year award for her efforts to uncover the unique and exciting cuisine of the Americas and for her help teaching Mr. Elijah Little, the newest member of the royal Order of the Peacock. No one clapped louder than Helena—even *she* realized that Penelope had worked harder than she had that term.

Mabel Pilkington could not help herself from giving Helena a small dig as they watched Penelope accept the plate-shaped bronze sculpture from Lady Rutland. "I suppose the best Culinarian won," she said, hoping to goad Helena into saying something she'd regret. For her part, Mabel would be staying on as personal culinary consultant to Princess Adelaide after graduation, and she was feeling quite pleased with herself for being right about Elijah's feelings for Penelope and hers for him. That she'd been wrong about Penelope's origin and had perpetuated an exaggerated rumor about her parents bothered her not one whit. Like Helena, Mabel was never overly prone to introspection.

"My dear Mabel," Helena said, turning to her, "you've never been more correct."

Mabel closed her mouth and kept it shut until they'd all dispersed after the ceremony.

Helena stopped waving to her parents and brother as they disappeared into their carriage sitting at the dock. They'd accompanied her, Elijah, and Penelope to meet the Pickerings in Liverpool. "I sincerely hope we shall be able to survive on the ship's stores until we put in for our first port of call. I know the captain has asked us to dine with him, but I do worry that it won't be"—she looked around them at the crew members walking the decks and lowered her voice—"quite what we're used to," Helena said to Penelope and Elijah.

"I doubt we will have as much variety as we'd prefer, but shipboard fare has improved markedly in recent years," Penelope said.

"I just hope they'll have something besides salt pork for Elijah. Perhaps we should have brought some extra dried beef—just in case." Helena tilted her head at them.

"Don't worry over me," Elijah said with a hint of a smile. "I'll find something. I always do."

"Of course you do," Helena said. "I was only thinking."

"I appreciate it," Elijah replied. He winked at Penelope, still amazed that Helena could change—and grow. A part of him had never believed she'd accept him for who he was—and Penelope too. When they'd all met Penelope's parents, Elijah had watched Helena closely, but she'd shown no sign of disapproval or awkwardness. She'd curtsied to Penelope's mother, a striking woman who, though short of stature like her daughter, looked very little like her daughter at first glance. Her dark, raisin-brown hair was many shades darker than Penelope's, her nose lacked Penelope's bridge, and she was quite a bit tanner than Elijah had expected. But she had all her daughter's warmth and kind disposition, and she welcomed her daughter's friends with embraces and smiles. Penelope's father had folded Penelope into his arms as soon as he saw her, with no regard for the rest of the company. Penelope did favor him more in looks, as she'd said, though it took Elijah some time to see the resemblances of each parent in the girl he loved.

"We missed you, my girl," her father had said as they'd hugged.

"I missed you, Papa," Penelope replied, her eyes shining with unshed tears. She'd introduced Helena's parents, and Mr. Pickering recalled his manners, bowing to the marquess, marquessate, and Helena and her brother. Then Penelope introduced Elijah.

"And last, but not least, Papa, Nanay, this is Sir Elijah Little."

Elijah held his breath. He didn't know when he'd grow used to everyone using "Sir" before his name. Yet he was well and truly a knight now; he'd kneeled with his right knee on the investiture stool before the queen, and she had dubbed him with a sword. Penelope and Helena's applause had created quite a din during the ceremony.

Elijah bowed to Penelope's parents, hoping against hope that they wouldn't hate him.

"Sir Elijah Little," her father said, "we've heard a great deal about you."

Elijah swallowed. "From all Miss Pickering has told me about you and Mrs. Pickering, I think you must be remarkable people. I'm honored to meet you both, sir."

Mr. Pickering's eyes swept over him for a long moment. Then the lines at his brow softened, and he offered Elijah a smile. "We're glad to have you on the voyage, young man." He looked at his wife, who had linked arms with Penelope.

"Anyone as important to our Penelope as you must be well worth knowing," Mrs. Pickering stated.

Elijah let out a relieved sigh. "Thank you, ma'am." He nodded at Mr. Pickering. "Sir."

Elijah could hardly believe how thoroughly his life had changed in a few short months. Now as he gazed out at the open ocean beckoning to them, he held tight to Penelope's hand. She angled her chin up, the amber rings around her pupils gleaming up at him.

"I think I'll go below and start unpacking," Helena said, putting a hand on the crown of her bonnet as the wind picked up.

They both nodded, ignorant of the fact that she was actually going to speak to the captain to ensure they had something other than salt pork in the ship's stores.

"What are you thinking?" Penelope asked Elijah.

"That I can't quite believe my luck. I'm off on a voyage to see the world with the lady I love." He raised his brows. "I suppose Helena was right after all."

"About what?"

He let out an amused breath. "With the right training from the right person"—he winked at her—"anyone can have the moon." He raised his free hand and brushed a windblown curl away from Penelope's eye.

Her breath caught, but she tilted her head and said in a teasing tone, "You once said the likes of you never got the moon."

He shook his head at himself as he leaned closer to her. "The more fool me."

"By the way, I love you too," she whispered.

He smirked at her in that adorable way. "Would it be cliché to say that my heart went on a journey to the moon? I think that might be more accurate."

She giggled. "Yes, I rather think it would be cliché. But I quite like it all the same." Then, as the ship set sail, she raised herself up on her toes and kissed him. His lips brushed against hers with intoxicating softness, and she sighed against him, knowing there was nowhere else on earth she'd rather be.

The shouts of men on the rigging, gulls squawking overhead, and the scent of the briny sea air all fell away, leaving only the rhythmic beating of their hearts as they found themselves in each other's arms. Many years later, when they were older and graying, both Penelope and Elijah would agree that this moment marked the beginning of countless happy days filled with grand culinary adventures.

Elijah, Penelope, and Helena's (Slightly Modernized) Recipe for Chocolate Coconut Empanadas

For the filling:

- Grate a fresh coconut into small shreds.
- Toast one teacup's worth (about ½ cup measure) of coconut in a pan or in the oven until light brown in color.
- Grate or chop another teacup's worth (½ cup measure) of bittersweet chocolate (at least 60 percent cocoa solids) into small pieces.
- Grind another teacup full (½ cup measure) of untoasted coconut in a large mortar and pestle. Add room-temperature water to the ground coconut a spoonful at a time until you have a thick yet viscous paste. It should be the consistency of double cream.
- Warm the coconut cream in a pot until small bubbles start

to appear, then immediately remove from heat. Do not allow mixture to boil. Add chopped chocolate to coconut cream and let sit undisturbed for 5 minutes. After 5 minutes, stir until all chocolate has melted.

- Set aside to let cool to below body temperature, then add most of the toasted coconut, reserving a spoonful or two for garnish.

For the empanada dough:

- In a large bowl, mix together 6 teacups (about 3 cups measured) of flour, ¼ to ½ teaspoon salt, and 1 tablespoon sugar or honey.
- Mix 6 ounces cold, unsalted butter, into the flour mixture with your hands or a pastry cutter until butter is completely coated and crumbs are approximately the size of dried cherries.
- Add 1 egg to 2 ounces (¼ cup) of water or milk in a separate bowl and beat until combined.
- Add in small increments to flour mixture, stirring with a spoon or your hands until a clumpy dough forms. If needed, add more water or milk until dough is correct consistency.
- Split the dough into 2 large balls and flatten each slightly into disks.
- Roll out the dough into a thin sheet and cut out round shapes for empanadas using round molds or a small plate. Alternatively, make small, individual balls of dough, and

roll each into a circle (which needn't be perfectly round),
or use a tortilla press (if you have one) to flatten each
dough ball.

Assembling and baking the empanadas:

- Place a spoonful of filling in the middle of each empanada
  disk. The amount of filling will vary based on the size you
  cut your empanada dough, but avoid overstuffing.
- To seal, fold the disk over the filling to make a half-moon
  shape, and seal the edges by pressing the dough with your
  fingers. If dough edges do not stick together easily, brush
  the inside edges with egg white to act as a glue and/or use a
  fork to crimp around the edges. To attempt the curled seal,
  use your fingers to twist and curl the edges. Depending on
  the size of empanadas and amount of filling used, there
  may be dough or filling left over.
- For best results, let cool in an icebox or a very cold place
  (or refrigerator) for at least half an hour before baking. For
  an attractive golden finish, brush empanadas with an egg
  wash (a whole whisked egg or one egg yolk whisked with
  a few drops of water). Sprinkle tops with reserved toasted
  coconut.
- Bake the empanadas in a medium-hot place in a wood-
  burning oven, or on a flat pan in a gas oven heated to
  375–400 degrees Fahrenheit. Temperature will vary based
  on the oven and the size of the empanadas. If empanadas
  are on the smaller side, bake at 375 degrees Fahrenheit and

keep checking for color. Baking time will also vary based on oven and size of empanadas but will likely take 18–25 minutes. Finished empanadas should be golden.

Let cool slightly before devouring with friends!

HISTORICAL NOTE

For those of you asking yourself why you don't recall the Charlottian age of British history, let me assure you that your memory has not betrayed you! King George IV's only heir was Princess Charlotte Augusta of Wales. When she was born on January 7, 1796, she was, in fact, the only legitimate grandchild of King George III, and immediately became the heir apparent to the British throne. By all accounts, she was a clever girl who showed an interest in law and politics early on and was known for her lack of formality and hot temper. As mentioned in this story, she was almost universally loved by the people of Britain, who were growing increasingly disgusted with George IV's (who was at that point still the prince regent) excesses. The people saw her as a new hope for a new era.

Princess Charlotte married Prince Leopold of Saxe-Coburg in 1816 (who later became the King of Belgium and the uncle of Prince

Albert of Saxe-Coburg, who married Queen Victoria in 1840). The couple was very happy, and when the princess became pregnant in 1817, the country rejoiced. Unfortunately, the labor did not go well and on November 6, Princess Charlotte died five hours after giving birth to a stillborn baby.

The princess's terrible early death sent her family and the entire country into mourning. The prince regent was so grief-stricken, he couldn't attend her funeral. Her mother, Caroline of Brunswick, fainted when she heard the news. The people turned out in droves to line the streets of Windsor for her funeral.

Princess Charlotte is now almost a footnote in British history. Her death forced the prince regent's brothers into a race to marry and produce legitimate heirs—the first of whom became Queen Victoria in 1837. I find it rather fascinating to think that if Princess Charlotte hadn't died in 1817, Queen Victoria wouldn't have been born. In many ways, the repression of the Victorian age was a reaction to the "fast times" of the Regency era.

With this book, I wanted to explore a world where women wouldn't be so constrained by the strict expectations imposed on them by Victorian society. Upper-class women in Georgian and Regency society were gaining more and more freedoms, so I had a grand time imagining how a potential Charlottian age could have looked, and how a government and society less focused on imperialism and more focused on increasing gender equality, education, and international diplomatic relations might have evolved.

I was also keen to show how people like Elijah and Penelope would have fared in society, which led me to *The Jews of Georgian England 1714–1830* by Tom M. Endelman, which I highly recommend if you are looking to read more about this subject. The truth is that Jews were treated better in England during this time than in most countries in Europe, but as mentioned in this novel, they were not allowed to vote in parliamentary elections, enter into government service, hold a municipal office, sit in the House of Commons, study to become lawyers, or attend Britain's oldest universities, and thus, they did not have all the privileges of other British citizens.

Merchants in the city of London did, indeed, keep Jews from operating retail businesses there by requiring all tradesmen to take a Christian oath. Jews who wanted to work around this resorted to having their records claim a Christian employee as the owner of their business or styling their store as a warehouse, where they actually sold goods or services retail. For a number of reasons, however, the majority of Jews had little interest in gaining all the rights that other Englishmen had, so there was never a large push for emancipation during this era as there was in other European countries like Germany, France, and Italy, where they had discriminatory laws that made survival for Jews very difficult. The majority of Ashkenazi Jews who came to England between 1700 and 1830 came from Germany, and from the Netherlands and Poland in smaller numbers.

But even in Britain, antisemitism was rampant and pervasive. There was a very real stigma attached to the word "Jew," and many people like Elijah and his uncle did change their names to avoid these associations. Many also changed their appearances: men shaved their beards and adopted English fashions; women started wearing low-cut gowns and abandoned the custom of wearing wigs. Well-to-do

Jews bought country estates to achieve gentlemanly status, and those who moved to the country effectively cut themselves off from the institutions that allowed them to preserve traditional Judaism such as Jewish schools, synagogues, and kosher butcher shops. Prosperous and poor Jews alike often had to make accommodations to their eating habits to fit in.

Poor boys like Elijah hawked and peddled their wares on streets and in markets throughout the city of London, and by 1800 the public had firmly associated the lemon-and-orange street trade with Jewish hawkers. Even in the 1830s, upward mobility was possible for the Jewish poor, but in many cases it didn't last long. A person could make money peddling goods, only to have their savings or inventory wiped out by one stroke of bad luck like an assault or a break-in. When you weren't trained for any special trade, couldn't afford to educate your children for more than three to five years, or pay the fee to apprentice your children to an artisan, a place in the middle class was difficult to grasp, let alone keep hold of.

In England during the 1830s, most formal dining was not as we know it today. Instead, the fashion was to dine *à la française*, where all dishes, including what we would consider desserts, were laid out on the dining table at the same time. This was a way for the upper classes to show off their wealth in both the amount of food presented and in their expensive tableware. By the mid-1800s, however, most people had adopted *service à la russe*, which is essentially eating course by course—as is the custom in fine dining establishments in many places throughout the world to this day.

Technically, dining *à la russe* was first noted by French chef Antonin Carême when he visited the court of Tsar Alexander I in

1818, so I thought it possible for some English chef or Culinarian to have also visited Russia around that time and brought the dining method back to England a bit earlier. Culinarians, of course, are an invention of mine, as is the Glorious Kitchen at Hampton Court Palace. For a rendering of what a royal kitchen looked like in the 1820s, I recommend doing a web search for the Royal Pavilion at Brighton's Great Kitchen. George IV was so proud of it, he gave people who visited him at the Royal Pavilion tours so he could show it off. It even had an automatic rotisserie for all the different meats he loved.

Though there were certainly interracial marriages and mixed-race children in Britain at this time, I have taken some small leaps with Penelope's parents' marriage. Britain occupied Manila from 1762 to 1764 during the Seven Years' War, but when the war ended, the British eventually handed Manila back to the Spanish. Though British troops never returned to the Philippines, British merchant ships often traveled through the South Pacific, so I thought it possible that Penelope's parents might have crossed paths. Having Penelope's nanay come from the island of Panay was a personal point of privilege since my mother and her family come from Ilo Ilo.

Though I haven't yet been able to visit the homelands of my ancestors, food has always been a way for me to connect to their cultures. I truly believe that food can be the perfect gateway to learning about cultures and peoples you may know little to nothing about. Great food can open your eyes to all kinds of possibilities and break down barriers at the same time. Because, after all, what is a cachapa but a latke by another name?

My parents introduced me to musicals before I can remember.

Along with their love of film musicals (I'd seen all the Rodgers and Hammerstein movie musicals before I was seven), they made a point of taking me and my siblings to the theater whenever possible, and they had all their favorite musical scores on records or cassette tapes, which they would bring on every family vacation. I'm fairly certain I knew the music and lyrics to Lerner and Loewe's *My Fair Lady* and *Gigi* long before I fully understood the stories, thanks to those cassette tapes and my parents' love of travel.

But when I grew old enough to understand *My Fair Lady* and its source material, *Pygmalion*, it still remained one of my favorite musicals—even as I wished certain elements could be changed or turn out differently. *My Fine Fellow* is, of course, the result of my many years delighting in the journey that George Bernard Shaw created in 1912 for Eliza Dolittle, Henry Higgins, and Colonel Pickering—from my 21st century perspective. I hope you've enjoyed reading it as much as I adored creating it!

Wishing you love and cookies,

Jennieke

ACKNOWLEDGMENTS

Writing this book in the midst of a global pandemic had its challenges, not the least of which was figuring out how to adapt to a new routine while trying to stay motivated. One thing that kept me writing was the knowledge that people who had read *Dangerous Alliance* were eager to read this book. My first thanks, therefore, must go to you if you are reading this, and to everyone who read *Dangerous Alliance* and wrote a review, took amazing photos, messaged or Tweeted at me with your enthusiasm, or came to an in-person event before the pandemic. Your passion kept me going when I felt like doomscrolling or watching TV all day long instead of writing. Also, thank you so much to my extended family and friends who were so supportive of *Dangerous Alliance* and excited for *My Fine Fellow*. I love you all!

Of course there were many people who held my feet to the fire in a number of ways as I wrote this book, and my infinite thanks must go to all of them. To my wonderful agent, Jennifer Unter, who had faith in the potential of this book when it was only an idea I had summarized in less than a page: for your tireless support of me, *My Fine Fellow*, and *Dangerous Alliance*, you have my eternal gratitude.

Kristen Pettit, thank you for opening my eyes to new ideas and different ways of thinking about what my characters might do. Your feedback made the manuscript that much better by helping me get out of my own head for a while and persuading me to see things from another perspective.

Obvious thanks must also go to Jessie Gang and Kasi Turpin for yet another gorgeous cover. I also wish to applaud the entire team at HarperCollins who made this book possible, especially Clare Vaughn, Jessica Berg, Jen Strada, Gwen Morton, Alison Klapthor, Meghan Pettit, Allison Brown, Lisa Calcasola, and Mitchell Thorpe. And, of course, many thanks to Professor Nadia Valman for your expertise and insights on the historical authenticity of the story.

To my publicist, Kathleen Carter: thank you so much for everything you do and for being such an indefatigable advocate for *My Fine Fellow*. I'm forever grateful.

To the authors who took the time to read this book (and the last one) and write lovely blurbs, thank you for your generosity. Stacey Lee, Rachel Lynn Solomon, Alexa Donne, Jacqueline Firkins, and Tobie Easton, you are simply wonderful humans, and I appreciate you so very much!

I must also send shout-outs to my writer friends who kept me going and encouraged me while I was writing and editing *My Fine Fellow* in the throes of the pandemic. Alexa Donne, Shannon Price, Kalyn Josephson, Dallas Woodburn, Jacqueline Firkins, Samantha

Hastings, and Alex Samuely, your phone calls, video calls, DMs, and emails kept me sane, and you deserve all the virtual hugs! Tobie Easton, you're always the best, and I hope you know why. Thank you for listening while I agonized over writing the logistics of a competition story, for reading this book before anyone else, for always being there at the other end of the phone, and for being you. (I would say you're the true Penelope of our friendship, but that would make me Helena, so I'll have to mull over some better comparisons. 😉)

In 2020 and 2021, the littlest things people did to support each other truly stand out in my memory. Mom and Aaron, thank you for *all* your support and assistance while I was writing and revising. Mariella, thank you for always being excited to read my stories and swoon over covers, even when we're far apart. Aunt Shirley: Thank you for sending me your Filipino cookbook when so many libraries were closed, for brainstorming dish ideas with me, and for being one of the first adults in my life to share recipes with me—I love you! Thanks and tons of love must also go to the Boroumands for constantly being there and for standing by at all times to help at a moment's notice, despite the hardship and loss of the year.

I have endless gratitude for my parents for passing on their enjoyment of *My Fair Lady* (and musicals in general) to me. To my dad, Jonathan, occasionally known as "Rex" within the city of London, I know you'd have loved this one. Mom, thank you for always showing up at the opening night of every play or concert I've ever performed in with flowers and a huge hug, for your encouragement, and for always having the bravery to unapologetically be yourself in the face of other peoples' prejudices. With your marriage, you and Dad set an example for your children that we all try to emulate. I'm

READ ON FOR AN EXCERPT FROM

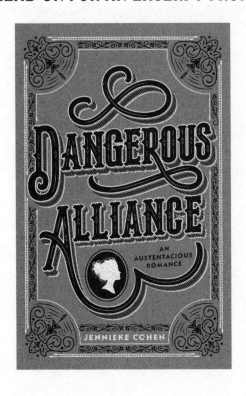

CHAPTER THE FIRST

The danger, however, was at present so unperceived, that
they did not by any means rank as misfortunes with her.
—Jane Austen, *Emma*

APRIL 1817

OAKBRIDGE ESTATE, HAMPSHIRE, ENGLAND

The lichen-kissed stone dropped onto the rock pile with a hollow clack. Lady Victoria Aston rested her aching hands on the rough stone. She wiped her muddy palms down the front of her thighs, smearing muck onto her father's old tan breeches. When attempting to save the lives of a particularly bothersome flock of sheep, one had to make sacrifices.

With two more sizable stones, she would close the gap in the wall. Then she could scour Oakbridge's 6,562 acres for the estate shepherd. Vicky narrowed her eyes at a shaggy old ewe: one of many she'd found out-of-bounds in the neighboring pasture. They'd jumped over the crumbling gap and gobbled a patch of indigestible clover. Soon, their bellies would bloat, and without the shepherd's aid, they would certainly perish.

Inhaling the clean morning air, redolent with the perfume of freshly drying grass, Vicky bent for another rock. This would never have happened to Emma Woodhouse. Or rather, Emma Woodhouse would never have *let* it happen to her.

Having just finished reading *Emma* for the third time since its publication, Vicky had lately found herself comparing her own country existence to the heroine of said novel. Not that Emma was her favorite heroine from the four novels written by the author known only to the public as "a lady" (but whom most of the local Hampshire society knew to be one Miss Jane Austen). No, Vicky reserved that honor for Miss Elizabeth Bennet of *Pride and Prejudice*.

A clear picture of Elizabeth Bennet muddying her gown to fix a stone wall darted into Vicky's mind—after all, Elizabeth had walked miles unaccompanied to see her sister, Jane, when she was ill and staying at Netherfield. Vicky's lips curved into a smile at the idea that her favorite heroine would approve of her behavior.

As Vicky straightened, movement far in the distance caught her eye. She squinted. Amid the emerald-green fields on the other side of the wall, a rider in a russet coat and dark hat cantered adjacent to a short hedgerow. She couldn't see his face, but his bearing looked familiar. She blinked.

Surely, it wasn't the *one* person she had no wish to see on such a morning. Fate wouldn't be so cruel.

She glanced down at her father's muddy breeches. They didn't exactly outline her legs, but they weren't particularly loose either. They hugged her hips just tightly enough to allow her to tuck a muslin shirt into them and actually stay up without other assistance. She'd buttoned the top half of her olive-green riding habit almost up to her neck for a semblance of decency, but by any stranger's standard, she was courting scandal.

She peered at the rider again. His attire proclaimed him a gentleman, and although she still couldn't make out his features, he rode a peculiar chestnut of medium height that looked something like a working horse. She had never seen the breed before.

Well, if he—whoever he was—felt scandalized by her appearance, that was his affair. Breeches afforded more comfort on her post-dawn inspections across the estate and allowed her to ride astride. That meant she could be more efficient helping her father, especially when something went wrong, like today. Their management strategies shouldered the livelihoods of more than a hundred individuals; if her father or his steward couldn't allocate funds or attention to one small piece of the puzzle making up the estate, someone less fortunate would suffer. Vicky helped wherever and whenever she could.

She hauled the stone up and set it on the pile with an involuntary squeak before glancing back at the rider.

He had jumped the hedgerow. Now he rode toward her, picking up speed. *What was he—*

Vicky's stomach tensed as his face came into focus. It was just as she'd feared: the rider was Tom Sherborne. Blast! She looked at her breeches again and winced.

Still some fifty feet away, Tom raised his hand and something fluttered in her chest. But he wasn't greeting her as she'd thought. With his whole arm, he pointed at something behind her.

She frowned. As she turned, something hard collided with the side of her head. White-hot pain burst through her skull. Her vision pitched sideways and her neck whipped to the right. As her knees smacked into the soggy turf, everything went black.

A rhythmic thudding invaded Vicky's head. Was it her heart? The rumble grew louder with each thump. She inhaled, and the smell of wet grass, mud, and sheep droppings flooded her nostrils. She groaned and forced her eyes open.

Her head sat askew on the ground, though it seemed she'd fallen face-first. A tender spot on the side of her head made her wince. She traced it with careful fingers, but that only intensified the pounding in her ears.

What had struck her? Through the blades of grass, a blurred movement caught her eye. Each motion was an agony, but Vicky pushed herself off the soggy ground with both hands until she sat upright. Blinking to clear her vision, she concentrated on the moving shape coming toward her.

Her cheeks blanched. The horse and rider she'd seen earlier—correction, Tom Sherborne and his horse—effortlessly jumped the stone wall. Her stomach dropped.

She'd never seen Tom riding at such an early hour—not a single time since he'd returned to England. Although his own estate bordered Oakbridge, she'd only glimpsed him twice in the last year: once in the village from opposite ends of the high street where he'd promptly disappeared into a tavern, and once at the village fair where he'd bought a gingerbread square and promptly ridden away.

Anyone else might have considered these circumstances coincidental, but Vicky knew better. She *knew* Tom Sherborne was avoiding her. *Unjustly* in point of fact, and he had been doing so for the last five years. Yet there he sat, reining in his odd-looking chestnut a mere two and a half feet away.

"Are you all right?" he bellowed from the saddle.

Her head whirled as she stared up at the face she'd known so well as a child. His hair fell in the same mahogany-brown waves around his forehead and ears, contrasting slightly with his light brown eyes. He was clean-shaven just as he'd been at fourteen, but his jaw and cheeks now had the angular sharpness of a man. His nose and forehead could have been copied from a marble bust of some Roman emperor.

Her pulse thrummed in her ears, so she pulled in a breath. "Er..."

His lips compressed into a frown, and his dark brows knit together.

How she'd missed that serious countenance. Yet that boy she'd known had thrown away their friendship and never given her a reason.

"My head," she muttered. She touched the lump materializing on her skull. "What happened?" She swallowed several times and wished for a glass of water.

"A man attacked you. I tried to warn you."

"What do you mean, 'attacked'? Who would possibly attack me?" She touched her head again.

Tom caught her eye for a brief moment before looking off into the distance behind her. "Whoever he was, he had a horse tethered at the edge of the trees."

Vicky shook her head. "But why—I don't understand—"

"I can still catch him," Tom interrupted. "Are you well enough to stay here?"

She inhaled and tilted her head gingerly. The pain had dulled a bit. "I think so." She looked up at him. "What do you mean stay—"

"*Stay* here," he repeated, kicking his boots into his horse's flanks. Clods of grass and mud flew into the air as they raced away.

"Wait!" But his horse had already carried him out of earshot.

Vicky clenched her jaw as she watched horse and rider disappear into a nearby copse of trees. How dare Tom hurry off and leave her sitting in a field? Especially if someone had attacked her! Well, if he thought she'd allow him to fight her battles for her, he was very much mistaken. She bent her knees and pushed herself off the ground. Stars reeled before her eyes. She swallowed an unladylike curse as she drew in a deep breath. Then she glanced in the direction Tom had disappeared.

If Tom had ridden that way, her attacker must have fled toward the road to London. If that were his goal, then the fastest way to head him off would be to ride across the field *around* the trees and intercept him. Tom should know as well as she did that he would never overtake the man by following him through the dense forest.

But she still could. Moreover, she was not about to sit here like an invalid just because her head hurt. Who did Tom think he was, trying to act the hero now? He'd been the one playing the coward these last five years.

Vicky stumbled to the tree where she'd tied her horse, Jilly. She unwound the reins, led her to an undamaged stretch of wall, and used it to jump into the saddle. A wave of dizziness washed through her head down into her stomach. She stilled and breathed, fully aware she was losing time.

Just get moving. Vicky gritted her teeth, pulled the reins to the right, kicked Jilly's flanks, and urged her to gallop across the field toward the attacker.

Jilly's ears pricked up, almost as though she sensed the urgency of the situation. They crossed the field in record time. The wind whipped Vicky's loose hair back as she steered Jilly around the edge of the trees. Her heart hammered in her chest. Would she catch the villain before he reached the road to London?

Vicky scanned ahead, her gaze narrowing in on the country lane that fed into the London post road. She glanced to the left, where Tom and the attacker should emerge. She couldn't see them yet, but they would soon arrive.

The thundering of hooves reached her ears.

With a satisfied breath, Vicky urged Jilly forward until they reached the edge of the road. But what could she do now that she had positioned herself in front of the chase? She looked around for something to give her an advantage. Just a smattering of broken twigs and dead leaves lay scattered on the road; she couldn't see one fallen branch or throwable rock—nothing she could use to slow the assailant.

Several yards farther down, trees lined her side of the road. Opposite those trees, a tall, overgrown hedgerow began. If she could maneuver Jilly to stand across the road in that narrow space, the man would have to stop. She guided her horse to the spot and made her stand so her head was near the hedgerow. The gap wasn't as narrow as it had looked. Just enough space for the man to maneuver around them remained, although there certainly wasn't enough width for a horse galloping at full speed.

Pummeling horse hooves resounded up through the earth as a man with a handkerchief tied around his nose and mouth charged down the road toward her, his black greatcoat flapping in the wind like the cape of a demonic villain straight from the pages of one of Mrs. Radcliffe's preposterous romances. Vicky's stomach quavered. It was too late to question her plan. Tom and his stocky horse followed close at the man's back.

Vicky swallowed hard. The man wasn't slowing.

She tightened her grip on the reins, causing Jilly to totter beneath her. She pressed her knees into Jilly's flanks, trying to steady her, but Jilly only jittered more. The horse sensed her fear.

Vicky closed her eyes and breathed. "Stand, Jilly. Stand and stay." Beneath her, the horse stilled. Vicky's eyes flew open in triumph, but as she looked to the side, the man still barreled down the road.

Only a few yards separated them now; they were so close she could see white foam outlining the horse's mouth. The man's eyes narrowed. He was not going to stop.

"Move," Tom shouted. "Move!"

In that moment, time slowed to a crawl. She wanted to listen, but she could no longer feel her legs. All she felt was her pounding heart and the leather of the reins cutting into her palms. The man would hit her!

Vicky closed her eyes, waiting for the impact. Then Jilly reared up on her hind legs, and the back of her head slammed into Vicky's face. Sparks clouded her vision as the weightlessness disappeared and a wave of dizziness took its place. A rush of air blew past her as the assailant and his horse careened in front of them. Then she was falling, falling until she landed with a bone-jarring thud onto a muddy patch of ground.

Vicky blinked. Once. Twice.

She vaguely knew Jilly hadn't yet trampled her, and through the pain and nausea, she forced herself to look to ensure she was in no more danger.

To her left, Tom pulled back hard on his reins to keep from colliding with Jilly. For a terrifying moment, Vicky thought he wouldn't be able to stop his horse. The muscles in the horse's legs bulged and its shoulders strained until it skidded to a halt merely feet away.

Vicky slumped back onto the ground in relief, not remembering the road's damp condition until her hair squished in the mud. Ugh.

Of the countless embarrassing moments in all her seventeen years, this one secured the prize for most ghastly.

Tom's mount pawed the ground with its front hooves. The horse's hind legs clenched in anticipation, intent on continuing the chase. Evidently considering it, Tom pulled the reins sideways to make his horse go around her.

Hope surged through her. Falling off her horse in such a useless fashion had dealt her dignity a serious blow, but if he continued on, at least she'd be spared the humiliation of conversing with him while caked in mud. To encourage him to leave, she pushed herself to sit upright, but an involuntary hiss of pain escaped her.

Tom cursed and jumped to the ground. "I cannot believe your

recklessness! Are you incapable of doing as you're told?"

Anger bloomed in her cheeks as she gaped up at him. He hadn't said one word to her in five years, and now he was berating her?

She squelched back the urge to lie down and cry. This wasn't supposed to happen. During the last fourteen months since Tom had returned to England and settled in at Halworth Hall, Vicky had prepared herself for their first meeting. She'd known it would happen eventually, with him living only miles away, and the prospect of speaking with him again had actually kept her in alternating states of excitement and nervous anticipation for weeks. Yet despite her nerves she had wisely planned for their meeting. As her sister, Althea, often said: planning was the mark of an evolved individual.

So Vicky had intended to be perfectly composed when she met Tom again—absolutely radiant in her favorite pale pink, satin ball gown—and graciously allow him to take her hand as he bowed in greeting. He would see she was no longer the improper little girl he'd deemed unworthy to be his friend.

She bit her lip until it throbbed. At the moment, she certainly wasn't doing a brilliant job of showing him how grown-up she was. The backs of her eyes started to prickle. No. She absolutely would not cry.

She lifted her chin and tried to look regal despite her pathetic, muddied position. "I do not take orders, Lord Halworth. Despite what you may recall, I am not a child."

"And I suppose many ladies lie down in puddles and dart about the countryside after they've been attacked by a madman."

She looked around her as though she'd only now realized where she sat. "Oh! Well, I may spend every pleasant spring day in mud puddles from now on! Doing so might be good for one's constitution, I daresay."

He blinked in surprise or annoyance, she couldn't decide which. Then his frown deepened. "How can you be so indifferent? You were knocked unconscious, fell off your bloody horse, were nearly trampled by mine—"

"There's no need to rehash it." She straightened to her full height, or as full as she could manage while seated. "My memory was not damaged in the fall."

He scowled. Then he looked away and looped his horse's reins through a branch in the hedgerow.

She sighed. He was right, after all. She'd been foolish. "I thought I could head the ruffian off. Which I succeeded in, by the way! I didn't bargain on him refusing to stop."

"How likely was it he'd stop to avoid harming you when that was clearly his original purpose?"

She exhaled. Blast him for his indisputable logic! She'd acted rashly and now fate was punishing her with this humiliating confrontation. If experience had taught her anything, it was that an apology went a long way. Nevertheless, her eyes narrowed when her mind tried to formulate the words.

"I am just as capable a rider as you are. As I recall, I bested you many times in the past and—"

"You. Fell. Off," he interrupted, "not I."

She wrinkled her nose but held his gaze. He was so insufferably . . . correct. Yet she absolutely refused to be cowed by his reasoning. If he thought she was about to apologize for something so inconsequential as this when he hadn't apologized for the past, he was sorely mistaken. She raised her chin even higher.

"I should go. I must tell my father about the brute who assaulted me. Not to mention tell our shepherd the sheep have gotten into the clover in your field *and* inform the steward about the wall." She slowly put one foot on the ground to stand up. "So, if you and my friend the puddle will excuse me . . ."

He seized her arms and leaned back until she stood. But when she was steady, he didn't release her. She couldn't bring herself to look into his eyes again, but as she stood there, the heat of his hands seeped through the leather of his riding gloves into her forearms. Warmth spread across her neck despite the chill leaching into her legs and shoulders from the mud. She stared into his white cravat, which was nothing more than the simplest knot, and realized he stood half a head taller than she remembered.

He pulled at her left arm, and her body pivoted to the side. The scent of toast, newspaper ink, and something else—cinnamon?— wafted toward her as he stepped closer. She craned her neck up in confusion and realized he'd turned her to inspect her from behind. His eyes traveled down her mud-caked, respectably clad back to her mud-coated breeches now adhering to her thighs. Blood rushed to her cheeks.

"What are you—"

"You need a physician. Where do you hurt the most?" he asked, turning her forward to catch her attention.

She cleared her throat. He'd been inspecting her for injuries.

What else would he be doing, you ninny?

His brows were pinched in the middle, his brown eyes serious. She could almost swear he looked concerned. For *her*.

Then his gaze shot away, and she remembered he'd been the one to toss her aside as though nearly thirteen years of friendship had meant nothing.

She tugged her arms away from him, but his grip did not loosen. "I am quite well. You needn't trouble yourself."

His eyes bored into hers. "If you think I'll let you gallop all over creation alone after you . . ." He looked away and released her. Her arms fell to her sides. "After you made me lose that criminal, then you are mistaken."

She felt her ears burning now. He may be right about her getting in his way, but it wasn't very gentlemanly of him to keep reiterating it. "You wouldn't have caught him anyway. He was lengths ahead."

He glared at her again, his eyes hard. "I was close enough to almost run you over. I *would* have caught him, Victoria." His cold stare made her want to squirm.

"We could debate this matter for the rest of the day, to be sure. If you wish to inform the magistrate of this incident, please do so. I shall tell my father, but I must go now and attend to my responsibilities. Kindly step aside," she stated with a scowl she knew barely rivaled his for intensity.

Tom's jaw hardened. "Whether you care for my company or not, I *will* accompany you home."

She bit her lip. "That is . . . kind of you."

"As a gentleman I can do no less."

She bristled and turned away with an irritated huff. Of course. No real gentleman would leave an injured lady on a muddied stretch of road without ensuring her safety. But the way he'd phrased it implied she was no more than some stranger he'd encountered whom he felt duty-bound to assist.

In some ways, she supposed she was.

Ever since Tom had stopped responding to her letters in what would otherwise have been a lovely summer in the year '12, Vicky had wondered what she could have done to drive him away. She'd moped around the house for weeks and neither her parents nor her sister had been able to cheer her. Then Tom's father had banished him to the Continent. Vicky had no way to contact him, no way to fix things.

She'd gone about her life at Oakbridge and tried, rather unsuccessfully, to forget him. But when his father died last year and Tom returned home as the new Earl of Halworth, he'd taken every possible measure to avoid her—no small feat since their estates shared a mile-long border.

Fine. It was all perfectly agreeable to her. He'd cut *her* off, after all. If he didn't care for her company, then so be it.